A SECOND BITE
AT THE APPLE

A SECOND BITE
AT THE APPLE

DANA BATE

KENSINGTON BOOKS
www.kensingtonbooks.com

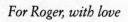

For Roger, with love

CHAPTER 1

Just when I think this morning can't get any weirder, I spot Charles Griffin skiing down Seventeenth Street. *Skiing,* like we're in Aspen. Or Vermont. But we're in Washington, DC, and unlike the rest of the residents of this city, who are drinking hot cocoa and snuggling beneath their fleecy blankets on this snowed-in December morning, Charles and I must subject ourselves to the vagaries of Mother Nature and the incompetence of the city's Department of Transportation.

"Hey, there!" Charles shouts as he glides through the mounds of snow, stabbing haphazardly at the ground with his ski poles. Even muffled by his scarf, his voice resonates with the deep gravitas of a TV news correspondent.

I wave and stumble toward the corner, plowing through a waist-high snowdrift as I clutch my notebook to my chest. Charles presses his knees together and manages to bring himself to a stop next to me.

"How about this weather?" he says, dabbing his forehead with his gloved hand. "When's the last time we got this much snow in December?"

"Someone at the *Chronicle* said 1932. They're calling it Snowzilla."

He laughs. "Where's Tony?"

"Grabbing the gear upstairs. He'll be down in a minute."

I pull my gray fleece hat tighter over my head as I glance down Seventeenth Street. Normally, at this time of morning, cars would barrel southward toward the bustle of K Street, that infamous east-west thoroughfare known for its lobbying firms and major office buildings. But today, instead of a thick flow of cars and taxis and buses, all I see is snow. As someone who once dreamed of penning articles about soufflés and famous chefs, I have to wonder how I ended up here, half-frozen and clad in snow boots, producing a live shot for a TV news correspondent on skis.

"I can't get over how quiet the city is," I say. "I've never seen the streets so empty."

Charles taps on his skis with the tip of his ski pole. "More people need to invest in a pair of these bad boys."

I roll my eyes. "How about we get you *out* of those bad boys and into position."

Charles raises his arm to prevent me from coming any closer. "The skis aren't going anywhere."

"Charles . . ."

"No—listen. I thought we could start with a tight shot of me skiing down Seventeenth, and then Tony could pull out to a wide as I approach the camera. To give people a sense of how much snow there is."

"Have you cleared this with New York?"

"I don't need to clear it with New York."

I raise an eyebrow. "I do."

"No, you don't. It'll be fine. Trust me. I do stuff like this all the time."

This is true. Charles is basically *The Morning Show*'s resident jackass, though officially, he is a general assignment reporter. He possesses an uncanny ability to make himself the center of every story, and, as his producer, my job involves, among other things, bailing him out of the binds that result from his asinine pranks. I'd say this behavior is part of his midlife crisis, but from what I gather, he has been acting like an idiot for years. Last year, when we visited a farm in Loudoun County to report on farm subsidies, Charles decided to do his standup while driving a combine harvester—a machine he had never driven before and that was probably bigger than my first apartment. Charles also happens to be a terrible driver. I begged him to choose another standup location (there is a reason he calls me "Square Sydney"), but when Charles gets an idea in his head, it is impossible to reason with him. He mounted the combine harvester, and the shot ended with him crashing through the poor farmer's fence. It was not one of my more enjoyable afternoons.

As Charles shuffles his skis back and forth, Tony trudges down the sidewalk from our bureau, gripping his camera gear with his big bear paws. Tony is built like a tank, with broad shoulders, a thick neck, and a perpetual five o'clock shadow. He regularly lugs multiple pounds of equipment from shoot to shoot, setting up and breaking down in record speed, and lifting boxes filled with lights and batteries as if they were filled with feathers.

Tony sets up Charles for his live shot, snapping the camera into the tripod and looping the wireless microphone through Charles's jacket. I tug the scarf away from Charles's face and apply a thick coat of foundation to his weathered skin, trying to smooth the peach-colored gunk out of the creases around his eyes and mouth. Not much of his face shows, framed as it is in fleece and wool, but his distinctive wide eyes peer out beneath his woolen hat, and a few tufts of his graying chestnut hair stick out around the edges.

"Up for a test run?" Tony asks.

Charles adjusts his hat. "I skied all the way from my apartment in Kalorama. I don't need a test run."

"Okay, man. Suit yourself."

Tony's attitude, always so laid back and calm, must be a requirement for his job. If reporters like Charles aren't complaining about their appearance on camera, producers like me are yelling at Tony for not getting enough video. But somehow he manages to take it all in stride, never raising his voice or saying a mean word. I don't know how he does it.

"What's our hit time?" Charles asks.

"The first is at 7:25, then every thirty minutes until ten. Unless there's breaking news."

Charles waves his ski poles in the air. "What could be more important than this?"

That pretty much sums up Charles's attitude in life: If he isn't involved in something, how important could it be? An intergalactic explosion, the defection of a political leader, the extinction of the human race—irrelevant when compared to the prospect of watching Charles slog through the snow on an old pair of cross-country skis.

At the top of the hour, Charles treks up Seventeenth Street, using the narrow tracks from his descent as his guide, and turns around when he reaches his self-proclaimed starting point. I call into the bridge in New York, where I hear Bridget, *The Morning Show*'s coordinating producer, moan at the sight of Charles on her preview screen.

"Is Charles really wearing skis?" she asks.

I sigh into the phone. "Yes. Unfortunately."

"Sydney . . ."

"It wasn't my idea—I told him not to do it."

Bridget clicks her tongue and doesn't say anything. She knows it wasn't my idea. I'm Square Sydney. Skiing live shots are not part of my vocabulary.

I hold my phone to my chest and yell up to Charles. "Five minutes!"

Tony finishes adjusting the camera. "Can you believe this guy? What a clown."

Thirty seconds before we go live, Charles rubs his skis back and forth into the ground, as if he is Bode Miller, preparing for the downhill race of his life. Every Olympic season, Charles catches Olympic fever something fierce, and this past year was worse than most. For years, he has been angling to travel to the main event as part of the network team, and for years, including the last one, he has been passed over in favor of another reporter. I'm sure these skis are his way, however small, of throwing up a symbolic middle finger at the network executives for having left him in Washington.

"That's right, Diana," Charles says, staring into the camera as he pushes off from his perch just below M Street. "This was how I got into work today—pushing my way through the snowdrifts that have brought the city to a *crippling* standstill."

As Charles speaks to the camera and, by default, our anchor Diana Humphrey, he picks up speed as his skis lock into the tracks made by his prior descent and ascent. He builds up momentum until, much to the surprise of both him and our viewers, he is moving at quite a clip, flying toward the camera, his eyes wild with terror. He stabs at the ground with his ski poles, but the mountains of snow lining the sidewalk rip them from his hands, and he loses them.

"Please fucking tell me he knows how to stop," Bridget yells into the phone, which is pressed tightly against my ear.

I wish I had an answer for her, but I am too busy watching Charles panic as he realizes he is heading straight for the camera.

". . . and as you can see, it's pretty treacherous out here. . . ."

He is fifteen feet away from the camera now and shows no sign of stopping. He continues to fly toward Tony, his arms flailing at his sides as he tries to keep his balance, his knees turned inward as he tries to bring himself to a halt. It worked earlier, but it isn't working now, not when his skis are stuck in the grooves of his track marks and he is coming at us like a freight train. When he is only a few feet from me and Tony, he surrenders and throws his arms over his face in a brace position.

"Oh, jeez!" he yells as he crashes full-force into the camera. Tony and the tripod go tumbling to the ground, and Charles lands on top of them.

It is just the sort of jackassery I've come to expect from Charles, and if past is precedent—and I believe it is—this will all be my fault.

After the show ends, I slog up to the fifth floor of our building, my fingers stiff and cold like spindly icicles and my nose the color of a maraschino cherry. I ran out of tissues around eight o'clock, so the sleeve of my puffy black ski parka is covered with crusted snot, and I may or may not be sporting a booger mustache. Some days in this job are definitely better than others.

When I reach my desk, I shimmy out of my coat and make my way toward Melanie, the show's senior Washington producer, whose desk is located at the far end of the newsroom. She hugs the phone to her ear as she types at her computer, speaking in a hushed tone, and sits up abruptly when she notices me approaching her desk.

"Gotta run," she barks into the phone. She throws the receiver into its cradle and leans back in her chair. "What the *hell* was that?"

"That was Charles."

She whips off her black-rimmed glasses and dangles them by one of the arms. "Bridget says New York is pissed."

"Charles says New York loves what he does."

"The skis?"

"His idea. I told him not to use them. And anyway, he took them off after the first live shot."

"After which he proceeded to throw a snowball at an old lady," she says.

"In his defense, she looked like a child all bundled up like that."

Melanie runs her hands through her chestnut, ear-length bob. She has the kind of hair I've always wished I could have: pin straight, always falling in exactly the same way no matter how windy or humid it is. A few months ago she added bangs, a style I haven't attempted since fifth grade due to my thick, unruly waves. I'm still traumatized by my class photo from that year, in which my forehead seems to have spontaneously grown a toy poodle.

"Come on—the snowball thing was kind of funny," I say.

Melanie rips open her file drawer and pulls out a Kashi bar. "Laugh all you want. You won't find it so funny when the suits make their announcement."

"What announcement?"

She stops halfway through peeling her snack and sits frozen in her chair. "You haven't heard?"

"Heard what?"

She bites off a hunk of the Kashi bar. "Suffice it to say, major changes are on the way."

"Major as in . . ."

"Think restructuring." She swallows. "Listen, I don't have any details. I shouldn't have said anything."

This is how Melanie operates: doling out a bit of juicy gossip, but then backtracking, assuring you she has already said too much, but ah, how lucky you were to catch her in a moment of weakness.

"They wouldn't do anything so close to the holidays, would they?"

She shrugs. "Who knows? Like I said, I shouldn't have mentioned it."

"I'm glad you did," I say. "Could you let me know if you hear anything else?"

"Sure. Assuming I hear anything. For now...I'd watch my step, if I were you. These are dangerous times." She picks up her coffee mug, and as she goes to take a sip, she narrows her eyes. "By the way," she says, "you have snot running down your face."

This day just gets better and better.

CHAPTER 2

Melanie may love gossip, but she also has a pretty good track record when it comes to knowing what's going on behind the scenes at our network. She knows which anchors are about to get the boot and which reporters are about to get a promotion and which correspondents are sleeping with the network executives. So if she says major changes are coming, major changes are coming.

I scoot back to my desk, which is wedged between a rectangular column and the wall: a less than perfect location for a less than perfect job. I know, I know—I shouldn't complain. It's a paying job, after all, and to most outsiders, it sounds fantastic. Associate producer for a national morning show? Who *wouldn't* want that job? Well . . . me, actually. It's not that I hate my job. In many ways, it's a great gig. I put together stories seen by millions of people every morning, regularly interact with on-air personalities like Charles Griffin and Diana Humphrey, and meet interesting people, from politicians to inventors, all the time. But the truth is, I ended up here by mistake, and if I had my choice, I'd be producing segments for the Cooking Channel or writing food columns for the *Washington Chronicle*. But I'm not. I'm here, working for a correspondent whose contribution to the journalistic profession includes a live shot on skis.

My fingers are still red and raw from our two hours in the snowy outdoors, so I sit at my desk, rubbing my hands together to thaw them. As I press my palms against each other, my cell phone hums and buzzes on my desk. It's my younger sister, Libby. I can only imagine what she wants to talk about this time.

Libby recently moved in with her boyfriend, relocating to an apartment in downtown Philadelphia only twenty minutes from the house where we grew up in the Philly suburbs, and has taken to calling me regularly with "crises" that involve crown molding and paint colors. I toy with the idea of ignoring her call, but I decide talking to her about Benjamin Moore's "Lavender Whisper" is better than talking to Charles, who is currently parading around the office in long johns.

"Syd—hi," she says, her voice tense. "Are you sitting down?"

As if by command, I sit up straighter. "Yes . . . Why?"

"I have news." She takes a deep breath. "Matt and I are engaged!"

My stomach curdles. This is an inappropriate reaction, I realize, but it is my reaction nonetheless. "What?"

"I'm engaged," she repeats. A brief moment passes. "Hello? Are you there?"

"Yes—sorry. Wow. Congrats, Lib. That's . . . great news."

"That almost sounded sincere," she says.

"Sorry, I'm just . . . How long have you known each other? Six months?"

"Seven," she says. "And they've been the most wonderful seven months of my life. I thought you'd be happy for me."

"I am. Sorry. I am. Really. Congratulations."

"Thank you," she says. I can hear her smile through the phone. "And to think, everyone thought you and Zach would be the ones to get engaged first!"

"Yeah. To think."

"Sorry—I didn't mean . . . It's just funny, is all."

Our idea of what is "funny" is one of the many ways Libby and I are nothing alike. We are three years apart, but to look at us you wouldn't think we were even related. She inherited my mother's honey-brown hair, her blue eyes, and her fair skin, whereas I am my father's likeness: thick, sable-colored hair, so dark it appears almost black, green eyes, and freckles, all set atop a wiry frame. At my best, I can look cute—the classic nice Jewish girl from a good family—but Libby is flat-out beautiful and always has been. She never went through an awkward phase, whereas I looked like a mutant Chinese crested dog for most of middle school.

To speak to us, you wouldn't know we were related either. Libby was the popular, sporty one in school, destined to become captain of the field hockey team and president of her sorority at Penn State. She dated with such frequency and enthusiasm that I could never keep track of the flavor du jour. One week it was James so-and-so, and the next it was Mike what's-his-face. With her bubbly laugh and outgoing personality, men flocked to her like a bunch of lovesick fools. Until now, she's had no interest in maintaining a long-term relationship with anyone, but that's because she knew she would always have a date, even if it was with a new person every time. She didn't even have to try.

Meanwhile, I had Zach. We met freshman year at Lower Merion High School when we both joined the school paper. Immediately I was attracted to his geeky, sideways smile and big truffle-colored eyes. Other girls probably laughed at the way his pin-straight brown hair stuck upright in the front, thanks to his severe cowlick, but I thought it was adorable. He must have thought the same about me because within a week of meeting, we were inseparable. We were like two black jellybeans in a sea of reds, two nerds who didn't really fit in with everyone else. We weren't outcasts. We were just ... different. Old souls. Rather than spend the weekend drunk in the woods around a bonfire, we would cook each other dinner and watch the original Japanese version of *Iron Chef*. When I went to Northwestern and he went to Princeton, we maintained a long-distance relationship all the way through graduation. Everyone assumed we would get married. I thought so, too. And then he lied to me and broke my heart.

"Obviously you will be the maid of honor," Libby says.

"Are you sure?"

"*That's* how you respond? 'Are you sure?'"

"It's just that work is so crazy, and you know I'm the worst when it comes to parties. I want you to have the maid of honor you deserve."

Libby grunts. "You're the maid of honor I *want,* okay? But if you'd rather I choose someone else, just say so."

Realistically, I *would* rather she chose someone else—not because I don't want to support Libby, but because helping with her wedding, after everything I've been through . . . it's too much. But I can't say that. Not if I want to avoid an onslaught of teary hysterics and a stern call from our mother.

"Of course I'll do it," I say. "I'm honored—no pun intended."

Libby squeals. "Fantastic! How do you feel about coming up here tomorrow morning to look at bridesmaids' dresses?"

"Already? Have you even set a date?"

"August 6," she says.

"But that's, what, eight months from now? What's the rush? Isn't a lot of stuff booked up already?"

"Matt knows the wedding coordinator at The Rittenhouse, so he called in a favor. We lucked out with the florist and photographer, too, so we're pretty much set."

The Rittenhouse. One of Philadelphia's fanciest hotels. That's where I always thought Zach and I might get married. Not that I fantasized about our wedding in any great detail. I wasn't lying to Libby when I said party-planning isn't my forte. But one time in high school, while Zach and I were having a picnic in Rittenhouse Square, we saw a bride and groom getting their photos taken in front of the hotel. And as I bit into my Di Bruno Brothers sandwich, I thought, *Who knows? Maybe that'll be us someday.*

Of course, as the years went by and I realized what a wedding at The Rittenhouse would cost, that fantasy gradually withered away. And then everything with Zach fell apart, so it hardly mattered.

"The Rittenhouse Hotel? Mom and Dad are okay with that?"

"Sure," she says. "Why wouldn't they be?"

"You know money has been tight. . . ."

"Yeah, but this is my *wedding.* And for all they know, it may be the only one they ever host."

"Thanks, Lib . . ."

"I'm just saying. Anyway, can you come up tomorrow?"

"I'm not even sure Amtrak will be running. The snow has shut everything down. And since I don't have a car—why don't we put a pin in that for now?"

She groans. "Fine. But I'm still going to need help with color schemes. I'm pretty sure I'm going with the jade chiffon for the bridesmaids' dresses. So the logical color accompaniment for the flowers is white and yellow. But now the florist thinks I need a third accent color, and I don't know what to do."

Libby pauses, and a long silence ensues. I pull my phone from my ear to make sure I haven't dropped her call. She is still there. And, apparently, waiting for me to say something.

"Syd? Hello?"

"I'm here," I say.

"Well, what should I do? What goes with yellow, white, and green?"

The only person less qualified than I to answer that question is someone who both is colorblind and has a penis. My work attire revolves around five pairs of slacks—two black, two gray, and one khaki—and a limited variety of solid color tops, the "wildest" of which is a red sweater. Style has never been a personal strength.

"Lib, you repeatedly tell me my entire wardrobe is a crime against fashion. I think you might be better served asking one of your other bridesmaids. Or Mom."

"Mom is more indecisive than I am, and my other bridesmaids are too worried about their own weddings. You're the only one left."

I lean back in my chair. "Okay ... What about ... lavender? Or violet?"

"Matt hates purple flowers."

"Wait, Matt has an *opinion* about flowers? What guy has an opinion about flowers?"

"Sydney—stop. Help me."

I clench my fist into a ball and bite my knuckle. "What about hot pink? That's bright and summery."

Libby goes silent, presumably mulling over this very important decision, upon which rests the fate of the human race.

"That's perfect!" she says. "See? There is a fashion sense somewhere in there. Just takes a little digging."

"Glad I could be of service."

"You're my maid of honor," she says. "Being of service is your job."

"Ah," I say. "Right."

This wedding is going to kill me.

When I hang up with Libby, Melanie storms over to my desk, her arms folded across her body.

"Hey—Boogerface," she barks. "You off the phone?"

It's at times like these that I remember Melanie grew up the youngest among five brothers. Sensitivity does not come naturally. Jokes revolving around poop and boogers, however, seem to flow with ease.

"Yeah, what's up?"

"Check your e-mail. Memo from the network prez. It's happening."

I scroll through my in-box and find a message from the network president, Andrew Halliday: "Structural Changes at the Network."

This can't be good.

Dear colleagues,

The past decade has brought massive changes to our industry—both in the way we cover news and the challenges we face from other news sources. So far, we have risen to the occasion and have served our audiences well. Our news coverage is stronger today than it has ever been. That is down to all of you.

However, the time has come to address these changes to the industry head-on—not by reacting to them, but by implementing a plan that will get ahead of them. The digital delivery of news poses both opportunities and challenges, and in order to overcome those challenges and embrace the opportunities, we must reconsider what we do and how we do it.

To that end, we will be reorganizing our network in the most cost-effective way possible to move into this new era. . . .

The e-mail continues, using expressions like "consolidate," "promote efficiency," and "eliminate redundancies." The bottom line? They are going to close bureaus, combine jobs, and fire people.

"Holy crap," I say as I finish reading the e-mail.

"I told you this was coming."

"Yeah, but I didn't realize . . . I mean, I didn't think it would happen *today*. Or be so extensive."

Melanie pushes her black-rimmed glasses up the bridge of her nose. "No one is safe. Every job is up for grabs."

"How many jobs are they eliminating?"

"How should I know?"

"You knew about the restructuring, didn't you?"

She tucks a pin-straight lock behind her ear. "I'm hearing at least four hundred positions."

My eyes widen. "Four *hundred?*"

"Apparently Halliday is calling the bureau chiefs today. He's delegating."

My heart rate quickens. This may not be my dream job, but I make a respectable salary and have decent health insurance. And given that I'm behind on rent and have a knee-high stack of bills, any job is better than no job.

"He's not telling us in person?"

"I think he wants to get this over with as quickly as possible. Out with the old year, in with the new."

Before I can exacerbate my anxiety with more questions, Charles waltzes past my desk, his thermal underpants only adding to my nausea.

"What's with the somber faces?" he asks.

"Check your e-mail," we say in unison.

Charles glances down at his phone, and his dopey smile morphs into a sober stare as he scrolls through the two-page memo.

"How long have you known about this?"

"I just found out," I say.

Charles nods solemnly, scrolling through the memo a second and then a third time. It's the most serious I've seen him in the four years I've worked here. Even when the Dow dropped almost eight hundred points in a day and all of our futures seemed to splinter before our eyes, Charles injected levity into the newsroom with an occasional bad joke or cheesy story. But not today. Today his face is as white as the snow outside, and he utters not a word.

As Charles reads through the e-mail for a fourth time, our bureau chief Linda McCoy—a woman I have spoken with a grand total of two times in my four years of working here—walks into the newsroom, dressed smartly in a black suit, baby-blue shell, and pearl studs. She is not smiling. The entire newsroom stares at her, none of us smiling either. We know why she's here. There's no need to pretend.

Linda smoothes her brassy bob with the palm of her hand and pulls on her suit jacket. "I just got off the phone with Andrew. I take it all of you have seen his memo."

We all nod, slowly and almost imperceptibly. No one wants to stand out. No one wants to let his or her anxiety into the open, to give off a vibe that says, *I'm nervous. I know I'm hanging by a thread.* But that's what we're all thinking. We're also thinking. *Don't get rid of me. Get rid of her. Or him. But not me.*

"I think it would be best if I spoke to each of you one-on-one to discuss your future here, and the future of *The Morning Show.*"

She drags her eyes across the newsroom and back again, until they land on me.

"Sydney," she says. "Why don't we talk in my office?"

As much as I try to tell myself that everything will be okay—that she wants to discuss the new duties I will assume and the cuts to my 401(k) match—I know from the pitying look in her eyes that we will not be discussing any of those things. We will be discussing something far worse. And everyone in this newsroom knows it.

CHAPTER 3

"Have a seat," Linda says, gesturing to the smooth, gray chair across from her desk.

I lower myself into the chair, gripping the cool, metal armrests for support.

"As you know, the network is going through some major changes," she says. "And one of those changes is to consolidate operations in the Washington bureau."

I nod soberly as my throat begins to close.

"They have decided to combine several of the producer and reporter roles and enhance our digital presence. As such, they are eliminating all of the associate producer and producer positions for *The Morning Show*."

A wave of nausea crashes over me. "All of them? Then . . . who is going to produce the morning segments?"

Linda presses her lips together and clears her throat. "Charles."

"*Charles?*" Linda nods. "What about Melanie?"

"Melanie will maintain some of her production duties, along with helping to maintain *The Morning Show*'s digital presence. It's where the business is heading." Linda folds her hands together and places them on her desk. "But, unfortunately, this means your position here is no longer needed."

A second wave of nausea knocks me over the head. This can't be happening.

I strain to speak through the ever-shrinking opening in my throat. "Is this . . . is this because I let Charles wear skis this morning?"

Linda rumples her brow and stares at me quizzically. "I— sorry?"

"The live shot this morning. When Charles knocked over the camera."

Linda slowly shakes her head, and from her expression I gather she did not see Charles's skiing fiasco. "No," she says. "This is purely a business decision. I hope you understand."

I try to come up with a response, but at the moment I cannot construct complete sentences. Besides, what am I supposed to say? Am I supposed to affirm her declaration, to say, *Yes, of course I understand?* That would be a lie. I don't understand. I've worked my butt off for four years. Frankly, if it weren't for me, Charles would probably have the network embroiled in some nasty lawsuit.

"You'll need to clear out your desk and leave the building within the hour," she says.

I look at my watch. "Within the *hour?*"

"I'm sorry. This isn't my decision. It's company policy."

I start to get up from my chair, but then I remember something I read for a recent unemployment story we did. "What sort of severance package should I expect?"

"Unfortunately, due to the financial strains on the network, the severance isn't as generous as it once was. You'll receive payment for your work through today, and then one month's salary—a week for each year you worked here."

I do the math in my head. That's barely enough to cover my rent, especially given how far behind I am on payments, thanks to some absurdly expensive oral surgery two months ago that my insurance didn't cover. Forget spending the money on anything else, like food or heating or other such luxuries.

Linda reaches into her file drawer and hands me a thick packet. "You'll find information in there regarding allocation of the severance, as well as a primer on unemployment insurance and resume building." She pushes her drawer shut and shakes her head. "I'm sorry about this. It isn't what any of us wanted."

I flick through the packet and then give Linda one last probing look, hoping there is even the slightest chance she will realize she's made a mistake. But Linda simply stares back, her lips pursed.

Finally, she reaches across the desk and grabs my hand, shaking it firmly. "Be well," she says. Then she gestures toward the door. "Please send in Abby on the way back to your desk."

Be well? *Be well?* No, I will not *be well,* Linda. I will be very, very unwell, thank you very much. I had misgivings about this job, but somehow that makes losing it even more painful. It's like being dumped by someone you don't like. All you can think is, *I should be the one dumping YOU.*

As I walk back into the newsroom, everyone's eyes follow me to my desk. I catch a glimpse of Charles, who still isn't wearing proper pants and yet is one of two people in this room who will still have a job in an hour. This has to be a sign of the apocalypse.

"Linda wants to see you," I say to Abby, dropping the unemployment packet on my desk. I yank open my top file drawer and begin stacking my folders in a pile next to my computer.

"What happened in there?" Melanie asks.

"I have an hour to clear out my desk. I'm toast."

Charles taps his pen against the side of his computer. "Did Linda say anything about the rest of us?"

"I'm not at liberty to discuss our conversation."

"Puh-*lease,*" Melanie says. "We're all going to find out within the hour anyway."

I turn to the Queen of Gossip, the only producer among us left standing. "Then you can wait."

The meetings are brief and orderly, and by the time Linda has finished speaking to everyone, the atmosphere in the newsroom approximates that of a funeral. Even Charles and Melanie, the two of us who still have jobs, look as if they've lost their childhood puppy and best friend on the same day. I don't blame them. They'll now be doing the jobs of two or three people for less money and fewer benefits, and neither of them signed up for that.

I manage to load all of my folders and tchotchkes into a large cardboard box I found in the storage room, the only downside being that the box now weighs approximately six hundred pounds, there are multiple feet of snow outside, I live twelve blocks from the office, and there is no one to help me.

"Would either of you mind if I stored this under your desk? I'll pick it up when they've done a better job clearing the streets."

"I don't think you're supposed to come back in the building," Melanie says. Then she waves me toward her desk. "Throw it over here and call me when you want to pick it up. I'll bring it down to you."

I shove the box behind her desk, give her and Charles each an awkward hug good-bye, and then say good-bye to Tony and the few other friends I have at the network.

"Where are you off to now?" Melanie asks as I throw on my jacket and gloves.

I give one last look around the office, pull my fleece hat over my head, and clap my gloved hands together. "To get drunk."

CHAPTER 4

The problem with getting laid off at noon on one of the snowiest days in Washington's history? There is nowhere *to* get drunk, other than your own apartment. And when the only drinkable alcohol in your apartment is a half-empty bottle of vodka and a few airplane miniatures of gin—well, let's just say the situation is less than ideal.

A high-speed wind whips at my face as I stomp through the piles of snow in my fat snow boots, my chin tucked tightly against my chest as the tears stream down my face. Renting an apartment twelve blocks from the office sounded like a fabulous idea when I signed my lease six months ago, in the balmy days of early June. Twelve blocks: a touch too close to justify public transportation, but more than a ten-minute walk. I told myself the walk would be my daily exercise, as if exercise had ever been a priority. Plus, the rent was surprisingly cheap—though, apparently, not cheap enough when combined with my payments to Dr. Larry Gopnik, DDS. But now I wish I'd spent a little more money on an apartment closer to a Metro stop, because between the wind and the snow, I cannot feel my face and may have permanently lost the use of my left index finger. Also, I now live twelve blocks from an office I will no longer visit.

My apartment sits on Swann Street between Fourteenth and

Fifteenth Streets, in a semi-undefined neighborhood sandwiched between Logan and Dupont Circles. For years, Fourteenth Street was known, informally at least, as Washington's "Red Light District," more famous for drug trafficking and prostitution than for organic markets and independent art galleries. But over the past decade or so, the neighborhoods have gentrified, and now Fourteenth Street is one of Washington's hottest areas, with a new restaurant or café seeming to open every week.

My street stretches from west to east and is filled from end to end with brightly colored town houses, all squashed together like crayons in a Crayola box, lying just beyond the red brick sidewalk. Unlike the towering, three-story row homes in Dupont Circle, the houses on my street are squat, two-story affairs with square, flat roofs and modest front stoops. Some of the homes lodge a single owner, but many, like mine, are broken up into separate apartments. I occupy the entire second floor, whereas the first floor houses a wiry, forty-something recluse named Simon.

When I arrive at my building, a butter-yellow house sandwiched between a maroon town house to the right and cobalt blue town house to the left, I find Simon shoveling the front walkway beyond our wrought-iron gate, humming what sounds like a slow dirge. Given the day I've had, I should probably join in with a funeral song of my own.

"Hi, Simon. Need any help?"

Simon looks up, his pale face blank as he stares at me with hollow eyes. "No. I'm fine."

"You sure?"

He digs into the snow with his shovel and tosses a heap over his shoulder. "Yes."

Simon was already living in the downstairs apartment of our town house when I moved into the second floor. We rarely see each other, given the private doorway to his apartment and the private, locked stairway leading to mine, so most of our interactions involve my saying hello and Simon's grunting an unintelligible reply. He looks a little like a rodent, with his pointy nose, bleached-blond hair, and beady eyes, the whites of which are often tinged with pink. But in a previous life, I lived in an apartment in Georgetown next door to a bunch of rowdy college students, and I would take a quiet introvert over a frat boy any day.

I march up the front steps and check my mailbox, where I find a folded piece of yellow paper. When I open it, I find, in bold capitals, a message from our landlord, Al:

NEED DECEMBER RENT ASAP. YOU ARE LATE. AGAIN.

Perfect. As if this day weren't already a kick in the ovaries.

I stick the note into my coat pocket and let myself through two sets of doors before trudging up the stairway that leads directly into my living room. As soon as I reach the top, I dump my coat and bag on the floor, kick off my boots, grab a handful of miniature gin bottles from the cupboard, and collapse onto my plush gray couch.

My feet propped on the armrest, I sip the gin straight from the toy-size bottles and reflect on all the ways in which this situation totally blows. I never even *wanted* to work on a morning news show. I wanted to be a food journalist, to write about the connections between food and culture, to interview chefs and bakers and food enthusiasts who would clue me in to new cooking techniques and food trends. That's the stuff that turns me on, the stuff I could read about for days. One time in college, I was so engrossed in Ruth Reichl's *Tender at the Bone* as I rode the "L" into Chicago that I missed my stop and ended up back where I'd started in Evanston. I loved immersing myself in her writing—the way I could almost taste the food she described through the pages—and I wanted to explore food and cooking through writing the way she did.

The problem, of course, was that I couldn't find a job like that after college, or at least not any job that paid anything. The only offers I got were "unpaid internships," which I couldn't afford to take without my parents' help, and I knew my parents didn't have the money to support me, so I didn't even bother to ask. I did interview for one job at a small online startup, but it was located in Fort Lauderdale, which, after four years of long distance, was farther away than I wanted to live from Zach, who was set to start law school at Columbia in New York City. I often wonder what would have happened if I'd taken that job: if I'd be the food writer I'd dreamed of being, or if that dream just isn't meant to be.

No other paid food-writing jobs came along, so I took the best journalism job I could get and figured with a little finessing, I could make the transition from general television journalist to paid food journalist. Naïve? Probably. But I thought I could make it work. Whenever I had the chance, I pitched *Morning Show* stories with a food angle—a piece on farm subsidies that would take us to Loudoun County, or a story about the cupcake craze hitting the nation's capital. Sometimes I felt as if I were trying to jam together two puzzle pieces that belonged to two entirely different puzzles, but I did my best to make the job and me fit. It wasn't a perfect match, but it was close enough, at least until I found the food-writing job I'd always wanted. Which, of course, I never did.

And now I'm unemployed.

Not just unemployed—unemployed in the only industry for which I have any real qualifications, which, as it happens, is also an industry that is hemorrhaging positions by the day. The other major networks have either already laid off hundreds of staff members or are planning to do so in the coming weeks. Where am I going to go?

I gulp down the last of the gin from the mini bottles and nestle myself into the couch cushions, determined to come up with a plan to pull myself out of this funk. All I need to do is close my eyes for a few minutes while I figure things out. Or, at the very least, forget why my life is a bit of a mess.

Four hours later, I jump as my cell phone hums and buzzes on the coffee table. A four-hour nap? This has not happened since I had mono freshman year of college.

I grab the phone and see it's Heidi Parker, one of my best friends from Northwestern who has been living in DC as long as I have.

"Hello . . . ?"

"Uh . . . hi," Heidi says. "Did I . . . wake you?"

I clear my throat and stretch my mouth wide to wake up my lips. "Kind of. Not really."

"Sleeping on the job? That's not like you."

"I'm at home. I got laid off today."

Heidi goes silent. "Oh my God," she eventually says. "Syd, I'm so sorry."

"Not half as sorry as I am at the moment," I say, breathing my stale, gin-laced breath into the phone.

"We need to get you out of that house. You need a drink."

I laugh. "Already have a head start on the latter."

"You've been drinking alone?" I don't answer. "Okay, we're calling in the troops," she says. "Bar Pilar is running some sort of blizzard special on beers for happy hour. Meet me there in twenty minutes."

"But I . . ."

"Ah, ah, ah—no objections. You're coming. End of story."

I contemplate interjecting with one more halfhearted protest, but I realize there is no point. Heidi will come to my apartment and physically drag me to the bar if necessary—probably by my hair, as she has done before—and in one day, there is only so much humiliation a girl can take.

Before I leave, I poke my head into the refrigerator to see if there is anything I can eat before I meet Heidi, since continuing to drink on an empty stomach will surely end in disaster. My choices consist of the following: a container of two-week-old Chinese leftovers, some bottles of mustard and ketchup, and several half-eaten containers of fruit preserves. I'm not sure what I expected to find. Ever since I landed a job on *The Morning Show,* work has consumed most of my waking hours, and I barely have time to do laundry, much less cook.

I haven't cooked much since Zach and I broke up, anyway. Cooking was our thing. Even if it was just a bowl of spaghetti and box-mix brownies, we would try to make dinner together every weekend in high school. Zach's mom, Alaine Pullman, is a famous Philadelphia caterer who regularly put on events for the mayor and other local celebrities, so while she was out on Saturday nights preparing filet mignon and arugula salads for Philadelphia's finest, Zach and I would raid her well-stocked pantry and whip up our own mini feasts. I developed an early fondness for candied walnuts and a definitive aversion to stinky cheese and learned there is, in fact, such a thing as too much cheesecake and that amount is equal to three slices. We made our own fun, even when that fun involved breaking a bottle of his mom's truffle oil from Piedmont, an incident that was not without consequences.

Once we left for college, seeing each other became more difficult, with him in New Jersey and me in Illinois, and our dorm kitchens lacked the swanky equipment and ingredients of his parents' kitchen. But we tried our best to make it work, even toward the end, when his heart wasn't in it anymore. The last meal we cooked together, on the night everything went wrong, was spaghetti carbonara, and to this day the smell of crisping bacon makes my stomach turn.

I slam the refrigerator door shut and decide I'll buy something at Bar Pilar, where the offerings will be more appealing than Chinese leftovers that smell like roadkill. I throw back one more airplane miniature of gin, pull on my coat and boots, and stumble woozily down the front steps, where once again I run into Simon, who is now beating our bushes with a meat mallet.

"Um . . . Simon?" I watch as he thrusts the tenderizer into the bushes again and again. "What are you doing?"

Simon whips his head in my direction, his vaguely rodent-like eyes glassy and pink. "Saving them."

"Saving . . . whom?"

"The bushes," he says. "This snow and ice will kill them. There's too much of it."

"Oh. Right. Do you need my help?"

He turns away from me and rattles the mallet around in one of the bushes. "No."

I wait for him to add a "thank you" or a "thanks for the offer," but he doesn't. "Well . . . have a nice night," I say.

And as I push past him onto Swann Street—me unemployed and soaked in gin, him beating at a bunch of shrubs with a meat mallet—I wonder which of us is the sadder case and how the contest ever got this close.

CHAPTER 5

The one-block walk to Bar Pilar requires the physical exertion of a two-mile hike, mostly because I am slightly buzzed from the gin and the sidewalks are covered with about four feet of snow. I have no idea how I'll make it home after another drink or two.

The overhang above the bar's entrance shoulders a good two feet of snow, the fluffy mounds bearing down with the weight of a small school bus. There's so much white that from where I stand below the entrance I can barely make out the block stencil letters punched out of the bar's copper nameplate. This is the kind of weather I loved as a kid. I remember missing two weeks of school in the seventh grade, when a major snow and ice storm pounded the East Coast. My mom and Libby baked chocolate chip cookies, while I looked on, peering over my copy of MFK Fisher's *The Gastronomical Me*. The three of us played cards and watched movies and curled up on our couch with steaming mugs of hot chocolate. It's one of the last memories I have of the three of us hanging out like that.

When I walk inside, I find Heidi sitting along the wooden bar, chatting to the bartender as he fills up a glass from the beer tap, his back to a long wall of exposed brick. A song by the Doves purrs through the bar's speakers, and as I tromp through the long, narrow bar in my snow boots, both Heidi and the bartender look up at me.

"There she is!" Heidi says, her blue eyes sparkling. She sips her beer and wipes a dab of frothy foam off her narrow freckled nose.

I look around for the many friends I assumed Heidi would bring with her, but the only people here besides the two of us are a thirty-something couple sitting at a table and a man in a puffy vest sitting at the far end of the bar.

"Where are the 'troops'?" I ask.

Heidi smiles sheepishly and tucks a stray strand of her stick-straight blond hair behind her ear. "Everyone is snowed in. We're an army of two tonight."

The bartender slides a beer to the man at the end of the counter and scratches his beard as he nods in my direction. "What can I get you?"

I scan down the list of beer specials scrawled on the black chalkboard, but I've never been much of a beer connoisseur, and at this point, I really don't care what I order as long as it contains alcohol. "Uh, the third one," I say. "Thanks."

Heidi helps me unwrap my scarf and stares at me worriedly. "Did you even look at yourself in the mirror before you left?"

"No, why?" I glance in the mirror behind the bar and notice a crease down my cheek, long and deep like the San Andreas Fault, and a mysterious streak of mucus in the corner of my eye. I look like an extra from *The Walking Dead*.

Heidi grabs my drink from the bartender and passes it to me. "To new beginnings."

We clink glasses, and I gulp down half my beer.

"Whoa, slow down," she says. "Happy hour lasts another two hours. We have time."

I slide my glass back and forth on the counter and sigh. "I can't believe I lost my job."

"Who did they keep?"

I roll my eyes as I take another sip of beer. "Fucking Charles."

"That's it?"

"Melanie, too. Although she's going to be some sort of quasi producer-slash-digital reporter, whereas Charles will produce his own spots. I almost feel bad for them, until I remember they will still be getting a paycheck."

"You will, too, soon enough. And anyway, you never loved that job. Maybe now you can give the whole food journalism thing a try."

I throw back the rest of my beer. "If it were that easy to find a job as a food writer, don't you think I would have left *The Morning Show* a long time ago?"

Heidi rubs my back. "Fair enough. But you'll get another job. Don't worry."

We both know she has no idea whether or not I'll get another job, but I suppose these are the stock phrases you say when a friend loses one. *You'll be okay. You'll land on your feet. You'll find work soon.* People say those phrases so often they almost lose meaning. Really, the only response that resonates at all is, *That sucks.*

On some level, I should trust Heidi knows what she's talking about. She works at an education nonprofit, her third in the four and a half years since we graduated college. She knows all about budget cuts and empty coffers and organizational mismanagement. At one point, between her last job and her current one, she was working three different side jobs—restaurant hostess, dog walker, and farmers' market cashier—just so that she could make the payments on her many student loans. Yet each time her company let her go, she managed to land on her feet, continuing to supplement her meager income with her weekend job at the farmers' market. If she has made it work, then maybe I will too.

Heidi takes another swig of beer and sets her glass on the counter. "Gotta run to the ladies'. You'll be okay?"

"I'm unemployed, not suicidal."

"You're a pain in the ass, is what you are," she says. "I'll be back in a minute."

She scoots down the narrow hallway to the bathroom, and I redirect my gaze to the counter as I swirl my empty glass by the base. There is an inch or two of beer left in Heidi's glass, and, not caring if it's rude or wrong, I grab her glass and finish it.

"Looks like you need a refill."

The man from the end of the bar is standing behind Heidi's chair, his hands tucked into the pockets of his puffy black vest. His hair is the color of milk chocolate, wavy and thick with narrow sideburns, which frame his slender face. He looks vaguely familiar.

"I guess I do," I say, looking into the bottoms of my glass and Heidi's.

The man flags the bartender. "Hey, Eli, another for the lady and her friend," he says. "Add it to my tab."

I dismiss him with a wave of my hand as I let out a small burp under my breath. "Thanks, but I've got this. I can manage four bucks."

"I'm sure you can. But I overheard you and your friend talking, and it sounds like you've had a rough day."

I raise an eyebrow. "You were eavesdropping?"

His cheeks flush, and he rubs his narrow chin. "It was hard not to. Your voice—let's just say it carries."

"Oh, so now I'm a loud talker? Great. Thanks. That's just what I needed to hear." The bartender places the filled glasses in front of me. I clear my throat. "I'VE GOT THIS," I shout. "BUT THANKS FOR THE OFFER."

The man's face turns even redder. "Suit yourself," he says. "But don't tell me chivalry is dead. I tried."

"Badly," I mumble into my beer.

"What's that?"

"BADLY," I shout. "FUNNY, IF I'M SUCH A LOUD TALKER, THEN WHY CAN'T YOU UNDERSTAND WHAT I'M SAYING?"

"Sydney . . . ?" Heidi pokes her head out from behind the man in the vest. "Why are you shouting?"

"Gee, I don't know. I guess I can't help it. According to this a-hole, I'm a LOUD TALKER."

Heidi smiles nervously. "How many of those gin bottles did you drink before you got here?"

"What do you care? I can do what I want. It's a free country."

Apparently in my buzzed and self-pitying state, I have resorted to the rhetorical sophistication of a six-year-old.

"Maybe another drink isn't such a good idea," Heidi says, eyeing the bartender and giving him a not-so-subtle sign to cut me off.

"Oh, yeah? And why's that?"

Heidi shifts her gaze from the bartender to me to the guy in the vest and back to me again. "Because I think we need to get something in your stomach."

"They serve food here," I say, now invoking the stubbornness of a three-year-old. At this rate, I'll be on the floor in the fetal position by the time we leave.

Heidi pats my shoulder. "I think you're more in the market for Taco Bell tonight."

"I thought you hated fast food. I thought you only ate organic."

"Tonight, for you, I will make an exception." She reaches into her pocket and throws twelve dollars on the counter. "Thanks," she says, waving at the bartender as she lifts me out of my seat. She smiles at the guy in the vest, who is staring at the two of us. "And thanks to you for the offer."

"Yeah, thanks for ruining *everything!*" I shout, fighting Heidi as she tries to stuff me into my gigantic coat.

He lifts his hands defensively. "Listen, I'm really sorry. I was just trying to be nice."

"Yeah, well, mission *un*-accomplished."

I don't even know what I'm saying at this point.

Heidi grabs me by the elbow with her pale, bony fingers and pulls me toward the front door. "Come on, lady. Let's get some food in you."

I whip my head around as Heidi pulls me through the front door and stick my tongue out at the man in the vest. He smirks and shakes his head and offers a small wave.

"Jerkface," I mutter under my breath.

Heidi drags me out the door and onto Fourteenth Street, but I slow my step as I stare at the man's figure disappearing through the closing door.

"What are you staring at?" she asks, her hand clasped around my arm.

I wriggle free from her grasp and readjust my hat. "Nothing. I thought I recognized that guy for a second."

"Who?"

"The jerk in the vest."

"I don't think you're in a state where you can recognize anyone right now. . . ."

I teeter as I try to walk through a small mountain of snow and nearly lose my balance at the corner of T Street. "I don't know. I can't put my finger on it. He just looked really . . . familiar."

Heidi grabs my arm to keep me from falling over. "Easy there, boozehound." She guides me onto a cleared patch of sidewalk and wraps her arm around my shoulder. "Forget about the guy in the vest, okay? He's an idiot. We have more important things to do."

"Like what? Buying a bunch of eighty-nine-cent tacos?"

Heidi grins. "Precisely."

She pats my shoulder with her gloved hand and holds me tight, and together we slip and slide along the icy pavement as we make our way up Fourteenth Street.

CHAPTER 6

The next morning, my cell phone starts ringing at the unholy hour of 5:45 a.m. It's Heidi.

"If this is some sort of joke, I'm not laughing," I mumble into the phone.

Heidi doesn't answer, and I hear an aria of retching in the background.

"Heidi?"

"Auuuugh," she groans.

I sit up and rub the sleep from the corners of my eyes. "Oh my God, are you okay?"

"Fucking gorditas," she says, letting out another moan. "I think I'm dying."

"You got food poisoning?"

Again she doesn't answer and instead offers the sounds of her gagging and heaving into the toilet.

"You should go to the ER," I say. "I'll come get you."

Heidi pants into the phone. "In what? Your Batmobile?"

She makes a good point. There are multiple feet of snow on the ground, and I don't own a car.

"Listen, I'll be fine," she says. "But I need you to cover for me at the farmers' market this morning."

"Cover for you?" I may not have food poisoning, but I am hungover and have no interest in standing outside in the cold at a farmers' market. "Isn't the market closed due to the snow?"

More retching noises, followed by what sounds like a dying cow. "They're open. West End market, near the Francis Park tennis courts."

I lie back into the softness of my pillow and race through different ways I can get out of this. "I'm sure they'll be fine without you," I say. "They'll understand."

"Not Rick the Prick. Someone needs to show up, and it sure as hell isn't going to be me."

"But maybe if you called him and explained the situation . . ."

Heidi lets out a burp and a long whimper. "Seven thirty, Wild Yeast Bakery," she says. "And don't be late."

Unfortunately, between the waist-high snowdrifts and my utter lack of motivation, I don't make it to the market until 7:45, and by the time I get there, I am out of breath from trundling through the snow for a mile. The weekly market operates next to a small park with public tennis courts and playing fields, just west of Dupont Circle. Shapeless piles of snow cover the grass and dirt paths where the market usually runs, so today the vendors set up along the sidewalk, just beside the parking meters, which poke their heads through the snow mounds like little meerkats.

I trudge along the sidewalk past a series of tents and scan the vendors for Wild Yeast Bakery. There are no signs, and I have no idea where I am going.

"Excuse me," I say, approaching a man about my age standing beneath a green-and-white striped tent. He whirls around and smiles, and my stomach flutters as his eyes land on mine. A red knit hat covers the bulk of his dark, wavy hair, and a few stray bits peek out above his round eyes, which are the color of black coffee. His chiseled jaw is covered by a smattering of stubble, and with his red-and-black plaid jacket, he looks a bit like a lumberjack, if lumberjacks also looked like Abercrombie and Fitch models. "Are you Rick?"

The man smirks. Definitely more model than lumberjack. "I'm

Drew," he says. "Are you looking for Wild Yeast? They're all the way at the end, with the red checkered tent."

I spot it. "Great, thanks."

Drew nods, studying me with his eyes. I am suddenly very aware that I am not wearing makeup and, in related news, also look like death.

"Good luck," he says. From his tone, I'm guessing I'll need all the luck I can get.

I make my way over to Wild Yeast's tent, where I find a plump man wearing a black down parka and furry brown Ushanka unloading a stack of bread-filled crates from his truck. It's parked across from one of the meters, in the middle of what normally serves as Twenty-third Street.

"Rick?"

He throws two crates onto one of the cloth-lined tables. "Who the hell are you?"

"I'm Heidi's friend, Sydney. I'm filling in for her today?"

He lets out a sarcastic laugh, revealing a set of tobacco-stained teeth. "Is that so?"

"She got food poisoning last night. She's really sick." I wait for him to reply, but he says nothing and instead stares at me, the wrinkled skin around his eyes drooping like melting wax. "I thought maybe she called you about it?"

Rick shuffles back to the truck and grabs another stack of crates. "And what if she did? Doesn't change the fact that it's seven-freaking-fifty, and you're just getting here."

I clutch my bag closer to my body. "Sorry—the snow slowed me down."

"Like I care? Maybe Heidi didn't tell you, but I'm a real son of a bitch when it comes to being on time."

No, Heidi never told me that specifically, but I'm guessing the epithet "Rick the Prick" didn't come from nowhere.

"I'm sorry," I say.

"I'll give you a pass this time. But in the future, show up late and I will make your life hell."

I am about to inform Rick there will be no future for him and me, that today is a one-time favor for a friend, but I decide my survival over the next four and a half hours depends on my keeping my mouth shut.

Rick grabs another stack of crates from the back of the truck and slams them onto the table. He stares at me and raises an eyebrow. "These crates aren't going to unload themselves, sweetheart. Let's *go*."

I rush to the back of the truck and toss my purse inside. Grabbing a handle for support, I lift myself into the back of the truck, where the warm, sweet smells of freshly baked baguettes and pumpkin muffins waft past my nose. It's how I imagine heaven must smell, the perfume of yeasty bread and cinnamon-laced muffins filling the air as little angels float by on pillows made of billowy croissants.

Rick bangs on the floor of the truck with his hand. "Jesus—are you deaf or something? Move!"

On the other hand, perhaps this is hell.

I grab a crate of cranberry-walnut bread, and my knees nearly buckle under the weight of the glossy oval loaves.

"Wow, these are heavy," I say.

Rick reaches for the crate. "Hand them over."

Rick and I start an assembly line: I grab a crate and hand it down to him, and he lugs it over to the table beneath the tent before coming back for another. Once I've unloaded all the crates from the truck, I start on the baskets and wooden cartons we'll use to display the bread and pastries. The baskets come in all shapes and sizes—round, square, shallow, deep—and I am 100 percent certain I will fill them in a manner that is not to Rick's liking.

"Do you think you'll get a lot of customers today?" I ask, though immediately after I do, I realize this is a stupid question Rick will not enjoy.

He narrows his eyes. "What do you think?"

"Maybe people will want to get out of the house. There's a lot of cabin fever going around. And it's the last Saturday before Christmas."

"Maybe," he says, loading a stack of chocolate chip cookies into a square wicker basket. "Hey, what are you doing over there? Never line up the chocolate croissants like that. You want a total mess?"

"Sorry."

He growls and shakes his fists at the heavens. "I swear, one of these days . . ."

I'm not really sure what that's supposed to mean, but Rick, I am learning, is not a man one questions. He talks and sings to himself. He fake punches the air. He laughs at nothing in particular. Rick, I am learning, is completely certifiable.

"Okay, here's the deal," he says. "Cookies, muffins, and croissants are two dollars. Cupcakes are three dollars. Scones are a buck. Plain loaves are six dollars, ones with fruit or nuts are eight dollars, and that big one over there is sixteen for the whole thing, eight for half, and four for a quarter. Brioche is eight bucks. You can do half loaves of everything but the baguettes. And don't come asking me every five seconds about the price on this or that. Otherwise I might as well work the stand myself. Got it?"

I clear my throat. "I think so. Sure."

"Good. Now stop staring at those muffins like they're gonna unload themselves and get them in the fucking basket. I'm running out of patience."

That makes two of us.

CHAPTER 7

One thing becomes clear very quickly: I am not good at this. I can spend hours reading and writing about pastries and bread, and I am happy to eat significant quantities of both, but when it comes to selling them, I am completely out of my element.

"Don't just stand there," Rick mutters under his breath. "Offer samples. Get the bags ready. Do *something*."

The problem is, there isn't much to do. When the bell rings at nine, the market is nearly empty. The customers milling along the sidewalk are diehards who come to this market every weekend and know what they want. No amount of smiling or cajoling from me is going to make them want to buy a lemon ginger scone, unless they wanted one already. This, combined with the numbness of my toes, makes me seriously question my need to be here.

The traffic picks up around nine thirty, at which point a few customers pass our stand, perusing the loaves and pastries. Rick immediately turns on the charm, transforming himself from a disgruntled troll into a smooth-talking ladies' man.

"Hello, sweetheart," he says to a middle-aged woman who, unless my eyes deceive me, appears to be growing a mustache.

She offers an uneasy smile. "Hello."

"If I weren't a married man . . ." He trails off. "Woo-*ee*."

Oh dear God. This is painful to watch.

Out of pity, hunger, or a combination of the two, the woman orders a loaf of brioche, two oatmeal cookies, and two pumpkin muffins, and Rick offers more nauseating flattery as he hands her the bag of goodies along with her change. From his demeanor, it is clear he fancies himself a modern day Don Juan, a perception that, as far as I can tell, is completely at odds with reality.

As the morning goes on, Rick offers more of the same, each female interaction increasingly embarrassing and unbearable. Thankfully, around ten o'clock the foot traffic picks up, which means I can focus on the small mob descending upon our tent instead of Rick's stomach-turning chauvinism.

People push their way to the front of the crowd, and my eyes race up and down the table as I try to figure out who is next in line. I settle on a tall man standing directly in front of me, his gray wool hat pulled snugly over his head. Our eyes catch, and he smiles.

"We meet again," he says.

"Sorry?" I narrow my eyes and study his face, and then I realize who he is. "Oh, right. From Bar Pilar. The jerk in the vest."

He winces. "Ouch."

"What can I get you?"

He rubs his chin as he studies the table. "Good question. Anything new today?"

"I've never worked here before. I'm just filling in for a friend—which, by the way, I wouldn't have needed to do if you hadn't ruined everything and forced us to eat at Taco Bell."

"I didn't force you to eat anywhere. And, anyway, after last night, I'm surprised you have the energy to fill in for anyone."

"After last night, I'm surprised you think I'd have any interest in talking to you."

He grins. "I'm sorry I called you a loud talker. Okay?"

I cup my hand to my ear. "Sorry? I didn't catch that."

He juts out his jaw and holds back a smirk. "I'm sorry I called you a loud talker," he repeats, louder this time. "Really, *really* sorry. Though maybe that still isn't sorry enough."

I shake open a paper bag, holding back a smile. "No, I think that should do. For now, at least."

"Yeah?"

I relax into a full smile. "Yeah. So what'll it be?"

"A loaf of the ciabatta and two pumpkin muffins. And an oatmeal cookie. Wild Yeast makes the best."

I grab a piece of tissue paper and start stuffing his baked goods into the paper bag. "You come here often?"

"As often as I can. I live around the corner."

"You've probably met my friend Heidi, then. She usually works here on Saturdays."

"Is she the friend from last night? I thought she looked familiar."

I nod and glance up at his face. "Speaking of looking familiar . . ."

But before I can finish, Rick interrupts. "This ain't social hour, kids. Save the chitchat for the bar. Sydney? Let's move it."

I roll up the top of the paper bag and hand it over the table, tallying the total in my head. "Twelve bucks," I say.

He leafs through his wallet and pulls out a twenty. I head over to the cashbox, where Rick is sorting through a stack of singles and cursing under his breath. I swap the twenty for a five and three ones and head back to hand the man his change.

"Nice running into you again," he says.

I nod. "You too. Stay warm."

He lingers for a moment, but other customers are waiting for me to take their orders, so I smile quickly and turn to a young couple standing behind the basket of French boules. As they rattle off their order, I can't shake the idea that I've seen the man in the vest before, but when I glance back over my shoulder to take another look, he is gone.

I bag up a bunch of pumpkin muffins and molasses cookies for the young couple, and as I grab their money to make change, a young woman approaches me from the other end of the table.

"The last guy you waited on left this for you," she says. She holds out a folded-up piece of bakery tissue paper.

"For me? What is it?"

"No idea. But he left it on the table and said to make sure you got it."

I take it from her hands and unfold it. Inside, in barely legible writing, are his phone number and a brief message:

Sorry again about last night. I'd like to make it
up to you. Call me some time.
    —Jeremy

I stare at the message for a few seconds, wondering if I should
call him, at least to apologize for giving him such a hard time. But
then I remember Zach, and how horribly wrong all of that went,
and how I promised myself I'd never let anyone hurt me like that
again. I crumple up the tissue paper and toss it into the trash bin.

"What did it say?" the girl asks.

I take a deep breath and consider my answer. Then I shrug.
"Nothing important," I say, and then I wait on the next customer.

"Wake up, sugar," Rick says, slapping my ass. "Time to pack up."

I look up from my perch behind the basket of walnut spelt
bread, trying to ignore the fact that Rick's hand just made contact
with my backside, as the market manager rings the cowbell at the
far end of the market.

"It's over? Already?"

Rick waddles over to the cash table. "No, the chick in the parka
is ringing a cowbell for kicks."

I follow Rick to the cash table and begin bagging up the leftover
half loaves and samples, which he plans to donate to a local soup
kitchen. Given my rocky start and my initial disinterest in being
here, I'm surprised at how quickly the morning has passed. Last
time I looked at my watch, it was 10:15, and now it's already noon.
Aside from the fact that I have lost all feeling in my face and feet, I
actually had . . . fun? More fun than I had standing in the snow
with Charles, at least. Rick may be nuts, but he bakes some of the
best bread I've ever eaten. One bite of his light, feathery brioche,
and I swear I heard angels singing.

"Where else do you sell your stuff?" I ask as I box up the leftover pumpkin muffins.

"Other farmers' markets—Dupont, Penn Quarter, Annapolis,
Crystal City."

"Any retail shops?"

"Nah. We do a little wholesale here and there. But that's about it."

"Have you ever thought of opening your own store?"

"Too much overhead. Don't need the hassle." He stacks two crates on top of one another and toddles through the snow to the truck.

"I wonder if one of the specialty markets around here would be interested in selling some of your stuff. I bet—"

"You aren't here to bet," he says, heaving the crates onto the truck. "You're here to help me pack up this truck, and at this rate, we'll be here until September."

"Sorry."

"They always are . . ."

I help Rick finish loading the truck and fold up the tables and tent, and as I gather my things together and prepare to leave, Rick digs into his pocket.

"Normally I pay a hundred dollars a market, but since this is your first day, and we didn't do much business, I'm only giving you sixty." He reaches for a paper bag. "Oh, and here are two loaves of walnut spelt bread. Those puppies didn't move for anything today."

Great. First I lose my job, and now this guy wants to pay me in leftover bread. Newsflash: Flour and yeast will not pay my electricity bill.

"I could use some extra help around the holidays, though," he says. "If you help at Penn Quarter and Dupont this week, I'll give you the standard hundred per market, plus the extra forty I owe you from today."

I clear my throat. When it comes to getting a job in the food world, working for a lunatic for three hundred dollars a week isn't exactly what I had in mind. "Um . . . well . . ."

"Hey—if you don't need the money, that's fine by me. I'll find someone who does." He turns and throws his cashbox onto the passenger seat of the truck and then walks around the truck to the driver's side.

I curse myself for what I'm about to do and scurry after him. "Wait."

I don't want to work for a chauvinistic misanthrope for, quite literally, crumbs. But I'm no fool. Three hundred dollars is better than zero dollars, and at this point, other than my severance, zero dollars is what I am currently making. I'm still playing catch-up from my oral surgery boondoggle, and my severance won't last long enough to keep me in that apartment for more than a month or so. My parents are dealing with their own financial strains, so I can't ask them for help. I could definitely use the extra cash, at least as a temporary stopgap.

"I'm in," I say. "I'll see you on Thursday at Penn Quarter."

Rick sticks a cigarette in his mouth and lights it with a bright purple lighter. "Good. But you'd better not be late, or you're finished. Got it?"

I nod. Rick lets out a grunt and heaves himself into the driver's seat. He slams the creaky door and fires up the motor, which sputters as he lowers his window.

"One freaking thirty," he says, the cigarette dangling from his lips. "And not a minute later."

"Got it."

"And next time you see your blond friend, tell her she'd better get her ass here on time too." He steps on the brake and pulls the truck into gear. "I don't need this bullshit."

Then he raises the window, steps on the gas, and jerks the truck down Twenty-third Street.

CHAPTER 8

Here's a little truth bomb: I don't need this bullshit either. What I need is a real job that pays more than three hundred dollars a week and doesn't entail interacting with a chain-smoking lunatic who verbally molests every female he encounters.

Unfortunately, such a job eludes me. Christmas and New Year's pass, as does all of January, and all I have to show for it is some under-the-table cash from Rick the Prick and some new croissant-induced cellulite on my thighs. Everyone assured me no one hired around the holidays, so I understood when New Year's came and went without any employment leads. But apparently no one is hiring *after* the holidays either, because now it's February, and I still don't have a job. Everyone has said the same thing, more or less:

"No open positions right now."

"Not hiring."

"Budget cuts."

"Looking for someone with more relevant experience."

Now nearly two months have passed since I lost my job at *The Morning Show,* and I'm basically in the same position I was on that snowy morning when Heidi got food poisoning, only now I'm well-versed in Rick's panoply of baked goods and their corresponding price structure. Baby steps?

If there is a small silver lining to my continued unemployment, it is that I have increased my hours at the farmers' market, where I am surrounded by people who love growing and making food as much as I love eating, reading, and writing about it. Every market brings with it a new sensory adventure: the toothsome crunch of Rick's millet muffins, the brazen tang of his sourdough, the sharp and herbaceous scent of his cheddar dill scones. Instead of trying to force a food connection like I did at *The Morning Show,* I now live and breathe an agricultural smorgasbord on an almost daily basis, poring over luscious apples and lumpy, bumpy squash and fat loaves of buttery brioche. In a strange way, despite the meager pay, I finally feel as if I'm where I belong.

Another upside of working at the market is that I've been able to spend more time with Heidi, whom I rarely saw while I worked at *The Morning Show.* For four years, we maintained nearly opposite schedules: I was usually up before sunrise and in bed by nine or ten, and she didn't get to work until 10:00 a.m. and was out until at least eleven at night. We did our best to meet up, but I was so tired by dinnertime that I frequently bailed on our happy hour and dinner dates, and on weekends she was usually tied up with farmers' market work and get-togethers with her knitting group. But now we catch up between sales and sneak nibbles of chocolate chip cookies together and fall into the familiar comfort of our friendship.

On the first Saturday in February, Heidi's is the first face I see as I cross Twenty-third Street and approach the market, which at 7:20 is already filled with colorful tents and crates of pastries and produce. I've arrived ten minutes ahead of schedule to spare myself Rick's wrath, but unfortunately, despite my miraculous timing and punctuality, I have still managed to arrive after him. I am convinced he shows up five minutes earlier each market just to torture me.

"Come along, slowpoke!" he yells as I make my way toward the truck. "This tent isn't going to pitch itself."

I toss my bag onto the front seat of the truck and, with Heidi's help, Rick and I pitch the tent over the triangular patch of grass just behind the dirt walking path, before the lawn descends into the vast grassy expanse of the park below. Rick and I pull in opposite directions, hoisting the red-and-white checkered canopy across our allotted space while Heidi snaps the legs into place.

Once we've secured the tent and set up the tables, Heidi starts unloading the bread off the truck, and I arrange the baskets along the table, lining each one with a cloth napkin. Rick sidles up next to me, surveying my work with narrowed eyes as he tucks his shirt into his baggy trousers. "Make sure you put the croissants in one of these big rectangular baskets, okay?"

"Got it."

He looks over his shoulder and spots Heidi unloading a crate of baguettes. "Sweet Jesus—would you help her unload those baguettes before she drops them all in the mud? Help me, Lord, for I'm surrounded by morons."

I rush to the back of the truck and help Heidi with the baguettes. "Thanks," she says, dusting off her hands on her jeans as she hops down. Specks of flour cover her puffy olive-colored coat, and she follows me beneath the tent to begin filling the baskets. "So what's the latest on the job search? Any leads?"

"None. At this point I'm applying to anything that will pay me."

"You've added 'high-end escort' to the list, then?"

I whack her arm with the lid to the cheddar dill scones. "I haven't, actually. Maybe I should."

"Are you kidding? You're way too uptight. One mention of handcuffs, and you'd be all, 'You want me to do *what?*'"

"Touché." I start arranging the scones in a wicker basket lined with a baby blue napkin. "I'm just so sick of sending out resumes and meeting for 'informational interviews,' you know? This whole process is eating away at my soul."

"Have you asked Rick about adding more days to your schedule? At least until you find something more permanent."

"I'm already working every winter market he does. Which, frankly, is about all the Rick I can handle right now."

"I'll ask around and see if any friends have leads. We'll find something."

"Thanks. I'm running out of ideas."

The chilled February air nips at my nose as I finish unloading the scones and place the signs in front of the various baskets and crates: seeded rye, peanut butter cookies, cinnamon raisin bread. The smell beneath the tent is intoxicating, a combination of sweet butter, yeast, and toasted flour.

"By the way," Heidi says as the opening bell rings, "did you realize people are still commenting on your blog? You haven't updated that thing in more than four years, but I stopped by the other day, and there are tons of recent comments."

"Yeah, I get e-mails whenever someone writes in. I'm shocked anyone still reads it."

"You should start blogging again. You certainly have the time these days."

"Oh, sure—devoting more of my time to yet another enterprise that doesn't pay. Great idea."

"At least it would get your mind off the job search for an hour or two. And you write about food so well. If you're trying to get your foot in the food-writing door, maybe the blog could help. It certainly couldn't hurt."

"I guess. I'll think about it."

"Ladies, enough with the yammering," Rick says, jabbing me in the side. "In case you haven't noticed, there's a line ten customers deep. Let's get to work."

I rub my hands together and wait on the first customer I see, who orders a loaf of chocolate chunk brioche and two millet muffins. I'm getting better at handling the crowds with each passing week, but I still haven't mastered the art of customer service. Somehow working at my fastest still doesn't seem fast enough, and every time someone makes a snide or impatient remark, I have fantasies of chucking a muffin in his or her face. I've never followed through, but that has less to do with my self-control and more with my complete lack of coordination and aim.

Baked goods and money fly across the table all morning— "Next please!" "What can I get you?" "Anything else for you today?"—and I try to ignore the people who slowly count their change in front of me, as if I am a lowly farm girl and therefore could not possibly do math properly in my head. To be fair, I couldn't find my hat this morning and had to buy a cheap one en route, and I ended up with a Washington Redskins hat that, aside from being two sizes too large and made of some sort of highly flammable furry material, resembles a wizard's cap, with a droopy pointed top festooned with a large yellow pompom. I can't really fault people for thinking I'm a little slow.

About an hour before the market closes, Drew, the model-cum-lumberjack I met on my first day, stops by our tent, a large red crate filled with apples resting on his forearms.

"Hello, ladies," he says, resting it on the edge of our table. "I come bearing gifts."

"Oh, Drew, your mere presence is gift enough," Heidi says.

"In that case . . ." He pulls the crate off the table.

"Not so fast." I reach out and draw the apples closer to me, rooting through the basket. "What exactly do we have here?"

"Ah, so apparently my presence isn't enough for *some* people at this stand."

"Your presence isn't going to feed my empty refrigerator and bank account," I say.

"Fair enough." He reaches into the crate and pulls out an apple with rough gold-and-brown skin. "A few different kinds of apples here. This one is a Goldrush. Kind of like a Golden Delicious but with a bit more acid. It keeps pretty well."

I pick up another from the heap. "And this one?"

Drew reaches out and delicately takes the apple from my hand. "This is a Smokehouse, an antique Pennsylvania Dutch variety. You can pretty much use it for anything—pies, cooking, sauce. It tastes like fresh cider. Really good. So are the Mutsus and Pink Ladies."

"And these are all for us?" I ask.

"Sure. In exchange for some bread and muffins—assuming you get the okay from Rick."

At the mention of his name, Rick trundles over to our corner of the tent. "What's going on over here? We still have forty-five minutes left. This isn't playtime."

"Maggie and I were hoping to do a little swap," Drew says. "Some apples for some of your olive bread and millet muffins. What do you think?"

"You know I can't resist Maggie's apples." He winks. "And her fruit ain't half-bad either." He waves Drew over to the truck. "Come on. I'll hook you up with a bag of goodies."

Drew follows Rick over to the truck, and they disappear behind the loading area.

"So Drew is pretty hot, huh?" Heidi says.

"He is definitely easy on the eyes."

"And very sweet. You should go for a drink with him."

"Me?"

"No, the other Sydney."

"You're the one who should go for a drink with him. You were like a dog in heat as soon as he came over."

Heidi cackles. "Been there, done that."

"Oh, so I get your sloppy seconds? No, thanks."

"He isn't my sloppy seconds. We went on one date, had a drunken smooch, and realized it would never work out between us, so we're just friends. But he's a sweetheart. I think you'd like him."

"Maybe. Mentally I'm not really in a place to date right now."

Heidi moans. "Because of Zach? That was years ago, Sydney. We've been over this. It's time to move on."

"It isn't because of Zach," I say, even though we both know it is. "I should be devoting my mental energies to finding a job, not to finding my way into someone's bed."

"Whatever. Just promise you'll think about it. We could go on a double date. It would be really low-key."

"Okay. I'll think about it."

Drew and Rick emerge from behind the truck, and Drew hands me and Heidi a white plastic bag filled with apples. "Enjoy, ladies," he says with a smile. Then he turns to me. "It's Sydney, right?"

I nod.

"Great seeing you again," he says. "You'll have to let me know what you think of the Smokehouses next time you see me—which I hope will be soon?"

"Sure. I'm here every weekend."

Heidi clears her throat as if she is about to say something, but I kick her beneath the table.

"Cool," Drew says. "I'll see you next weekend, then."

He grabs his brown bag filled with bread and pastries and turns to leave, then turns back quickly, as if he has forgotten something. His big brown eyes run up and down my face and land on the top of my head. He breaks into a broad smile. "By the way," he says, "sweet hat."

When I get back to my apartment that afternoon, I flip open my laptop and log on to *A Perpetual Feast,* the food blog I started freshman year of college. It was a mix of personal essays, recipes, and trend reporting, an extension of the column I began in high school while working on the school paper. I'd worked on the paper for four years at that point, but once we were high school seniors, Zach encouraged me to start a food column, and with his help, I launched "Zest," which ran articles on everything from our cafeteria food to restaurants around town. One of my first pieces blasted our cafeteria staff and launched an investigation into their hygienic practices after I found a dirty bandage and a fingernail in my baked beans. The column won a local award and compelled our school board to strengthen their health and safety rules, and I'm pretty sure the story helped me get into college.

Once I got to Northwestern, though, the competition was steep, and I couldn't convince the editors of *The Daily Northwestern* or the producers of the Northwestern News Network to make me the resident food journalist. So instead, I created my own food blog. At first, I didn't have many readers, but within a few months, my audience ballooned, and by my junior year, I was able to leverage my clout as a food blogger to produce my own weekly food show on NNN. Even with all of that experience, I still couldn't land a paying job as a food journalist after college, but I kept up the blog for a few months after graduation anyway. I still enjoyed writing about food, but if I'm being honest, I also saw the blog as an extension of my high school column and therefore an extension of Zach. Keeping up the site made me feel close to him, even once we'd broken up and I knew he wasn't reading it anymore.

As I scan my site today, I see the most recent post is dated four years ago, a week before I started at *The Morning Show.* I reread the first sentence:

> Few things will make you feel as lonely as the
> sound of a place setting being cleared at a table set
> for two.

The post goes on to detail the art of eating alone, of finding peace at a table for one. It reads like a piece of post-breakup therapy, even though I'd written it six months after Zach and I split. I click on the fifty-seven comments, the bulk of which are from people sharing their own experiences eating alone, which I remember comforting me at the time. I wasn't a freak for feeling the way I did. Lots of people felt that way after losing their best friends, and even though I'd never met those people, knowing they were out there had made me feel less alone. My eyes land on the last comment in the queue, which someone left last week: "Is this blog dead? Or are you still out there?"

My fingers hover over the keyboard as I ponder a reply. Is this blog dead? Heidi doesn't seem to think it should be. Maybe she's right. I do have plenty of time to maintain it these days. And with all of my work at the farmers' market, I have a new perspective on food and the farming system, not to mention all of the crazy characters who work there. I rub my hands together, crack my knuckles, and click Reply.

"I'm still out here," I write.

Then I click New Post and let my fingers fly.

CHAPTER 9

In the first week, my first post in more than four years garners a total of twenty views and one measly comment, which is actually from a spam bot promoting drugs for erectile dysfunction. Considering the post is about heirloom apples, this is both disappointing and confusing.

One of the twenty readers happens to be my sister, who calls me the Friday after I post, with what I can only assume is some sort of wedding-related query.

"Leave it to you to turn apples into a history lesson," she says as soon as I pick up the phone.

"Hello to you, too."

"Come on. You didn't expect me not to comment on that post. Antique apples? What a snoozefest."

"Just because you don't care doesn't mean no one else does. Some people enjoy reading material beyond *Bachelorette* recaps."

"Oh my God, did you see this week's episode?" she gushes.

I sigh. "No."

"You should. So much drama. Anyway, I didn't know you'd decided to start blogging again. Where'd that come from?"

"I guess I missed it. I've been working at the farmers' market, so I realized I had plenty of new material. Like those apples. One of the other vendors gave them to me, and it got me thinking about why we have, like, five kinds of apples in the grocery store when there are dozens and dozens of varieties out there."

Libby fakes a snore. "Only kidding," she says. "It was actually kind of interesting. Needed a recipe, though. Or are you still on your cooking strike?"

"It isn't a cooking strike."

"Oh, really? When was the last time you actually cooked something other than Easy Mac?"

I consider her question and come up blank. "I don't know. I can't remember."

"You can't remember because it's been years. Four years and seven months, if I had to guess."

"Libby . . ."

"It's just weird. All through high school, we couldn't get you out of Zach's kitchen, and now you won't set foot in one."

"That isn't true," I say.

"You're right: In high school, you wouldn't really cook in Mom's kitchen either. So I guess now you've just extended the policy across the board."

"Jesus, Libby, would you lay off?"

"I'm just saying."

Libby is always "just saying." The phrase is one of her most annoying retorts. But she isn't entirely wrong. In high school, Zach's was the only kitchen in which I spent much time, mostly because his mom's gear was so much nicer than mine. But I also felt, from a very early age, that our family kitchen was Mom and Libby's domain. They always had so much in common—the same hair and eye color, the same cadence in their voices, the same interest in clothes and shopping and soap operas. Over school breaks, the two of them would powwow about what culinary adventure they would take up next, whether it was a chocolate soufflé or a croquembouche, and it was clear their bond over cooking was something I could never be a part of. Whenever I tried to help, I felt like an intruder. So instead of nosing around every time they decided to cook together, I gave up and left them alone, even though, deep down, I wanted to join in the fun.

"Anyway," Libby says with a protracted sigh, "the main reason I'm calling is to ask if you can come to my tasting at The Rittenhouse in June."

"Isn't that for couples and parents only?"

"They said I can bring anyone I want. And Matt is sort of fussy about food, so I could use your input."

"If he's the groom, though, shouldn't the menu be something he'd enjoy?"

"If it were up to Matt, we'd serve chicken fingers and French fries. And that is so not happening."

"I thought you two were soul mates."

"We are. We just have different ideas about wedding food."

I glance at the ceiling. "Yeah, okay, I'll be there. When is it?"

"June 10—a Friday. I know you'd normally be working that day, but given how all of that is going . . ."

She trails off. Normally I'd say she was trying to wind me up, as she always does, but considering she wants me to do her a favor, I know it's just Libby's typical self-absorption combined with her complete lack of interest in my career.

"I'll mark my calendar," I say.

"Yay! I'm so excited. And it'll be even more fun for you because you don't have to worry about fitting into a wedding dress."

"Thanks for reminding me."

"I'm just saying," she replies.

Of course she is.

The next morning, Rick greets me at the West End farmers' market with his signature blend of cantankerousness and misogyny.

"Hurry up, sweet cheeks," he bellows from the cavernous interior of the truck. "I don't have all morning."

I meet Heidi beside the loading area and grab a crate of oatmeal raisin cookies. Their sweet, toasty aroma makes my stomach growl. They are nearly five inches in diameter and packed with plump golden raisins and fat rolled oats, the perfect balance between crispy and chewy. Every bite is perfumed with vanilla and just a touch of cinnamon, and I can see why Rick sells out at every market.

"So I have a job lead for you," Heidi says as she arranges a stack of apple streusel muffins on a porcelain cake stand.

"Really? Where?"

"I was talking to Julie—the woman who runs the whole farmers' market consortium in DC—and she mentioned they need someone to manage their weekly newsletter. She's looking for someone to write a few columns about what's fresh at market, profile a few farmers, stuff like that. I pointed her to your blog, and she liked what she saw."

"Really? Any idea how much it pays?"

"No idea. My guess is not much. But it's something. If not full-time, then at least a resume builder."

I sigh. "Considering I worked on a national news show for four years, writing a farmers' market newsletter doesn't exactly feel like a step forward."

"It's a step in a different direction—the right direction, from what you've said you'd actually like to do."

"True. Do you think she'd mind if I e-mailed her?"

"She'd love it. I'll send you her contact info."

The opening bell rings, and as Heidi helps a few customers at the other end of our tent, a man in a navy North Face jacket and Red Sox baseball cap approaches my corner. His face is vaguely familiar, but his hat covers so much of his forehead that I can't place him.

"Hey there," he says with a grin as he tucks his hands into the pockets of his coat.

"Hi . . . Can I help you?"

"Don't you remember me?"

I search his face and realize he is the guy from Bar Pilar—Jeremy, the one who tried to slip me his number on a piece of bakery tissue paper back in December. I haven't seen him since.

"Oh—hi. Jeremy, right? I haven't seen you here in a while."

"Things got a little crazy at the beginning of the year with work. You know how it is."

"I wish," I say. He looks as if he wants me to elaborate, but I decide against boring him with my unemployment sob story. "Anyway, what can I get you?"

"Wow. Down to business. Okay." He scrunches his lips to the side and scans the table.

"The apple streusel muffins are relatively new. So is the Finnish pulla."

He rubs his chin, which is covered with the barest whisper of brown stubble. "Those sound good, but that's not really what I want. . . ."

"Oatmeal raisin cookie?"

He fixes his eyes on mine. "I was thinking more along the lines of a date with you."

I swallow hard. "A what?"

"A date. You and me."

"I'm sort of . . . busy lately."

This, clearly, is not true, unless I am qualifying as "busy" working at the farmers' market and maintaining a social life that primarily involves *Law & Order* reruns.

"Is that why you never called me?" he asks. "I left you my number."

"You did? I never got it," I lie.

"Ah. Well, that would make calling me a little difficult."

"Usually does."

He grins and leans back on his heels. "What are you doing Friday night?"

"Friday? As in six days from now?"

"Unless there's another Friday I don't know about . . ."

I rack my brain. Friday, Friday, Friday. What do I have going on this Friday? Oh, right: nothing, because I have to work at the farmers' market the next morning. Also, I am boring and currently have no life.

"Hadn't thought about it," I say.

"Let me take you to dinner."

I clear my throat. "Yeah, the thing is, I might be—"

"Lame?"

I furrow my brow. "No, I was going to say I might be—"

"Lame. You might be lame and make up some excuse as to why you can't have dinner with me. Am I right?"

I pick up a piece of bakery tissue paper and rub it between my fingers. Before I can confirm that yes, in fact, I was about to make up an excuse as to why I can't have dinner with him, mostly because I don't *want* to go out to dinner with him, Rick yells at me from the other side of the tent.

"Come on, Chatty Cathy. People are waiting!"

"Sorry!" I yell back.

Jeremy grins. "How about this: Meet me Friday night at Birch and Barley at seven o'clock. If you're bored after fifteen minutes, you can leave. No strings attached."

"Fifteen minutes?"

He nods. "Fifteen minutes."

"Sydney, let's *go!*" Rick shouts.

"Okay, okay!" I yell over my shoulder. I look back at Jeremy. I could say no. I probably should say no, given that he called me a loud talker and will probably decide I am an undateable nerd after two minutes. But there is something about him—his penetrating eyes, his unapologetic boldness, his endearing smile. I could say no, but something in my gut won't let me.

"Okay," I say. "I'll be there. But I'm holding you to that fifteen-minute rule."

"Then I'd better bring my A game," he says with a smirk. "See you Friday. And as long as I'm here . . ." He points to an oatmeal raisin cookie.

"You got it." I stuff the cookie into a bag, and as I study the devilish grin on Jeremy's face, I decide I either just made the best decision I've ever made, or the worst.

CHAPTER 10

The following Friday night, I show up at Birch and Barley looking as good as someone with a supremely limited fashion sense who doesn't really want to participate in this dinner can look: bland and unremarkable, other than my raging under-eye circles and stubby nails, which I've bitten down to the quick. Were this a date with my dream man—whatever rare specimen might fit that description—I would have used my meager salary to buy a new dress and new underwear and new shoes. I would have popped for the fifteen-dollar anti-frizz pomade, instead of the five-dollar pot-o'-grease I have applied to my unruly, dark brown waves, and I would have spent two hours grooming myself into my most attractive state.

But this isn't my dream man. This is some guy who seems to be stalking me, and so I haven't done any of those things. And, by decree, I only have to spend fifteen minutes with him before I can go home, change into fleece pants, and flip through reruns of *Law & Order* and *The Office*. Part of me wishes I could dispense with this entire charade before it begins.

The good news is that Birch and Barley sits only seven short blocks south of my apartment, on a stretch of Fourteenth Street teeming with restaurants, bars, and home furnishing shops. This part of Washington has always felt more like New York or Philadelphia to me, with its urban bustle and density, each storefront pressed tightly against the next. I think that's why I chose to live in this area of town. Even if I worked crazy hours, rarely dated, and spent most of my free time in my apartment by myself, I had at least the illusion of companionship. Surrounded by so many people, I could pretend I wasn't completely alone.

I squeeze past a group lingering in front of the restaurant's warehouse-like edifice, with its two-story birch door and large-paned front window. The front vestibule is cramped and narrow, and I line up behind the crowd waiting to speak to the hostess. The interior of the restaurant is warm and dark, with exotic wood panels interspersed between long stretches of exposed brick walls. Small globe lights dangle from the ceiling, their twinkling orbs casting a warm glow on the plush olive booths and Lucite chairs. The room is hip and sexy and polished—everything I currently am not.

I make my way up to the hostess, who is aggressively tapping her touch-screen computer. She glances up at me. "Can I help you?"

"I'm supposed to be meeting someone. A guy named Jeremy? Reservation for seven o'clock?"

She raps her finger against her computer screen. "Unfortunately, you're the first to arrive, and we can't seat you until the entire party is present. But if you want, you can—"

"Looking for me?"

I glance over my shoulder and find Jeremy standing behind me, the jacket to his gray suit slung over his shoulder. He wears a lilac shirt with a navy grid and matching navy tie, along with a pair of shiny silver cufflinks. I feel massively unstylish in my black pants and black boatneck tee, which are slightly different shades of black and are both at least three years old. Also, even on my wiry frame, the pants are too tight. Not in a sexy way. In an "I've-been-eating-a-lot-of-free-brioche" kind of way. An "I-may-need-to-unbutton-my-pants-when-we-sit-down" kind of way. This outfit was a terrible mistake.

I smile at Jeremy and motion toward the hostess. "I was just checking in."

"Perfect timing then."

The hostess leads us to our table, one of five two-tops lined up against the side wall, with a plush bench stretching from end to end and Lucite chairs perched on the opposite side.

"Bench or chair?" Jeremy asks, gesturing to the booth against the wall and the chair on the outside.

"Chair," I say. An easier escape.

I sit down, and as soon as the hostess hands us the menus, Jeremy grabs mine out of my hand. "Ah, ah, ah—not so fast," he says. "I might only have fifteen minutes with you. I don't want to spend the majority of it reading the menu."

I fold my hands in my lap. "Fair enough."

"So tell me a little about yourself. How long have you been working at the farmers' market?"

"Two months today, actually. Since you saw me there for the first time in December."

"How'd you get into that?"

"Long story. My friend Heidi got food poisoning, and I had to fill in for her, and then working there became a good way to make a few bucks while I look for a real job."

He raises an eyebrow as he takes a sip of water. "You're still out of work?"

"What do you mean 'still'?"

"That night I met you at Bar Pilar, you mentioned losing your job...."

"Oh, right. When you were eavesdropping." He starts to object, but I cut him off. "Sorry—you weren't eavesdropping. I was just talking REALLY LOUD."

The couple at the table next to us jumps, and Jeremy flushes. "Here we go again...."

"Sorry," I say. "Bad joke."

He grins and relaxes. "So back to the farmers' market..."

"Right. The market. I've been working for Wild Yeast for two months, a few days a week. And this week I've been e-mailing with the woman who manages most of the markets in DC, and she may pay me to write their weekly newsletter."

"That sounds cool. Would that be a temporary thing too?"

"Not sure. Ideally the work on the newsletter would help me

land a job in food journalism, which is what I've always wanted to do anyway."

Jeremy's cheeks flush. "Ah."

"What's that supposed to mean?"

"I . . . nothing."

"What, you have something against food writers?"

His expression darkens. "No. I used to be one."

"Really?" I study his face. I'd thought he looked familiar. "Where?"

He clears his throat. "The *Washington Chronicle*."

"Wow—seriously? That's like my dream job. Why did you leave?"

"Long story." He glances down at his watch and grimaces. "And one we don't have time for because apparently I only have five minutes left to convince you I'm not a loser. As far as I can tell, I'm doing a really bad job."

"I'll be honest. The situation is not looking good."

Jeremy slaps himself across the face. "Come on, man! Pull it together!"

I bite my lip to keep from laughing. "Tell you what. I'll give you a five-minute extension. So you have ten minutes left."

"Really?"

"Really."

Jeremy pumps his fist under the table. He shakes out his shoulders and loosens his neck, tilting his head from side to side. "Okay," he says. "Time to do this right."

He rubs his hands together and fixes his blue eyes on mine, and I'm struck by both how familiar he seems and how much better looking he is than I'd realized. "Okay," he says. "Tell me about the best and worst things you ever ate, and where you ate them."

"Ever?"

"Ever," he says. "And I'll go next. Think fast. We only have ten minutes. Ready? Go."

Somehow, ten minutes morphs into thirty, and before I know it, we've drunk a beer each and have ordered starters and entrées off the menu. I've learned that the best thing he's ever eaten was fresh ricotta on a small farm outside Scanno in Abruzzo, Italy, and that his worst meal involved Hamburger Helper, minus the hamburger, when he was a poor college student and couldn't afford to splurge on beef. He is a beer nerd who brews at home and brought me here because he loves their draft list, and in the thirty minutes of our date, he has already taught me the difference between brewing a porter and brewing an IPA. I've learned that he loves Fitzgerald and Hornby, Bach and Death Cab for Cutie, autumn and *Seinfeld* and Humphrey Bogart movies. I've learned we have a lot more in common than I thought.

"So wait," he says, as he takes a sip of his second beer, a Kasteel Tripel. "Let's go back to this cigarette spaghetti situation. I'm seriously confused as to how this could have happened."

I laugh and almost spit my porter back into my glass. "I know. It's a mystery. But I'm telling you: It tasted like eating a plate full of cigarettes."

"And this was at band camp?"

"No—not band camp. It was more like a band . . . festival." Jeremy starts snickering. "Shut up! It was a big deal. Only a few kids from each high school were chosen."

"Hey, you're talking to a former tuba player. I'm not judging."

"You played the *tuba*?"

He blushes. "It's an important instrument—and, I'll have you know, one that's difficult to play well."

"Tell me about it. I learned a lot those years at band ca—sorry, band *festival*."

"So what did you play?"

"Clarinet."

He smiles. "That fits."

"What is that supposed to mean?"

"All of the clarinet players at my high school were cute girls. And none of them would go on a date with me."

The waitress returns with our grilled octopus and tuna tartare appetizers, cutting off Jeremy before I can point out that I *am* on a date with him—the first date I've been on in ages, actually. I could blame my dating misfortune on the intensity of working on a daily news show, but that would be an easy excuse, and it wouldn't be entirely true. I could also blame Zach, and although he started me down this path of mistrust and loneliness, I'm the one who has continued on it for so long.

What happens, if you're me, is at a young age you let someone know you, totally and completely, and then that person breaks your heart. So you don't date for a while, and you blame the breakup, which is true but eventually sounds lame as the months pass. So then you blame your job for being too time consuming, which is only partially true but sounds more reasonable to an outsider than blaming an ex-boyfriend you haven't seen or talked to in a year. And then, even once the early sting of betrayal wears off, it becomes easier not to date. To opt out. To protect yourself from rejection. Publicly you still blame your job, and you hide behind that story, until that hidden space becomes warm and cozy, and you don't want to come out from behind it. And the more time that passes, the cozier that space becomes, until the dating world seems like a wild jungle, full of traps and hazards and scary things. So what do you do? You burrow deeper into that space and spend your nights alone, fantasizing about an ex-boyfriend who probably doesn't even think about you anymore.

And then, by some combination of pressure and guilt and decidedly peculiar luck, you end up on a date with a guy named Jeremy, who proves dating isn't scary after all.

"This octopus is to die for," he says, cutting into a fat tentacle. "Here, try a bite."

He cuts off a large hunk and deposits it on my bread plate, and I poke my fork into it and stick the slice into my mouth. The meat is tender and juicy and slightly sweet, with a smoky kick from the charred grilled bits.

"Wow, you're right," I say, washing the octopus down with a sip of my beer. "That's fantastic."

"I take it you've never been here before?"

I shake my head. "I don't get out a lot."

"No?"

I consider the best way not to sound socially incompetent. Given my track record, this will not be easy.

"No," I say, opting for a one-word answer, simple and true.

He grins as he cuts into another piece of octopus. "Then we'll have to change that, won't we?"

The alcohol rushes to my cheeks, and I can hear my heart thumping in my ears. "Sure," I say.

I smile and fix my eyes on his, and then, to dispel any ambiguity in my response, I add, "Yeah. I'd really like that."

CHAPTER 11

On a good day, an appetizer, entrée, and two beers would put me into a full-fledged food coma, but the warm and gooey chocolate peanut butter tart we share for dessert puts me over the top. I can barely breathe. The button to my pants gave up two courses ago.

But I don't even care because, wow, I forgot how wonderful it is to dine at a nice restaurant. And I forgot how nice it is to sit across from someone of the opposite sex who is attractive and interesting and engaging and actually seems to like me. That, of course, suggests I knew what such an experience was like with anyone other than Zach, which—let's face it—I didn't. So, on all fronts, the evening has been a success.

Jeremy pulls out my chair and helps me into my coat. "You look great, by the way," he says. "I should have said that earlier. I kind of panicked under the whole fifteen-minute rule. But you really do look terrific."

I feel myself blush. "Thanks. Although I'll let you in on a little secret. I'm wearing two different shades of black. And these pants are at least three years old."

I have no idea why I am sharing this with him. I blame the beer, along with my general social awkwardness.

"Well, I'll let *you* in on a little secret," he says, lowering his voice as he comes in close. "This tie is five years old. And I bought it at the Leesburg outlets."

I widen my eyes, feigning shock. "You're a discount shopper?"

He shrugs. "What can I say? I like a good deal."

It's about now that I feel an overwhelming urge to lean in and kiss this man, this adorable smooth talker who managed to cajole me into going to dinner with him. But we're still standing in the middle of the restaurant, and though I may lack the ever-elusive quality of grace, I possess at least a modicum of self-awareness that tells me making out in the middle of a restaurant is trashy.

Jeremy and I make our way toward the exit. As we pass the hostess stand, he touches the small of my back, ever so gently, and sends a thrill shooting through my body like lightning.

"Where to?" he asks.

I hesitate outside the front door. Is this a your-place-or-mine type of question? Or does he actually want to *do* something, like go to a jazz club or share a nightcap? I have very little experience with this. I don't know the rules.

"Um, not sure..." I look at my watch. "Holy crap—it's ten thirty already."

He chuckles. "Is that late for you?"

"Kind of." I catch myself. "Wow. That sounded even lamer out loud than it did in my head. The thing is, I used to work on a morning news show. My bedtime was nine o'clock. Ten at the latest."

Only when I say this do I realize how little we discussed our careers—current and former—over the course of our three-and-a-half-hour date. I mentioned wanting to be a food writer, and he talked a little about his job in PR, but mostly we just talked about our lives. We talked about our favorite foods and college memories, where we've been in the world, and where we'd still like to go. We talked about what movies and books have shaped our views and what sort of music makes us happy. We talked about what makes us... well, *us,* without any mention of our vocations. In a city where what you do and where you work often defines you, I find this very refreshing.

Jeremy claps his hands together. "Well, I'd hate to keep you up past your bedtime. I'll walk you home. We can stay out late another time."

He slips into his coat, and we stroll up Fourteenth Street, past the Studio Theatre and a bunch of closed storefronts, moving in silence through the chilled February air. As we reach the corner of Fourteenth and R, he brushes against my shoulder, and another bolt of lightning shoots through me from head to toe. I can't deny it: I *like* this guy.

But, as a general rule, nothing in my life goes smoothly when it has the potential to become excruciatingly awkward, and so as we proceed up Swann Street toward my house, I spot my crazy downstairs neighbor, Simon, standing on our front stoop, up to his usual freaky tricks. Tonight, he is applying duct tape over the doorbell to his unit.

"Is this your place . . . ?" Jeremy mutters as I turn through the hip-height gate in front of my building.

"Yep."

He lowers his voice and whispers in my ear. "Who is that guy?"

"My downstairs neighbor," I whisper back. "He's a little weird."

I pull away, and Jeremy raises his eyebrows without replying, as if to say, *You think?*

"Hi, Simon," I say as we approach the front steps. "What are you doing?"

He glances over his shoulder and drags his eyes across me and Jeremy. "My doorbell isn't working. It makes an annoying buzzing sound."

"Have you told Al?"

He smoothes the sides of the duct tape into place. "Yes. He'll fix it Monday. But until then, I don't want to be disturbed."

Considering I've never seen anyone visit Simon, I'm not sure what he's worried about.

Jeremy casts a sideways glance in my direction, unsure of what to say or do. The three of us are just standing on the front steps together: me, my date, and my supremely bizarre neighbor. I may not have much experience with dating, but I feel comfortable saying this is one of the stranger ways to end an evening.

Simon clutches his roll of duct tape and runs a hand over his buzz cut. "Well, good night," he finally says. He walks inside and slams the front door behind him.

"Dude, that guy is creepy," Jeremy says.

"He's harmless. Just a loner who keeps to himself."

"If you say so . . ."

We stand next to each other on the top step, grinding our heels in the pavement. I'm not sure what to do next. Every topic for discussion that enters my head is both inane and banal—beer and flowers, neighbors and music, anything to keep him standing here until one of us makes a move.

"Thanks for giving me a shot tonight," Jeremy says.

I try to smile as naturally as possible, even though my heart is racing. "Thanks for being persistent."

"Persistence is one of my many fine qualities," he jokes, fiddling with his tie.

"So . . . do you want to come upstairs for a bit?"

My forwardness catches me by surprise. The words, to me, sound like a canned script from a bad romantic comedy. But the truth is, I want him to come upstairs, and for more than a bit. I want him to spend the night.

Jeremy juts out his jaw and manages a wry smile. "I'm not sure that's such a good idea."

My stomach drops. "Oh. Okay."

"Don't get me wrong—I would love to come upstairs. But . . . I don't want to jinx this. I've made that mistake before."

What he doesn't understand is that I've *never* made that mistake before. I've never let someone stay the night at my apartment. Any dalliances over the past four years have involved a drunken kiss in a bar or a random venture to someone else's apartment (which, admittedly, has only happened twice). I've proceeded with caution at every turn—not just with men, but with everything else too. As a child, I was never the first kid to jump in the pool. I was the last, and I would inch my way in, toe first. Recklessness does not come naturally to me.

So why, the one time I want to make a rash decision, won't this guy play along? Isn't playing along what men have been biologically programmed to do?

"You're sure . . . ?" I ask, hoping he'll change his mind.

He sighs. "Yeah, I'm sure. Though I'll probably kick myself later."

I nod, disappointed. "Okay."

"Hang on—you're not off the hook that easy. What are you up to next Tuesday?"

"I'm working at a farmers' market out in Virginia during the day, but otherwise, no plans," I say.

"Great. Maybe we can try a place in Penn Quarter. I'll give you a call Sunday or Monday, and we can work out the details. Which reminds me—what's your number?"

He pulls out his phone and punches in my number, and as he does, he reaches into his jacket pocket with his other hand and offers me two business cards. "Here's my info," he says.

I glance quickly at the card. "A business card? Seriously?"

"Two business cards, actually, in case you lose one. My e-mail is on there too. I know it seems formal but—"

I grab him by the tie and pull him in for a kiss. I don't know what possesses me to do that, but I can't help myself. The action is instinctual, impulsive, and unlike me in every way.

We kiss for a few minutes on the front steps, and eventually Jeremy pulls away and smiles.

"There's still time to change your mind about coming upstairs," I say.

"Nah, one step at a time." He tucks a lock of my hair behind my ear and kisses my forehead. "I'll talk to you soon, okay?"

I nod.

He kisses me once more on the lips and squeezes my hand. Then he hustles down the front steps and looks over his shoulder twice before disappearing down Swann Street.

I'm smitten.

I race up my steps, throw myself onto my couch, and let out a contented sigh. My heart flutters with excitement, and I cannot stop smiling. My whole body feels light and tingly, as if I could float up off the couch. I haven't felt like this since—No. I'm not going to think about that now. I'm not going to ruin the moment.

I throw myself upright and glance down at the business cards I'm still holding: JEREMY BRAUER, ACCOUNT EXECUTIVE, CARPER MASON. Looking at his name like that, something stirs in my gut. Jeremy Brauer. He couldn't be the same Jeremy Brauer as . . . No. Couldn't be.

I rush over to my laptop, flip it open, and punch "Jeremy Brauer" into Google.

And then I want to throw up.

> Disgraced food writer Jeremy Brauer, best known for his involvement in the "cash for comment" scandal at the *Washington Chronicle* . . .

> Jeremy Brauer, a former writer for the *Washington Chronicle*'s food section, whose reputation as the paper's young and promising talent was sullied by accusations of ethics violations . . .

> Jeremy Brauer . . . forced to resign from the paper . . . questions of integrity . . .

> Jeremy Brauer . . . journalist hack . . . rocked the *Chronicle*'s credibility. . . . no comment, no comment, no comment . . .

Great. I'm smitten with a scumbag.

CHAPTER 12

I should have known. I should have *known*. Not only because I thought he looked familiar, and not only because he seemed a little too smooth, but also because the laws of the universe demand that my love life be an utter shambles. Of course Jeremy couldn't wind up being a normal, nice guy who liked me. Of course not.

I first heard Jeremy's story about six years ago, when the food blogosphere was all a-titter over the *Chronicle*'s bright young talent and his fall from grace. The scandal surrounded a series of columns he'd written for the paper's food section, in which he reviewed a bunch of products and eateries at the behest of some PR firm that paid him for his reviews. When it came out that he'd received "cash for comment," food writers—and the journalism community more generally—went nuts, and there was an uproar calling for his dismissal. He was fired from the paper, and I never heard about him again.

Until he conned me into going on a date with him.

If I'd known who he was, I never would have agreed to that date. But the scandal had broken while I was in college, so my memory of the incident was a little hazy, and he never told me his last name anyway. I'd had no idea my Jeremy—the man I kissed tonight and with whom I was momentarily smitten—was the infamous Jeremy Brauer.

I'm pissed I didn't make the connection sooner, but what grates most of all, what really burns, is how much I liked him. How could my instincts have been so wrong? And why did the one person I finally let peek behind the curtain have to be even less trustworthy than Zach?

I drift in and out of sleep that night, my mind a whirring mess of anxiety and disappointment, until my alarm goes off at six thirty the next morning, rousing me for my shift at the West End farmers' market. After last night, I have neither the interest nor the patience to deal with Rick and a bunch of cranky customers, but if this latest romantic debacle is any indication, my wants don't exactly rank high on the universe's "To Do" list.

"There she is," Heidi says as I approach the tent, which she and Rick have already pitched. She tugs at her green-and-white knit hat. "You look terrible."

"Thanks."

"Sorry. You just look . . . tired."

"That's probably because I didn't get any sleep last night."

"No?"

I wave her off. "Long story. Do you need help with that crate of rye?"

"Nah." Heidi manhandles the big, black crate, then thinks better of it. "Yeah, actually. Could you grab the other side?"

I help Heidi and Rick unload the bread off the truck, noticing that Rick is in a particularly quiet mood this morning, which feels like a gift from the Almighty. As we arrange the bread and pastries in baskets, Heidi casts sideways glances in my direction, as if she knows there is a juicy story behind my intense under-eye circles and ratty hair.

"So . . . what did you do last night?" she asks.

I heave a sigh. "I had a date. Okay?"

"Seriously?"

"Don't sound so surprised."

"It's hard not to, given your track record. You wouldn't even go for a drink with Drew. Who's the lucky guy?"

I stack a pile of pumpkin muffins inside a deep wicker basket. "Do you remember the guy we ran into the night I lost my job back in December? The one at Bar Pilar?"

Heidi purses her lips in a moment of deep thought and then widens her eyes. "The guy who called you a loud talker? In the vest?"

"That's the one."

"No way! How did that come about?"

I shove an empty crate under the table and reach for the container of snickerdoodles. "He stopped by the market the other week, while you were helping a bunch of people on the other side of the tent, and conned me into going out with him."

"And? How'd it go?"

I let out a sarcastic laugh. "Well, the date went fine. Great, actually. Until I got home and Googled him and discovered he is a total shill."

"Explain?"

"Do you remember the whole 'cash for comment' scandal at the *Chronicle*? In their food section? It happened back when we were in college."

Heidi arranges a stack of oatmeal loaves. "I think so. . . . Some young reporter got paid by a PR company to write a bunch of reviews, right?"

"Yep. His name was Jeremy Brauer."

She pounds one loaf against another. "Yes! Okay. That rings a bell."

"Well, that's who I went out with last night. Jeremy Brauer."

"No shit."

"Yep. Total disaster."

She stacks the loaves in a basket. "I hadn't thought about that story in years."

"Well, if you have any interest, it's all over the Internet, so you can refresh your memory at any time."

"That's the glory of the Web, right?"

"Something like that." I sigh. "We are supposed to go out again on Tuesday, but clearly that isn't happening. I can't believe I fell for his act. I actually thought I liked him."

Heidi pats my shoulder. "I've been there. Approximately eighty-seven times. Totally sucks."

I nod in agreement, knowing that Heidi is somewhat of a professional when it comes to poor dating choices. She frequently falls madly, irrationally in love with complete losers, only to discover too late the full extent of their freakishness and potential mental instability. Hence my hesitation in going for a drink with this Drew character, who for all I know is a total psycho.

"Do you think Jeremy will stop by this morning?" she asks as she reaches for a cake stand.

"Oh dear God. I hope not." The thought hadn't even occurred to me.

"If he does, just hide in the truck. I'll cover for you."

"That's the best plan we can come up with? Hiding in the truck?"

"You have a better one?"

"No. Unfortunately."

"Didn't think so."

We finish setting up the tables, arranging the baskets of almond croissants and raisin bran muffins at one end and the loaves of oatmeal bread and ciabatta at the other. Rick's tattered Wild Yeast sign, whose ends are frayed and whose letters are faded and smudged, hangs on the back of the tent, flapping lightly in the chilled February air.

The market bell rings, and a short man with olive skin and jet-black hair begins playing classical guitar on a grassy area abutting the park, filling the market with smooth, calming melodies. As much as I wasn't looking forward to working this morning, I've come to realize my market gig is like therapy for me. I've always loved being surrounded by food, but what I have come to cherish most at these markets is the sense of community. I know Frank the cheese guy and Barbara the mushroom lady. I swap muffins for raspberry jam with Josie at Jefferson Family Farms and ciabatta for apples with Maggie and Drew at Broad Tree Orchards. They've started to accept me as one of their own, at a time when I could use the company.

Two hours into the market, as I refill a muffin basket with more pumpkin muffins, a woman dressed in a red down parka approaches our tent. Her mousy brown hair is twisted into a knot atop her head, with a few wisps framing her heart-shaped face. Her skin is a study in wrinkles and laugh lines, but rather than aging her, they make her face look worldly and lived in and delightfully at ease. She smiles at me as she slows her step.

"You must be Sydney," she says. "I'm Julie, the market founder and director."

"Oh, right—hi!" I dust my palms on my jeans and reach out to shake her gloved hand. "So good to meet you in person."

"I figured it would be easier to chat in the flesh instead of e-mailing back and forth a dozen times." She reaches into her coat pocket and pulls out a piece of paper. "I had some ideas for the first few newsletters, if you can read my chicken scratch. There are lots of exciting developments on the horizon here."

I stare at her, wide-eyed. "Wait . . . so it's official? I'm writing the newsletter?"

"Sorry—yes. Was that not clear from my last e-mail?"

I feel my cheeks redden. "Not really . . ."

"See, this is why I'm not writing the damn thing myself. I'm great in person, terrible in writing." She sighs. "But anyway, yes, it's official. I love what I've seen on your blog, and I think you'd be perfect."

"This is so exciting—thank you!"

I glance down at the crumpled piece of paper in my hands. Her handwriting is completely unintelligible. The notes consist of a series of bullet points, the first three of which are as follows:

- Dust dial w GG

- Wipo spender farm flask?

- Winkly prof—RICK

"So . . . about this list . . ."

"Right. The list." Her eyes flit in the direction of the bullet points.

"What are 'dust dial' and 'winkly prof'?"

"What and what?" She snatches the list from my hands and scans it. "Wow, my handwriting really is appalling. I'm sorry. That first item should read 'distribution deal with Green Grocers.'"

"And the second and third?"

She glances down. "*Washington Chronicle* to sponsor Farmland Festival, and weekly profile starting with Rick. Sorry—I abbreviate a lot and use unconventional shorthand. Doesn't help that my handwriting looks as if I've had a stroke." She looks up. "I haven't, by the way."

"You want all of this in the first newsletter?"

"No. Here's what I'm thinking. Every newsletter should have a rundown of what's fresh at market that week, a few recipes, and a weekly profile of one of the market vendors. I realize at some point you'll run out of people to profile, but then you can move on to profiling some aspect of their business—a particular product they sell, a new farming technique they're using. Something to humanize the market. All of this will go on our Web site, too."

"Okay. So what about this distribution deal?"

"Ah. That's one of the potential exciting bits of news on the horizon—though we'll have to tread carefully. I don't know how much you've read about Green Grocers' new CEO, but he has made a big stink about prioritizing 'local' food more than his predecessor. There used to be so much red tape for any of these guys to sell their goods at Green Grocers, which is why they sell at these outdoor markets around town. But this new CEO—Bob Young—is lowering the barriers to entry for a lot of farmers across the country."

"But how is that good for you? I mean, if people can buy the same stuff at Green Grocers as they can buy here, why would they bother braving the elements?"

She nods. "A fair point, which is why it's taking a while to work out the details. But there is a huge customer base that never comes to the farmers' market, so this will allow the producers to reach a wider audience. And the people who do come will keep coming because they love the one-on-one interaction with the people who grow and make their food. Plus, the profit margin at our markets is pretty thin, so by giving these guys more of a cushion, it helps us stay in business too."

"How do you want me to play it? As a quick news item? A full story?"

She scrunches up her lips and wiggles them from side to side. "Nothing yet. Our family of DC markets is part of the pilot project, and we're still working out the details of how all of this would work. Let's see what happens in the next month or two, and we can go from there. In the meantime, you can start pulling together recipes and profiles." She grins as Rick hobbles over to my side of the tent. "You can start with Rick—I'm sure he has plenty to share with you."

Rick hikes his pants up around his waist and licks his fat lips suggestively. "You bet I do."

I ignore his nauseating innuendo and tuck Julie's notes into my coat pocket. "By the way, what sort of compensation are we talking about . . . ?"

"You mean how much will I pay? I'm looking at fifty dollars a newsletter, plus reimbursement for any extra costs, like transportation or whatever. It's not a lot, I know, but it's all we can manage in the budget for now. And hey, it's better than nothing, right?"

I smile politely and nod, but as I look up at Rick, who is eye-raping me as he scratches his balls, all I can think is, *I'm not so sure.*

CHAPTER 13

That isn't fair. Fifty dollars is better than zero dollars. Although when I divide fifty by the hours I'll need to spend writing and formatting this newsletter, it's basically slave labor. But at least I can use the columns as clips for an actual food-writing or producing job. By now, the stories I wrote and produced at Northwestern are almost five years old, so having fresh material will make me more employable. At least I hope so.

The following Monday, I borrow Heidi's car and drive out to Rick's bakehouse in West Virginia, about an hour and a half outside Washington, DC. As part of my first profile, Rick agreed to let me visit the place where all of the "magic" happens, but as I turn onto a narrow, bumpy road in what seems to be the middle of nowhere, I sense this afternoon will be anything but magical.

I bounce along in Heidi's 1999 Honda Accord, swerving around potholes the size of Texas as I pass seemingly endless stretches of rolling hills and farmland. As I careen around a bend in the road, I spot Rick's driveway, a dirt lane that winds up a broad hill to a white clapboard farmhouse at the top.

From a distance, the house looks quaint, a bright white cottage perched atop a grassy knoll, looking down upon the apple orchards and cornfields. But as I get closer, the charm wears off. The roof shingles cling precariously to the top of the house, standing on end like flakes of dandruff. Several of the black shutters hang at a crooked angle, dangling by one corner like loose teeth, and the white clapboard exterior is covered in dust and dirt. It's what I imagine the "Little House on the Prairie" might look like if it were run by Miss Havisham.

I pull up beside an old, rusty pickup truck and make my way to Rick's dusty black front door, where I rap a dingy brass knocker to announce my arrival. Flakes of black paint sprinkle to the ground like confetti.

"Well, well, well, look who it is." He frowns as he glances down at my tote bag, which is filled with a reporter's notebook, pens, a digital voice recorder, and a small video recorder I bought in college, along with a mini tripod. "You know I'm not paying you extra for this, right?"

"Julie said she'd pick up the tab for the gas."

"All this for some dinky newsletter?"

"It isn't dinky. Apparently the subscriber list is huge. You should be thrilled—your profile will be front and center."

"Do I look like the kind of person who gets thrilled?" I stare at him blankly. "Exactly," he says. "Come on—let's get to work."

I follow Rick around the front of the house and continue onto a crushed gravel path, which leads to a converted barn adjacent to the main farmhouse. Like the main house, the outside of the barn is made of white clapboard and, also like the main house, appears to be falling apart. But as Rick slides open the thick, black barn door, the glint of stainless steel and bright lights catches my eye as the interior of the bakehouse comes into view. Glistening, rectangular stainless steel tables fill the room, which is lined with wire bakers' racks, fancy ovens, proofing racks, and dozens of scales, scoops, and plastic tubs. Two mixers sit in the back corner, both so large I could fit inside the mixing bowl and still have room for a friend. There are baskets and barrels of flour and more mixing bowls than I've ever seen. And unlike the rest of the property, which seems to be on the verge of collapse, the inside of the barn is immaculate.

"Wow, Rick—this is amazing."

"For the amount it cost me, it'd better be. I'll be paying off the loans on that oven until I die." He points across the room to an enormous metal contraption that is attached to a wide chimney at the back of the barn.

"Is that a wood-fired oven?"

"You bet your tits it is."

I'd rather not involve my tits in any of today's happenings. Frankly, when it comes to Rick, I'd like to keep my tits to myself.

Rick gives me a quick tour of the bakehouse and a brief history of his business. He started Wild Yeast a decade ago, but before that he'd been baking for more than two decades, having spent time in France learning from many of the bread-baking greats: Lionel Poilâne, Bernard Ganachaud, Jean-Luc Poujauran. He has served his bread to four US presidents and two dictators, and in recent years, he has toyed with the idea of milling his own grain.

"But unless a wad of cash drops from the sky, that ain't happening," he says.

"I heard Green Grocers might start selling more local products. Maybe it'll be a windfall for you."

"Doubtful," he says. "And even if it were, I'm in debt up to my eyeballs. Between the loans for this damn bakehouse and the bills for my wife's surgery, it'll take a freaking miracle to get me out of this hole."

"I didn't realize your wife was sick."

More to the point, I didn't realize Rick had a wife. That poor woman. Either she is some sort of masochist, or she is as batshit crazy as he is.

"She isn't sick. The old cow needed a knee replacement. I've needed a hip replacement for years, but she got her surgery first. We lost our health insurance, so Lord knows when we'll be able to afford mine. I used to be a much nicer guy before my hip started hurting like hell."

"Ah," I say. *For the sake of humanity, someone get this man a hip replacement immediately.*

"Anyway," he says, "enough business talk. I thought you wanted to bake bread."

"I do. Let me just . . ."

I pull out my video camera and tripod and begin setting up next to one of the stainless steel tables.

"What's all this?" Rick asks. "I thought this was for some stinking newsletter."

"It is. But I have a food blog, too, and I wanted to post a little video on it. Let people peek behind the Wild Yeast curtain."

He winks. "You can peek behind my curtain any time."

I set up my camera and begin filming as Rick pulls a large tub of sourdough starter from his walk-in refrigerator. The starter—or "levain," as he calls it—is based on a strain of yeast more than a hundred years old, and as he dips his hands into the bubbling, liquidy mixture the color of café au lait, the air fills with the tangy, sweet smell of fresh yeast. He transfers a hunk of starter into a large blue plastic bowl and begins adding more flour and water, using his fat bear paws to knead the flour into the loose, sticky dough. He works quickly but with care, and I zoom in to make sure I get enough close-up shots of the silky smooth dough to edit into the sequence later. I have to admit: It's refreshing to see Rick in this setting, to confirm that he can be someone other than a misogynistic troglodyte.

"This batch won't be ready to go into the oven for another ten hours," he says as he removes the tacky dough from his fingers with a white plastic bench scraper.

"Ten hours?" There's no way in hell I'm staying here for ten hours.

"Don't get your panties in a bunch," he says.

Again: I'd really, really prefer it if Rick wouldn't talk about my tits *or* my panties.

"I have another batch ready to go in the oven in a few minutes," he continues. "Relax."

He pulls out a proofing rack lined with baskets called bannetons, each filled with a puffed mound of pale dough, and as he does, my cell phone rings from within my tote bag. I pause the camera. "Can you hold on just one second? I need to take this." For all I know, it could be a response to one of my many job applications.

"Oh, sure. Because I don't have better things to do . . ."

"I'll just be a sec."

I run over to my tote and grab my phone. I don't recognize the number. "Hello?"

"Hey, Sydney? It's Jeremy." He waits for me to respond, but I don't. "I just wanted to touch base about tomorrow night." He waits again. "Hello?"

"Hi—sorry." My mouth goes dry. I'd forgotten he might call about tomorrow night. I guess I'd been hoping he'd forgotten, too. "I think . . . I think we have a bad connection."

"I can hear you fine," he says. "Can you hear me?"

"I . . . Yeah, I can hear you." I am my own worst enemy.

"Okay, cool. Anyway, I was thinking we could meet up at Rasika—assuming you like Indian. It's hard to get a table, but I managed to pull a few strings."

"Um . . . actually . . . I've had a change of plans. I can't meet up."

"Oh. Okay. How about Thursday?"

I hold my breath and rack my brain for an excuse. "That's not going to work either. I have . . . a thing."

A thing? What does that even mean?

Jeremy goes quiet on the other end of the phone. "Oh," he finally says. "That's too bad."

Rick slaps a huge hunk of dough onto one of the other steel tables, smacking it repeatedly against the surface with a loud bang. "You're missing another crucial step, sweetheart," he shouts above the din. "Post-mixing, pre-banneton."

"Where are you?" Jeremy asks as Rick slams the dough again with a loud *thwack*.

"In West Virginia. Long story." I glance over my shoulder as Rick heaves the dough onto the table, beating it into submission against the cool, steel surface. "I'm actually in the middle of something, so I can't really talk right now."

"Oh. Okay." Jeremy waits for me to fill the silence, but when I don't, he says, "I'd really like to see you again."

"Sometime *today*, sweetheart?" Rick shouts across the room.

"Listen, I have to go," I say.

"Okay . . . Should I call you later?"

I hesitate, wondering if I should tell him the real reason behind my sudden disinterest. But as Rick gives me the evil eye from across the room, I decide I don't have time for a full-fledged confrontation. So instead, I simply say, "Probably not."

Before Jeremy can say anything else, I hang up and head back to my camera, trying to fix my mind on the task at hand. I focus the lens on Rick as he continues to wrestle the huge slab of dough, and as I do, I tell myself cutting a shill like Jeremy loose was the right decision, even though a small part of me isn't so sure.

Four hours later, after shaping two dozen loaves of sourdough and baking off two dozen more, I head back to DC, the passenger seat of Heidi's car covered in bags filled with leftovers and castaways from Rick's bakehouse. As I gnaw at a hunk of day-old cranberry pecan bread, my mom calls. Normally I wouldn't attempt answering the phone while stuffing my face with one hand and driving someone else's car with the other, but I owe her a call. Also, considering I just spent five hours with Rick, I could use a little interaction with someone who doesn't belong in an asylum.

"Hi, sweetie," my mom says. "How are you?"

"Pretty good," I say, my mouth full of cranberry-studded bread.

"Did I catch you in the middle of something? I can call back."

"No, now is fine." I swerve around a pothole, steering with one hand as I grip the phone with the other, and accidentally run over a huge tree branch. "Shit!"

"Excuse me?"

"Sorry—I just nearly blew out one of Heidi's tires."

"You're driving? Sydney, we've been over this. What have I told you about talking on the phone while driving?"

I tuck the phone between my shoulder and ear and reach for a broken oatmeal raisin cookie. "Stop worrying." I toss a chunk of cookie into my mouth. "I'm fine."

"No, you're not fine. You're driving. And apparently eating! Are you even holding the steering wheel?"

"I'm using my knees."

"Sydney!"

I giggle. "I'm kidding. Of course I'm holding the steering wheel."

"I'm hanging up. We can talk later."

"Don't hang up. I'll put you on speaker. I could use the company right now."

She sighs. "Fine. But you keep your eyes on the road, understood? And no eating."

"I don't know. . . . These oatmeal raisin cookies are pretty amazing. Like toasty little bites of heaven."

"Sydney . . ."

"Okay, okay. No eating." I put the phone on speaker and rest it on the dashboard.

"So why are you in Heidi's car?" she asks. "Job interview?"

I groan. "I wish. No, I was interviewing the baker I've been helping at the farmers' market."

"For that newsletter thing?"

"And my blog."

"Your blog? I thought you gave that up years ago."

"I did. But I've resurrected it."

"Shouldn't you be focusing on enterprises that are more . . . lucrative?"

I grip the steering wheel tightly with both hands. "Listen, I know you think my blog is silly—"

"I don't think it's silly. I think it's great. I've always loved your food columns. But you've been out of work for two months now, and it doesn't sound as if these farmers' market jobs pay all that much."

"That's for sure. . . ."

"I just don't want to see you get in over your head, money-wise."

"Trust me, neither do I. But the job market is really rough right now. Especially for someone trying to shift career tracks."

She grunts. "Don't I know it."

Normally I'd say my mom, who has been a stay-at-home mom for the past twenty-six years, knows as much about the job market as she does about x-ray crystallography. But something about her tone piques my curiosity.

"What's that supposed to mean?"

"Well . . ." She clears her throat. "You know things at home have been a little . . . tight, money-wise. . . ."

"Yeah, Dad mentioned business was down."

"Down? Try over. Ford is closing his dealership."

"What? Since when?"

"Since a few months ago. The dealership in Conshohocken is doing better, so they've decided to make that the primary dealership in the area. He'll be out of work by July."

"Wow, Mom—I don't know what to say."

"Neither do I. It's been rough on your father, to say the least. And with Libby's wedding coming up in a few months . . . Well, we thought it might be a good idea for me to get out there again and make a few bucks."

"Teaching?"

"Not necessarily . . . I haven't been in a classroom in almost thirty years. And anyway, teaching jobs aren't all that easy to come by these days."

"So, if not teaching, then . . . what?"

"Well, you know I've always loved food and cooking. . . ."

"Are you thinking of starting a catering company? Libby and I always thought you should."

"No. . . . I was thinking more along the lines of . . . a position at Williams-Sonoma."

"Aren't they based in San Francisco?"

"Not the corporate end. A position in the store." She hesitates. "A salesperson."

"Oh," I say, trying to sound supportive. "That sounds cool, too. I bet you'll get a good employee discount."

"That's what everyone keeps saying." She lets out another sigh. "Oh, who am I kidding? This is humiliating."

"No, it isn't. Don't say that."

"Well, it is. Your father and I have lived a comfortable life for so many years, and now, for everything to change so suddenly . . ." She sniffles.

I try my best to comfort her, but all I can think about is what a blow this must be to my parents, especially my dad. His auto dealership has been like his third child, older than both me and Libby and a fixture in the area. The tagline for his business—"No stress, just Strauss"—was everywhere growing up, whether it was in radio ads or on bumper stickers. Business started to slow about ten years ago, but he carried on and managed to dodge the wave of dealership closings following the recession and auto bailout. Still, from everything he's told me, business never got back to where it was during the "good old days," and I knew that, despite his catchy slogan, there was plenty of stress about sales figures and inventory. But I hadn't realized it was this bad. I hadn't realized three quarters of the Strauss family would soon be unemployed.

"I can talk to Libby about the wedding," I say. "I'm sure there are a few places she can cut down on expenses."

"Don't you dare say a word to your sister."

"Why not?"

"Because your father doesn't want her knowing about any of this until after the wedding. She is so excited and happy, and he wants to make the day special for her."

"But that's ridiculous. The day can be special without spending a zillion dollars. I'm sure Libby will understand."

My mom snickers. "Are we talking about the same Libby?"

I can picture her face simply by listening to her voice: her left eyebrow raised, her thin lips pressed together in a wry smile. Her glossy hair is probably styled in its signature shoulder-length cut, the front swept across her narrow forehead and held in place by a hefty dose of hairspray.

"True," I say. "But maybe I could try to talk her out of some of her more ridiculous requests."

"Just leave it alone for now. Your father doesn't want his misfortune to ruin her big day."

"But—"

"Anyway," she says, moving swiftly along, "speaking of Libby's wedding, the reason I called in the first place was to update you on her bridal shower. We have a date: Saturday, July 16."

"I'll mark my calendar. . . ." At this point, July sounds as far away as 2052.

"Libby dropped a few hints that she wants you to put together a few shower games."

"Games?"

"You know—a Q&A, the toilet paper game, stuff like that."

"I have no idea what you're talking about."

"Look it up online."

"Can't one of the other bridesmaids do that?"

She blows a gust of air into the receiver. "I'll ask around. But it would mean a lot to Libby if you did *something* special for her shower."

"I'll work on it."

"Good," she says. "One of us in this family deserves a pleasant surprise."

"That's for sure."

But as I pull the car onto the highway, the stretches of farmland fading into the distance, I wonder why, as far as my family is concerned, that person has never been me.

CHAPTER 14

The Rick profile is an instant smash. Within hours of my sending out the new-and-improved newsletter the following Tuesday, his stand at the Crystal City market teems with hordes of hungry customers, everyone clamoring for sourdough loaves and oatmeal cookies by the handful. With Julie's permission, I included a link in the newsletter to my blog, where I uploaded an edited video of Rick making his sourdough boule, documenting the process from beginning to end and providing plenty of close-up shots of the bread's airy, custardy crumb and crisp, blistered crust. I don't think it's a coincidence that we sell out of boules in the first hour.

Before we've even made it through the first week of March, traffic on my blog is up 1000 percent, and the comments section explodes with people wondering where they can find Rick's bread and asking what other breads and pastries he sells. Even Libby sends an e-mail, asking if I could ship a loaf of brioche to Philly. Of course she then e-mails back fifteen minutes later telling me to forget it because she has decided to cut out all carbs before the wedding. Which, she reminds me, is in twenty-one weeks, four days, and six hours. Just in case I'd forgotten.

When I get to the Penn Quarter market Thursday afternoon, the first day of its reopening after a two-month hiatus in January and February, Rick is grumbling to himself as he yanks the folded-up tent off the truck. I never enjoy the weekday markets as much as the ones on the weekend, mostly because Heidi works at her real job during the week, leaving me to deal with Rick on my own. Plus, whereas the weekend markets attract a low-key crowd—people out for a stroll on their Saturday or Sunday mornings—the weekday markets draw high-strung professionals on their coffee breaks, people who want their muffin *yesterday,* thank you very much. Given the Penn Quarter market's location, surrounded on all sides by the FBI, the Justice Department, and dozens of nonprofits and swanky law firms, the crowd is particularly intense.

The market sits on a narrow one-block stretch of Eighth Street, which descends at a gradual slope toward Pennsylvania Avenue, coming to a dead end at the tree-lined plaza in front of the US Navy Memorial. The street is blockaded to the north and south by vibrant orange cones, and brightly colored tents line each side, from one end to the other. Rick's truck is parked on the eastern side, in front of an outpost of CVS.

"You trying to kill me?" he gripes as I pull myself onto the back of the truck.

"No," I say, though I'd be lying if I said the thought had never crossed my mind. "What did I do this time?"

"Thanks to your little profile and video, I'm selling out early at every market, and Julie is up my ass about some pilot project with Green Grocers."

"And this is a problem how?"

"I can't keep up with demand. And to sell at Green Grocers, I'd need to up my volume by at least 75 percent, but I don't have the manpower."

"So hire some more people."

"Oh, really?" He raises his arms and gestures to no one in particular. "Attention, please: Someone give this girl a fucking MBA."

"I'm just trying to help."

He lifts his eyes to the sky and sighs. "If I could hire more people, don't you think I would?"

"I guess so. . . ."

"More people means more salaries, which means more money,

which means more loans, which means more credit, which I sure as shit don't have." He sneers as he shakes out one of his red cotton tablecloths. "Unless you want to help me out for free."

"No, thanks," I say.

I can't think of anything worse. Between my work for him and Julie, I might as well already be working for free, and my blog sure as hell isn't making me any cash. I don't need to take on yet another unpaid position—particularly not for a guy who will make my life a living hell.

"Then stop setting me up for failure," he says.

"What about interns from one of the local culinary programs? I know L'Academie de Cuisine is always looking for apprenticeships. Those are all unpaid."

He frowns. "Maybe."

"At least that would allow you to get ahead of the demand. And it would get you in the door at Green Grocers, which could help your cash-flow problem."

"Well, aren't you a regular Warren Buffett," he says.

Clearly Rick is unaware of my current bank account balance. Also, my guess is Warren Buffett never spent his time writing unpaid blog posts about apples.

"I'll think about it," he says. "You make a good point."

He turns and heads back to the truck to grab another crate of rye, and with his faint praise still ringing in my ears, I'm not sure whether to smile or die from shock.

Rick's stand is on fire today. Loaves of brioche and sourdough fly across the table, with dozens of tender muffins and fudgy brownies nipping at their heels. I'm not sure why I care so much about seeing Rick succeed, especially given that he is ... well ... *Rick,* but I love watching his business thrive. Some of that is down to the fact that I've woven myself into the fabric of the farmers' market and feel as if I'm a part of this growing family. But I also like seeing the direct impact of my writing. When I worked on stories in high school and college, and even at *The Morning Show,* I'd pour my heart and soul into them and never know if anyone read or watched, much less cared. But here, I have tangible evidence, in the form of empty baskets and long lines, that I've reached at least a few people.

Mere moments after the words *Morning Show* enter my mind, I nearly drop a bag of muffins on the ground as I spot Charles Griffin ambling down the market thoroughfare toward the Navy Memorial, as if I've conjured him to this very spot. I haven't seen him since I lost my job almost three months ago.

"Just the gal I was looking for," he says as he approaches the Wild Yeast tent.

I can't imagine why Charles would be looking for me, unless perhaps he needs to locate a tricycle for a live shot. "How did you know to find me here?"

He smirks. "I have my ways. I'm a reporter after all."

This is true, though I'm tempted to remind him that our last reporting adventures together involved skis and snowballs. "So what's up? Melanie's toilet humor got you down?"

"Ha, no. Well, yes, but that's not why I'm here." He considers this for a moment. "Have you noticed she's really into booger jokes?"

"They're sort of her specialty."

He nods, conceding my point. "Anyway, the reason I'm here: I don't know if I ever mentioned this, but my buddy Stu is the food editor over at the *Chronicle*."

My heart nearly stops. "You know Stu Abbott? Since when?"

"Since forever. We met when we were young, scrappy reporters in Washington. He sort of fell into food journalism by accident."

"I can't believe you never mentioned that before."

"I guess it never seemed relevant."

And why would it? It's not as if Charles and I sat around pouring our hearts out to each other and sharing our innermost hopes and dreams. We were colleagues. Our relationship was all surface. Sure, we worked together for four years, driving out to farms in rural Virginia and standing in the middle of record-breaking snowstorms, but beyond our shared experiences, we didn't share much else. For all I know, in his spare time Charles is into bondage and role-playing. Having said that, for many, many reasons, I hope he is not.

"Stu and I keep up with each other a fair amount," he says, "especially since our network now has a content-sharing agreement with the *Chronicle*. The two of us mainly vent about the state of journalism and our bureau chiefs, but the other day he forwarded me a link to a video on your blog with a note saying, 'Didn't you use to work with this girl?'"

"Really?"

"Believe me, I was as surprised as anyone," he says, his inner diva apparently still intact. "But Stu subscribes to all those foodie e-mail lists, and he came across the profile you did of that baker guy and the video you put on your site. I guess there's a push at the *Chronicle* to add more multimedia to their food page? I don't know. But Stu sounded interested in chatting with you, at least to pick your brain."

"Seriously? Oh my gosh, Charles—you have no idea. This is like a dream come true."

"You did always love those food stories. Remember the one we did at that poultry farm?"

"The one where you got attacked by a turkey? Yeah, I'm pretty sure that image is tattooed on my brain forever."

"I still have a scar, you know," he says, lifting up his jacket and shirt.

I hold up my hand. "I'll take your word for it."

He shrugs as if to say, *Your loss,* and tucks his hands into his coat pockets. "Anyway, I assume your e-mail and number are still the same?"

"Yep. No change."

"Good. Stu will probably be in touch in the next day or two."

I beat my fists together and bounce up and down. "I can't believe this is happening. Thank you, Charles. This is so exciting!"

"Hey, I'm just the messenger," he says. He glances down at the table. "I will, however, take two of those chocolate chip muffins."

"Done and done."

I bag up the muffins and hand them to Charles, who smiles as he grips the bag with his wrinkly, weathered hands. "And don't worry," he says, a strange glint in his eye. "Washington is a small town. It won't be long before I'm asking you to return the favor."

CHAPTER 15

An entire week passes before Stu Abbott calls, but when he does, I have to muster all my self-control to keep from squealing into the phone.

"I'd love to meet for coffee," he says. "You free next week?"

"Yes!" I blurt at a deafening pitch, unable to control my excitement.

Stu hesitates, apparently flustered by my manic gusto. "Okay, then . . . How does next Thursday sound?"

"I work at the Penn Quarter market from about one thirty until seven thirty, but otherwise I'm around."

"Hmm . . . Afternoons are usually better for me. . . ."

"Or I could bail on the market—whatever is easiest for you. I'm at your disposal. Whatever you want. I'd love to meet. I'll make it work." The words fire out of my mouth like bullets.

"How about Friday afternoon?"

"Perfect. Just tell me where and when, and I'll be there."

"The coffee options by my office are kind of lame. Where will you be coming from?"

"Fourteenth and Swann."

"Oh—that's right by Peregrine. They don't have a ton of seat-ing, but I can try to get something by the window. Want to say three o'clock?"

"Perfect."

"I'll be the guy with the black-rimmed glasses and reddish beard."

"I'll be the girl with dark hair and freckles who will probably be tripping all over herself." I pause. "With excitement. Not because there is anything wrong with me. Although I'm not particularly co-ordinated."

Oh my God, why can't I shut up?

"Sure. Okay."

He goes quiet for a few seconds, and I bite my lip to keep from saying anything to fill the void because everything that comes out of my mouth is awkward beyond belief.

"I'll see you Friday at three, then," he finally says.

"Yepper!" I say.

There's no way this guy doesn't think I'm completely insane.

The following Friday I show up at Peregrine Espresso at three on the dot, figuring this guy already thinks I'm a lunatic, so I might as well be a punctual one.

When I approach the gray brick storefront, I spot Stu sitting in the front window, stirring a foamy cappuccino with a small silver spoon. I take a deep breath as I smooth my lightweight trench coat and pull open the front door, hoping I can keep Psycho Sydney at bay, at least for thirty minutes. If our prior conversation is any indication, this won't be easy.

I enter the coffee shop, which is bright and airy, flanked on one side by exposed brick and on the other by natural wood panels lined with mugs, filters, and bags of coffee beans. A glass pastry case sits atop the blond wood counter and is filled with croissants, scones, and muffins, and the entire shop bears the rich, slightly smoky smell of freshly ground coffee beans.

Since Stu is already here, I am in the awkward position of either (a) pretending I don't see him and ordering a drink, (b) saying hello, but then making him wait while I order a drink, or (c) sitting down and not ordering a drink, but wishing I had as I watch him sip his luscious cappuccino. This meeting is a disaster before it has even begun.

I decide I cannot ignore him, especially since he already thinks I'm nuts, so I make my way toward the front window, where he sits in a wooden chair in front of a small table.

"Stu?"

He looks up from his mug and smiles, the reddish stubble from his beard folding into thick creases. He is about Charles's age—mid-forties, maybe a few years younger—though with his black-rimmed glasses and plaid shirt, he looks a lot hipper than Charles ever did.

"You must be Sydney," he says. He reaches out and shakes my hand. "I didn't see you come in. I was looking for someone tripping all over herself."

I feel my cheeks flush. "I made sure I did all my tripping before I crossed the street."

"Ah. Got it. Good plan." He gestures to the bench across from him. "Have a seat. Or did you want to order a drink first?"

Is this a test? It must be a test. Although if he minded if I ordered something, he wouldn't have offered it as an option, right? Then again, he is a journalist, and of all people I should know that journalists have deadlines and don't have all day to hang around while some wannabe food writer orders a fancy espresso-based beverage. On the other hand, he is a food writer, so maybe he wants to see what I order. Like, am I super boring with a plain black coffee, or do I order something overly elaborate and over-the-top, which makes it look as if I don't really like coffee and am trying to disguise the taste?

OH MY GOD, WHAT IS WRONG WITH ME?

"Would you mind if I ordered something real quick?" I say.

"No problem. Take your time."

I order a cappuccino, which comes out with a little heart drawn into the foam on top. When I bring it to the table and take a seat, Stu smiles. "Good choice. They make a mean cappuccino."

"That's what I hear." I give my drink a quick stir and take a sip. "So Charles says you liked the video on my site."

"I did. It was cute."

Cute? *Cute?* No. Puppies and kittens are cute. Babies are cute. I'm not saying my little video was Edward R. Murrow's "Harvest of Shame," but it was a decent piece of production work.

"Thanks . . ."

"Sorry—that came out wrong. What I meant was it was fun. Made me interested in that crazy baker and his bread. And it got me thinking about what we're trying to do over at the *Chronicle*. The new editor-in-chief wants to make our page a real destination. Right now it's more of an afterthought, and we're really falling behind, especially with all of the food sites online these days."

"So where does my blog fit in?"

"Well, that's the thing. I'm not really sure it does."

"Oh." Not exactly the response I was hoping for.

He takes a sip of coffee and wipes a mustache of white foam from his lips with a small napkin. "We're experimenting with some things behind the scenes right now, but I'd love to throw a few of them against the wall to see what sticks. One idea I had was for a blog called *Buying the Farm*—something tied into the DC farmers' market scene. You seem pretty plugged in to what's going on over there. I was thinking maybe we could use you as a stringer and have you contribute a weekly post."

I sit up straight. "That would be amazing!" I catch myself mid-outburst. "Only . . . I'm sort of already doing that for the market's weekly newsletter. I'm not sure how Julie would feel about double dipping."

He nods. "Fair point. I know Julie. I'll give her a call and see what she thinks." He smiles. "I'm glad you brought that up, though. Shows you have a good moral compass. As you may know, our food section has . . . well, a bit of a spotty record in that regard."

My cheeks flush at the reference to Jeremy Brauer. "I—I think you do a great job."

"We do now. In the past . . ." He waves his hand back and forth. "Anyway, we'd be looking for more multimedia and a slightly newsier angle, so my guess is there wouldn't be a ton of overlap with the newsletter."

"I'm sure I could bring something fresh to the table for your site. The video stuff alone would be different. And I could take a more critical angle with what I write for you."

"That would be great. Not that I expect you to dig up dirt on everyone at the market, but if you did . . ." He waves me off as he takes another sip of his cappuccino. "I'm getting ahead of myself. Let's work on putting together a few posts we can launch in April and go from there."

"Sounds great." I fiddle with the handle on my cup and take a deep breath. "In terms of compensation . . . what are we talking?"

"Yeah . . . about that . . ."

Great. Here we go again. Apparently I've chosen a field desperate to survive and content not to pay anyone willing to help it do so.

"This is all experimental right now," he says, "and we'd only be using you as a stringer, so we're looking at like one hundred dollars a post, max."

My heart sinks. A hundred dollars is better than Julie's fifty, but it's also the same amount I make working one of Rick's markets, which requires very little use of my brain.

"Oh," I say, unable to mask the disappointment in my voice.

"Listen, I know a hundred bucks isn't the jackpot, but it's the best I can do right now."

"Do you think there's potential for something more . . . lucrative in the future?"

"Depends on how this goes. But yeah, there could be opportunities. We'd want something bigger than a farmer profile, but assuming you came up with something meaty . . ." He leans forward. "Again, I'm getting ahead of myself. For now, a hundred bucks is all I can offer for what we're talking about. You game?"

I nod, my spirits lifted by the prospect for future work. "Definitely."

He smacks his hand against the table. "Great. Shoot me an e-mail this week with some thoughts on a few posts, and we'll come up with a game plan." He reaches out across the table to shake my hand and smiles. "To a budding partnership," he says. "Welcome aboard."

CHAPTER 16

I can't believe it—a gig at the *Chronicle*! Okay, so officially it isn't really a job. And at a hundred dollars a week, there's a chance I'd make more money babysitting or standing on a street corner with a tin can. But after trying for so many years to break into this industry, at least I finally have a foot in the door. Granted, it's more like a toe in the door, and a pinky toe at that, but if I come up with a legitimate story—something "meaty," as Stu put it—I have a shot at breaking through that door in a serious way.

After my meeting with Stu, I head back to my apartment, but not before popping into a small creperie for a Nutella, banana, and coconut crepe because, let's be honest, I'm only human. The shop sits a few doors down from Peregrine Espresso, and even though I spend most days surrounded by flaky croissants and fudgy brownies, God help me, I still cannot resist the siren song of a sweet Nutella crepe.

I order it to go, but I dive in before I even leave the store because Nutella is my kryptonite. The rich chocolate hazelnut spread oozes from within the sweet eggy crepe, each bite filled with fresh bananas and bits of toasted coconut. I go in for another bite as I dash across S Street, the damp March air blowing my hair to and fro, and as I do, I walk smack into a guy charging down Fourteenth Street in the opposite direction.

"Whoa! Watch it!" he says as I accidentally smear a huge streak of Nutella down his white dress shirt.

"Oh my gosh, I'm so sorry." I fumble through my bag in search of a napkin, which I cannot find, so instead I grab an old, crumpled tissue and begin dabbing at his shirt. I glance up at his face to apologize, and that's when I notice the man in question is Jeremy Brauer. Perfect.

"Sydney—hi." He smiles awkwardly, as if my general demeanor isn't awkward enough for the both of us.

"Hi . . ." I continue wiping at his shirt because (a) I lack social skills, and (b) I have no idea what else to do.

He brushes my hand away. "Don't worry about the shirt. I'm heading back to the office anyway. I can change."

"Okay." I retract my hand and tuck the gooey, chocolaty tissue in my bag. "You work around here?"

He points down Fourteenth Street. "Fourteenth and K. I was up here meeting a client."

His eyes land on my upper lip, and it is at this moment I realize I am surely sporting a Nutella mustache.

"What are you doing out and about?" he asks as I attempt to blot my lip subtly with the back of my hand. Sure enough: Mustache Central. "Shouldn't you be working at a farmers' market somewhere?"

"I usually have Fridays off."

"Ah, got it."

He waits for me to say something, but I can't think of anything to say, so we just stand there, staring at each other in silence. It is very awkward.

Finally, when we have been standing across from each other for what feels like an eternity, he presses his eyebrows together gently and scratches his jaw. "Could I ask you something?"

"Sure," I say, tearing my eyes from his. I take another bite of my crepe because, apparently, I am trying to make this interaction as uncomfortable as possible.

"What did I do wrong? I thought we had a really good time together."

I gulp down a mouthful of Nutella and banana, refusing to meet his gaze. "We did. Dinner was fun."

He lets out a pained laugh. "Right. But then when I called you about hanging out again, you blew me off."

"No, I didn't."

"You told me not to call you again."

I glance up, and the intensity of his stare pulls me in like a tractor beam. "I didn't mean, like . . . never."

"No?"

"No."

Except that *is* what I meant. That is precisely what I meant. Why can't I tell him I don't want to see him again? That I know all about his shady past? That I could not possibly date someone whose Wikipedia entry makes him sound like a total sleaze?

I know why: because his glittery eyes and soft smile make my heart race, and because I cannot reconcile what I've read online with the man standing before me.

"If that's not what you meant, then is there really no way I could convince you to have dinner with me sometime?"

"I . . . It's complicated."

He blanches. "Is there someone else?"

My heart jumps. Someone else? Of course there isn't. I wish there were. That would make this so much easier.

"Not really," I say. Jeremy's face remains pale and tense. "No," I finally say. "There isn't anyone else."

"Listen, I don't want to nag you. I just thought we had so much fun the other night. At least give me one more shot."

I study his face—the almost imperceptible cleft in his pointy chin, the gentle sweep of his milk-chocolate hair, the way his lips curl ever-so-slightly to the left when he speaks. There is nothing but sincerity in his voice, and, though I try my hardest not to, I cave.

"Okay, fine," I say. "You win. I'll have dinner with you sometime."

He breaks into a broad smile, which deepens the laugh lines around his mouth and eyes. "How about this: You know how to get to the Smithsonian Metro stop from your apartment, right?"

"Yeah . . ."

"Great. Meet me outside the stop at seven next Saturday night. Sound okay?"

"Sure, I guess."

"I realize that gives you more than a week to back out, but I really hope you won't."

"I won't," I say. "I promise."

"Good. I'm glad. And, hey, you know what? Bring a flashlight."

"I'm sorry, what?"

His lips curl into a subtle smirk. "You heard me. A flashlight. Bring one."

Setting aside the fact that I don't think I own a flashlight, I cannot imagine why I'd need to bring one for what sounds like a tame evening of museum hopping. What am I signing up for?

My phone rings, and I glance down to see it's my sister, who is probably calling with a flower emergency. "Listen, I have to take this," I say.

"That's fine. I'll see you next Saturday night."

"Seven o'clock."

"With a flashlight."

"Right."

"And wear comfortable shoes," he says. "You'll need them."

CHAPTER 17

A flashlight? A flashlight. What kind of sick, crazy, creepy freak asks you to bring a flashlight on a date? This is a recipe for disaster already. I should have broken my promise and backed out while I still had the chance. But I didn't, and now I'm going to pay the price.

When Saturday night arrives, I board an Orange Line train, which whooshes through the underground tunnels, heading south to the Smithsonian Metro stop on the National Mall. I sit on one of the orange vinyl seats, across from a man wearing red, white, and blue, who is holding a sign that reads, TEABAGGING 4 JESUS. I'm not sure whether this is a parody or a case of linguistic confusion, but given that this is Washington, anything is possible.

My oversize purse sits in my lap, weighing about fifty pounds thanks to the flashlight hidden inside. I stopped by Ace Hardware this morning, hoping to find something petite and feminine and refined, but the manager informed me they didn't carry flashlights bearing that description. In fact, thanks to the snowstorms a few months back, combined with the threat of new storms that never materialized, they sold out of most of their smaller flashlights and have yet to restock. So, instead, I'm stuck with a seventy-dollar flashlight the length of my forearm.

The train reaches the Smithsonian stop at 6:55 p.m., and my teabagging buddy pushes ahead of me onto the platform and then rushes ahead of me onto the escalator, where he stands firmly on the left-hand side, breaking that holy Washington rule: Stand on the right; walk on the left. I try my best to squeeze by him, but his girth takes up nearly the entire stairway, and I cannot.

When we reach the top, Jeremy is standing a few feet from the entrance, wearing a black nylon bomber jacket and a pair of dark jeans. He holds a brown paper bag in his left hand and grips a backpack slung over his shoulder with his right. He smiles when he sees me.

"New friend?" he asks, nodding toward the Teabagger 4 Jesus, who is now holding his sign high and shouting as he marches down the Mall.

I offer a wry smile. "We're dating, actually."

"See? I knew there was someone else."

"Well, I mean, can you blame me?"

We watch the man thrust his sign up and down as he leads his protest of one. Jeremy grins. "I understand the attraction."

I glance around the Mall, which glows in the warm light of the sunset. The museums and other buildings are framed by a froth of blossoms on the cherry trees, which, on this final weekend in March, have finally started to bloom. "So . . . what's the plan? Time to bust out the flashlight?"

"Not yet," he says. "First I thought we'd have a little picnic. You game?"

"When it comes to eating, I'm always game."

"That's what I like to hear."

He leads me over to a wooden bench across from the National Gallery of Art and gestures for me to have a seat. He plops down and tosses his backpack next to him, leaving the paper bag between us.

"Okay!" he says, rubbing his hands together. "Here's the deal. I didn't know what you'd want to eat, so I made a few different things. First, since you mentioned you grew up on the Main Line, I decided to make some Philly-style sandwiches." He reaches into the paper bag. "Classic Italian hoagie, or chicken cutlet?"

"Hmm . . . not sure . . ."

"She's not impressed. Okay. Moving on."

"No, no—both sound good. I just—"

"There's more where that came from, so slow down." He reaches into the paper bag again. "You mentioned you've always wanted to visit Thailand, so I made a classic Thai green papaya salad. And"—he reaches into the bag one last time—"you said *The Godfather* is one of your favorite movies, so I made cannoli."

"You made cannoli?"

"Well, I only made the filling. I bought the shells."

I study the piles of food sitting between us on the bench. "How long did all this cooking take you? All day?"

He dismisses me with a wave of his hand. "Not important. What's important is that there is something among these choices that you actually might want to eat. Anything sound appealing?"

"All of it, actually."

He slaps his thigh. "Excellent. Take your pick."

I grab the Italian hoagie and a napkin. The sandwich reminds me of the ones my family would order almost every Friday night for takeout when I was growing up. Friday was "Mom's night off" from cooking because, she told us, even stay-at-home moms deserved a night off. Sometimes we'd order pizza or Chinese, but more often than not, we'd order cheesesteaks and hoagies, and my sister and I would strike the same deal: one turkey hoagie, one Italian hoagie, split evenly between the two of us. She would always complain that I got the bigger half of each sandwich, and I would correct her that, technically speaking, there cannot be a bigger half, so she was wrong. Looking back on it, I'm pretty sure that was one of many examples where, in a social context, I won the battle but lost the war.

I take a bite, and although the sandwich does not replicate the hoagies of my youth with outright precision, it comes pretty damn close. The spicy, garlicky Genoa salami is layered with thin slices of capocollo, prosciutto, and provolone cheese and sprinkled with shredded lettuce, thinly sliced onions, and tomatoes. The whole thing is doused in oil and vinegar and dusted with oregano and transports me to those Friday nights in my youth. I applaud Jeremy's boldness: Between the garlicky meat and the abundance of onions, my breath is guaranteed to smell horrible for the remainder of the evening.

Jeremy pulls two brown glass bottles from his backpack and pops off the caps with a bottle opener on his key chain.

"Homebrewed American wheat ale," he says, handing me a bottle, which is labeled *Brauer's Brew*. "Made by yours truly."

I hold the bottle up to what little light remains in the sky. "You even made the beer? Impressive."

"I've been working on this one for a while. I think I finally got the recipe right."

I take a sip, and the flavor of the beer blossoms in my mouth, bright and lemony with just a touch of bitterness. "Wow, that's really good. So is the hoagie, actually—considering it was made by an outsider."

He tries to contain his satisfied smile and takes a sip of his beer, and then he reaches out and clinks the neck of his bottle against mine.

"Cheers," he says. "To second chances."

By eight, we've finished our food, and evening has rolled in, snuffing out the light from the sky. Jeremy crumples up the napkins and trash and stuffs them into the paper bag, while I lick the sweet ricotta cannoli filling from my fingers.

"So what's next?"

Jeremy hops up and dumps the paper bag in a trashcan, then saunters toward the bench and reaches into his backpack. "Got your flashlight?"

"Yep." I reach into my purse and pull out my fourteen-inch abomination.

Jeremy's eyes widen. "Dude, that's like . . . a light saber."

"What? Shut up. It's a flashlight. It was the only one left at Ace Hardware."

Jeremy takes it from my hands. "Seriously, look at this thing." He flicks on the light, grips the shaft with both hands, and begins wielding it back and forth. "I am Obi-Wan Kenobi—feel my power!"

"You're imitating a *Star Wars* character? And I'm the loser in this scenario?"

"Hey, George Lucas was a visionary."

I snatch it back from him. "Just—give me the damn flashlight."

"Listen, I like a girl who's prepared. If anything, I'm impressed." He grabs a much smaller flashlight from his backpack. "Okay," he says. "Let's do this."

We wander west across the National Mall, guided through the darkness by the piercing white of the Washington Monument, the towering obelisk lit up like a searchlight. I haven't spent any time down here at night, and I cannot believe how dark it is, how different everything looks in the camouflage of night. Before the sun set, the Mall bustled with activity and color—the fluffy white-and-pink cherry blossoms, the green lawn, the museums made of maroon bricks and pale limestone. But now, it's as if someone turned out the overhead lights and flicked on the monuments, which punctuate the city like a series of reading lamps.

Jeremy leads me down Independence Avenue and then cuts across a dark, grassy area studded with trees, heading toward the Tidal Basin. As we draw closer, the moon peeks through the branches, huge and bright, but soon I realize it isn't the moon at all; it's the Jefferson Memorial, its smooth dome glowing on the other side of the shimmering reservoir. We cross a busy road and come upon a small parking lot with a big, white tent, set just behind the broad wooden dock housing the Tidal Basin's paddle boats.

"I am not paddle boating in the dark," I say.

"Neither am I." He shines his flashlight in my eyes. "They aren't open, anyway."

I swat his hand away. "Then what *are* you doing?"

"Taking you on a lantern tour around the Tidal Basin. The Cherry Blossom Festival just started today. Come on."

He grabs my hand and pulls me toward a small group of people standing in front of the white tent. A mustached park ranger wearing a padded, olive-green jacket stands at the center of the group, holding what appears to be an asymmetrical wooden cross with a lit Japanese paper lantern dangling from the end. He is in the middle of telling the group some scintillating factoid about the origins of the Tidal Basin, but he stops mid-sentence when he sees us approach.

"Greetings, latecomers!" he says. "Welcome. Do you have your flashlights handy?"

I wave mine in the air. The park ranger raps his wooden cross against the pavement and lets out a belly laugh. "Well, how about that? Look at that thing! It's bigger than you are. You could light up the whole city!"

The crowd turns and stares at my enormous flashlight, confirming that, yes, it is enormous and, yes, I could light up the whole city.

"Anywho," the ranger says, "come along. We were just getting started."

He leads us around the basin, walking north as he talks about the tulips in the surrounding flowerbeds. Even with my light saber, I have trouble seeing where I'm going and what this guy is talking about.

"Now, folks, if you look straight north from this spot, that's where they originally wanted to construct the Washington Monument. If you draw a straight line south from the White House and a straight line west from the Capitol, that's where they wanted it to be. But it didn't end up there. And do you know why?"

"Because the ground wasn't structurally sound," I say.

Everyone turns and looks at me. The ranger beams. "That's exactly right." He lets out a hearty laugh. "She's 'bright' in more ways than one, folks."

The crowd chuckles in unison, amused by a man who resembles a bloated cartoon character and who, in spite of this fact, feels comfortable making jokes at my expense. He gives me a jovial pat on the back, lets out a toothy guffaw, and raises his hand to give Jeremy an awkward high five.

This date cannot end soon enough.

CHAPTER 18

Unfortunately, our nocturnal expedition continues for what feels like days. By the time we reach the site where the first cherry trees were planted in 1912, we've been at this for forty-five minutes and have only covered a quarter of the walking tour. We have also acknowledged the immensity of my flashlight on at least ten occasions.

As our park ranger discusses the first cherry trees, Jeremy nudges me in the side.

"Hey," he whispers in my ear. "Follow me."

He takes my hand and gently backs away from the crowd, slipping into the darkness. He tiptoes around the Tidal Basin's western bend, slinking with me along the narrow path and away from the crowd.

"What are you doing? He was just saying something interesting about Helen Taft."

"I want to show you something," he says.

"Aren't you already showing me something? Aren't you the one who brought me on this tour to begin with?"

"Stop arguing with me and come on."

We follow the curve of the Tidal Basin, ducking beneath the branches that stretch over the path. As we move along, we come upon a knotted cherry tree that leans diagonally across the walkway, as if it is trying to dip its fluffy, flower-coated branches into the reservoir.

"Watch it," Jeremy says, pressing his palm against the back of my head and forcing me to duck. "You almost whacked yourself on that branch."

"Maybe if it weren't pitch-black, I would have been able to see it."

"Maybe if you weren't trying so hard not to have a good time, you'd be able to see how cool this is."

We reach a broad granite stairway, on the opposite side of the Tidal Basin from the Washington Monument, and he pushes me up the steps, his hand on the small of my back. As I grip the railing, I hear the unmistakable crash of a waterfall, the whoosh of water cascading to the ground. The sound intensifies as we reach the top and continue straight ahead, guided by the gentle uplighting and shadows across the expansive slate plaza.

Jeremy pushes ahead, his hands tucked into the pockets of his nylon jacket, and stops before an illuminated waterfall to his left, where a wide sheet of water crashes to the ground.

"The FDR Memorial," he says. He points to the waterfall. "This is supposed to represent the economic crash that led to the Great Depression."

He leads me across the exhibit, a sprawling display documenting the four terms of FDR's presidency, each term occupying its own outdoor space. We meander from section to section, weaving our way through the waterfalls and sculptures and plantings. Jeremy shuffles toward a wall with a series of tactile reliefs and runs his fingers across the surface.

"I love it here at night," he says. "There's a certain magic you miss during the day."

I glance up, taking in the stars, which shine brightly in the clear night sky. As I trace the outlines of the constellations with my eyes, I feel him move closer, the warmth from his body tingling the back of my neck. I whip my head around and meet his stare, halting his approach. He smiles nervously and scratches his jaw.

"You can really see the stars out here, huh?"

I nod and walk toward another installation in the exhibit, keeping the distance between us. I look up at the sky again. "When I was about five or six, I wanted to be an astronaut," I say. "Isn't that weird?"

He grins. "Not at all. I did, too."

"Really?"

"What kid didn't want to be an astronaut? Floating through space, eating space ice cream—it sounded like the coolest job ever."

"Exactly."

He smiles and draws closer. "See? We have more in common than our interest in Bach and food writing."

My cheeks grow hot at the mention of food writing. I wonder if he knows that I know about his past.

"So do you want to rejoin the tour?" Jeremy finally says, nodding over his shoulder.

"Oh. Sure. I guess?"

"We don't have to," he says. "We could always just walk around the Tidal Basin by ourselves. Or go home."

"Let's just wander toward the Jefferson Memorial and see if they catch up with us. Okay?"

He smiles. "Sure. Okay."

We walk back down the granite stairway, our shoulders nearly touching, and turn right at the bottom, heading back along the narrow path surrounding the Tidal Basin. Jeremy stands to the left of me, providing a buffer from the edge of the basin, and I reach into my bag and pull out my battery-operated monstrosity, lighting the path in front of us. Jeremy reaches down and grabs my left hand, caressing my fingers, and for a moment my entire body stiffens. I shouldn't be on this date. We shouldn't be holding hands. But as we walk along, my shoulders relax, and I remember why I fell for him after our first date.

He rubs his thumb against mine. "You look beautiful tonight, by the way," he says.

My mouth goes dry. I'm not the kind of girl people call beautiful. Interesting, maybe, or cute, but not beautiful. My face is too narrow, and I have too many freckles, and my ears stick out a little too much. No one except my parents calls me beautiful, and even they tend to favor gentler words like "pretty" and "lovely." I guess Zach used to call me beautiful sometimes, but look how that turned out.

Given that I've never been good with accepting a compliment, especially one about my looks, I'm not sure how to respond. So, instead of saying "thank you" like a normal person, I reply in the awkward fashion I seem to have mastered. I say, "You're just saying that because you want to get in my pants."

Jeremy whips his head around, his mouth hanging open. "What?"

But before he can indulge his shock, he walks smack into a thick cherry tree branch that stretches across the path, cracking his forehead against the gnarled piece of wood.

"Jesus!" He lets go of my hand and grips his head, hunching over as he groans.

"Sorry—I'm sorry." I'm not sure if I'm apologizing for my ill-chosen words or for walking him straight into a cherry tree, but either way, I'm pretty sure this is all my fault.

"Ouch!" he shouts, as he continues to massage his head.

"Here—let me help." I reach out and grab his arm, but when I lift him up, I knock his head into the branch for the second time.

"Damn it!"

He stumbles backward, gripping his head, and I find myself in the midst of one of those moments when I know exactly what is about to happen but, like in a nightmare, can do nothing to stop it. I see him stumbling, I see the water, and I see the cracked edge of the pathway at the water's edge, but before I can say anything—before I can shout "Stop!" or "Water!" or "Look out!"—Jeremy takes one more step backward, and the next thing I hear is a yelp and a plop and a splash, as he plunges into the Tidal Basin.

CHAPTER 19

"Jeremy!"

Silence. I creep toward the edge of the walkway and peer into the water, but it's too dark for me to see anything, so I shine my flashlight across the reservoir. I wave the light back and forth, illuminating the pool of water, which is black as a tar pit. What if I killed him? What if he drowned? I may not want to date the guy, and I may not respect his life choices, but that doesn't mean he should *die*.

Then, in the stillness of the night, I see a ripple and hear a splash.

"Jeremy!"

There is another splash and a hiss of water, and then I hear a husky groan. "Get me *out* of here," Jeremy says.

I squat by the edge of the walkway and extend my hand, and Jeremy grabs hold. Using all my strength, I pull him upward, until he can grab the edge and lift himself out of the water. He lies on his side in the middle of the path, shaking and shivering in the cool evening breeze.

"Jeremy—oh my God. I'm so sorry. Are you okay?"

"I'm f-f-f-freezing. I c-c-can't f-f-feel my t-t-t-toes."

"Do you want to go to the ER? I can take you to the ER."

His head bobs from side to side. "N-n-no. T-t-t-take m-m-me home."

I reach down to help Jeremy off the ground, and as I do I hear a loud whoop. "Hey, what's happening over there?"

Our doughy park ranger approaches, the throng of tour partici-pants congregated behind him. He glances down at Jeremy, who shivers violently by my side.

"Have you been in the water?"

"I f-f-f-fell," Jeremy says.

The ranger shakes off his padded green jacket and throws it over Jeremy. "This boy needs to get out of these wet clothes stat. He should probably see a doctor."

"I'm f-f-f-fine."

"I'm taking him home," I say.

The ranger looks unconvinced. "He really should see a doctor."

I implore Jeremy with my eyes, hoping he'll relent and agree to see a doctor, but he shakes his head. Not going to happen.

"He was in the water for less than a minute," I say. "I'll keep an eye on him, and if he gets worse, I'll take him to the emergency room."

The ranger frowns. "Okay. But keep a close watch, you hear? Stay with him a good long while."

"Yes," I say. "Of course."

But as the ranger grabs Jeremy around the waist and escorts him toward Ohio Drive to hail a cab, I realize I just signed myself up for an evening at Jeremy's place. And a part of me, however terrible and small, wonders if this was part of his plan all along.

The cab pulls up to the corner of Twenty-fourth and M Streets, next to a tall, crisp condo building. This stretch of M Street is wide and dark and quiet—almost eerily so, when compared to the vi-brant bustle on the same street, only three blocks west, at the entry point to Georgetown. But here, aside from a few hotels and restau-rants, the area feels deserted.

I pay the cab driver, ignoring Jeremy's protests, and help Jeremy out of the backseat. He is wrapped in a thick, wool blanket, one lent to us by one of the other sightseers, who'd brought it for a picnic before the tour. Jeremy pulls it tight as we walk toward the door to his building, his entire body still quivering.

I usher him through the lobby, a sharp, corporate space with dark leather couches, angular light fixtures, and beige tile floor. We move toward the elevator bay, my hand resting on his back.

"What floor?" I ask as we step into the elevator.

"S-s-s-seven."

I press the button and glance up at Jeremy, whose face I haven't seen in the light since he fell into the Tidal Basin. His complexion, once smooth and warm, is now pale and mottled, his lips a faint purply blue.

"I'm so sorry," I say for the twentieth time.

"S-s-s-stop s-s-s-saying that," he says. "It w-w-wasn't your f-f-f-fault."

"Okay," I say, even though we both know that isn't true.

Jeremy leads me down the seventh-floor hallway until we reach apartment 707. His hand jiggles as he tries to fit his key into the lock, and I reach out and wrap my hand around his, steadying his grip. He smiles, and for a moment I think he might kiss me. But instead he turns the lock and says, "Th-thanks."

His apartment is big and clean and masculine. The entryway leads directly into the living room, which features a tan leather couch, walnut coffee table, and plush chocolate-colored armchair. The walls are painted a rich taupe, with framed posters of old movies and concerts hanging around the room—*North by Northwest,* The Doors, *The Big Chill,* Radiohead. At the far end of the room, a large window looks onto a courtyard in the middle of the apartment complex.

Jeremy shuffles toward a short hallway to the right, rubbing his hands up and down his arms. "I'm g-g-g-going to t-t-take a sh-sh-shower."

"Okay. I'll . . . I'll make you some tea. Or coffee? Whatever you want."

"Th-thanks," he says, and then shuts the bathroom door.

The kitchen sits just to the left of the entry foyer and, at a first glance, looks like a chemistry lab gone wild. Three huge glass jugs sit in the far corner of the shiny gray-and-white granite counter, tucked beneath the cabinets in the darkest part of the kitchen. All three are draped with large gray towels, and when I peer underneath, I encounter frothy concoctions in varying shades of brown. The counter wraps around the kitchen and extends into the living room as a breakfast bar, with two barstools on the other side. The entire surface is covered with jars of bottle caps and corks and several tall and narrow metal contraptions whose purpose I cannot for the life of me ascertain. There are tubes and hoses curled up like snakes, coils of copper wire standing on end, and, perched at the edge of the breakfast bar, a bright orange Rubbermaid water cooler, the kind they use at professional football games. If I didn't know better, I'd say I just stepped into a meth lab.

As I root through his kitchen drawers, I spot two packets of Ghirardelli instant hot cocoa tucked beneath a jar of bottle caps. I fill the kettle and set it on the jet-black stovetop to boil, then empty the packets of hot cocoa into two bright red mugs. As I pour the boiling water into each mug, Jeremy trudges out of his bedroom in a hoodie and sweatpants, his hair still damp and disheveled from his shower. The color has started to return to his cheeks.

"I couldn't find any coffee or tea," I say, lifting the mug of cocoa by its handle. "I made hot cocoa instead. Hope that's okay."

Jeremy reaches out and takes the mug from my hands. "Perfect."

He clutches it, hunching his shoulders as he shuffles over to his leather couch. The steam pours off the top of his mug in thick swirls, and he brings his face in close, soaking up its warmth. I give my cocoa a stir and then join him in the living room, sitting at the other end of the couch.

We both take long sips of our cocoa, and then Jeremy glances into his mug and back at me. "So . . . that was not how I saw this evening going."

I place my mug on the coffee table. "I don't know. You managed to lure me back to your apartment. It all seems very suspicious to me."

He takes a sip of cocoa and laughs. "I was willing to do many things to get you to come home with me. Contracting hypothermia was not one of them. Besides, no offense, but after falling into a reservoir, all I want to do is drink this hot cocoa and go to bed. Under, like, five comforters."

"You won't need five comforters. You'll be back to normal in an hour or so. At which point I'm heading home."

"Understood." He takes another sip and narrows his eyes. "You really think all I care about is 'getting in your pants'?"

My face grows hot. "I . . . I don't know. Not really . . ."

"Because, believe it or not, I actually like you, Sydney. I'm not sure why you find that so shocking."

"Shocking is the wrong word."

"Then what's the right one?"

"I don't know. . . . Odd? Unfortunate?"

"Unfortunate?" He furrows his brow. "Am I really that horrible?"

"No . . ." I grab my mug off the table. "It's . . . Well, I know who you are. What you did."

"What I did?"

"At the *Chronicle*. The whole 'cash for comment' scandal."

He goes quiet for a long while. Then he nods slowly. "Ah. I see." He drinks some more of his cocoa. "That was a long time ago."

"It wasn't that long."

"Six years," he says. "A lot can change in six years."

I want to ask him more about the scandal. Didn't he know that what he was doing was wrong at the time? Does he regret what he did? Why did he do it in the first place? But before I can say anything, he lets out a loud sigh.

"Listen, if that's why you don't want to go out with me . . . I don't know what to say. That's part of my past. It always will be. But a journalism scandal from six years ago doesn't make my interest in you any less sincere."

"I know, but . . ."

"I'm not asking you to marry me," he says. "I just want to get to know you. Take you out to dinner a few times. Have a normal date that doesn't end with running into an albino housemate or falling into the Tidal Basin. That's all."

That may be all he wants, but all I want is to find someone I can trust. Someone who won't break my heart. How can I trust him if he's already on record as being a fraud?

"Okay," I say, because despite my misgivings, I cannot deny my attraction to him. "We can try once more for a normal date. But three strikes and you're out. Got it?"

He grins. "Got it."

"Good." I play with the handle on my mug. "You might as well pick a night now, before I change my mind."

"Oh, so it's gonna be like that, huh?" He puts his mug on the coffee table. "Fine. Allow me to consult my social secretary."

"Oh, please. Like you're that important."

"You have no idea who you're dealing with. I'm kind of a big deal." He pulls out his phone and begins flipping through his calendar. "I'm out of town this week for work, and I'm in New Orleans next weekend for my brother's bachelor party."

"Naked dancers on Bourbon Street? Eww."

"That isn't what we have planned. But thanks for the vote of confidence." He continues flicking through his calendar. "How about the weekend after next?"

"Sure. Okay. As long as I won't need a flashlight."

"You won't. I promise." He rests his phone on the coffee table. "I'd better make this next date count, huh?"

"It's sudden death, my friend."

He smirks and scoots closer to me on the couch, his eyes locked on mine. He tucks a strand of my hair behind my ear, leans in, and kisses me softly on the lips. A voice in my head tells me to pull away, that this is a huge mistake, but something about Jeremy—the tenderness of his touch, the softness of his lips, the piney smell of his freshly washed hair—sucks me in, and instead of pulling away, I lean in closer. Before I know it we are lying on his couch, our legs intertwined, our faces pressed together. Our bodies burrow into his thick leather cushions, and as he kisses me, I kiss him back, even though I know, with near certainty, that this will come back later to bite me in the ass.

CHAPTER 20

The next morning, I roll over to find myself staring at the back of Jeremy's head. I bolt upright.

"Oh my God!"

Jeremy starts and turns over to face me, his eyes half open as I pull the sheets up around my shoulders. "What's up?" he says, rubbing his eyes.

"I shouldn't be here. What time is it?"

"No idea." He reaches for his phone on his nightstand. "Almost nine."

"Shit!" I leap out of bed, draping my arms across my naked torso to prevent him from catching a glimpse of my pasty body. "I should have been at the Dupont market half an hour ago. Rick is going to kill me."

"The market doesn't open for another hour. You'll be fine."

I grab my marled gray sweater off the floor. "You don't know Rick. He's an asshole on a good day." I glance around the floor. "Where are the rest of my clothes?"

Jeremy rolls over and reaches down to the floor on his side of the bed. "There's a bra over here." He tosses it in my direction. "I think your pants are at the foot of the bed."

Jesus Christ. "How did this happen?"

"Well, it was dark, so I guess it was hard to see where the clothes ended up. . . ."

"No, I mean how did I end up spending the night? I remember us making our way from the couch to your bed, but once we'd . . . you know . . . you offered to walk me home."

"I did. And then I went to get you a glass of water, and when I came back you were sound asleep. You looked so peaceful. I figured it was better to let you sleep than to wake you up."

I let out a loud groan as I clasp my bra with my back to Jeremy and throw on my sweater. "This is such a disaster."

"Thanks. . . ."

I turn around. "Sorry—I didn't mean . . . I just didn't plan on sleeping over."

"Yeah, well, I didn't plan on falling in the Tidal Basin, so I guess we're even."

I smile in spite of myself and pull on my jeans. "Listen, I have to get to work. But I'll see you in about two weeks, okay?"

"Sure."

I slip through the bedroom door into the living room, where I throw on my coat and grab my bag. When I look over my shoulder, Jeremy is standing in his bedroom doorway, dressed in a faded gray T-shirt and a pair of black boxers.

"Would it be okay if I called you before our next date? Just to talk?"

"Yeah, sure, of course." I think back to our phone conversation at Rick's bakehouse and how I basically told him never to call me again. "From now on, you don't have to ask if you can call me. You can just call. Honestly."

"You just seem so . . . I don't know. Guarded. I don't want to overstep."

"If you overstep, I'll let you know. And hey, if I really don't want to talk to you, I'll just ignore your call."

He grins. "Fair enough."

He escorts me to the front door and holds it open as I step into the hallway. "I'll talk to you soon, then," he says.

He leans in to kiss me, but I turn my head awkwardly to the side and give him a quick peck on the cheek. Then I walk down the hall toward the elevator, wondering if someday I'll explain to him why I am the way I am.

As predicted, Rick rips me a new one as soon as I arrive at the Dupont Circle market.

"What did I tell you about being on time?" he says as he heaves a wooden crate of sourdough onto the table. It lands with a loud bang.

"Sorry—I forgot to set my alarm."

"I don't care if your apartment caught fire. Eight thirty means eight thirty. I'm docking you half your pay for this."

"Half my pay? But I'm here. The market doesn't open for another forty-five minutes."

"Oh, so you're gonna argue with me now? You're late. End of story."

"But Rick—"

He slams another crate onto the table. "End. Of. Story. Now go help your blond friend unload the rest of the truck. I'm too tired and sore to listen to your bullshit."

I head over to Rick's truck, which is parked behind the tent on a blockaded stretch of Twentieth Street, just north of Dupont Circle. The Dupont market is arguably the biggest farmers' market in Washington, DC, operating year-round and selling everything from thick spools of wool and handcrafted soap to fat hunks of artisanal cheese and heritage meats. Colorful tents pack Twentieth Street from one intersection to the next and spill over into an adjacent parking lot, which is flanked by tall, wrought-iron gates. Unlike the West End market, which maintains a calm, unhurried atmosphere, the Dupont market always feels like a celebration, with throngs of people jamming the aisles and a vibrant chatter filling the air. Even on the last Sunday in March, with forty-five minutes to go until the market actually opens, it is full of energy, as farmers and craftsmen breathe life into the weekend morning air.

When I reach the back of Rick's truck, Heidi emerges from the cavernous interior carrying a black plastic crate filled with almond croissants. She glances at her watch. "Living on the edge," she says. "I'm surprised Rick didn't impale you with a baguette."

"The day is still young."

She hands the crate down to me and hops off the truck. "So where were you? You're never late." She drags her eyes up and down my figure. "And you look kind of dressed up. For you, at least."

I lay the crate on the table and unload the almond croissants into a basket, their sweet, nutty scent wafting across Rick's tent. I clear my throat. "I didn't make it home last night."

"What? Where did you sleep?"

My cheeks flush. "Jeremy Brauer's."

"The shady food-writer guy?" I nod, and Heidi stamps her foot, her hands on her hips. "*Sydney*. What is wrong with you?"

"I ask myself this question at least ten times a day."

"Well, I mean, seriously. I Googled Jeremy after your date last month, and he's even sketchier than I thought. What kind of guy sells his opinion to the highest bidder, and then pretends his views are totally unbiased? He seems like a total shill."

"I know. Believe me, I know. He does not Google well. But the thing is . . . in person he isn't like that. He's actually really nice."

"I'm sure Robert Mugabe's wife thinks he's really nice, too."

"Jeremy is a disgraced food writer, not a Zimbabwean dictator."

"Potato, po-tah-to." She grins and jabs me in the side. "I'm only kidding. But after all these years of closing yourself off and refusing to date, why are you choosing this guy, who seems about as trustworthy as Bernie Madoff?"

"Again with the hyperbole . . ."

"Whatever. The point is the same. This is self-sabotage."

I unload a basket of millet muffins. "You're probably right. There's just something about him, you know? He's very charismatic."

"You know who else is charismatic? Drew. And unlike Mr. Brauer, Drew isn't haunted by an unsavory professional history that's plastered all over the Internet."

"So you've Googled Drew, too? Do you Google everyone?"

"Pretty much." She tosses an empty container beneath the table and grabs a bucket of biscotti. "Why don't you let me set up a group date for next Saturday—you, me, Drew, and one of Drew's buddies. Something casual."

"I don't know. . . ." I glance up and spot Drew setting up a few stands away, unloading a crate of bright red apples off the back of Broad Tree Orchards' truck. He wears a gray flannel jacket, and his dark mop of hair is tucked beneath a black knit hat. He catches sight of me staring at him, and when he does, he smiles and waves. I wave back.

"Hey! Stop flirting with your boyfriend!" Rick yells from the other end of the tent, in full earshot of Drew and pretty much everyone else at the market.

My face is, without question, the color of a tomato. "Sorry . . ."

"Not as sorry as you will be if you don't get those oatmeal cookies in a basket, *capisce?*"

I quickly begin organizing them. "Got it. Sorry."

Rick grumbles an unintelligible retort under his breath and hobbles toward the back of the truck.

"So? Are you in?" Heidi asks when Rick is out of earshot. "I know Drew will be into the idea."

I watch as Drew grabs three apples and begins juggling them like a circus performer, an admittedly adorable smirk blooming on his face as his coworkers hoot and holler and applaud his dexterity. His eyes flit in my direction, and his smile broadens as he catches all three apples in one hand and presses them against his chest. He winks at me, and my heart races.

"Okay, fine," I say. "I guess it isn't the worst idea."

What's sad is that lately, that's about the strongest endorsement I can give.

CHAPTER 21

The following week, I send Stu Abbott a list of ideas for blog posts and video segments for the *Chronicle*'s experimental *Buying the Farm* blog:

- Broad Tree Orchards' cold storage facility
- Following crop from farm to market
- Profile of new food entrepreneur
- Trend piece—the next kale?

The list goes on with a few more ideas, and Stu writes back within the hour.

"Start with the cold storage piece," he writes. "Would love to see where/how they store their apples."

Julie signs off on my contributing content to the *Chronicle*, too, as long as I give the market newsletter precedence on all market-related announcements and news. I'm a little worried I may run out of ideas and that by contributing to both, I will spend all of my waking hours on two enterprises that collectively will pay me about $150 a week. But Stu assures me there will be more lucrative opportunities on the horizon, so as long as I keep my ears open for a big story, I could be on my way to the career I've always wanted but that has somehow eluded my grasp.

To jumpstart the cold storage piece, I coordinate with Maggie to visit Broad Tree Orchards' facility on Friday, since I don't have to work for Rick that day. We arrange to meet in front of Eastern Market, a year-round public market housed inside a nineteenth-century brick building on Capitol Hill, where Maggie delivers a bushel of apples every Friday morning before heading back to her farm in Maryland. But when I arrive in front of Eastern Market that morning, neither Maggie nor her truck is anywhere in sight.

A gentle drizzle begins to fall from the sky, so I scurry along the uneven sidewalk in front of the market's sturdy brick edifice, peering around the corner in case I misunderstood which entrance Maggie meant. But as I stare down C Street, I don't see any sign of her there either. I head back toward the main entrance, taking cover beneath the green metal awnings that stretch along the sidewalk in front of the market from end to end. On the weekends, these sidewalks fill with vendors selling everything from cabbage to jewelry, and crowds flock to the outdoor market, particularly in the spring, when the entire block comes alive with activity, a beating heart pumping life into the surrounding streets and alleyways. On a weekday like today, however, the area beneath the awnings is empty, and I pace beneath them as drops of rain ricochet off their tops.

Once I have been waiting fifteen minutes, I decide to head inside. Either I misunderstood Maggie's instructions or, it being April 1, this is some sort of cruel April Fools' joke, but regardless, I'm sick of standing in the rain and would like some answers. Or, at the very least, a cup of coffee.

Even at nine thirty, the market bustles with activity, as people mill up and down the long, narrow thoroughfare and browse the numerous food stalls. The cement-paved market is a straight shot from end to end, lined on either side by butchers, cheesemongers, and grocers selling everything from chicken feet to lettuce. The steep, hipped roof rises nearly fifty feet, traversed by white metal scaffolding, and what little sunlight there is today pours through the skylights and windows lining the walls. The air carries a funky mustiness, the combination of aged cheese mixed with fresh fish and bread hot from the oven. A crowd is gathered at the far end of the market in front of the Market Lunch, which serves some of the best blueberry pancakes and crab cakes in town.

As I make my way toward Capitol Hill Produce, I feel a tap on my shoulder. I whirl around and find myself standing face-to-face with Drew. He wears a weathered pair of khakis, New Balance sneakers, and a heather-gray hooded sweatshirt, his face covered by a layer of stubble just shy of a full-blown beard. As always, I'm enchanted by his dark eyes and warm smile.

"Drew—hi." I glance at my watch. "What are you doing here? I was supposed to meet Maggie at 9:15."

"Yeah, I know. That's why I'm here. Maggie ran into a problem with the supply truck, so she couldn't make her usual delivery. She asked if I could give you a ride out to the orchard instead."

"Oh. Okay." My heartbeat quickens. "Isn't that really inconvenient for you? Don't you have work today? Heidi said you work at the Alaska Wildlife Fund during the week."

"I do. But my boss is cool. She has a really lenient leave policy— especially for something like this. She's a big supporter of the local food movement."

"Ah. Got it."

Great. Aside from the fact that I didn't wash my hair this morning and look like a hungover college student in my comfortable "journalist clothes," Heidi arranged our group date for tomorrow night, so seeing Drew a day in advance—and sitting alone in a car with him for an hour and a half each way—officially ruins all of my plans. I have an extremely limited first-date repertoire, and after today, I will possibly have nothing left to talk about.

"I'm parked down the block on Seventh," he says, nodding over his shoulder. "You ready?"

I smile awkwardly. "I was born ready," I say.

This is going to be a disaster.

By the time we have been driving for thirty minutes, I have officially sweat through my shirt. I keep my arms glued to my sides to prevent Drew from seeing the dark green circles staining my long-sleeved olive-green T-shirt, but as a result, I look like a spooked robot. Throw in some greasy hair and a few zits, and I officially look like an explosion of hormones.

"So what is it like to work for Rick?" Drew asks once we have been driving for forty-five minutes.

"Exasperating and delicious."

He laughs. "He's such a character. Bakes a mean sourdough, though."

"And some pretty amazing brioche."

He taps the steering wheel with his thumbs. "What kind of music do you listen to?"

"Mostly pretty mellow stuff. A little Bon Iver, a little Fleet Foxes. A lot of Elliott Smith."

"Elliott Smith? Didn't he play at the 9:30 Club recently?"

"Definitely not."

"You sure?"

"Positive." I glance in Drew's direction. "He's dead. He committed suicide."

"Oh. Right."

A lengthy silence hangs between us, probably because I somehow managed to steer our conversation in the direction of suicide. This is why I shouldn't date. By tomorrow night, I'll have us talking about the Holocaust.

I stare out the window as we pass long stretches of farmland, a light mist of rain spraying the car on all sides. Once we have been sitting in silence for an intensely awkward five minutes, we both attempt to restart the conversation, speaking at the exact same time.

"So," we say in unison.

"Sorry," Drew says. "I didn't mean . . . You were starting to say?"

"No, nothing. I was just . . . You first."

Drew scratches his jaw and pulls around a traffic circle. "Can we start over?" he says.

My shoulders relax. "That would be great."

"Tell me why you're visiting Maggie's cold storage facility. What's this all about?"

"I'm producing a short video along with a Web column for the *Washington Chronicle*'s new *Buying the Farm* blog."

"You work for the *Chronicle*?"

"Not yet. Maybe someday. For now, I'm sort of a freelancer."

"And they're interested in a cold storage facility because . . . ?"

"Basically, the editors want to show people how cold storage works, and why you can buy apples almost all year round, even though the harvest ended months ago."

Drew nods. "Ah, got it. Cool." He flicks his wipers to clear the mist off the front windshield. "How many of these columns do you think you'll write?"

"As many as they'll let me? The blog is sort of experimental at this point, but I'm hoping it catches on so that eventually they'll hire me."

"Ha, right. Wouldn't that be nice."

I shift uncomfortably in my seat. "That wasn't supposed to be a joke. . . ."

"No, I know. Sorry. I didn't mean it like that. I just know how hard it can be to break into food journalism. From what I've heard, it's an exclusive club."

He's right: It is an exclusive club. Back when I started my *Perpetual Feast* blog, I tried to attract readers by commenting on all of the food blogs I read daily—the super popular ones, with thousands upon thousands of followers and hundreds of commenters for each post. But none of them followed me back or commented on my blog. None of them acknowledged my blog existed. I felt like the new kid in school, who showed up in the lunchroom with her tray of food and tried to sit at the popular table, but all the seats were taken and no one tried to make room. I'm sure that's why I had so much trouble finding a job as a food writer after college. I didn't have the right connections with the right people, so unless I was willing to work for free, I had to look elsewhere.

But the *Chronicle*'s food editor asked to meet with me, and now I'm writing for him, so for the first time, I feel as if I'm part of the club—if not as a full-fledged member, then at least as a welcomed guest.

"I really think I have a shot at making it this time," I say.

"This time?"

"I tried to break in during college, but . . . well, it didn't really work out."

Drew smiles. "Well, I hope it does now. We're not getting any younger, right?"

I offer a faint smile in return and shift my gaze out the side window. "Right," I say. Thanks for reminding me.

We arrive at Broad Tree Orchards just after eleven o'clock, and Drew drives up a long dirt driveway, past rows of cherry trees covered with fluffy pink blossoms and bright blue netting. The farm stretches over a flat plain of more than a hundred acres, with barren, drab patches of still unplanted earth punctuated by vibrant swathes of pink from blooming peach and plum trees. We pass the main farmhouse, with its white clapboard siding and rust-colored roof, and make our way toward a large cement building with a flat roof and no windows.

Drew parks in a large paved lot, and as we get out of the car, Maggie emerges from behind the building, her spiky, salt-and-pepper hair sticking out in all directions.

"You made it!" she says as she approaches us. "So sorry about the mix-up. That damn truck makes my blood boil. If I had a nickel for every time it broke down and messed up my plans, I could retire."

"No worries," I say. "I still managed to get here."

"Thanks to this guy," she says, elbowing Drew. "I can think of worse things than spending an hour and a half in the car with this handsome devil."

My cheeks flush as Drew and I lock eyes.

"We had fun," he says, smiling, though I can't tell if he means it or is just being polite.

"Come on," Maggie says, waving us toward the cement building. "Let me show you around."

She waves us around the back and escorts us through a narrow doorway, which opens to a large warehouse, where a series of locked metal doors sit side by side. She explains that each door opens to a separate, controlled-atmosphere cold storage room, where they load freshly picked fruit before sealing the room and sucking out nearly all of the oxygen. Without oxygen, the fruit stops breathing and ripening until they reopen the room, keeping the fruit as fresh as it was when they plucked it from the tree.

"We opened the one at the end before you came to get the air moving," she says. "Otherwise, there isn't enough oxygen for us to breathe either."

She leads us into a small lockup at the end of the row, the right side of which is lined from floor to ceiling with large green crates, each one at least four feet on a side and filled to the brim with golden yellow- and blush-colored apples.

"We're actually down to our last round of apples, so it's a good thing you came today," she says. "At this point, our main focus is on getting ready for cherry and peach season. You'll have to come back in August, when we start harvesting apples again."

She checks the oxygen level in the room on a small digital monitor and gives a thumbs up. I set up my camera in an empty corner and begin to film as a mustard yellow forklift enters and removes a crate from the top of one of the stacks. I shoot from all different angles as the forklift empties the room crate by crate, making sure I get plenty of close-ups of the bright, crisp fruit and the lifting machinery in action. When the room is empty, I meet Drew and Maggie in the common area, where workers repack the fruit into smaller, wooden containers to take to the markets. I get more footage of the fruit being unloaded, dozens of golden orbs tumbling into weathered crates, and once I've followed the crates onto the freight truck with my camera, Drew and I pile in the back of Maggie's pickup truck, and she takes us out to the fields where she is planting more Goldrush and Pink Lady apples for next season.

As she barrels around a bend in the dirt road, I slide across the backseat and press up against Drew, whose knee grazes mine. My heart races as our bodies press against each other, my torso nuzzling his. He looks as if he might reach out and rest his hand on my leg, but before he can, Maggie brings the truck to an abrupt halt.

"Here we are," she says, throwing it into park. "My new babies."

We hop out and head for the new plantings, my camera armed

and ready. The rain stopped about thirty minutes ago, and though the sky is still tinged with gray, the sun has begun to peek through the clouds.

"We're boosting production on the assumption that this deal with Green Grocers goes through," she says as I pan across the rows of new trees.

"Julie mentioned a partnership might be in the works," I say, clicking the Pause button. "Any updates?"

Maggie shakes her head. "But I think the idea is to create a mini 'farmers' market' within the store. It'd be a huge windfall for us. The former CEO made it so hard for us to get our foot in the door, but this new guy seems intent on doing away with a lot of the red tape."

"Sounds like it would be great exposure."

"It would." She lets out a hardened laugh. "Hopefully the new guy won't let the skeptics muck it all up."

I get a few more shots of the orchard, and then Drew and I hop into the truck with Maggie and head back to the storage facility, where I take a few more notes on the cold storage process and do a brief on-camera interview with Maggie. By the time I've finished, we've been at the orchard more than four hours.

Drew helps me load my belongings back into his Camry, and we wave to Maggie as we pull back onto the dirt road in front of her farm and head back to DC.

"That was awesome," he says. "You're really good at interviewing people. You ask all the right questions."

"Thanks."

"Definitely send me the link once the story goes live. I'd love to see it." He reaches into his sweatshirt pocket and pulls out his phone. "Oh, and while you were shooting, I downloaded an Elliott Smith album. I figured we could listen on the ride home."

He taps on his phone with one hand as he steers with the other and rests the phone on the dashboard. The mellow harmonies of Elliott Smith's guitar hum through the speakers on his phone, and as we turn onto the highway back toward DC, I think this ride might not be nearly as bad as I'd imagined.

* * *

An hour and a half later, Drew pulls up in front of my house and turns on his warning flashers.

"Door-to-door service," he says with a smile.

"Thanks so much for the ride. I'm sorry you had to take a day off for this."

"Are you kidding? You made my day."

"Really?"

"Yeah, really. I don't know what I expected when we headed out there today, but seeing you in action . . . it was cool. Gave me a whole new perspective on Maggie's business."

"Oh. Well . . . I'm glad."

"We'll have to continue the conversation tomorrow night. Heidi said eight o'clock? At Estadio?"

"That sounds right."

"Cool." He clears his throat. "I guess I'll see you tomorrow, then."

I smile and move to take off my seat belt, but before I do, he leans in and kisses me. His breath is warm, and he tastes of mint chewing gum, and his stubble tickles my chin, not enough to bother me but enough for me to notice. He kisses me softly as Elliott Smith's voice hums through his speakers, and as his lips press against mine, an uneasy feeling arises deep in my chest, a sensation I cannot place, something that prevents me from giving in fully to this moment. What am I afraid of? Why can't I just let go? What is *wrong* with me?

Drew rubs his thumb gently along my jawline, and then he pulls away and smiles and reaches across me to open my door. I undo my seat belt, grab my bag, and slip out of the car, but as I watch him drive away, the uneasy feeling in my chest hardens into a tight ball, and I finally place it. It isn't fear or anxiety or even insecurity.

It's guilt.

CHAPTER 22

I shouldn't feel guilty for kissing Drew. But I do, and it's all Jeremy's fault.

No, I take that back. It isn't Jeremy's fault. It's Zach's.

What Zach and I had . . . it was special. We were best friends. We grew up together. I experienced so many of my firsts with him by my side: my first byline, my first Thai curry, my first time watching *The Godfather* and *Casablanca*. We lost our virginity to each other. When Libby got invited to parties by my cooler classmates, who were three years her senior and never invited me to anything, I didn't care because I had Zach. We had each other. For a long and crucial stretch of my young adult life, his existence and mine were inextricably linked, and I cannot reflect on my development into the person I am today without looking through the prism of our relationship.

Which is why his betrayal still stings after all these years. Looking back on it now, I should have seen it coming. Everyone told me high school relationships rarely survive four years of college. But I told myself Zach and I were different. We weren't a couple of horny teenagers who were obsessed with one another, two kids who thought we were the first people to discover sex. Our relationship was deeper than that. We talked about our hopes and fears and dreams. We cooked together and went on walks in the park together and read books together. We were soul mates. At least that's what I'd thought.

When freshman year of college went by without a hitch, I thought we had it all figured out. We'd agreed to see each other at least once a month, alternating visits at Northwestern and Princeton so that neither of us had to shoulder the cost of a plane ticket every time. There were, of course, the obvious comparisons between our colleges at every visit—The Keg versus The Street, the preppy allure of Princeton versus the artsy character of Evanston—but we both appreciated that each of our respective universities suited our personalities. We were happy to see each other finally fit in, after feeling like outsiders in high school.

The only thing that didn't sit right with me during freshman year was Zach's growing obsession with Ivy, Princeton's oldest and most selective eating club. He took me to a few parties there when I visited, leading me through the tall iron gates on Prospect Avenue into the three-story brick manse. We'd drink glasses of wine and scotch in the billiard room, surrounded by red leather club chairs and preppy, well-heeled members, the mahogany walls lined with oil paintings of thirties-era men playing lacrosse. I felt like I'd stepped into a Fitzgerald novel.

The Zach I knew had nothing in common with those people—he was a geek with a cowlick, who wore plaid shirts and corduroys and suede Wallabee shoes, who used to love watching *The Princess Bride* with me in his living room—and yet he made a point of getting to know all of the Ivy upperclassmen, those juniors and seniors who were already members and would decide whether Zach would ever become a member himself.

"You'd really want to become a member of a club that makes you go through ten rounds of interviews?" I asked during one of my visits.

"Sure," he said. "Why not?"

"It just seems so . . . elitist."

"You know I'm not like that."

"Exactly my point."

He sighed. "It'll be like an inside joke between you and me. I can send you pictures of all these guys in their tweed jackets and wingtip shoes, and we can laugh about it."

I smiled weakly and let the subject drop, even though it didn't seem like a very funny joke to me.

Then, in the spring semester of sophomore year, Zach was selected by Ivy in the "bicker"—the club's process for choosing new members—and after his ten rounds of interviews eventually became a member. That was around the same time his visits to Northwestern became less frequent. Our monthly rendezvous became bimonthly at best and often trimonthly, as he stopped flying to Chicago and my funds for flights back east withered away. We still spoke on the phone nearly every day, and whenever we were home for holidays or summer break, we spent nearly every waking hour together, so I told myself we were still going strong.

But over the next two years, our ties began to fray. Instead of cooking together in his kitchen like we used to do, my visits to Princeton mostly involved us eating four-course meals at Ivy, served by a uniformed staff. The other Ivy members—many of whom were the offspring of Fortune 500 CEOs or world leaders—didn't seem like the butt of a joke between Zach and me. They seemed like Zach's friends. When I'd try to poke fun at them, I was the only one laughing.

"Check out that chick's diamond earrings," I whispered in his ear one night. "It's a wonder her earlobes aren't on the floor."

"Who, Georgina?" He waved me off. "Nah, she's cool."

But she wasn't cool. She was tall and thin and gorgeous, with thick chestnut hair and deep-set brown eyes and an ass so tight you could bounce her diamond studs right off it. Her dad was some real estate mogul in New York who regularly rubbed elbows with Michael Bloomberg and Donald Trump. She was everything I was not.

As months went by, Georgina appeared in more of Zach's stories: something funny she'd said while everyone was having dinner the previous week, a reference to a new wine she'd introduced the group to. Finally, when he'd mentioned her name in a phone conversation for what felt like the ten thousandth time, I'd had enough.

"Are you sleeping with Georgina?" I asked.

"What? Are you kidding? Of course I'm not sleeping with Georgina."

"Then why do you mention her in every conversation we have?"

"Because we're friends." He sighed. "Syd, you know me better than anyone. You can trust me."

And I did. But as graduation neared, he became more and more distant. He had stopped visiting me entirely by senior year, and he called maybe once a week, always claiming he'd meant to call a bunch of times but had fallen asleep. Meanwhile, I was busy trying to land a job as a food writer or producer, without success, so I distracted myself from Zach's aloofness with job applications and resumes.

Then one night after graduation, we were cooking spaghetti carbonara in his mom's kitchen. He was heading to Columbia in the fall for law school, and I still didn't have a job, so we decided we'd make the most of our summer, cooking together like old times. Or at least that's what I'd decided. As I pulled together my ingredients, I couldn't remember whether my favorite carbonara recipe used three eggs or four, so I flipped open Zach's laptop, which was sitting on the kitchen table, while he stirred the fat cubes of bacon sizzling in his mom's frying pan. He glanced over his shoulder as the grease hissed and popped, and his eyes widened.

"Hey, wait a sec—don't—"

But it was too late. His e-mail account was open to an e-mail from Georgina, a topless photo of her staring back at me through the screen. When are you going to get your ass to NYC so you can fuck me?? the e-mail said in bold.

I slammed the laptop shut, ran to the bathroom, and threw up in the toilet, as the smell of frying bacon wafted beneath the door.

"Sydney, listen—I can explain."

He told me it had all happened so fast, that they'd always had a connection, that eventually it became too much for them to ignore. I found out later they'd been sleeping together for nearly two years, but that night, it wouldn't have mattered if it had been two years or two weeks. He'd cheated on me, he'd lied to me, and, according to what he told me that night, he'd fallen out of love with me. After all of our years together, after all of the cooked meals and long walks and four-hour phone conversations, that was it. It was over.

That was the last time I saw Zach. He e-mailed and called a few times, but when I was too inconsolable to respond to his first few attempts, he gave up. He didn't try to win me back, and he didn't try to make it up to me. He didn't do anything. But what hurt most of all, what still stings to this day, is that he never said he was sorry. Not once. He explained and rationalized and apologized for the way I found out, but he never apologized for what he'd done. He never said, "I'm sorry I lied to you. I'm sorry for breaking your heart."

And so as much as I know my relationship with Jeremy is not analogous to my relationship with Zach, as much as I am aware that Jeremy and I don't even have a *relationship,* I can't help but feel guilty for kissing someone else while he is away—even if that person is generous and sweet and looks like an Abercrombie model.

Which, as far as I can tell, basically means I'm doomed.

Later that afternoon, I download the video from Broad Tree Orchards onto my laptop and begin cobbling together a piece for the *Chronicle*'s Web site. My floor vibrates from Simon's trance music below, my entire apartment quivering with a low-level buzz, which makes it difficult to focus on pretty much anything. After about an hour of deafening electronica, my phone rings—though, with Simon's music still raging, I only know this because I see Jeremy's name appear on my screen. Part of me wants to ignore his call (*Do I tell him about kissing Drew? Do I mention Drew's name at all?*), but to my surprise, a bigger part of me misses him and wants to hear about his trip. I'm also glad to have an activity that will distract me from my vibrating floor.

"Greetings from The Big Easy," Jeremy says when I answer the phone.

Simon's music thumps in the background. "Greetings."

"You throwing a party or something?"

"No. I wish. I'm working, believe it or not. The music you hear is from my downstairs neighbor, who has been blasting bizarre German trance music all night."

"Okay, wow. I have so many questions about that comment. First of all, I thought your downstairs neighbor was 'harmless'?"

"No, you were right. He's super weird."

"Ah. So I was right about something."

I hold back a smile. "Maybe."

"And as for the music," he says, "I'm curious as to how you know he's playing *German* trance. That's very specific and indicates a knowledge of trance music I can't help but question."

"You're questioning my musical taste now?"

"I think I am."

The music thumps on in the background. "I don't know for sure that it's German. But German, French, Swedish—whatever. The point is, it's annoying, and it's distracting me from getting any work done."

"Which leads me to my next question: Why are you at home doing work on a Friday night?"

"Because I'm a loser?"

"Well, yeah. Obviously."

"Hey!"

"You said it, not me."

I close my laptop lid. "If you must know, I'm trying to edit some footage I shot earlier today."

"Footage? Of what?"

I hold back for a moment, but decide there is no harm in telling him about my visit with Maggie. "Broad Tree Orchards' cold storage facility," I say.

"Ah, very cool. Is that for the newsletter thing?"

"No, it's for the *Chronicle*'s new food blog."

Jeremy hesitates. "Oh. You're working for the *Chronicle* now?"

"Just as a freelancer." I bite the end of my pen. "I'm working for Stu Abbott."

There is a break in the conversation, just long enough to be uncomfortable. "Stu's a good guy," he finally says. "Doesn't think much of me, though."

"No?"

"Let's just say we didn't part on the best terms."

I wait for him to continue with an explanation, to say, *I didn't actually do anything wrong—the whole "cash for comment" thing was a big misunderstanding.* But he doesn't, and an uneasy silence hangs between us.

"Could we . . . talk about all of that?" I say. "What actually happened?"

He lets out a long sigh. "Yeah. We can talk about it. But not now. Not over the phone."

"Okay. That's fair." Because really, I'd rather talk about it in person, too.

"So tell me more about this shoot," he says. "How'd you get out to rural Maryland?"

I clear my throat. "One of Maggie's helpers gave me a lift."

"Oh, cool. That was nice of her."

"Him."

"Sorry? Maggie is a dude?"

"No—the person who gave me a lift. It was a guy."

"Oh, okay, whatever," he says, unfazed. "Anyway, what was it like?"

I move swiftly on from any mention of Drew and tell Jeremy all about the controlled-atmosphere storage rooms, the towering crates of crisp Goldrush apples, and the rich, earthy smell of the blossoming orchards.

"They're even planting more trees because they may start selling at Green Grocers," I say. Then I stop myself. "I'm not sure I was supposed to tell you that."

"Your secret's safe with me. My firm does Green Grocers' outside PR, so I know all about the pilot project. That's actually what I've been working on for the past three months."

"Oh. Really? Is it a done deal?"

"Not yet. It will be soon, though. Assuming the new CEO doesn't derail the whole thing."

"Why would he derail it?"

"He wouldn't intentionally. There's just some stuff in his past, and if it became public—" He cuts himself off. "Now I'm the one who's said too much."

I sit forward, thinking back to my conversation with Stu Abbott about a bigger, meatier story. "What happened in his past?"

"Long story. Nothing I can talk about. Not right now, anyway."

"I'm a very good listener, so when you're ready to share . . ."

He laughs. "Thanks. I'll keep that in mind."

I hesitate, hoping he will fill the silence with another juicy tidbit or two about the Green Grocers deal, but when he doesn't, I decide to let it go for now and lean back against my plush gray couch cushions. "So how is your brother doing? Having the time of his life?"

"I sure hope so. Jake has always been a little more reserved and uptight than the rest of us. We're trying to get him to let loose this weekend."

"Any success so far?"

"Some. He's getting there."

"Does it freak you out at all, having your younger brother settle down before you?"

"Nah, not really. Jake has always been an old soul. Dave, on the other hand . . ."

"Dave?"

"My youngest brother."

"Wait, remind me—how many brothers do you have?"

He laughs. "Just two. And we couldn't be more different."

He starts to tell me about Jake, the crazy genius of the family who is getting a PhD in mathematics at MIT and may or may not win the Fields Medal someday. The conversation eventually drifts to Dave, his youngest brother and the family clown, who is still trying to figure out his life while he parks cars for a restaurant in Boston and lives with their parents in Watertown. I tell him about Libby and her fiancé Matt, about my parents and their employment woes, about our family dog Boots, who died last year. We talk about what it's like to be the oldest sibling, our thoughts on growing up in the suburbs, our mutual fondness for the summer camps of our youth. We talk and talk and talk, until my throat is parched and my tongue feels thick and sticky. Somewhere in the middle of a discussion about drivers' tests, I glance at my clock and realize we've been chatting for an hour and a half.

"Wow—did you realize it's almost seven o'clock?" I say.

"Seriously? Crap. I'm supposed to meet the guys in the lobby in five minutes, and I haven't showered or shaved."

"I'm guessing your brother won't care."

"I kind of look like the Wolf Man right now, so I'm guessing the general public might."

"Then I'd better let you go. I hear it's a full moon tonight."

He howls into the phone. "Sorry. That was lame. Forget I just did that."

"Did what?"

"Exactly." He covers the phone and calls out to someone in the background. "Listen, I've got to run, but I'll call you in a few days about getting together next weekend, okay?"

"Sounds good."

I hang on the line, feeling like a teenager again, not wanting to be the first to say good-bye or hang up. When Zach and I first started dating, we'd talk on the phone for hours, and at the end I'd say, "You hang up first," and he'd say, "No, you hang up first," and we'd go on like that for a nauseating period of time until his mom picked up the extension and made him hang up. There are a hundred ways my conversations with Jeremy are nothing like my conversations with Zach—in good ways and in bad—but talking to him like this makes me feel fifteen again.

"Well, off I go," he says. "Later alligator."

"Later."

I hesitate for a moment. I can still hear Jeremy breathing.

"Hey, Sydney?"

"Yeah?"

"It was really great talking to you tonight. I'm glad I called."

A smile grows on my face, and I let myself fall deeper into the couch cushions, and without a trace of snark or cynicism in my voice, I say, "Yeah. Me too."

CHAPTER 23

Well, now I'm really in trouble.

If Jeremy weren't so damn charming, I could cut him loose and never look back. But he is charming, and I like him, and despite his shady past and highly unflattering Wikipedia entry, I don't want to cut him loose. Which, given that I'm supposed to meet up with Drew tonight, is kind of a problem.

Given my penchant for lists and order, I sit down Saturday afternoon with a pen and paper and make a list of Jeremy's and Drew's pros and cons:

JEREMY

Pros: Smart, charming, interested in food, creative, has cooking skills, good-looking, persistent, might have useful information for *Chronicle* story, makes me laugh

Cons: Questionable morals, has very bad Wikipedia entry, on the outs with Stu Abbott (aka future dream boss), possible *Star Wars* fanatic

DREW

Pros: Kind (gave ride to orchard), extremely
attractive/looks like model, interested in food,
works at farmers' market, cares about environment,
million-dollar smile

Cons: Beard is kind of scratchy

I try to come up with more cons for Drew, but I can't think of
any. He hadn't heard of Elliott Smith, but lots of people haven't
heard of Elliott Smith. And anyway, he downloaded *Either/Or*
while I was shooting, so that's almost a pro. On the other hand, I
don't really know enough about him to decide whether he is a good
or bad person. To be fair, I don't really know enough about Jeremy
either.

As I continue to obsess over whether or not I should bail on
tonight's group date, my cell phone trills loudly on my kitchen
counter with a text from my dad. Before reading it, I know it will
be about Libby's wedding because that's all anyone in my family
seems capable of discussing these days.

> **More than two grand for CHAIRS??? Are you
> telling me you support this insanity??**

Last night, Libby e-mailed my dad and copied me and my mom,
saying the women of the family all agreed the Chiavari chairs were
a necessary expense for the wedding reception. I had to Google
"Chiavari" to know what she was talking about, and I had no idea
how expensive they were.

Instead of texting him back, I decide to give him a call to clarify
my position on this chair-rental boondoggle.

"So you've gone to the dark side," he says when he picks up the
phone.

I laugh. "Hey, I had nothing to do with that e-mail."

"More than two thousand dollars on *chairs?* Are you kidding me?"

"I had no idea chairs could be that expensive. I mean, I guess they're pretty. . . ."

"You know what else is pretty? The Hope Diamond. But your sister isn't getting that for her wedding either."

"I hope you break the news to her gently."

He lets out an exasperated sigh. "I'm trying my best here, Syd. I'm trying to give your sister what she wants. But she sure isn't making it easy."

"Why don't you just tell her about the dealership closing?"

Silence. "How do you know about that?"

"Mom told me."

He groans. "I didn't want you girls to know about any of that until the dust settled."

"Libby doesn't know. I haven't told her, and neither has Mom."

"Good," he says. "Keep it that way."

"Wouldn't it be a lot easier if you just told her what's going on with your job? Maybe then she wouldn't want two-thousand-dollar chairs."

"I want to give Libby the wedding of her dreams. I want to do that for her. And anyway, there's a chance I might be able to move over to the Toyota dealership once we close in July. I'll find a way to make it work."

"I'm sure you will. I just . . . I don't want you to bankrupt yourself over one night. And I don't want you to feel like you have to keep stuff like this a secret from me."

"There are some things parents shouldn't discuss with their children," he says.

"I'm not a child anymore," I say, though sometimes I wonder if that's true.

"I know you're not. But your sister . . . She doesn't always understand the way things work in the real world."

"That's putting it mildly," I say, my voice tart.

"Yes, well . . ." He trails off.

And whose fault is that? I want to say. Because anyone with a brain knows the blame lies with him and my mom. My parents always spoiled Libby more than they spoiled me. She was the one Mom would take on shopping excursions to the King of Prussia

Mall and New York City to buy pretty clothes for all the parties and dances Libby planned to attend. I spent much of my adolescence watching my family obsess over Libby's every social engagement: Libby's bat mitzvah, Libby's sweet sixteen, Libby's graduation party. As the older sister, I reached all of those milestones first, and yet Libby always had the bigger party, mostly because she always had more friends. She was pretty and popular and athletic, and I was awkward and studious, and so when it came time to make up guest lists for our respective bat mitzvot, she had ninety friends on her list, whereas I'd only had twenty-five on mine. I didn't even have a sweet sixteen because I was too afraid no one but Zach would show up.

For some sisters, that would probably breed lifelong resentment. And, okay, I have always been a little jealous of how easily things fell into place for Libby—her instant popularity in every circumstance, her field hockey scholarship to Penn State, her engagement. But on some level, I always knew my parents' coddling would ultimately result in her inability to handle adult life, and so at some point all of this would come back to bite her in the ass, and then she'd need me. That hasn't happened yet, and maybe it never will, but given the direction this wedding is headed, my guess is it'll happen sooner rather than later.

"Anyway," he says, "what are you up to tonight? Big plans?"

"I'm meeting up with Heidi and some friends."

"I always liked Heidi. She's a motivated free spirit."

I smile. "That is a perfect way of describing her."

"And how is the job search going? Any luck?"

"Sort of. I don't know if Mom mentioned the newsletter I'm working on, but now I'm writing a freelance blog for the *Chronicle*'s food section, too."

"She did mention that. Sounds like a great opportunity." He clears his throat. "She did express some . . . concern about the pay, though. And I'm guessing none of these positions provides health insurance . . . ?"

"No. But don't worry. I've managed to cobble together enough money with my farmers' market gig to keep me afloat. It isn't a long-term solution, but it's fine for now."

"Okay..."

"What about Mom? How's her job search going?"

He sighs. "Not well."

"No? Why, what happened?"

"I'd better leave that for a conversation between you and your mother—who unfortunately is in the shower at the moment because we're going out with the Hansons tonight. But I'll have her give you a call. She's taking all of this very hard."

"Sounds that way."

He lets out another sigh. "Anyway, now I need to go explain to your sister why the chairs the Rittenhouse provides for free are just fine."

"Good luck with that."

"Something tells me I'll need more than luck."

"Something tells me you're right."

He laughs. "But hey, have fun tonight. Will there be any... you know, guys in the group?"

"Uh huh."

"Anyone... special?"

I glance down at my list of pros and cons. I consider telling him about Jeremy and Drew and how I'm not really sure how I feel about either, but instead I fold up the list and stick it in my junk drawer.

"Nah," I finally say. "Not really."

Because my dad was right: There are some things parents shouldn't discuss with their children.

At three minutes to eight, I barrel down the front stairs and burst out of the house, slinging my purse over my shoulder as I lock the door behind me. The walk to Estadio only takes about eight minutes, so I've timed it perfectly: I'll be a fashionable five minutes late, increasing the likelihood that I won't be the first one there. As much as I don't like being late, I don't want to sit at the bar by myself or, worse, have to converse with Drew on my own. I still feel awkward about our kiss last night.

As I hustle down Fourteenth Street, I think back to the conversation with my dad and his interest in my date tonight. My parents always loved Zach and probably thought, as I did, that we would end up together. Early on, they worried we were too serious for a high school couple, but when they saw our relationship up close, I think they knew we had something special, and they must have appreciated that he prevented me from sitting home alone on Saturday nights.

Libby, on the other hand, never took to Zach. "He's kind of a dweeb," she said during her freshman year, when I was a senior. Then she quickly added, "I mean, so are you, so it makes sense, but I really don't get what you see in him."

That's probably because she was being hit on by my cooler classmates—the varsity soccer players and the captain of the swim team, the sort of guys Zach would have loved to befriend in high school but who barely spoke two words to him. What Libby never understood was that for every maternal instinct I felt toward my baby sister, Zach, by association, felt a paternal instinct. When she called me at Zach's house one Saturday night, slurring her words in a drunken stupor, Zach was the one who pulled the plug on our attempt to make mushroom risotto and drove to pick her up and take her home.

"You guysssarrr such goody goodiessss," she said in the car, her words thick and sloppy as gravy. "But thasss okay. I should prolly be more like you." Then, just before she puked all over the backseat, she said, "I misssyou, Syd."

When Zach and I broke up, Libby seemed to take the nature of Zach's betrayal as confirmation he was never good enough for me. She ran out and bought me five pints of Ben & Jerry's Peanut Butter Cup—my favorite at the time—and amassed a stack of feel-good DVDs for me to watch and did all of the things a supportive sister would do. But beneath it all, there was an air of, *See? I told you so.*

My parents, on the other hand, were in a state of shock. I was light on details, but they got the drift: Zach had cheated on me, and it was over. At first they supported me as any parents would, striking a surprisingly perfect balance between providing consolation and space. But as one year passed, then another and another, without my having so much as a cup of coffee with another guy, they began to worry. On a few occasions, they attempted to set me up with some of their friends' sons, but when I blew up at them for meddling, they let it drop. Hence my dad's delicate mix of hope, interest, and trepidation in inquiring about tonight's date. I know deep down he is hoping I have finally met Zach 2.0. I guess I am, too.

As predicted, I reach Estadio five minutes after eight, but when I check in at the hostess desk, I discover I am the first to arrive—just the scenario I had hoped to avoid. I wander over to the bar, a rectangular concrete counter situated in the middle of the room, surrounded by thick iron and wood stools and flanked on either end by columns made of Spanish tile. Bartenders hurry back and forth within the bar's concrete confines, beneath huge legs of *Jamón Ibérico* that dangle from the bar's wrought-iron trellis. The entire room has a rustic feel, with stone walls, wrought-iron chandeliers, and heavy wooden chairs. I order a glass of Tempranillo, which I sip as I survey the crowd, mostly young people in their twenties and thirties. The wine is fruity and rich, and as I take another sip, I feel a tap on my shoulder.

"So sorry I'm late," Heidi says as she unravels a cream linen scarf from around her neck. "Today has been a disaster."

"Things seemed fine this morning at the market."

"It's all been downhill since then. Trust me." She stuffs her scarf into her oversize purse and sighs. "Oh, but this is Sam. I don't think you've met before." She nods to the blond-haired man standing to her left.

"No—hi, I'm Sydney." I shake his hand and glance over her shoulder. "Any word from Drew?"

Heidi throws her eyes to the ceiling. "Yes. That's part of why today has been such a disaster. Drew can't make it."

My shoulders slump. I'm not sure whether I feel disappointed or relieved. "Oh."

"His grandmother lives out in Leesburg, and she had a stroke this morning, so he had to go and see her. Apparently it's really bad. Like, this could be the end."

"I'm so sorry—that's terrible."

"I know. And he feels really bad about bailing at the last minute, but he's really close with his grandmother, so he kind of had to drive out there." She gestures toward Sam. "Anyway, you're stuck with the two of us tonight. I hope that's okay."

"Of course it is."

"Good. We'll make the Drew thing happen another time. Promise."

"I'm going to hold you to that," I say, but as I grab my glass of wine and follow her and Sam to our table, I wonder if she already knows I won't.

CHAPTER 24

If there is an upside to my being the third wheel on Heidi's date with Sam, it is that I have an easy excuse to leave early and crawl into bed by ten o'clock. It being the first weekend in April, the Dupont farmers' market now opens at eight thirty in the morning, meaning I need to meet Rick by seven at the latest. I could pretend this is the reason I'm in pajamas at ten on a Saturday night, but let's be honest: I was doing this long before I ever heard of Rick or Wild Yeast Bakery.

The next morning I show up five minutes ahead of schedule, wandering up Twentieth Street in the dull morning light, the sky a muted gray. To my surprise, I've arrived before both Rick and Heidi, so I sit on the edge of the curb, pulling the sleeves of my charcoal gray sweatshirt over my hands to keep warm in the chilled spring air.

"Did you get everything you needed Friday?" asks a voice over my right shoulder.

I glance up and see Maggie standing above me. I get to my feet and rub my hands together. "I did. Thanks."

"When do you think it'll be online?"

"By the end of the week. I think we're aiming for Friday."

"Very cool."

I'm about to ask whether Drew is working today, but before I can, Rick's truck charges down the street, the wheels rattling and clanking as Rick attempts—unsuccessfully—to maneuver around all the potholes. He careens toward his station like some sort of wild cowboy, and Maggie and I jump out of the way as he races headfirst into his parking spot.

"Morning, ladies," he grunts as he rolls out of the front seat. He tosses the stub of his cigarette to the ground and stomps it out with his foot as he hikes up his pants. "Where's your blond friend?"

Given that Heidi has worked for him for more than two years, I don't know why he insists on referring to her as "your blond friend." Then again, "your blond friend" is better than "Tits McGee," one of his other favorite epithets.

"She'll be here any second," I say, unsure if this is true. If I had to guess, she spent the night with Sam, so her ETA could be any time between now and never.

"Likely story," he says. He unlocks the back of the truck and sends the door flying upward with a loud rip. "C'mon, sweet cheeks. Let's get this party started."

Maggie heads back to her stand, and I help Rick unload the cases of bread and pastries. He rattles off the new items at market this week—almond poppy seed muffins, rhubarb streusel tea cakes, asparagus and goat cheese quiche—and instructs me to push the olive bread because it didn't sell well yesterday and he needs to move it.

"Any luck with getting an intern or two from L'Academie?"

He heaves the cashbox onto the center table. "Yeah, actually. Hired two guys yesterday." He sneers. "Let's see how long they last."

"At least you'll have a few extra hands."

"Assuming they don't screw everything up," he says. "But yeah. It'll help. Especially since this Green Grocers thing looks like it might actually happen."

"That's what I heard, too."

He throws a crate of cookies next to a rectangular wicker basket. "I'll believe it when I see it."

I unload the almond poppy seed muffins into a cloth-lined basket, and their sweet, vaguely nutty perfume fills the air. Unlike his sturdy raisin bran muffins, which are dense, dark, and chockablock with plump raisins, the almond poppy seed muffins are delicate and cakey, their crumb so light and tender they threaten to float right out of the basket. When Rick isn't looking, I sneak a bite of one of the broken muffin tops, and before I know it I've eaten the entire thing, the flavor as rich as the texture is light, bursting with sweet almond essence.

"You have crumbs on your face."

Heidi throws her canvas bag beneath one of the tables as I wipe my cheek with the back of my hand. "Where have you been?"

"Sam's place."

"Predictably."

She grins. "Oh, come on. You met him last night. He's cool, right?"

"He is. That said, you don't exactly have the best track record."

She raises an eyebrow. "Pots and kettles, my friend . . ."

"Hey, your dubious track record is much longer than mine."

"At least I never dated someone who made national headlines for some journalism scandal."

"What about Drew? You're the one who set me up with him because he's supposedly 'nice.'"

"He is nice." She casts a sideways glance as she places a sign in front of the rhubarb streusel cakes. "Speak of the devil . . ."

I look up and see Drew ambling toward our tent, his hands tucked into the center pocket of his hooded navy sweatshirt. His stubble appears about as thick as it did on Friday, which makes me wonder how much effort must go into maintaining a vaguely unkempt appearance. He hunches his shoulders and smiles sheepishly as he stops in front of my table, leaning back on his heels.

"Hey," he says. "Apologies about last night. Heidi told you about my grandma?"

"She did. I'm so sorry. Is she okay?"

He waves his hand back and forth. "Unclear. She's improved since yesterday, but she's been in poor health for a while now, and she's eighty-seven. We have to be realistic."

"I'm sure Maggie would give you a pass on working the market today, given the circumstances."

"Honestly? Hospitals really freak me out. The docs don't think the end is as imminent as they did yesterday, so I'm happy to have an excuse to do something else for a few hours." He brings his hands out from within his pocket, one of them clasped around a fat golden apple with a light pink blush. He tosses it back and forth between his hands. "But I feel really bad about bailing on last night, so I was thinking ... What are you doing after the market?"

My heart flutters. "Finishing up this week's newsletter and editing more of the cold storage video. But that's about it."

"Wanna grab a cup of coffee or something? I have to head back to the hospital at three, but we could hang for a bit before that."

My palms begin to sweat. Part of me felt relieved when he didn't show up last night. There was no reason to feel guilty anymore for dating behind Jeremy's back, and I didn't have to choose between them. But my parents aren't the only ones who hope I find Zach 2.0. Part of me hopes so too, and at this point, Jeremy has a lot more cons going for him than Drew does. And besides, we'd only be having coffee. What's the harm in an innocent coffee?

"Sure—coffee sounds great," I say, with so much enthusiasm I fool even myself.

Heidi and I finish packing up the truck after the market is over, and Rick slips us each one hundred dollars.

"Those poppy seed muffins were unreal," I say. "They were seriously some of the best muffins I've ever eaten in my life."

"They're basically cake," he says.

"Call them whatever you want. I could eat a whole batch in a single sitting."

"But then you wouldn't have that cute ass," he says, flashing his tobacco-stained smile. He clears his throat as he heads back toward the truck and spits a huge hunk of mucus onto the ground. The man has a seemingly inexhaustible repertoire for making my skin crawl.

As Rick seals up the truck, Drew wanders over, a big crate of apples resting on his arms. "Today's leftovers, courtesy of Maggie."

Heidi's blue eyes brighten. "Come to mama," she says, waving Drew in her direction.

She grabs a dozen and tosses them into a plastic bag, and I do the same. "So where are we heading?" I ask Drew.

Heidi tucks her bag of apples into one of her totes. "Who's heading where?"

"Sydney and I are going to grab a quick cup of coffee," he says, his eyes shifting between the two of us. "You're welcome to join us, if you want."

"Oh—no. I'm . . . Never mind. You two have fun."

She gives me a gentle nudge and waves to Drew before disappearing behind Rick's truck.

"So where to?" I say.

"If it's okay with you, I wanted to drop these apples at my apartment first. I live just off Columbia Road on Biltmore."

"Sure. Isn't that right by Tryst? We could go there after."

"Perfect," he says.

I grab my bag and head up Connecticut Avenue with Drew, breathing in the fresh spring air as I huff and puff my way past Dupont Circle's myriad shops and cafés. The walk from the market to Drew's apartment in Adams Morgan is mostly uphill, and though I try to conceal my acute lack of fitness, it quickly becomes clear I possess the athleticism and vigor of a Care Bear.

"You okay?" Drew asks as we pass a French café on Columbia Road, whose tables spill onto the sidewalk around it, each one filled with young Washingtonians enjoying their Sunday brunch.

"Fine," I pant, calculating how much farther we have to go until we reach his apartment. We've been walking for about fifteen minutes, so by my estimation, we have about another block ahead of us.

We pass a few more restaurants and cafés and round the corner onto Drew's street, which is just one block shy of the infamous intersection between Eighteenth Street and Columbia Road. That's where the rowdy strip of bars on Eighteenth begins, as if a slice of Miami Beach somehow made it to Washington, DC. On Saturday nights, cars and raucous crowds fill the streets and sidewalks, as the intoxicated masses make their way from one bar to the next.

Drew's building is an eight-story brick structure, dappled with air-conditioning units, which jut out from the windows like pushbuttons. He leads me beneath the green awning above the entrance and into the sparsely adorned lobby, which looks as if it hasn't been updated since 1979. We ride the elevator to his studio apartment on the fourth floor, and when I step inside, I think, for a moment, that I have entered a seventeen-year-old boy's bedroom. Random socks and T-shirts litter the floor of the apartment, and empty glasses and dirty plates cover his coffee table, whose blond wooden surface is streaked with coffee and wine stains. I had thought Drew carefully constructed his haphazard appearance, but given the state of his apartment, I am seriously questioning that assumption.

"Sorry the place is kind of a mess," Drew says as he kicks what appears to be a crumpled wad of tinfoil beneath his futon. "I didn't expect to have company."

"That's okay...."

I notice a pizza box sitting on a side table and wonder how long it has been there.

Drew nods toward the futon. "Have a seat. I'm just going to throw these apples in the fridge."

I push aside an old T-shirt and sit down as I survey the rest of his apartment. A large, grid-shaped bookcase stands across from the futon, lined with books on US history and environmental policy, with a few books by Tom Friedman thrown into the mix. I also notice several framed photos of Drew dressed up as various animals: Drew as polar bear, Drew as moose, Drew as wolf, Drew as seal. I grab the framed photo on the table beside me, next to the pizza box, in which he appears to be dressed as some sort of whale.

"That's me as a beluga," he says, sitting beside me on the futon.

"As in the caviar?"

"No. I mean, yeah, the name is the same, but caviar comes from beluga sturgeon. That's me as a beluga whale."

"Right. Sorry. Dumb question."

"Can you guess which beluga whale I am?" He raises his eyebrows expectantly.

"There's more than one kind . . . ?"

He widens his eyes. "Uh . . . yeah. There are like twenty-nine subpopulations."

I hunch my shoulders. "You've got me. Which kind?"

"Cook Inlet. There are only like four hundred of them left in Alaska. They're on the critically endangered list."

"So . . . what's with all the other animal costumes?"

"That's part of my job."

"Your job is to dress up like animals?"

"Well, I mean, that isn't the main part of the job. Most of the time I work on conservation issues. But at fundraisers and stuff, I dress up as animals to increase donor interest."

"Oh." I glance down again at the photo of him dressed as a beluga whale. "So what's your favorite costume, then?"

He scratches his chin. "Tough call. The polar bear tends to get everyone pretty excited. And most people can't pass up a good sea otter. We all agreed the porcupine was a mistake."

"I can imagine."

"Yeah, that didn't go over so well. And some of the costumes are kind of uncomfortable. The sandpiper was pretty tough because of the beak."

I start to laugh, but stop myself when I notice Drew isn't smiling. I clear my throat. "I can see how that would be . . . difficult."

He takes another glance around the apartment. "So should we head to Tryst?"

"Sure," I say, happy to relocate to someplace that doesn't make me question his hygiene.

We head down Eighteenth Street, passing all of the bars that twelve hours ago were probably packed to the brim with drunk twenty-somethings. The façades of the buildings burst with color—red, blue, gray, yellow—and a few are covered by giant murals, from the bawdy, redheaded "Madam's Organ" to the scarf-clad Frenchman à la Toulouse-Lautrec. Adams Morgan always reminds me of a girl you might meet one night at a bar who comes across as vibrant and wild and fun but who, the next morning in the daylight, seems a little worn, a little garish, a little partied out. The sidewalks around me are littered with receipts, gum wrappers, and grease-stained paper plates, remnants of the so-called Jumbo Slice, a culinary abomination in the form of an oily piece of pizza the size of one's torso.

Drew holds open the door to Tryst, a coffee bar cum lounge whose interior is filled with big couches, barstools, and large wooden communal tables, where people sit with laptops and steaming mugs of tea and coffee. The space has a warm glow from the rust-colored walls, which are lined with contemporary works by local artists. Drew spots a table for two by an old fireplace in the middle of the room and races to save it before someone else takes it.

"What can I get you?" he asks.

"Oh. Um . . . a café au lait, I guess?"

"Anything to eat?"

"I've had my fair share of Rick's almond poppy seed muffins today."

He smiles. "I'll be right back."

He saunters over to the bar, which is lined with coffee makers, espresso machines, and every kind of liquor imaginable. A series of chalkboards lines the wall, outlining the various menu options in funky handwriting and wild illustrations. When Drew returns, he places my steaming, bowl-shaped mug in front of me and slides into his chair, holding a pint of Guinness.

"How much do I owe you?"

He waves me off. "My treat."

"Are you sure? I have plenty of cash from the market."

He smirks. "Considering I bailed on you at the last minute, a three-dollar coffee is the least I can do."

I cup my hands around the bowl. "That's sweet of you. Thanks."

"My pleasure," he says as he takes a sip of his beer. "So anyway, I was starting to tell you about the short-tailed albatross."

"Oh. Right."

"Habitat loss is a huge problem, but so is pollution. And the fisheries? Don't get me started."

He goes on to outline the many threats to the short-tailed albatross and what his organization is doing to save the species, and as I sip my coffee I try very hard to focus and not let my mind wander to other things, like which Radiohead song is playing in the background or what Drew would look like dressed as a walrus.

"So have you spent much time in Alaska?" I ask during a break in the conversation.

"A bit. I spent the summer there in college. It was totally amazing." He gulps more of his beer and wipes a bit of foam off his top lip. "Oh, but I meant to say—about the albatross? A major oil company is trying to drill near one of the nesting colonies, which would be totally detrimental to the species."

"Maybe you could dress as an oil executive and hang an albatross around your neck."

Drew frowns. "Why would I do that?"

"As a joke. You know . . . the Coleridge poem. 'The Rime of the Ancient Mariner.'" Drew stares at me blankly. "You didn't read that in high school?"

"I don't remember. Is it about habitat loss?"

"No. Never mind. It was a joke."

"Ah." He takes a sip of beer. "Well, unfortunately, this whole drilling controversy isn't very funny."

"Right. No. Of course not."

"Anyway, as I was saying . . ."

He regales me with more facts about the short-tailed albatross and its habitat, and once we finish our drinks, he offers to walk me home. As we meander through Adams Morgan toward my apartment, we talk more about the Alaskan wilderness and a bit about Maggie's farm, and by the time we reach my building, we've talked for a good hour and a half, and yet I still feel as if I don't know much about him, other than the fact that he could talk about the short-tailed albatross for days and looks mighty fine in a beaver costume.

"Well, I'd better head back to the hospital," he says.

"Send your family my best," I say. "Sorry. That's weird. Your family doesn't even know me."

He smiles. "But maybe they will at some point, right?" He leans in and kisses me before I can answer, and as he does my shoulders stiffen. Eventually he pulls away. "I'll see you soon, okay?"

He heads down my front walkway, and when I enter my apartment, I head straight for the kitchen and open my junk drawer. I pull out the list I made yesterday and scan Drew's pros and cons again:

> **Pros:** Kind (gave ride to orchard), extremely attractive/looks like model, interested in food, works at farmers' market, cares about environment, million-dollar smile
>
> **Cons:** Beard is kind of scratchy

Then I pull out a pen and, under cons, I add, "Isn't Jeremy."

CHAPTER 25

Apparently I want to die alone. It is the only explanation. Drew is not Jeremy, but why would I view that as a "con"? Drew wants to save the planet. He is willing to dress as an albatross to do so. Jeremy, on the other hand, is willing to take money from anyone who will pay him. Or at least that's what his Wikipedia entry says. And Stu Abbott, my future dream boss, hates him. What the hell is wrong with me?

Wednesday morning, I send Stu the edited cold storage video, along with an accompanying column, replete with links and photos. Stu e-mails back right away with a few editorial comments, but overall he loves it.

"This is great," he writes. "When can you send me the next one?"

We bat ideas back and forth and try to line up an editorial schedule, but after seven e-mails back and forth, he finally calls me.

"This is the problem with the digital revolution," he says. "No one wants to pick up the phone anymore."

"At least we weren't trying to do this by text message."

"Yes, at least there's that." He takes a sip of something and smacks his lips. "So I'm hearing a lot of buzz about this Green Grocers partnership with the farmers' market consortium. What's the word on the street?"

"I think it's nearly a done deal. Maybe a matter of weeks before an announcement."

"I'd love to get ahead of that. Could you poke around and see what you can find out?"

"Sure."

"The business section would probably cover the story from a commercial perspective—what it means for the company's stock, their overall business direction, blah, blah, blah—but I'd love to do something from the farmers' perspective. Like that Rick guy, or the apple lady—what would this mean for their business? And what does this say about the food movement as a whole?"

"I'll see what I can find out." I pause. "But this sounds like a bigger story. Given the amount of time I'd need to spend on it, I'd need more than one hundred dollars."

He sighs. "Let's see what you come up with. I'd love to give you more than a hundred bucks, but I don't control the purse strings. Believe me, I wish I did."

I'm about to tell him I understand but I'm running out of savings. Then I remind myself there are dozens of other hungry wannabe food journalists who would happily take my place. If I don't want to do this for pennies, someone else will. So instead, I try a different angle.

"What if I gave you something really juicy?" I say, remembering my earlier conversation with Jeremy about Bob Young, the new Green Grocers CEO.

"What do you mean, 'juicy'?"

"Something about the new CEO's past and what it could mean for the deal—an angle or tidbit no one else has. Some sort of inside scoop."

"Keep talking."

"I'd have to look into it, but if I could get you an exclusive angle, is that something that could get me on the payroll in a more serious way?"

He takes a deep breath and exhales into the phone. "If you can bring me a big story that I can sell to my superiors, I'll make sure you are appropriately compensated. How does that sound?"

I break into a broad smile and pump my fist back and forth as I press the phone tightly against my ear with the other hand.

"That," I say, "sounds wonderful."

The problem with dangling a juicy story in front of Stu? Now I actually have to deliver a juicy story. And if I'm being honest with myself, sexy investigative journalism isn't my thing. Those aren't the stories I want to write. I want to write people stories, stories that humanize some aspect of our food system. But if a salacious story is what it will take to get my foot in the door at the *Chronicle*, then that's what I'll write.

I spend early Wednesday afternoon looking into Bob Young's background, but as far as I can tell, the guy is a virtual Boy Scout: bachelor's degree from Stanford, MBA from Harvard, a run in the marketing department at Kroger before joining the Green Grocers team, where he has worked for the past fifteen years, first as the director of marketing and then working his way up the ranks to CEO. If there is an issue in Bob Young's past, I can't find it.

As I plug various permutations of "Bob Young + scandal" and "Bob Young + controversy" into Google, Jeremy calls. This is the first I've heard from him since he returned from New Orleans.

"So how was NOLA?" I ask. "Sufficiently wild?"

"Pretty tame, actually. Ate some amazing food, though. New Orleans truly is one of the best food cities in the world."

"I hope you had some beignets at Café du Monde."

"Like a boss. Twice a day, every day."

"Ugh. I'm so jealous."

"You've been, then?"

"I went with my mom and sister while my dad was at a sales conference down there. But that was like ten years ago."

"Well, take it from me: Even a decade later, the beignets are still to die for."

My stomach growls as I think about the beignets I ate that day, those magical deep-fried pillows of dough, covered in half an inch of powdered sugar. The exterior was crisp and golden, and when I took a bite—the airy, cloud-like interior still warm from the deep fryer—the powdered sugar fell into my lap like snow. I'd known the beignet was a cousin of the doughnut, but somehow without the hole in the middle, it managed to surpass any notion I had of what a doughnut could be. My mom and Libby bought the baking mix at the Café du Monde gift shop and tried to recreate the beignets when we got home, but they weren't the same. Zach suspected it had something to do with the leavening in the batter, but since my mom and Libby made them without me, as they did with nearly all of their cooking endeavors, I couldn't be sure.

"So what's the plan for Saturday?" I ask, shaking myself out of my sugar-filled reverie.

"We're brewing beer, baby."

"Excuse me?"

He laughs into the phone, sensing my uneasiness. "My place. Five o'clock. I'm teaching you how to brew beer. Then we'll have dinner and, I don't know, watch a movie or something."

"Beer. We're brewing beer."

"Hells yeah, we're brewing beer. And you're going to love it."

"Should I wear my corset and lederhosen?"

"You own a corset and lederhosen?"

"*No.* Don't get all excited."

"Ah. Bummer." He hums into the phone. "You know, I could probably hook that up for you . . ."

"I'm not wearing a corset and lederhosen. It was a joke. Let it go."

"Okay, okay. Fine." His voice is smooth and relaxed, and I can tell he is smiling. "Anyway, it'll be fun. I promise. Plus, my Flemish red ale will finally be ready for drinking. I've been working on that puppy for eighteen months."

"Eighteen months? It takes eighteen months to brew beer?" What am I signing myself up for?

"Some beers—not most. Don't worry, I don't plan on keeping you in my apartment for eighteen months."

"Yeah, well, thank God for that."

"We'll have fun. Trust me. It couldn't be worse than falling in the Tidal Basin, right?"

I picture that night: the pitch-black walking tour, my gargantuan flashlight, the plop and splash of Jeremy plunging into the water, his trembling shoulders. "No," I say. "It couldn't be worse than that."

Because it couldn't be. Right?

No more than two hours after I get off the phone, I change my mind. Of course it could be worse than having Jeremy fall in the Tidal Basin. I could scald myself or ruin his beer recipe or spill his prized eighteen-month red ale all over the floor. But worse than any of those possibilities—worse than spilling boiling liquid all over myself—is the prospect of falling for him.

Sure, he makes me laugh and makes me happy, but every time I type his name into Google, I'm given 1,256,789 reasons why I have clearly lost my mind. I don't want to judge him, but it's so easy. All of his mistakes, all of his transgressions, they're at my fingertips, with a few strokes of my keyboard. Some days I wish I could hide from all this history, but I can't. His past is just so . . . *available*.

By the time Saturday arrives, I am downright stressed about the evening of beer making and awkwardness that awaits me. But despite the voice in my head telling me to stay away from Jeremy, I can't bring myself to cancel. I am, quite clearly, my own worst enemy.

Just as I am about to make what is surely a poor wardrobe choice, my mom calls. I've tried her a few times over the past week, ever since I spoke to my dad, but she never picked up and, uncharacteristically, never called back—until now, exactly forty minutes before I'm supposed to leave for Jeremy's apartment.

"I was beginning to worry about you," I say, holding up a taupe cardigan as I look at myself in my full-length mirror.

"Worry? Oh, please. You have nothing to worry about. Worrying is a mother's job."

"Speaking of jobs," I say, discarding the taupe cardigan and grabbing another top from my closet, "how's the job search going? Dad mentioned you'd run into a little trouble."

"Trouble doesn't begin to describe it."

"What's the deal?"

"There is no deal. There isn't anything. Nada. Zip. The Williams-Sonoma by us doesn't have any openings. Neither does the one downtown. I'm checking with the one at King of Prussia, but I'm not holding my breath."

"Have you checked out Sur La Table? Or the home section of one of the department stores?"

"Oh, that's just what I need. To wait on all of my friends at Macy's."

"So what? You guys need the money, right?"

"There are jobs, and then there are jobs."

"You're talking to a girl who is working at a farm stand so that she can chase her dream job."

"That's different."

"Oh, yeah? How? Last I checked, Libby wanted you to spend two thousand bucks on chairs. Where's that money coming from?"

She sighs. "You and your father are all burned up about those chairs. Poor Libby."

"Poor *Libby?*" Classic. My mom always takes Libby's side. When Libby got a bad grade on an exam or paper, my mom would claim the teacher was incompetent, even when I'd had the same teachers and had aced their classes. When Libby's field hockey tournament was the same weekend as my clarinet recital, my mom chose Libby's tournament because, she said, Libby needed her support more than I did. And when Libby and her girlfriends ate the chocolate mousse I made as part of a project for French class senior year, my mom said it was my fault for leaving it in our refrigerator without a note. How was Libby to know?

"Mom, Libby lives in fantasyland. And anyway, if you cared so much about getting her the damn chairs, you'd take a job at the gas station if you needed to." I catch myself. "I take that back. If Libby cares so much about the damn chairs, *she* should get a job at the gas station."

She clicks her tongue. "Sydney."

"What? Maybe it's time for Libby to grow up and realize she needs to take responsibility for things. Maybe it's time for you to tell her the Bank of Strauss is closed."

"When it comes to our children, the Bank of Strauss is never closed."

"Except if your name is Sydney and you want to pursue a career in food writing."

"What?"

I let out a sigh. "Never mind. I don't want to get into this right now. And anyway, I have to run—I'm behind schedule."

"Behind schedule for what?"

I clear my throat. "A date."

"A *date?*" Her tone brightens. "Oh, that's wonderful. With whom?"

"Just ... a guy."

"Yes, well, I assumed it was a guy. Not that I would have a problem if it *weren't* a guy. Your father and I are very progressive when it comes to our views on gay marriage."

I roll my eyes. "Mom."

"You know, I always thought your Aunt Ina was gay. Remember her good friend Selma? Anyway, in this day and age—"

"Mom," I say. "Enough."

"Sorry, sorry. I don't want to make you late." She squeals. "For your *date.*"

Her tone, so downtrodden only moments ago, now brims with enthusiasm and joy, her spirits seemingly lifted by the prospect of my courtship. The level of her excitement threatens to grate, with its edge of surprise and profusion of eagerness, but I'm willing to indulge her relief—her palpable, unapologetic relief—that someone out there wants to date her awkward daughter. I will allow her this moment of satisfaction because, with every squeal and encouraging remark, with every indication she approves of my activities this evening, she makes it easier for me to tell myself this date isn't a terrible idea, brimming with problems and potential pitfalls and certain to end in disaster.

CHAPTER 26

The date is a disaster before it even begins. The moment I open my
front door, I know the hour I spent grooming myself—beating my
hair into submission with a blow-dryer and brush, carefully covering the zits on my chin, and choosing the right outfit—was entirely
a waste of my time. The temperature has bounced around all week,
throwing the mercury up and down the Fahrenheit scale as spring
sputters to a start, and today the air is a tepid fifty-six degrees and
heavy with the smell of grass and rain. The sky is one thick sheet of
gray stratus clouds, which hover ominously and threaten to blanket
the city with rain, and the humidity is approximately 5,000 percent.

This wouldn't be a problem if my hair weren't a sponge, sucking
every last droplet of moisture out of the air and swelling like a Chia
Pet. But my hair is a sponge, and I do look like a Chia Pet, and I
wish I hadn't tried so hard. The fact that I did try hard is, in and of
itself, an issue, but it is one I choose not to address because it
brings up a host of other issues I'd rather not deal with.

I hop down my front steps, and as I walk along the path toward
Swann Street, I spot my crazy downstairs neighbor Simon staring at
the front of our house from the sidewalk. He stands with his arms
crossed over his chest, transfixed by something I cannot identify.
For all I know, he is staring at his doorbell, which still bears the

duct tape covering he put in place back in February. It looks trashy and terrible, but I decide it's not my problem. If neither Simon nor our landlord Al can bring himself to fix the stupid bell, then I can live with the hideous block of silver tape. Knowing Al, the doorbell will look that way for months.

If I had any sense, I would ignore Simon and hurry to the L2 bus stop, but, as I have established on many occasions, I do not have any sense, so I sidle up beside him and join him in staring at our building.

"What are we looking at?" I ask.

Simon shoots me a sideways glance. "Why do you care?"

"Because I live here too?" He doesn't respond. "Is something wrong? Is one of the windows leaking?"

"Why would one of the windows be leaking?"

Sweet Lord. "I don't know. You tell me. You're the one standing out here staring at the house."

He narrows his pink-rimmed eyes. "Your hair is very large," he says. Then he stuffs his hands into his black leather jacket and scurries toward our door.

If this is an omen for the rest of the evening, I might as well give up now.

Thanks to my run-in with Simon, I am ten minutes late in getting to Jeremy's place, which adds to my state of disarray. At this point, my hair has swollen with so much moisture that I could hide a squirrel in there and no one would know.

Jeremy lives in Washington's West End, a small neighborhood just east of Georgetown. For the most part, the area is home to upscale condos, hotels, and restaurants, with the odd embassy thrown in. Unlike the buildings bordering the West End, which bleed history and age from every crack, the construction in Jeremy's neighborhood is mostly new, with smooth concrete fasciae and swathes of glass. The neighborhood is only a mile and a half southwest of my apartment and yet, with its wide streets, level sidewalks, and multistory buildings, feels like part of a different city.

I hurry through Jeremy's lobby and ride the elevator to the seventh floor. As soon as I step out, I hear the pulsating rhythm of

Dave Brubeck's "Take Five" filling the hallway, emanating from Jeremy's apartment at the end. His door is ajar, and when I knock, it opens further.

"Hello?"

I poke my head inside and hear loud clanking sounds coming from the kitchen. I slip into his entryway, close the door behind me, and creep toward the kitchen, where I find him standing in front of his sink dressed in a sleeveless *Star Wars* T-shirt and mesh Adidas shorts.

"Jeremy?"

He whips his head around. "There she is! I was beginning to think you'd had second thoughts."

My eyes land on his sleeveless shirt, which features an enormous photographic rendering of Harrison Ford as Han Solo, surrounded by a rainbow.

"I am now . . ."

He glances down at his shirt. "You're not a *Star Wars* fan?"

"I have no problem with *Star Wars*," I say. That is true. What I have a problem with is the lack of sleeves on his shirt and the nonexistent barrier between me and his armpit hair.

"Good," he says. "Because like I said before: George Lucas was a visionary." He studies my taupe cardigan and dark jeans. "Your outfit is going to be a problem."

"*My* outfit is a problem? *Mine?*"

"It's my fault," he says. "I forgot to tell you. Making beer . . . My apartment gets a little warm."

"I'm sure I'll be fine."

He raises an eyebrow. "I don't know. . . . There's a lot of steam. . . ."

"If this is your plan to get me to take off my clothes, allow me to disabuse you of that notion right now."

"Why do you always assume I have some sinister plan? I'm not that crafty. Trust me."

"You say this, and yet history suggests otherwise."

He flushes and rumples his brow. "How do you mean?"

"Never mind," I say. Now isn't the time to discuss his past. "So where do we begin?"

Jeremy clears a spot on one of the barstools for me to lay my purse and finishes arranging all of his brewing equipment on the counter. Once everything is in the proper place, he rubs his hands together.

"So, I figured for your introduction to homebrewing, I'd start with something interesting but basic. I remember you ordered a porter on our first date, so I thought we could start there."

"You remember what beer I ordered?"

His cheeks redden, and he scratches at his temple. "I'm not a stalker or anything. I just . . . I like you. I pay attention to the things you seem to enjoy."

I think back to the cannoli and hoagies he made for our picnic and the obvious thought he has put into all of our activities. "Thanks. That's very thoughtful." My eyes drift to his sleeveless shirt. "Now might be a good time to mention I prefer men's shirts to have sleeves."

He groans. "It's not like I wear this to work."

"But you would if you could. Am I right?"

"No." He glances down at the image of Han Solo. "Maybe. I don't know. The point is, this is my brewing shirt. It's part of the magic. You'll see."

He pulls out a large mesh bag and begins filling it with three different types of grains that he weighs on a digital scale. He twirls the bag around to seal the top and tosses it into a large metal pot, which he has filled with several gallons of water, and begins heating everything up on the stove. It is clear from his quick, precise movements that he has done this many times, to the point where each step is almost instinctual, requiring little thought or explanation.

The boiling grain fills the kitchen with a sweet, toasty aroma, and once the pot reaches 170 degrees, I help Jeremy remove the soggy bag of grain. He cranks up the heat and instructs me to pour in the malt extract, holding his hand over mine to steady my grip as I tip the pitcher over the pot. His hands are warm and sticky from all of the heat in the kitchen, and as the steam rises toward the ceiling, beads of sweat develop along my hairline, helped along by my increasing anxiety over the proximity of Jeremy's body—and, by default, his armpit hair. As I put the pitcher back on the counter, I feel his other hand graze my hip.

"What's next?" I ask, unsure whether to lean into his touch or pull away.

Jeremy steps back and nods toward the big metal pot. "We add some hops when that comes to a full boil, and then we let it boil for an hour."

"An hour?"

He nods. "An hour. And while that's going on, you're going to help me make dinner."

My stomach churns as memories of Zach and me cooking together come rushing back. I've barely cooked anything in the nearly five years since we broke up, and I certainly haven't cooked with another potential suitor.

"Now I have to cook my own dinner?" I say, trying to sound relaxed even though I hate this idea. I don't think I'm ready for this. Sleeping together, fine. But cooking together? That's different. That's intimate. That means something. To me, at least.

"I already did the heavy lifting," he says. "You just have to help me put it all together."

He reaches into his refrigerator and pulls out a bright red, lidded pot, which he puts on the burner diagonal from the simmering beer. He peers beneath the lid, takes a whiff, and then replaces the lid and cranks the heat to medium.

"Are you sure?" I say. "I don't want to ruin whatever you have planned."

"That would be impossible. I've already braised the pork and pickled the peppers. I'll fry the eggs, so all you need to do is cook the rice. Unless you don't know how to cook rice."

I purse my lips, suddenly defensive. "I know how to cook rice."

"Then we'll be fine."

But given the uneasy feeling in my stomach, I'm not sure we will.

One thing is definitely not fine, and that thing is my outfit.

Between the gallons of rapidly boiling beer and the bubbling pork—not to mention the simmering rice—Jeremy's apartment is a whopping eighty-six degrees, and I am basically wearing a sweater. I never thought I'd envy a sleeveless shirt with a photo of Harrison

Ford circa 1977, but right now I would murder for that sartorial eyesore.

By the time we add the second bag of hops to the beer boil, I am having trouble breathing. The cream camisole beneath my cardigan is sheer and skimpy, but I have reached a point where self-consciousness is trumped by potentially life-threatening discomfort. This cardigan cannot remain on my body for another second.

Jeremy's eyes flit in my direction as I throw my cardigan over the back of one of his barstools. "Don't get any ideas," I say. "I just need to cool down."

He holds his hands up defensively. "I didn't say anything."

"I know what you're thinking."

"I'm thinking you should borrow a pair of shorts. That's what I'm thinking."

I lift the lid off the rice and fluff it with a fork. "I'm guessing we don't wear the same size."

"You could borrow a pair of boxers. Roll them up around the waist?"

I put the lid back on the rice and place the pan on the counter. "You want me to wear your underwear?"

"Why do you have to make it sound so gross? They're boxers—clean, unworn boxers. I have a new pack I haven't even worn yet."

I place my hands on my hips and tap my toe on the floor. As much as I want to say no, as much as I do *not* want to get any more undressed than I already am, I must admit that boxers—airy, cottony boxers—sound glorious right about now.

"Fine," I say. "Where are they?"

Jeremy leads me back into his bedroom, where the white duvet is pulled up over the bed, each pillow properly arranged against the dark walnut headboard. The top of his dresser is bare, apart from a small black leather valet case containing a watch, some loose change, and a set of keys. There are no clothes on the floor, no stacks of old bills or piles of old batteries, no expired credit cards or licenses. Drew could learn a thing or two from this guy.

"Try a pair of these and see if they work," he says, handing me a three-pack of cotton boxers.

"Thanks."

He glances over his shoulder toward the kitchen. "I'm going to head back out there and finish cooking dinner. By the time you come out, everything should be ready."

He heads for the door, but I stop him before he crosses the threshold. "Hey, Jeremy?"

"Yeah?"

"Thanks."

"For the boxers?"

"For everything." I fidget with the packet in my hands. "I haven't cooked like this in a long time. The beer, the dinner. It's just—it's nice."

His cheeks flush, and his smile seems to take up the whole room, and I can't help but believe this is the real Jeremy Brauer—this man right here, who made me dinner and taught me to make beer and is letting me borrow a pair of his boxers. The man I read about on Wikipedia, well, I don't know who he is, but he isn't the Jeremy I know.

"You're welcome," he says. "It's my pleasure. Truly."

He smiles again, his hand resting delicately on the door handle, and then he turns around, closes the door behind him, and heads back into the kitchen.

CHAPTER 27

I am wearing boxers. Not just any boxers: Jeremy's boxers. Jeremy's red boxers with bright yellow chickens, which are now rolled up around my waist, beneath my skimpy camisole. I'm not sure how I could look any worse or if that's even possible. Maybe if I'd chosen the turtles? No. The chickens are worse. Probably the worst of the three. But I'm not changing now. I don't want to seem like I'm trying too hard, as if that's even an option when I am wearing a grown man's underwear.

I take a deep breath before opening the bedroom door and heading back into the living room, where the ambiance has undergone a noticeable transformation. The room is still a sweltering eighty-some degrees, but Jeremy has dimmed the lights and lit a few candles on the small, square table behind the breakfast bar. The table is set for two, with two tulip-shaped glasses filled with mahogany-colored beer, each topped with a thick crown of white foam. The apartment smells of sesame, eggs, and yeasty beer all at once.

Jeremy puts the finishing touches on our dinner, taking care to keep everything as far away from the brewing beer as possible. He moves quickly, sliding a fried egg on top of each dish and scattering some sort of garnish over the top. Then he carries the bowls, one in each hand, to the table.

"Bon appétit," he says as he places a bowl in front of me.

Steam rises from the surface, smelling of soy and ginger and hot peppers. A fried egg sits atop the slices of braised pork, the golden yolk loose and glistening in the light of the candles. A thick layer of white rice covers the bottom of the bowl, sopping up the rich, porky juices.

"So what exactly is this? Bibimbap?"

"Similar. It's a riff on a Japanese dish—donburi. Meat and an egg with rice."

"Sounds delicious."

"I thought it would go well with the beer. Speaking of which, tell me what you think of the red ale."

I take a whiff before swallowing a large gulp. The beer smacks of sourness but with a fruity kick, reminiscent of raisins or plums. "It's good," I say. "Fruity."

"I added some prunes during the fermentation. It just about works."

I rest my beer on the table and tuck into my meal, poking the egg so that the gooey yolk bursts and trickles down into the rice. "When did you get into homebrewing?"

"A few years back. I was always into beer and science—I almost majored in chemistry in college—and I'd always wanted to try my hand at homebrewing. And then a few years ago I had a lot of time on my hands due to some . . . career changes, so I decided to join a local brew club and give it a whirl."

I push the rice around my bowl with the tines of my fork. "Can we talk about that now? Those 'career changes'?"

He takes a long sip of beer and then places the glass back on the table and sighs. "Sure. What do you want to know?"

"Well . . . what happened, exactly?"

"You've read the articles, right? You've seen Wikipedia? That's pretty much it. A PR company paid me for columns I wrote, and the *Chronicle* found out and fired me."

"Yeah, but . . . what *really* happened?"

"That is what really happened."

"But why did you do it?"

He swirls his tulip glass around by the base. "I was broke, and almost all of my *Chronicle* salary was going toward my student loans. It seemed like a good way to make a few extra bucks."

"But you were basically selling your opinion."

"I never wrote anything I didn't actually believe. All of those reviews, whether they were of a product or a place, were my honest opinions."

"It isn't honest if you're effectively being paid by the subject of your review—and if you didn't tell your employer about it. You had to know the *Chronicle* wouldn't be okay with that."

He picks at his pork. "I should have. But I was twenty-five and needed the cash, and at the time it didn't seem like the end of the world. I wasn't hurting anyone. I wasn't writing lies."

I rub my fingers around the edge of my glass and look into his eyes. "Did you know, at least on some level, that what you were doing was wrong?"

He tears his eyes away and shovels a forkful of pork and rice into his mouth. "Yeah, but it's . . . At first, it was just one piece. A little story on Pizz-o-rama's national rollout of their new gluten-free pizza crust. My mom has celiac, so I'm always looking for new products for her, and the crust was really good. I figured, what the hell? What was the big deal in getting paid extra for something I'd write anyway? But once I wrote that one piece, my PR contact kept sending me new pitches, and with all the bills and debt I had piling up, it got really hard to say no. It's not that I thought what I was doing was right, but at the time I didn't necessarily think it was wrong either."

"And what do you think now?"

He drops his fork on the table. "That I made a mistake, okay? A bunch of mistakes. And it used to be that if you made a mistake, you'd have a second chance. You could wipe the slate clean. Some people would forgive you, others would forget, and you could move on. But that isn't true anymore. The Internet isn't written in pencil. It's written in ink, and now no matter what I do, no matter what I achieve, I will always be the sleazebag who got fired from the *Chronicle*. Forever."

I glance down at my bowl. "I'm sorry."

"Me too. I've done a lot of good work since I left the *Chronicle*. I did a lot of good work *at* the *Chronicle*. But it's like my whole identity is caught in an Internet trap—a time capsule of a fraction of the work I've done my entire life."

I think about what an Internet snapshot of my life would look like. In first grade, I would have been the space-crazed introvert. In high school, the food columnist glued to her boyfriend's side. In college, the driven broadcaster. And a snapshot taken today would be different than any of those three. But does that make any of those prior snapshots less true? Aren't all of those moments a part of who I am today?

Jeremy shovels another forkful of pork, egg, and rice into his mouth and washes it down with a long sip of beer. His movements are sharper now, brimming with frustration. It isn't clear whether he is annoyed with me for bringing this up or with himself for what he did, or a combination of both. But whatever the reason, he is irritated, and to my surprise, I feel worse about having possibly contributed to his mood than I do about being on a date with food journalism's persona non grata.

I glance down at my watch. "About two hours into date number three, and I've already ruined it, huh?"

He smirks. "I wouldn't say that...."

"I just ... I had to ask about it. I didn't mean to upset you."

"It's okay. The subject was bound to come up eventually. Better to get it out of the way now."

He polishes off the rest of his beer, and, in the silence that follows, I load my fork with a heap of pork, peppers, and rice. "So what's it like now, working on the other side?"

He shrugs. "Took a while for me to get used to pitching ideas rather than being pitched, but I caught on pretty fast. Frankly, I was happy anyone would hire me after what happened."

"Do you like working in PR?"

"Most days. But lately ..." He trails off.

"Lately what?"

He shakes his head. "Nah, it's nothing."

"No, what? You can tell me."

"One of my projects is sort of stressing me out, that's all."

"The Green Grocers deal?"

He fixes his eyes on mine. "Yeah, how did you know?"

"You mentioned on the phone that you'd been working on the farmers' market partnership."

He lets out his breath. "Oh, right. I forgot."

"What's going on? Is the deal not going through?"

"Oh, no, it isn't that. It's . . ." He bites his lip. "Never mind. I shouldn't talk about it."

"Listen, if something is bothering you, you can tell me."

He rubs his temples and leans back in his chair. "Okay, but this is just between you and me, got it?"

"Sure."

He leans forward again and rests his elbows on the table. "So I'm working on the rollout of this pilot project, which is going to be a pretty big deal, and we're helping the company plan a big launch campaign. Since I'm the company's point person, Green Grocers sent me a bunch of documents to help with the launch, but someone obviously didn't scrub the correspondence too closely because I've definitely seen something I shouldn't have."

I lean forward, suddenly alert. "Something . . . like what?"

He rubs his eyes with his palms. "Apparently before Bob Young became CEO, when he was the chief operating officer, he found out one of the suppliers for Green Grocers' private label was using horse meat instead of beef in their frozen meals. But instead of going public, he just sort of . . . swept it under the rug."

"Wait. Green Grocers' 'organic beef bourguignon' is actually 'horse bourguignon'?"

"Not anymore. At least I don't think so. But it was for a period of time."

"How is that even possible? I thought horses weren't slaughtered in the US."

"They aren't. But they are in China and Mexico, and that's where these frozen meals were made."

"But . . . Green Grocers is all about 'local.' That doesn't sound very local."

"Another reason this is really bad." He grabs his beer and takes another sip. "I went to my boss to ask how I should handle this, but he basically told me to keep my mouth shut because it isn't my business. Our job is to focus on the launch of this new initiative, and we shouldn't do anything that would scupper or detract from the launch." He sips his beer. "The whole thing is really stressing me out. If I say anything, I could lose my job, but keeping this a secret—it just seems wrong."

My ears are burning. "So . . . what are you going to do?"

"I don't know. Probably nothing. I'd love to say something, but I don't think anyone will ever hire me again if I get fired from another job."

"But this time it would be for a good cause."

"I guess." He lets out a long sigh. "Anyway, I don't really want to talk about it anymore, if that's okay. I shouldn't have told you in the first place."

"Sure. I understand."

And I do understand. But as we finish our meal and make our beer and start kissing each other passionately, there is only one thing on my mind:

I just landed the scoop of a lifetime.

CHAPTER 28

This is huge. The new CEO of one of the biggest grocery chains in America, the guy everyone thinks is an Earth-loving, local foods guru, knew his company was selling horse meat instead of beef—produced abroad, no less—and, instead of owning up to it, covered the whole thing up. This isn't a one-off column for some experimental food blog. This is the sort of story that could make a career.

I spend the night at Jeremy's apartment, but the entire time I am preoccupied with what Jeremy has told me. Even as I lie in his bed, our bodies twisted together, all I can think is, "I need to call Stu Abbott. I have to tell him about this story." This, I will admit, is kind of a problem because (a) I am now sleeping with my source, and (b) Jeremy shared this information in confidence.

But here's the thing: Jeremy knows I'm a journalist. He knows I'm working for Stu Abbott. And he is obviously very uncomfortable with what Bob Young has done. Subconsciously, he probably *wants* this story to come out. Otherwise, he wouldn't have told me. Right?

The wheels in my head spin wildly all night, as I watch the digital clock on Jeremy's nightstand and wonder how early I could reasonably call Stu Abbott on a Sunday morning. I have to be at the Dupont farmers' market at seven. That's probably too early. Unless he is a morning person? No, I'd better wait until at least eight. Or maybe I will text him. Yes, that's what I'll do: I'll text him on my way to the market, and then he can call me when he gets up. Which, if I'm lucky, will be soon.

I roll out of Jeremy's bed at just after six thirty and sift through the pile of clothes on the floor, casting aside the Han Solo T-shirt and chicken print boxers. The bed creaks as Jeremy rolls over.

"Come back to bed," he croaks, his voice scratchy with sleep.

"No can do. I have to work at the market this morning."

"Oh, right. I forgot." He yawns. "Couldn't you skip this morning? I could make us breakfast in bed."

I consider this, the idea of Jeremy and me curled up in bed together, him feeding me toast, me feeding him bacon. Instead of bristling at the idea, like I might have done a few weeks ago, I find myself comforted by it. I like him. I can't deny it. He might have made some pretty bad decisions in his past, but he thinks Bob Young's cover-up was wrong, so his moral compass isn't completely out of whack. If I write up this story and credit him as the whistle-blower, maybe I could even redeem him. At the very least, I can redeem myself for letting Zach talk me out of covering a similarly juicy story in college, something I've always regretted.

"So? How about it?" he says.

"Not this morning." I creep over to his side of the bed and kiss his forehead. "But maybe another time."

"Your loss," he says. "I make a pretty mean eggs Benedict."

"Or so you say."

"Hey, did you or did you not enjoy that donburi? And what about those cannoli?"

"Not bad for a beer nerd."

"Not *bad*? Oh, you're in for it now." He grabs me and tosses me onto his bed, rolling on top of me and pinning me down as I squeal. "Wait . . . Are you . . . ticklish?"

He wiggles his fingers beneath my arm, and I wriggle and shriek with laughter. "Stop—*stop!*"

He lets go and rolls off me. "Okay, okay—I don't want the neighbors to get the wrong idea." He grins. "Though my guess is, if they heard you last night, they know everything is fine."

I elbow him. "They didn't hear anything."

"I don't know. . . . There was a lot of moaning. . . ."

I elbow him again. "You're the worst, you know that?"

"That's not what you said last night. . . ."

I throw a pillow in his face and hop out of bed. "All right, I'm out of here. I have muffins to sell."

"Okay, okay. But I'll see you later this week?"

"I don't know. I'm not sure you've earned a fourth date."

"Oh, really?"

"Really."

"So this is it. The end of you and me. *Sayonara.*"

I shrug. "Might be."

But as he smiles at me and I smile back, we both know, with absolute certainty, that nothing could be further from the truth.

In an entirely unexpected turn of events, Rick is in a frighteningly jolly mood when I arrive at the market. I say frightening because this is Rick the Prick, whose curmudgeonly ways I have come to expect and tolerate. Seeing him smile, with those yellowing teeth and that pervy grin, is enough to make my stomach turn over. Toss in a few inappropriate epithets and a bit of over-animated whistling, and I am thoroughly uncomfortable.

Thankfully, Heidi arrives only three minutes after I do, so I don't have to deal with Rick's friendliness for very long.

"Dude, what's up with the boss today?" she says as Rick sneaks behind the truck for a cigarette break. She tosses her canvas tote beneath one of the tables.

"No idea. But I want no part of it."

"And here we thought we'd like him better if he weren't such a Grumpy Gus."

"Who knew?"

She laughs and grabs for an empty basket. "So Drew says he hasn't heard from you in a while. I thought you had fun at coffee the other weekend."

"I did. It was fine."

"Fine isn't a ringing endorsement."

"He's just . . . I don't know."

"Gorgeous?"

"I was going to say bland."

"The guy is, like, saving the wilderness. How is that bland?"

"Do *you* want to talk about the short-tailed albatross for two hours?"

She snorts. "I don't know. Is Drew naked while this is happening?"

I knock her playfully in the shoulder. "You are ridiculous."

"Whatever. At least he is trying to improve the world, unlike your other gentleman caller. . . ."

"Here we go again." I unload a crate of molasses cookies, their puffy tops sparkling with glittery turbinado sugar. "For your information, Jeremy Brauer is a decent guy."

"Says you."

"Yes, says me."

"So he *didn't* do all those things we read about online?"

"No, he did. But he's sorry."

"Aren't they all?" Heidi purses her lips as she arranges a stack of fudgy brownies on a white porcelain cake stand. "What makes you think he's changed? How can you trust him?"

"Because he's told me things that show he isn't morally bankrupt."

"Like what?"

I break off a piece of cookie and, when I'm sure Rick isn't looking, pop it in my mouth, every chewy morsel laced with a sweet, burnt-sugar flavor. "I can't say."

"Oh, you can't *say*." She dusts off her hands. "Well, perhaps someday you can enlighten me. Until then, I stand by my warning: Stay away."

"Trust me—in a few weeks, everything will be a lot clearer."

"And why is that?" She waits for me to respond, but when I don't she grins. "Let me guess: You can't say."

And though I'm dying to tell her, to let her in on this massive secret that could upend an entire company, I know I can't. Not yet. So instead, I simply nod and say, "No. But I will soon. I promise."

* * *

During a lull in the market foot traffic, Rick shares the reason behind his uncharacteristically good mood.

"Hey, sugar tits, guess what? Looks like Green Grocers is going to take a massive order for my sourdough." He arranges a stack of twenties in the cashbox. "They want it in all their mid-Atlantic stores."

"That's amazing—congratulations!"

"Of course, now I need to up my volume like crazy. But those interns are actually great. I'm working them like slaves."

I ignore Rick's special brand of political incorrectness and sidle up to the cashbox. "What does this mean, in terms of profit for you?"

He gives me a snide look. "Well, aren't you a nosey one. . . ."

"Sorry—I'm looking into an article about the upside for farmers and vendors if this partnership goes through. I figured you'd be a good case study."

"I haven't crunched the numbers, but if this pans out, it'll give me enough pad to pay off my loans. Not immediately, but in the long term."

I'm about to ask if he can get me more specific numbers when my cell phone rings. It's Stu Abbott.

"Do you mind if I take this?"

Rick frowns. "You know my policy on cell phones."

"I know. But it's important."

He lets out a grunt. "Fine. But just this once. Understood?"

"Understood. Thank you so much." I rush behind the truck and answer Stu's call.

"What's so important that you needed to text me at 6:45 on a Sunday morning?" Stu asks.

"I have a story for you. A big one."

"Okay. I'm listening."

I tell him what Jeremy told me about Bob Young and the horse-meat and the frozen dinners made in China and Mexico. When I finish outlining the facts, there is silence on the other end of the phone.

"Hello? Stu?"

"Who told you this?" Stu finally says.

I bite my lip. "A source. I can't say."

"Is he or she willing to go on the record?"

"I don't know. I don't think so."

"Have you verified this story with anyone else?"

"Not yet."

"And have you seen these alleged documents?"

"No."

Stu lets out a bitter laugh. "Then it sounds to me like you don't have much of a story."

My heart sinks. "But . . . assuming my source isn't making this up, this story is a huge scandal."

"It is. But I need more than a little anecdote. These are serious accusations."

I lean against the truck and bite at my thumbnail. "What if I confirmed the story? Got people to go on the record. Got a copy of the relevant documents."

"Then we'd have a story."

"Something worth more than a hundred bucks?"

He laughs. "If you can bring me a bulletproof story showing that the new CEO of one of the biggest grocery chains in the country knowingly sold horse meat to his customers when he was COO and covered it up—yeah, I'd say that's worth more than one hundred dollars. That's probably worth a job."

"Seriously?"

"We'll see. Don't get ahead of yourself. Bring me a solid story, and then we'll talk."

I hang up and slip my phone into my jacket pocket. Then I head back beneath Rick's tent and wonder how I can make all of my professional dreams come true without ruining all of Jeremy's.

CHAPTER 29

I need to get my hands on those documents. That is the only solution.

If I see copies of the alleged correspondence, I can prove that what Jeremy said is true without having to involve him in the story. And if Stu asks where I got the documents . . . well, I can just say my source doesn't want to be named. Woodward and Bernstein had Deep Throat. I'll have Deep Fryer.

As I sit in front of my computer that afternoon, scheming and outlining and stuffing my face with leftover molasses cookies, Libby's name pops up on my screen as she calls for a video chat. She left me a voice mail yesterday about her bachelorette party, for which she wants to rent a bright pink stretch Hummer, but I still haven't returned her call. I wish I were more enthusiastic about her bachelorette, but somehow I cannot muster the appropriate level of interest about an event that will involve feather boas and penis necklaces.

I click Accept, and Libby's face appears on my screen, her honey-colored hair spilling in thick waves over her shoulders. Growing up, I was always jealous of Libby's hair—the way it would glitter with gold flecks in the sunlight and never frizzed, even on a hot, sticky August night. Frankly, I was jealous when it came to most of Libby's physical attributes: her boobs, her button nose, her flawless complexion, her muscular arms. I've spent nearly my entire life having friends and classmates tell me, "Wow, your sister is *gorgeous*," followed at some point by, "I can't believe you two are sisters—you look nothing alike." Our relationship has always seemed a little backward in that way—the older sister envying the younger; the younger knowing it and using it to her advantage. Sometimes I wonder if Libby even respects me, or if I'm just a fact of life she has to tolerate.

Libby beams as my face appears on her screen. "How was your hot date last night?" she asks.

"How did you know I had a date?"

"I talked to Mom. She sounded very excited."

"I'll bet she did."

"She just wants you to be happy. We all do."

"I'm plenty happy," I say. "At one time I was happy with Zach, and you didn't seem too thrilled about that."

"Zach was a douchebag."

"No, he wasn't. Not until the end."

"Whatever. He's dead to me. I don't want to talk about him."

Classic Libby. To her, everything is black-and-white: good and evil, wrong and right, friends and enemies. She has always had a tight-knit group of girlfriends, and if you aren't with them, you're against them. When she was a high school freshman, Libby and her friends turned on a girl named Jess Kline, who had made the cardinal mistake of kissing the object of Libby's affection at a party. Jess was banished to social Siberia, and they never spoke to her again. They never considered for a second that perhaps Libby's crush had made the first move or that maybe, just maybe, Jess was an insecure girl who'd been happy to discover someone out there actually wanted to kiss her.

"Then what do you want to talk about?" I say. "Let me guess: your bachelorette party."

She tosses her hair over her shoulder. "No. I called to hear about your date. I'm interested. Who is this guy? What is he like?"

"He's . . ." I sigh. "He's great, actually."

"Why the hesitation?"

"Nothing. His past is a little . . . dubious, that's all."

"Dubious how?"

"He was involved in a journalism scandal a few years back. Kind of a big one, at least in foodie circles."

She rolls her eyes. "Great. Another shady loser. Just what you need."

"People make mistakes, Libby. No one is perfect."

She cackles loudly. "This coming from Miss Perfectionist."

"Hey—that isn't fair. I'm far from perfect."

"Oh, I know. Trust me, I've seen your closet."

"Yeah, well, maybe if Mom took *me* shopping all the time, my closet would look more like yours."

Libby shrinks back from the screen defensively. "Mom takes me shopping because we both like to shop. You hate shopping. You always have."

"Or maybe I never felt welcome."

"What? That's crazy. You were always welcome. You never wanted to come."

"That's not how I remember it."

Libby pulls her hair into a low ponytail. "You always think I somehow get special treatment from Mom and Dad."

I let out a huff. "Uh, maybe because you do?"

"That's totally untrue. Like with the wedding? Dad is refusing to pay for those chairs, and he isn't budging."

"I'd hardly call that an act of cruelty. They're chairs. Their main function is to serve as a resting place for your ass."

"No, their main function is to look beautiful."

"Perhaps you are unfamiliar with what a chair does. . . ."

"Sydney—stop. The point is, Dad isn't giving me special treatment. Frankly, I feel like he's trying to cheap out on this entire wedding."

I consider how to respond without spilling the beans about my dad's job loss. "He's paying for the wedding," I finally say. "Isn't that enough?"

"Of course he is paying for the wedding. Who else would pay?"

"You and Matt?"

She recoils. "Uh, no. The father of the bride pays for the wedding."

"Not always. Not anymore."

"Well, that's what's happening for our wedding. And anyway, Mom and Dad can certainly afford it."

I take a deep breath and hold it in, trying to keep my dad's secret from spilling out.

"What's with the face?" Libby says.

"Nothing. It's just . . . you know money has been tight."

"Since when?"

"Since always. Or maybe not always, but at least the last ten years or so. Why do you think I took a job in Washington after college instead of trying to make it as a food writer?"

"Because you're weird?"

I lean my forehead on my hand. "No, because I knew Mom and Dad couldn't bankroll my dreams. Not after they'd paid for college."

"Did they tell you that?"

"No. They didn't have to."

"See, that's your problem," she says. "You never ask, and then you blame me when I get what I want because I do. I ask for the chairs, and then I'm the spoiled brat because I ask for one little thing."

"Libby, with you, it's never just one thing. Next it'll be the flowers. Or the invitations. Or, I don't know, live swans."

"The Rittenhouse doesn't allow swans. I already checked."

I massage my temples. "Do you hear yourself? Do you actually hear the words coming out of your mouth?"

"I do, and I don't care. Maybe if you weren't so afraid of asking for help, you would have given the food-writing thing a try a long time ago, instead of wasting four years in a job you didn't even really like."

"I liked working at *The Morning Show*."

"But you didn't love it."

I stick out my jaw as I meet her eyes, which stare back at me through my computer screen. "No," I say. "I didn't love it."

"See? So maybe if you were a little more like me, you'd be a lot happier."

I'm about to tell Libby that I'm just fine the way I am, but I realize there is no use belaboring a point she will never concede. She isn't accustomed to being challenged, to having anyone prove her wrong, and as far as she is concerned, she is perfect. But as exasperating as it is to listen to her preach about my reticence and insecurity, as much as it makes me want to reach through the computer screen and slap her across the face, what frustrates me most of all, what really burns, is that on some profoundly uncomfortable level, she might actually be right.

Wednesday night, after working Rick's stand in Foggy Bottom for four hours, I head to Jeremy's apartment, which lies five blocks north of the market. We are cooking dinner together again, and he asked me to pick up some salad greens and a loaf of something "Italian-ish," so my tote bag is brimming with bunches of peppery arugula and tender lamb's lettuce and a half loaf of Rick's pane pugliese, a crusty Italian peasant bread with a delicate, open crumb and slightly sour, caramel flavor. For dessert, I decided to buy half of one of Rick's rhubarb crumble tarts—vanilla custard encased in a tender shortbread crust and topped with roasted chunks of ruby rhubarb and a buttery oatmeal crumble—which Rick sold to me at a discount. Working for him does have its perks.

When I reach Jeremy's apartment, I ring the doorbell with one hand as I grip the white pastry box in the other. He opens the door, and, as he notices my overflowing tote bag and the pastry box, he smiles. "Wow. Looks like you cleaned the place out."

"I came pretty close." I glance into my bag. "I traded two oatmeal cookies for the arugula, so you know it has to be good."

"Two of the best cookies on the planet for a bunch of green leaves? I don't know—I think you got a raw deal on that one, my friend."

"Or maybe this arugula will change your life."

"Will it do my laundry? Because otherwise, I think you got played."

Jeremy ushers me into the apartment, and I make my way toward the kitchen, where I plunk the tart box on his counter next to my bag of goodies. I rub my hands together as my eyes land on his stovetop, where a tall pot hisses with simmering water.

"What's on the menu?"

"Nothing fancy," he says. "Spaghetti carbonara."

My stomach somersaults as I survey the ingredients lining his counter: eggs, Parmesan, spaghetti, pancetta. I haven't eaten carbonara since that fateful night with Zach when everything fell apart, and the mere thought of it makes me want to vomit.

Jeremy studies my expression, and his smile fades. "Shit—do you not like carbonara?"

"No. Well, I mean, yes." I try to compose myself. "It's complicated."

"Crap. I'm so sorry. I just figured, with everything else I've seen you eat . . . Carbonara is usually a safe bet."

I take a deep breath and let it out slowly. "It is a safe bet. It's fine. I'm being silly."

"Is it the pork thing? Because I thought about that, but then I remembered you ate the Japanese pork last weekend, so I thought it would be okay."

"It has nothing to do with pork. It's fine. Really. I like carbonara."

"Are you sure?"

"Positive."

"Because I have other things we could—"

"Jeremy? It's fine. I swear."

He holds up his hands defensively. "Okay. Then let's get cooking, shall we?"

He hands me a hunk of Parmesan cheese, and I begin rubbing it back and forth along a box grater, creating a fluffy pile of Parmesan snow, whose nutty, slightly funky smell fills my corner of the kitchen. Jeremy stands at the other end of the counter, slicing into the pancetta in a crosshatch pattern, creating a bunch of even cubes with a few smooth strokes of his knife.

"Do you come from a family of cooks?" I ask as I rasp the

cheese against the prickly grater, trying to distract myself from the familiar smells and sounds.

"Kind of. My grandma used to be an amazing cook. Her mother had emigrated from Alsace-Lorraine, so she knew how to make all of these incredible French-German dishes—curly endive salad with bacon dressing, sausages with sauerkraut, green bean stew with potatoes and bacon. When I'd come to visit for lunch, she'd make me radish sandwiches on white bread with salt and butter."

"Sounds like the answer is yes, then."

"Not exactly. That was my dad's mom. My mom's mom stored cereal and wine in her oven."

I laugh. "I see."

"What about you? You seem to know your way around a kitchen."

I tap the hunk of Parmesan against the box grater to knock off the excess flakes of cheese. "My mom and sister have always been big cooks."

"But not you?"

"I cooked a lot in high school. Not with them, though."

"No? Why not?"

I shrug. "It was sort of their thing. Libby was my mom's Mini-Me—is her Mini-Me, I guess. They both loved shopping, both loved baking, both loved reading fashion magazines. My mom had been a teacher at one time, and now Libby is a teacher. So whenever they embarked on some cooking project, I felt like the third wheel."

"Then where did you learn to hold a whisk like that?" he asks, nodding in my direction as I beat the eggs together in a glass bowl.

I glance down at my hand, which grips the whisk handle like a pencil as my wrist flicks quickly back and forth. My uneasy feeling returns. "Zach," I finally say. "My ex-boyfriend."

Jeremy hesitates. "Oh."

"We broke up a long time ago," I say. "We dated in high school. His mom was—is—a famous Philadelphia caterer."

"Ah. Got it." He places a stainless steel frying pan on the stove and coats it with a slick of olive oil. "How long ago did you guys break up?"

"Almost five years ago."

He dumps the cubes of pancetta into the frying pan, which shimmers with hot oil. "Oh, wow. So you dated all through college?"

I nod. "We were together eight years."

"Wow," he says again. He pushes the bits of pancetta around the pan. They sizzle and pop in the hot oil, the streaks of white fat melting into translucent, bubbling grease. "If you don't mind my asking . . . what happened?"

My wrist tenses as I beat the eggs, whipping them into a golden yellow emulsion. "He cheated on me."

"Oh," he says. "I'm sorry."

"Don't be. He wasn't."

Jeremy pokes at the crackling pancetta with his wooden spoon. "I just meant . . . that must have been hard."

"It was."

He scratches his temple with his free hand. "I guess you guys don't talk, then?"

"Not since . . ." I clear my throat. "I haven't seen him since the night I found out about everything."

"Ah," he says.

I take a deep breath, and my lungs fill with the rich, smoky smell of frying bacon, and in a flash, the intense aroma transports me back to that horrible night: Zach's kitchen, his laptop, Georgina's e-mail, that photo. I tell myself what I'm smelling is here, now, in Jeremy's kitchen, but the memory of that evening is so entangled in this same smell, these same sounds, that I cannot bring myself out of that horrible memory. All I see are Georgina's huge, perfectly round breasts and the panicked look on Zach's face as he realized I'd discovered his secret. I try to push those images from my brain, but I can't, and the more I try, the more vivid they become—Georgina's boobs, Zach's face, his mother's glistening stove, her cold porcelain toilet. I want to separate that moment from this one, but as the snap, crackle, and pop of the frying pancetta intensifies, my breath shortens, and the walls of Jeremy's apartment seem to close in on me.

"I'm sorry," I say, clutching my chest. "I have to—"

But I can't finish the sentence, not unless I want to have a full-fledged panic attack in the middle of Jeremy's kitchen, so instead I rush out of the kitchen to the bathroom and slam the door behind me.

"Sydney? Are you okay?"

Jeremy's muffled voice emanates from behind the closed bathroom door as I sit on the toilet with my head between my knees. "Fine," I say, my eyes closed. "I'll be out in a minute."

"Do you need me to get you some water?"

"Maybe in a second." I take a few deep breaths. "I'll meet you back in the kitchen. I just need a minute. Okay?"

"Yeah. Okay. Sure." He hesitates. "Let me know if you need anything."

"Will do."

Jeremy's footsteps grow softer as he heads toward the kitchen, and I take a few more deep breaths before standing up and flicking on the tap to splash some cool water on my face. I catch a glimpse of my ashen complexion in the mirror, my freckles sitting in sharp contrast to my wan skin, like the inside of a dragon fruit.

"You're being ridiculous," I whisper to my reflection. I stare at my face, my jaw tense. "And now you're talking to yourself. Like an asshole. Way to go, Sydney."

I open Jeremy's medicine cabinet, hoping to find a lifeline in the form of Valium or Xanax, but all I find are shaving cream and aftershave and a bunch of razor cartridges. I begin rifling through his bathroom drawers, quickly searching through one after the next. To be honest, I'm not really sure what my plan is, exactly. To take someone else's antianxiety medication? Assuming he even has any? The fact that I see this as a viable plan only confirms that I should be taking some psychotropic drugs of my own.

As I yank open the top right drawer, I manage to pull the drawer off its track, and the contents crash to the floor.

"Everything okay in there?" Jeremy yells from the kitchen, his voice getting closer.

"Everything's fine!"

"You sure?"

"Yep! Be out in just a sec."

I squat down and begin shoving everything back into the drawer, but somehow a container of talcum powder managed to explode in the crash, and so now everything is covered in mounds of baby powder—his deodorant, his nail clippers, his hair gel, everything. I, too, am covered in it, my indigo jeans now stained with streaks of white.

I grab a hand towel and dust off my pants and the contents of his drawer before scooping up the mountain of talcum powder on the floor. Unfortunately, the towel is a bit damp, and so the dark gray fibers are now coated in a pasty white glue that smells like diapers. At this point, I might as well smash the mirror and clog the toilet because I am on the road to destroying everything else in this bathroom.

Once I've swept up the floor and thoroughly wrecked his towel, I decide to hide the evidence by dumping it in his laundry hamper. This, admittedly, is a lame plan, considering the bathroom now reeks of baby powder and the towel looks as if it's been dredged in flour. But given my emotional state, I have neither the energy nor the inclination to explain why I was snooping through his drawers, so I'd rather hide the soiled towel beneath his dirty underwear.

Jeremy's bathroom opens both to the hallway and to his bedroom, so I slip into his bedroom, dumping the gummy, powdery towel in his wicker hamper. As I close the lid, my eyes land on his laptop, which sits atop his dresser next to a tall stack of papers. I creep over to the dresser and glance at the top piece of paper, which bears the Green Grocers logo, along with the heading FARM-ERS AT MARKET.

"You still okay in there?" Jeremy calls from the kitchen.

I scurry back toward the bathroom and project my voice from behind the other bathroom door. "Yep! Just washing up!"

I hurry back to his dresser and lift the top piece of paper to find another document related to the farmers' market partnership. I lift that document, and then another, and another, and another, until I reach a series of e-mails between Bob Young and someone named Louis Frieback at Everly Foods.

From: Louis Frieback
To: Bob Young
Cc: Katherine Reed
Subject: Problem with supplier

Bob,
Looks like Mr. Ed made it into the bourguignon
and lasagna. Not sure yet about the chili con carne.
Checking, but doesn't look good. Will let you
know ASAP.
Lou

From: Bob Young
To: Louis Frieback
Subject: Problem with supplier

Lou,
Let me know ASAP. I cut Katherine on this corre-
spondence—let's keep this between you and me.
Bob

From: Louis Frieback
To: Bob Young
Subject: Problem with supplier

Bob,
Bad news—chili con carne has problems too. How
do you want to handle?
Lou

From: Bob Young
To: Louis Frieback
Subject: Problem with supplier

Lou,
I'll take care of it.
Bob

Holy crap. I just hit the freaking jackpot.

CHAPTER 30

It isn't stealing if you leave something where you found it. That is a fact.

What is less clear is whether taking a photo of something with your phone—several photos, actually, one more detailed than the next—constitutes stealing in some indirect way. But I'm too excited about this story's potential to care. I have the e-mails. I have names and dates and wheres and whens. I have a story.

The next morning, as soon as Jeremy leaves for work, I head back to my apartment and call Stu Abbott en route.

"I saw the e-mails," I blurt out as soon as he picks up the phone.

"What e-mails?"

"The ones between Bob Young and his supplier. Some guy named Louis Frieback? He works for Everly Foods. Anyway, there was definitely horsemeat in Green Grocers' beef bourguignon, lasagna, and chili con carne, and Bob Young definitely knew about it."

I hear Stu press his phone against his chest and tell someone he can't talk right now. "You have a copy of these e-mails?"

"Yeah. Sort of. I have photos of them on my phone."

"What do you mean, photos? You don't have the actual e-mails?"

"My source . . . didn't feel comfortable making copies of the documents, so I took photos of them with my phone. But you can see everything clearly. It's all right there."

In truth, I waited until Jeremy had fallen asleep to sneak out of bed and capture the images on my phone, not wanting to ruin the evening any more than I already had. As it was, Jeremy ended up serving me plain, buttered spaghetti because he feared setting off another panic attack with a plate of carbonara. He was correct in assuming I didn't have much of an appetite, but that had more to do with my excitement over the incriminating e-mails I'd discovered and less to do with Zach and Georgina. But given that I'd ruined his plans for a romantic evening and managed to cover his entire bathroom in baby powder, I didn't think bringing up Bob Young's cover-up, currently his least favorite topic, was a wise choice.

"Can you send me a copy of the photos, then?"

"Sure."

"Once I see what we're working with, I'll circle back with you, and we can come up with a game plan." He goes silent for a moment. "If these e-mails are as damning as you say, we have a huge story on our hands."

"They are," I say. "We do."

"I'll probably have to get legal involved at some point."

My throat tightens. "Legal?"

"Any time we do this kind of story, we bring them on board."

"Oh. Sure. Of course."

"Don't worry—it shouldn't be a problem. It's not like you hacked this guy's e-mail account and stole his e-mails, right?"

I shift uncomfortably from one foot to the other as I wait for the light to change at the corner of New Hampshire and S.

"Right," I say.

"Good," he says. "Then we're fine."

But as I hang up the phone and head toward Swann Street, I'm not so sure we are.

I barely make it inside my apartment before Stu calls me back.

"Sydney—these e-mails. Oh my God." He hums excitedly into

the phone. "You'll be able to write your own ticket after this one. Christ."

"So I have a story?"

"You have more than a story. You have a bombshell."

We come up with a list of people to contact, including Louis Frieback and Katherine Reed, Louis's assistant who was copied on the first e-mail. Bob Young is last on our list. We don't want to go to him for a comment until the story is airtight, and we don't want to give the company extra time to cover up anything else. Because when this story comes out? It's going to be a total shit storm.

Jeremy, meanwhile, has no idea what I've been up to, which is making me increasingly uncomfortable. Then again, a lot of things about Jeremy make me uncomfortable. Number one: his career history. Number two: how much I like him. Number three: how much he seems to like me. Number four: his *Star Wars* obsession. So, really, what's a scandalous e-mail exchange in the context of all that?

Friday morning, as I continue my research into Everly Foods and their supply chain, Jeremy calls me during his lunch break.

"I owe you another apology," he says.

"You owe *me* an apology?" Something tells me he has this backward.

"For Wednesday. The carbonara. I still feel bad about that."

"I've told you a zillion times—it wasn't a big deal."

"You spent twenty minutes in the bathroom. I kind of think it was."

"I told you, that wasn't because of the carbonara."

It was because I went on a psycho rampage in search of Valium, smothered your bathroom in talcum powder, and found a stack of career-making e-mails in your bedroom. Duh.

"Well, anyway, I wanted to treat you to my famous roast chicken tonight." He pauses. "Unless you have issues with roast chicken too?"

"I have no issues with roast chicken."

"Excellent. I'll see you at six, then."

I'm about to hang up when Jeremy jumps in with one more thing. "Oh, and I have some exciting news," he says. "There's been . . . a development. I think you'll be interested."

My ears perk up. "Oh, yeah?"

"Yeah. I'll explain when I see you."

I stare at my computer screen, which has five open windows relating to Bob Young and Everly Foods and Louis Frieback, and as I drag my index finger along the keyboard, I say, "I can't wait."

When I show up at Jeremy's apartment, the entire place already smells of caramelizing onions and earthy thyme, the rhythmic jazz emanating through his speakers punctuated by the hiss of chicken skin rendering its fat as it crisps.

"Should I get the smelling salts?" Jeremy asks as I toss my bag on one of his chairs.

"Enough with the jokes about Wednesday. I'm fine."

"Sorry. I promise not to mention it again. I promise not to bring up that guy either. Zeke?"

"Zach."

"Right. That's the last time I'll mention his name."

"Somehow I doubt that."

He shrugs. "I'll do my best."

I make my way into the kitchen and peek into the oven, where the chicken sits on a bed of onions and carrots, the skin puffing up and sputtering as it turns a deep golden brown. Roast chicken was one of my favorite meals growing up and a dish my mom often made on Sunday night, along with her famous crispy roasted potatoes. Libby liked her roast chicken flavored with lots of lemon and a little garlic, but I preferred mine with lots of garlic, no lemon, and a bit of paprika under the skin. In an unusual meeting of the minds, that's how my mom preferred it too, so that's how she made it most often. I loved that Sunday night dinner. I loved how it made me feel closer to her for once.

"Looks great," I say as I flick off the oven light. "What else is on the menu?"

"Roasted carrots and mashed potatoes. Oh, and . . ." He lifts up a brown glass bottle with fanfare. "My Munich Helles."

"I have no idea what that means."

"It's a German-style lager. Tastes really good with roast chicken."

He pops off the top with a bottle opener and takes a swig. "It might even be an *award-winning* lager, if things go my way."

"Oh, yeah?"

"*Ohhh* yeah." He places the beer on the counter and rubs his hands together excitedly. "That's the big news I wanted to share with you: I submitted my Helles and my oatmeal stout to this year's National Homebrew Competition, and both made it past the first round."

"Wow—congrats." I try to mask the disappointment in my voice. I'd really hoped his news had something to do with Bob Young or Green Grocers. "What do you get if you win?"

"Eternal fame and fortune." He smirks. "I think they give you a medal or a ribbon or something. Maybe some free beer."

"On top of eternal fame and fortune? Not too shabby." I grab a bottle of the Helles lager off his counter. "So when do you find out if you won?"

"Not until June. It's part of the National Homebrewers Conference."

"You guys have conferences? Wow. That's . . ."

"Nerdy?"

"Very."

"I know. But I love it. I go every year. It's so much fun."

He starts to tell me more about the conference, which is in Philadelphia this year, and the seven other members of his brew club and how they all go together. His enthusiasm is infectious, and I suddenly find myself caring more about fermentation and mashing and bottle conditioning—terms I'd either never heard or rarely considered before tonight—than I ever have before. The impassioned sound of his voice, punctuated by his enthusiastic hand movements and animated facial expressions, draws me into his world of barley and yeast and hops, until nothing seems more important or exciting than the process of turning malted barley and water into a bottle of Munich Helles.

"Have you ever considered turning brewing into more than a hobby?" I ask.

"You mean like going into business?"

"Sure. Starting a microbrewery. Something like that."

"I've toyed with the idea. Part of me thinks it would be the perfect job. But I like my current job, and it's definitely more stable than starting a business."

My stomach curdles. "But if your job ever became less stable . . ."

"Why would my job become less stable?"

"No, I didn't mean—you mentioned work has been stressing you out, that's all. Like you weren't totally happy there."

"Nah, I'm happy. It isn't perfect, but it's a good job."

"But your boss basically told you to hush up a scandal."

He takes another swig of beer. "He didn't tell me to hush it up. He told me not to make a huge stink about it."

"But . . . don't you think that's wrong?"

He hunches his shoulders. "Yeah? But after everything I've been through, keeping a low profile isn't the worst thing. I'm not ready to be a hero. I'd rather be anonymous for a while."

"There's nothing wrong with being a hero."

"True. But I'd rather be a hero for something that matters right now. Like this farmers' market partnership? That's going to be huge for a lot of these farmers and artisans."

"So it doesn't bother you that the new CEO of a company you represent is a total hypocrite?"

"He made a mistake in his past. I know what that's like."

"Yeah, but your mistake didn't have an impact on thousands of people. Don't you think his customers have a right to know the truth?"

Jeremy sighs. "Of course I do. But I'm not ready to be in the spotlight again. And I'm not prepared to upend a deal that could benefit a bunch of hardworking people. Like your boss Rick—how do you think he'd feel if we pulled the rug out from under him? All of these vendors have been working under the assumption that this partnership is going forward. They've made investments. Financial projections. I don't want to be the guy who blows all of that up."

I fiddle with the label on my beer bottle. "Why would telling the truth blow all of that up?"

"Because that's what always happens. This whole partnership

was Bob Young's brainchild. But when a scandal becomes public, that's all anyone cares about. You worked in news. You know how it goes. So this scandal comes out, and Bob apologizes and then steps aside, and some new bozo takes his place and claims things will be different on his or her watch, and then any program or initiative Bob touched will be like fucking anthrax, and no one will want anything to do with it. At least not for a very long time."

My chest tightens as Jeremy's words ring in my ears, their veracity undeniable. He's right: When this story comes out, that's all anyone will want to talk about. No one will care about the plans Bob Young has for the company and the people those plans might benefit. No one will care about Rick or Maggie or the impact on their businesses. But I've let someone talk me out of doing a major story before, and I've lived with that guilt for more than six years. I can't let it happen again. Which means no matter how much I agree with what Jeremy is saying, no matter how right he is, I can't change course. I've started down the road to delivering this story, and now, for better or worse, there's no turning back.

CHAPTER 31

The story at Northwestern started out as an innocent little feature. I decided to do a segment on the annual Wildcat Chili Cook-off run by Professor Arthur Ferguson, one of the university's superstar professors, who held a named chair in the economics department and regularly appeared on TV and in major newspapers. His work focused on Africa, and for more than a decade he'd run a nonprofit whose mission was to build schools in Tanzania and Kenya. He started the Wildcat Chili Cook-off as a way to fundraise for his pet project.

When I started working on the feature, I was a junior, doing a spot for the weekly food show I produced for the Northwestern News Network. As someone who loved telling "people stories," I wanted to profile not only the students and professors who were whipping up their best chili recipes, but also the children in Africa who would benefit from the money the university raised. I knew there was no way we'd be able to travel to Africa, but I figured with enough advance notice, I could get one of the schools to send me some promotional video of their own.

And that's when things started to get weird.

When I asked Professor Ferguson for a list of schools I could contact, he instead put me in touch with someone in media relations at his nonprofit, who then sent me a small snippet of video that looked at least ten years old. When I asked for something more recent, she said that was all they had. And when I asked for a local contact in Kenya or Tanzania, she kept saying she'd get back to me, but never did.

I finally did some digging on my own and found one school Professor Ferguson had mentioned in an interview with Charlie Rose, but when I tried to e-mail the principal there, I discovered the school had closed—five years earlier.

When Zach and I spoke a few days later, I told him I'd stumbled across a potentially major story—one that could tarnish not only Professor Ferguson's reputation but the reputation of the entire university as well.

"Leave it alone," Zach said, without skipping a beat.

"Why?"

"You'll just open a can of worms and get yourself into trouble. Someone as important as Arthur Ferguson isn't going to be brought down by some scrappy twenty-year-old. You don't even know he's done anything wrong."

"It looks really bad, Zach."

"Doesn't matter. You'll be the one ruined by this story, not him. Let it be."

So I did.

I'd never loved covering hard news stories anyway, so I told myself Zach was right. I had no business covering a story like that. But the guilt gnawed at me until one day, three years later, when I opened my daily *New York Times* digest to find a front-page story on how Arthur Ferguson's nonprofit was a total sham. He hadn't built three-quarters of the schools he claimed he had, the ones he did build had closed years ago, and he'd absconded with the remaining funds. Boom.

At the time, I was still reeling from my breakup with Zach, and this reignited all of the hurt and anger. What right did he have to call me off the story? If I hadn't listened to him, I could have exposed the scam earlier and saved millions and millions of dollars from being wasted. Maybe schools would have been built to help those children. Maybe that money could have been used for something good, instead of lining Arthur Ferguson's pockets.

But that didn't happen. Which is why, this time, I have to do the right thing the first time around. I can't let another scandal slip through the cracks. The public has a right to know the truth.

I spend the week finding out everything I can about Everly Foods and its supply chain—how a frozen "Green Grocers Country Lasagna Dinner" gets from the processing plant to the shelf. I talk to regulators; I track down former employees through Google and Facebook; I call up business professors and financial analysts. I've never wanted to be an investigative journalist, but aside from wanting to make right on my past wrongs, I'm spurred on by the knowledge that if I get this right, a dream job awaits me at the other end.

According to my sources, Everly has been in financial straits for a few years and has been looking to cut expenses. They recently began outsourcing some of their processing and packaging to China—the largest producer of horsemeat in the world. Everly then imported the frozen meals, branded them with the Green Grocers private label, and shipped them out to Green Grocers, who sold them to millions of people looking for a quick and healthy microwave meal. From what I can put together, someone at the Chinese processing plant cut a few corners and swapped cheaper cuts of horse for the pricier beef.

Once I've nailed down a timeline and the basic facts, I reach out to Katherine Reed, Louis Frieback's assistant. When I call the company, however, I'm told she no longer works there. I search for her on Google and Facebook, and feeling as if I've been running in circles for days, I finally find a number for her, which I call first thing Friday morning.

"Katherine?"

A long pause. "Who is this?"

"My name is Sydney Strauss. I'm a food writer for the *Washington Chronicle*." A chill runs up my spine as those words come out of my mouth—words I've longed to say for more than a decade.

"What do you want?"

"I have a few quick questions for you about your time at Everly Foods."

Silence.

"Hello?"

"I can't talk about that," she says.

"I'll be quick—just a few questions."

"No, you don't understand: I can't talk about that. I signed a nondisclosure agreement."

"Oh." I twirl my pen in my hand. "So you can't tell me about the e-mail you were copied on, dated June 28 of last year, between Bob Young and Louis Frieback, entitled 'Problem with Supplier'?"

A beat. "What did you say your name was?"

"So you were copied on that e-mail. Right?"

Silence.

"Can you tell me why you left the company?"

"Like I already said, I can't talk about that."

"Was it to spend more time with your family, or to take another job, or . . . something else?"

A heavy sigh. "Listen. I can't tell you anything. I wish I could, but I can't." She pauses. "Call Pete Hamilton. We worked together. He might be able to help you."

She gives me his number and hangs up, and all I can think is that the better this story gets for me, the worse it gets for everyone else.

Pete Hamilton is a gold mine. Until two months ago, he worked in Everly's IT department, meaning he can confirm the e-mails I found in Jeremy's apartment are genuine. He was also good friends with Katherine and knows why she left: She caught wind of a potential horsemeat scandal, confronted Louis Frieback, and faster than you can say "chili con carne," was out the door with a nice severance package. Pete doesn't want to go on the record, but he says I can use him as an unnamed source. With his interview in my pocket, all I need are a few more on-the-record quotes and facts for this story to come together.

What unfortunately has not come together is the Green Grocers pilot project, something Rick has proceeded to complain about for the past week. When I show up at the West End market Saturday morning, he is already grumbling to himself as he rolls out of the front seat of the truck.

"Another day, another chance for someone to screw me," he says.

"Good morning to you, too."

He unlatches the back of the truck. "Tell me something: Do I look like the kind of guy who enjoys being dicked around?"

I shake my head.

"Do I look like the kind of guy who has patience for idiots?"

I shake my head again.

"Then tell me: Why are these idiots dicking me around?" He raises his arms and faces the other vendors, who, at the early hour of 7:00 a.m. on a Saturday, are minding their own business as they set up and pitch their tents. "Can *some*body *fuck*ing *tell* me?"

A few of the other farmers look up and then carry on with their morning business, apparently unfazed by Rick's latest outburst. Rick's status as resident lunatic may be well established, but I wish this deal would go through as much as he does, and I hate to think how much he has riding on it and how much he stands to lose if everything falls apart.

Heidi shows up ten minutes late, carrying approximately five different tote bags, as per usual, at least two of which bear PBS and NPR logos. Rick interrupts his tirade at a stack of poppy seed muffins ("Could you stay put? Could you fucking do that for me? *Could you?*") to acknowledge her tardiness with his signature chauvinism.

"Hey, Blondie—can't you read a clock? Or are the numbers too complicated for your pretty little head?"

"I'd ask you to teach me, but my guess is you'd be too busy scratching your balls."

I gasp and drop a chocolate chip muffin on the ground, certain I am about to witness my friend's murder, but instead, Rick smirks and says, "Thanks, Blondie. I needed that this morning."

Heidi throws her canvas bags beneath the table and grabs the muffin I dropped on the ground. "Thirty-second rule," she says, before popping a hunk into her mouth.

"I'm pretty sure it's called the five-second rule."

She takes another bite. "Too late now."

I stack a few more muffins on a cake stand. "So how are you? How was Houston?"

Heidi was at a conference last weekend, and I've been so busy with my research into the horsemeat story that I haven't seen or talked to her in two weeks.

"Total waste of time," she says, pulling her wheat-colored hair into a ponytail while a black elastic band hangs out of her mouth. She ties it into a messy bun on top of her head, looking the picture of bohemian chic in her loose floral tunic and black leggings. "But it was good to get out of town for a few days. What about you? How are things?"

"Things are good. Busy."

"Newsletter stuff?"

"No. Well, I'm still working on the newsletter for Julie, but that isn't what's been keeping me busy. It's this story I'm doing for the *Chronicle*."

"Oh, right, for the blog."

"This is actually for the paper."

"Really? Wow, that's awesome. What's the story about?"

I arrange a row of flaky almond croissants in a long basket and wonder what I should tell Heidi. On the one hand, I shouldn't say anything to anyone about a story that could hurt other people's careers and potentially make mine. On the other, Heidi and I have been friends since college, and I can't imagine keeping this from her. I also desperately want to share the story with someone because the secret is killing me.

"It's . . . complicated," I say.

"What do you mean? Like, it's a complicated story? Or it's complicated because you can't talk about it?"

"Both."

Heidi is about to say something when Rick interrupts us. "Hey, my little *chiquitas*. Less chitchat, more hustle. *Comprende?*"

"Sorry," I say.

"I'm heading over to Broad Tree to discuss something with Maggie," he says. "But when I get back, I want everything set up. Got it?"

"Got it."

Rick waddles over to Maggie's tent, and when he is out of earshot, Heidi clears her throat as she tosses an empty crate beneath the table. "So about this story . . ."

"Like I said, it's complicated."

She sticks a sign in front of the rhubarb crumb cake. "How complicated can it be? You're writing about farmers' markets. It's not like you're covering Watergate."

"Not exactly."

She smirks. "What, is there some big farmers' market scandal afoot? Trouble in foodie paradise?" Her smile fades when I don't respond. "Wait. There's a scandal?"

I walk over to the cashbox and begin organizing the stack of twenties. "I can't really talk about it."

Heidi sidles up beside me. "Sydney. Come on. It's me."

"I know it's you."

"And have I ever betrayed your confidence? Have I given you any reason to mistrust me?"

I bite my lip as I close the cashbox. Heidi is right. In nearly a decade of friendship, she has never been disloyal. In college, when my period was late after one of Zach's visits, she bought me a pregnancy test and didn't tell a soul. And when the test came back negative, she hugged me, destroyed the evidence, and never mentioned the incident again. The girl may be capricious and free spirited, but she is damn good at keeping a secret.

"Okay," I finally say, letting out a sigh. "But you can't say a word to *anyone*."

Heidi mimes locking her lips and tossing away the key.

"You know the new CEO of Green Grocers? The one spearheading the whole farmers' market partnership?" Heidi nods. "Well, when he was COO, he discovered a bunch of Green Grocers' frozen meals contained horsemeat from China, and he covered it up."

Heidi's blue eyes grow as big and round as two silver dollars. "Shut. Up."

"Apparently one of Green Grocers' suppliers had an issue with their supply chain."

"Uh, ya think? How the hell did Chinese horsemeat end up here?"

"The supplier outsourced frozen meal production to China, and the Chinese subcontractor cut a few corners to keep costs down."

"Jesus." Heidi takes a deep breath, her eyes still wide. "How did you find out about this?"

I clear my throat. "Well, that's the thing. . . . You know how I've been seeing more of Jeremy Brauer?"

"Don't tell me he's the shady contractor in question." She rests a hand on her hip. "I *told* you to stay away from him. I *told* you he was bad news."

"No—Heidi, jeez, calm down. Jeremy isn't the shady contractor. He's the one who came across the e-mails between Bob Young and the supplier. His company is doing PR for Green Grocers, and he saw the e-mails by mistake."

"Oh. So he's helping you with the story?"

"Not exactly."

"But he gave you a copy of the e-mails."

"Not exactly."

"He knows you're doing the story, though."

"Not exactly."

Heidi raises an eyebrow. "Then what *exactly* is he doing?"

"Working on the PR for the farmers' market partnership."

She huffs. "So he knows Green Grocers was putting Seabiscuit into its frozen dinners, and he isn't planning to say anything about it? What a slimeball."

"No—it isn't like that. He went to his bosses about it, but they told him to butt out. And given his past, he doesn't want to be part of a media circus again. Plus, he's worried that if the scandal comes out, the company will call off the pilot program with the farmers' market. He doesn't want to screw everyone."

"Sounds like he doesn't want to screw himself."

"It isn't like that. I swear. He really does care about these people. He isn't the sleaze you read about online."

"If you say so . . ." She grabs the remaining signs and begins sticking them in front of the corresponding loaves of bread. "So if he didn't show you the e-mails, how do you know they even exist?"

"Because I found them in his apartment."

Heidi snorts. "Ah, so you were snooping."

"I was not." I rearrange the stack of quark bread. "Okay, I was kind of snooping. But only because I was having a panic attack and ended up locked in his bathroom."

"He kept the e-mails in his bathroom?"

"No—he . . . I . . . Never mind. It isn't important. The point is, I have copies."

Heidi titters. "So Miss Goody-Two-Shoes stole her boyfriend's e-mails while he thought she was having a panic attack in the shitter? This is hilarious."

"I didn't steal them. I took photos of them with my phone while he was sleeping."

Heidi bursts into laughter. "Even better."

"And he isn't my boyfriend." I stop and consider this as I dust the powdered sugar from the strawberry muffins off my hands. "Or maybe he is. We haven't officially discussed it."

"Sounds like you've been too busy trying to sabotage his career."

"Hey—that's unfair. I'm trying to redeem him. He's my whistle-blower." I pause. "Although I'm not really sure it counts if he doesn't know he's blowing the whistle."

She bursts into another fit of laughter. "Sorry," she says, wiping the tears from her eyes. "Sorry. I shouldn't laugh. I can't help myself. It's just too good. This has disaster written all over it."

I roll my shoulders back. "Not necessarily."

"Really? Describe one scenario in which this thing doesn't go nuclear."

I fidget with the sign in front of the chocolate chip cookies, even though it's already straight and doesn't need adjusting. "Okay, maybe you're right. But it doesn't matter. From past experience, I know telling this story is the right thing to do."

"Are you at least going to tell him you're working on it?"

I sigh. "Eventually. I just don't want him to talk me out of writing it. I've made that mistake before. And anyway, if I nail this piece, I'll be on my way to the career I've always wanted."

"Maybe you should break it off with Jeremy until the story comes out."

"No. I couldn't do that."

"Why not?"

I play with the edge of the tablecloth and then look up at Heidi. "Because I really like him. He's smart and thoughtful and funny, and when I'm with him, I feel . . . well, like me again. The way I used to feel with Zach—alive, happy. He's really into food and brews his own beer. He makes me laugh." I pause. "I think . . . I think I'm falling for him."

Heidi chokes on the air and holds up a finger while she grabs her bottle of water and takes a big gulp. She stares at me with wide, glassy eyes, as if she cannot believe that I, Sydney Strauss, could possibly be falling in love again, and with Jeremy Brauer of all people. But more than disbelief—more than blatant astonishment—the look on her face expresses pity wrapped in dread, as if my fate has been sealed, and confirms what I was beginning to suspect: that I'm skydiving without a parachute, tumbling ass over tits toward a pool of bloodthirsty sharks, and there's nothing anyone can do to save me.

She takes another swig of water and smirks as she shakes her head. "Sydney, my friend, I have but one request."

"Sure. Anything."

"I won't tell a soul about any of this, and you can talk to me about it any time you want. But when this thing blows up in all of its messy glory?" She screws the cap on her water and winks, a grin spreading across her face. "I want a front row seat."

CHAPTER 32

There is no reason why this situation has to end badly. Okay, yes, there are a million reasons why it *could* end badly or *should* end badly, but that doesn't mean it definitely will. Then again, this is me, and these days my life and disaster seem to go hand in hand.

Case in point: Two weeks later, just as the horsemeat story is beginning to coalesce, I run into Charles Griffin at the farmers' market. This, in and of itself, is not a disaster, but whenever Charles is involved, disaster is never far behind.

He moseys up to the Wild Yeast tent around 10:00 a.m., his hands tucked into the pockets of his baggy chinos as he breathes in the balmy May air. I haven't spoken to him since he linked me up with Stu Abbott more than two months ago, but I've caught a few of his recent spots on *The Morning Show.* The last one I saw had something to do with the national debt and involved Charles dressed in a dollar bill costume made of skintight spandex, which confirmed my dismissal from *The Morning Show* had been a blessing in disguise.

"The Sydster!" he crows as he parks himself in front of the basket of brioche.

"Well, well, well. Chaz Griffin. Long time, no see."

Back at *The Morning Show,* Melanie, Charles, and I prided ourselves on coming up with the most annoying nicknames we could think of for one another. He would call me The Sydster and Square Sydney, and Melanie and I used to call him "Chaz" and variations thereof: DJ Chazzy Jeff, Chazberries and Cream, Chaz-been. One of the few times I saw Charles get really angry involved a particularly stressful in-studio live shot, when Melanie called out during a break, "How you doing over there, Princess Chazmin?" I've never seen his face turn redder.

"Stu tells me you have a major scoop," he says as he scans the basket of cinnamon-speckled snickerdoodles.

"He told you about my story?"

"A bit, yeah. I told you we have a content-sharing agreement now, right?"

"You did. Sorry. I forgot."

"He's been light on details, but it sounds like you're ready to drop a pretty big bombshell. We've been talking about how the network plans to cover this, and I'd love to get the exclusive for *The Morning Show*. Interview you the morning the piece comes out—something like that."

"An interview with me?"

"It's your story, isn't it?"

"It is. But . . ."

I'm about to say I didn't expect the story to become about me, but that isn't entirely true. Aside from wanting to expose a fraud, I also pitched this story to gain entry into the exclusive club of serious food writers. I wanted to tell a story, but I also wanted people to know I was the one telling it. But that was before I realized my reporting could hurt other people's businesses and reputations. That was before I knew how far-reaching the impact of this story could be.

"I'm not sure I'm camera-ready," I say.

"Of course you are." He narrows his eyes as he studies my face. "You could use a haircut. And some tooth whitener. But with some good lighting and a lot of makeup, I think you'd be fine."

I wait for him to break into a laugh and say he is kidding, but he doesn't. The Charles Griffin ego is alive and well.

"I'll have to think about it," I say. "There are . . . some moving pieces."

"Understood." He glances down again at the snickerdoodles. "Are these cookies any good?"

"The snickerdoodles? Epic."

"Then I'll take three."

"Coming right up."

I bag up the cookies, each one nearly an inch thick and the size of a DVD, and Charles hands me a twenty, which I take over to the cashbox to make change. As I tuck his bill into the fat stack of twenties, Heidi sidles up beside me with a ten-dollar bill in her hand.

"Is that Charles Griffin?" she asks, nodding over her shoulder.

"The one and only."

"What is he doing here?"

"Buying snickerdoodles. And trying to convince me to come on *The Morning Show* as a guest when my story comes out."

Heidi snorts. "You're joking, right?"

"Nope. The network has a content-sharing agreement with the *Chronicle*. Charles wants the 'exclusive' with me."

Heidi bursts into a full-fledged laugh, her eyes filling with tears.

"Is there a problem over here?" Rick asks, creeping up behind Heidi and me. "What's so freaking funny?"

"Nothing," I say, grabbing Charles's change from the box.

Heidi brings her laughter under control. "Sydney is dealing with some highly entertaining first-world problems."

"Well, hey, here's a newsflash: I don't give a shit." Rick pulls a lit cigarette out of his pants pocket and takes a quick puff. "Get back to work."

He stuffs the lit cigarette back into his pocket, as if it were perfectly normal to keep close to one's groin an object that is, technically speaking, *on fire*.

I head back to the corner of the table where Charles is standing, and he smiles as he stuffs the bills in his pocket. "Let's stay in touch about this story," he says. He wiggles his eyebrows up and down. "This could be your ticket to stardom."

"A ticket to stardom?" says a voice to my left.

I whip my head around and feel the blood rush to my face. "Jeremy—hi." My stomach sours. "What are you doing here?"

"I thought I'd swing by to say hello. But given your expression . . . I'm thinking I should turn around and go home."

"No, no—you just surprised me, that's all."

"So what's this about a ticket to stardom?"

I open my mouth to answer, but Charles butts in before I can speak. "Our friend Sydney is working on a big story."

Jeremy locks eyes with me. "Oh, really?"

My stomach churns. "It's not that big," I say.

"She's being modest," Charles says. "It's huge. At least from what I know."

Jeremy looks Charles up and down. "I'm sorry—who are you?"

Charles stares at Jeremy in utter disbelief. "Who am I? Who are *you?*"

"I'm Jeremy. Sydney's . . ." He trails off as his eyes search mine.

"Boyfriend," I say, surprised at how easily that word rolls off my tongue.

"Ah. Well, I'm Charles Griffin." He waits for Jeremy to acknowledge him, but when Jeremy doesn't bite, Charles lets out an exasperated huff. "From *The Morning Show?* With Diana Humphrey? I used to work with Sydney?"

"Oh, right. You're the guy who always does those crazy stunts."

"It's called visual storytelling." Charles tightens his grip around the bag of cookies. "And I assure you, the story Sydney and I are working on is far from a stunt."

I ignore the fact that Charles just took credit for a story he has had nothing to do with and try to steer the conversation in another direction. "Hey, Charles, remember that time you got attacked by a turkey?" I laugh nervously.

Charles and Jeremy look at me and then back at each other. "So what's this big story, then?" Jeremy asks.

"We can't talk about it," Charles says. "Sorry."

My jaw tightens as I glare at Charles, unsure whether I'm more upset over his spilling the beans about my story or his appropriation of a story to which his contribution has been zero.

"That's too bad," Jeremy says. His eyes drift over my shoulder and land on Heidi, who is making her way to our corner of the tent.

"Everything cool over here?" she asks.

"Fantastic," I say through a tight smile.

Heidi's eyes land on Jeremy, and she pushes forward, extending her hand in his direction.

"I don't think we've been formally introduced," she says. "Heidi Parker."

"Jeremy Brauer. Sydney's—"

"Boyfriend," she says, cutting him off as she shakes his hand.

"Right."

Charles leans back on his heels as he waits for Heidi to extend her hand in his direction. When she doesn't, he puts on his cheesiest smile and reaches out his hand.

"I'm not sure if you recognize me, but I'm—"

"Charles Griffin. I know. Nice to meet you." She shakes his hand matter-of-factly and shifts her attention back to Jeremy, Charles visibly put out by her disinterest. "So what are we talking about? You all look so serious."

"Apparently Sydney and Charles are working on some big story together," Jeremy says.

"I don't think it's fair to say you're working on that story together," Heidi says.

"We are." Charles catches my stare. "Well, sort of. We will be."

"What story?" Jeremy asks. "What are we talking about?"

I clear my throat. "It's nothing. Really. Charles is blowing this out of proportion."

"No, I'm not," Charles says, completely missing all of my cues to *shut the hell up*. "You're honestly going to tell me that—"

But before Charles can continue, Jeremy's eyes wander to the opposite side of the tent. "Sorry to interrupt, but . . . Sydney, I think your boss's pants are on fire."

I spin around and see that, indeed, Rick's pants have begun smoking in the vicinity of his left jean pocket. Rick, unfortunately, is in the middle of chatting up a lithe brunette in spandex pants, and thus the only fire in his pants of which he is aware stems from his underserved libido.

"Um . . . hey, Rick?"

Rick carries on with his pointless flirtation, ignoring me.

"Rick?"

His face reddens, but he does not tear his eyes away from the attractive woman in spandex, and it is clear he does not want to be interrupted.

"RICK!"

He whirls around to face me, his jaw clenched as he forces a fake smile. "*Yes,* dear."

"Your pants are on fire."

He takes a quick peek and notices they are smoldering in an area precariously close to his crotch, and then he glares at me and rushes out of the tent to the area behind the truck.

I look back at Jeremy and Charles, whose mouths are hanging open as they follow Rick with their eyes. I hear Rick rattling through the ice chest in the back of the truck, followed by a series of muffled expletives involving "Jesus Christ" and "son-of-a-bitch" and "mother-bleeping-balls." And then I hear what I have been waiting for:

"Sydney! Could you come *back* here, please?"

On any other day, dealing with Rick and his singed pubic hairs would approximate a punishment worse than death. But in an indication of how far I've backed myself into a corner, I'd rather attend to Rick than continue this conversation with Jeremy, Charles, and Heidi. It is a sad commentary on the current state of affairs, and not something I'm proud of, but there is no denying the fact that, today at least, I am very glad to contend with Rick's flaming crotch.

Which, as far as I can tell, means I have lost my will to live.

CHAPTER 33

What is wrong with Charles?

That isn't a rhetorical question. I'm seriously asking: What is wrong with him? Is he demented? On drugs? Because otherwise I honestly don't understand what just happened. What kind of person takes credit for a story that isn't his? And what kind of person, when I make it abundantly clear I do not want to discuss said story, proceeds to blather on about it?

And now Jeremy thinks I'm working on some juicy story. Which I guess I am, but he doesn't need to know that. Well, okay, he does need to know eventually, but not because Charles threw a hissy fit in the middle of the farmers' market. Jeremy deserves to hear the news from me, on my own terms. And he will. But not before I make sure the story is airtight.

Later that evening, I meet Jeremy outside his apartment before the two of us head to the Georgetown waterfront for a picnic. Both he and Charles quickly fled the scene earlier this morning, Rick's flaming nether regions a prospect too gruesome for either of them to contemplate. I don't blame them. I had to avert my eyes to prevent the image of Rick unbuttoning his pants from tattooing itself on my brain forever.

I stand on the corner of Twenty-fourth and M, grinding my flats into the pavement as a balmy breeze blows through the sleeves of my silky white tunic. May has ushered in a spell of warm weather, and the fresh spring air feels delicious against my pale skin. Jeremy bursts through his front door, carrying a large paper bag by its bottom and looking characteristically handsome in his dark jeans and gray-and-white plaid button-down. I take no pride in admitting I'd feel less guilty about this whole situation if he were ugly.

He pulls a small paper bag out from within the larger one and passes it to me. "Can you handle the beer?"

"Sure." I glance inside and spot four bottles bearing the Brauer's Brew label. "Another Brauer creation?"

"A Brauer-*Strauss* creation."

"This is the porter we brewed last month?"

He smiles. "Yep. I think you'll be happy with how it came out."

He leads the way down M Street and over the Rock Creek Parkway, entering the bustle of Georgetown. As we cross Twenty-eighth Street, the air fills with the incongruous scents of Ethiopian berbere and Middle Eastern falafel, which emanate from two restaurants on the corner and are otherwise foreign to this decidedly preppy neighborhood. We cross the street and make our way south toward the waterfront, treading along the uneven brick sidewalk as we pass tall brick office buildings and squat Federalist town houses festooned with shiny black shutters.

When we hit the water, we follow the narrow wooden boardwalk until it dead ends and continue onto a paved pathway that runs along the edge of the river at a higher elevation. To the right of the path, a wide expanse of grass extends toward K Street, studded with curved granite benches, walkways, and beds of butterfly milkweed and tall grasses and reeds.

Jeremy guides me down the pathway until we find an empty spot on one of the granite benches beneath a large metal and glass trellis. When we sit down, he pulls out five Tupperware containers and arranges them on the bench beside him.

"Dude, no one with testicles should own that much Tupperware," I say.

"Says who? The Tupperware police?"

"I'm just saying. That's a lot of plastic storage for one man."

"What would you prefer? A crinkled wad of aluminum foil?"

"Maybe."

"Do you try to be difficult, or does it come naturally?"

"It's a gift."

"One that, unfortunately, didn't come with a return receipt."

I nudge him. "Oh, come on, you love my quirks."

"Yes, in what may be considered one of the great mysteries of our time."

He pulls the lids off the five containers, revealing an assortment of provisions that includes, among other things, an enormous stack of fudgy brownies.

"Come to mama," I say, reaching for a brownie.

Jeremy pushes my hand away. "Not so fast—those are for dessert."

"Which is why I should eat them first. I'd rather spoil my appetite with brownies than with potato salad."

"Fine." He lifts the container toward me. "Salted fudge brownies. Enjoy."

I sink my teeth into the thick, fudgy square, whose velvety crumbs coat my gums. The brownie is sweet and salty, with a slightly bitter edge from the dark chocolate and the texture of the silkiest fudge. It is, quite possibly, the best brownie I have ever eaten.

"Wow. You could give Rick the Prick a run for his money with these." I lick a few crumbs from my fingers. "Seriously. Are you sure you're in the right line of work?"

"Somehow I don't think beer and brownies are the basis for a viable business plan."

"You're kidding, right? Chocolate and alcohol? That sounds like the *best* business plan."

He laughs. "Maybe you're right."

"Not maybe. Definitely."

I scoff down the rest of the brownie, savoring each chocolaty bite, and wonder if it would be too piggish to have a second now, before dinner.

"Have you ever thought of putting beer *in* the brownies?" I ask, after deciding, yes, a second now would be a bit too gluttonous.

"Beer in the brownies? Uh, no."

"You should try it. I used to make these Guinness brownies in college with Zach, and they were off the charts."

I don't realize I've mentioned Zach's name until I notice the blush in Jeremy's cheeks.

"They weren't as good as these," I quickly add.

He smiles awkwardly. "It's okay if they were better. My feelings won't be hurt."

"They weren't better. Just different."

Jeremy's expression relaxes. "I'll have to try it some time. Maybe with my oatmeal stout."

"Correction: your *award-winning* oatmeal stout."

"Let's not get ahead of ourselves," he says with a grin. "I won't find out if I made the finals for another week or two. In the meantime . . ." He reaches into the paper bag and pulls out two bottles. "Let's give this porter a whirl, shall we?"

He pops off the caps and hands me a beer, whose malty, almost coffee-like flavor catches me by surprise. "This is really good," I say.

"You helped make it."

I take another sip. "Obviously I am a brewing genius."

"Obviously."

The two of us begin assembling pulled pork sandwiches from the ingredients in the containers, layering the jalapeño-lime slaw on top of piles of chipotle pulled pork and capping it off with a fluffy white bun. The sandwiches are smoky and spicy, with a slight tang from the slaw, and we wash them down with hefty swigs of our full-bodied porter. Between bites, Jeremy hands me a fork and the container of Yukon gold and purple potato salad, which we pass back and forth until there is nothing left but a few scallions in a pool of mustard-laced vinaigrette. I'm tempted to compare the experience to the times Zach and I had picnics along the Schuylkill River or Lake Carnegie, but I decide comparing the two experiences is a futile exercise. Like the brownies, one experience isn't better than the other. They're just different. And if I don't stop comparing every guy I meet to Zach instead of judging him on his own merits, I'm going to drive myself crazy.

As we eat, we watch a series of eights row by on the river, the oars splayed like the legs of a bug, moving in sync as the boats glide through the water toward the Key Bridge. From this distance, the movement looks effortless, like a knife cutting through a stick of softened butter. The boats press onward, the bows cutting through the stillness of the water until they disappear beneath the bridge. I cannot see the effort involved in propelling them forward—the contorted faces, the blistered hands, the throbbing veins, and rivers of sweat. From this distance, all I can see is the illusion of grace.

Jeremy wipes his hands on a paper napkin and takes another sip of beer. "So tell me about this big story you're working on."

His words cut through the peaceful tableau in front of me, and my throat tightens. Of course he would ask about the story. After this morning, who wouldn't?

"It's okay if you don't want to tell me," he says.

"It's just . . . complicated."

"I get it. Trust me. I used to be a journalist, remember?"

I let out a nervous laugh. "Yeah."

"I guess I was a little surprised you hadn't mentioned it before. Charles made it sound like a big deal."

"Charles is good at that. He once pitched a story on winterizing your pets as if it were worthy of a Pulitzer."

Jeremy laughs. "Ah, so consider the source, huh?"

"Something like that."

He picks at the Brauer's Brew label on his beer bottle and then takes another sip. "Well, like I said, we don't have to talk about it. I was just curious."

The spicy slaw gnaws at the lining of my stomach. I should tell him. I know I should tell him. He has opened the door, giving me the perfect opportunity to come clean, and all I have to do is walk through it. But I can't. Every time I open my mouth to speak, the words get caught in my throat. I could pretend my hesitation stems from the sensitivity of the story or the fact that he could warn his bosses or Green Grocers. But the main reason I can't bring myself to tell him about the story is because he is the first guy with whom I've felt a real connection in five years, and I'm too afraid of losing him.

"I'll tell you all about it sometime," I finally say. "Just not right now."

"Okay." He picks again at the label on his bottle. "I hope you feel like you can tell me things."

"I do."

"Yeah? Because . . . I don't know. You seem pretty private about stuff. This story, that guy Zach. I realize my Wikipedia entry probably doesn't make me sound like the most trustworthy guy, but you can trust me. I promise."

I study his face as he stares at me, the pink light from the setting sun casting a warm glow on his angular cheekbones and narrow chin. "I do trust you," I say. Then, before I can stop myself, I say, "You can trust me, too."

Jeremy smiles. "Good. I'm glad."

I tear my eyes from his and look out over the river, and as another boat disappears beneath the bridge, I wonder when I became such a good liar.

CHAPTER 34

I am a horrible person. After everything Zach and I went through, after all the lies he told me, how can I lie to Jeremy and then look him in the eye and tell him he can trust me?

What I have to remind myself is that this story is bigger than Jeremy and me. It's bigger than a job at the *Chronicle*. It's about fraud and the public interest, the same issues behind the story I didn't cover six years ago and should have. And anyway, technically I'm not actually lying to Jeremy. I'm just holding back the truth for a little while.

That said, I don't want this story to screw him royally when someone connects the dots and realizes he must be the whistleblower in question. Which is why, the Monday after my picnic with Jeremy, I call Stu and ask him to take my name off the story when it runs.

"Why would you want to do that?" he asks.

"Having my name on the story could get my source into a lot of trouble. People have seen us together. It wouldn't be all that difficult for his bosses to trace the story back from me to him. I don't want to expose him."

"But if we remove your name, no one will know you were the one who broke it," Stu says.

"You'll know. Your managing editor will know. Anyone who would hire me at the *Chronicle* would know. This isn't about getting the credit. It's about exposing a cover-up."

Stu hesitates. "Okay. If you're sure."

"I'm sure," I say.

And I am. It's the only plan that makes sense. The public will know the truth, right will triumph over wrong, I will get credit from the editors at the *Chronicle,* and Jeremy's identity will remain a secret. Everyone wins.

Stu and I keep working on the story separately, looping back to crosscheck our findings and pull everything together. After some nudging, Pete Hamilton, Everly Foods' former IT guy, sends me a copy of DNA test results showing that, between March and July of last year, Green Grocers' frozen beef bourguignon, lasagna, and chili con carne all contained horsemeat. Apparently after his friend Katherine got fired, Pete did a little digging of his own and found that his brother-in-law worked at the lab responsible for Everly's DNA tests, giving him a way to wangle a copy. The whole situation feels very cloak-and-dagger, and though I'm sure some reporters would find this story exhilarating, I can't wait to get it off my plate. I'd much rather be writing about heirloom apples.

While I work with Pete, Stu finds out more about Everly's Chinese supplier, and though we can't get anyone from the Chinese processor to go on the record, we do find information related to other problems at their processing plants, which bolsters my story. By the last full week in May, all we need are statements from Louis Frieback and Bob Young, and we're ready to roll.

The Monday I plan to call Everly Foods, Stu and I run through the questions I'll ask Louis Frieback, assuming I actually get him to talk to me. We both know there's a good chance that won't happen, but I have to be ready, just in case.

My palms sweat as I give a final look over my questions, but as I prepare to dial Everly Foods, my phone rings. It's Libby. She has called no fewer than eight times in the last twenty-four hours, but between working at the farmers' market and preparing for these last two interviews, I have ignored her. I am about to ignore her this time, too, when her name pops up on my computer requesting a video chat. And, as if that cacophony of rings weren't enough, she pings me with an instant message:

LadyLibRT: I know you're there. Pick up.

I have no idea how she knows that, but then I have never been able to figure out how Libby knows what she knows or does what she does. She possesses an uncanny ability to pin people down and call their bluffs, and yet she has chosen to use this skill solely in a social setting and never in a professional one. I've long suspected she would make a better journalist than I'll ever be, but she has never shown any interest—not in journalism, not in law, not in anything that would involve a lot of studying or hard work. She has always seen her intelligence as a burden rather than a boon, a trait that would push men away instead of reeling them in. She prefers to trade on her good looks and athleticism rather than her cunning and wits, a choice I've never understood, probably because it's one I never had the luxury of making.

I consider ignoring all of her calls and pings, but then I realize she will only keep bugging me until I pick up, and the last thing I need is my little sister interrupting an interview with a major food distributor.

"Fine, you win," I say as I answer the phone. "What do you want?"

"Ha! I knew you were there."

"I'm here, and I'm busy."

"Doing what? Selling blueberry scones?"

"Are you trying to get me to hang up on you? Because if you are, you're doing a great job."

She groans. "You sound like Mom."

"This coming from her clone."

"I'm not her clone. Especially not lately. Did you know I found an application on her counter for a job at Sur La Table? I mean, what the hell? Why would she need a job at Sur La Table?"

"I don't know—maybe because you want to spend two thousand dollars on chairs for your wedding?"

"Again with the chairs! Why is everyone up my ass about those freaking chairs?"

"I'm not having this conversation again. Sorry."

She lets out a sigh. "Whatever. That's not even why I'm calling."

"Then why are you calling? Please: Enlighten me."

"I'm worried Matt might be cheating on me."

I sit up in my chair, my pen clasped tightly in my hand. "Oh my God. Why? What happened?"

She hesitates. "I found an earring."

"Where?"

"On his nightstand."

"And you're sure it isn't yours?"

She clicks her tongue. "Sydney, seriously..."

"Okay, well, let's think this through. Maybe there's another explanation."

"Like what?"

I fiddle with my pen. I'm the last person to excuse infidelity, but given how much my parents have already spent on this wedding, I really hope Libby is mistaken.

"Like...maybe it belongs to one of the other lawyers at his firm," I say, "and it fell off during a meeting and ended up in his briefcase."

"Then why would it be on his nightstand?"

I try to come up with an answer, but I can't. "I don't know. It doesn't make sense. Have you confronted him about it?"

"Not yet. I'm not sure what to say."

"Uh, how about, 'Why the hell is there a random earring on your nightstand?'"

"And what if he says he slept with someone else?"

"Well, for a start, you cancel the wedding."

"I can't do that."

"Seriously? You'd have Mom and Dad pay thousands of dollars for a wedding with a guy who's cheating on you?"

"People make mistakes. You said so yourself. Remember?"

I glance up at the ceiling. "If you've already decided you aren't going to do anything about this, then why are we having this conversation?"

"Because I'm confused. I need advice."

"What do your other friends say?"

"You're the only one I've told."

"Why? Because my ex-boyfriend cheated on me, too?"

"No. Because . . ." She takes a deep breath. "Because you're my big sister, and you know me better than anyone, and I respect your opinion more than anyone else's. Okay?"

I sit back in my chair, momentarily stunned by Libby's praise. "Okay," I finally say.

She gives a long whimper. "So you really think I should confront him?"

"I do."

She goes quiet for a few moments. "I don't think I realized how much the Zach thing must have hurt. It must've been pretty horrible."

I stare down at the notepad in front of me. "It was."

"I'm sorry if I wasn't there for you."

"You were."

"Not as much as I could have been. With Zach . . . I don't know. I guess I always resented him a little bit."

"For what?"

"For stealing my big sister."

I lay my pen next to my notepad, Libby's distrust and dislike of Zach finally coming into focus. It's not as if she and I were attached at the hip until Zach came along. But she was only eleven when he and I met, at which point I spent a lot more time at his house than I did at my own. Part of me assumed Libby didn't want me around—that I wasn't cool enough for her, that she wanted Mom to herself—but maybe I had it wrong. Maybe she clung to Mom because she couldn't cling to me.

A bout of silence hangs between us, and I pull the phone away from my ear to see if Libby is still there. "Lib? You still there?"

"I'm here. Listen, could you not tell Mom and Dad about this?"

"It's not my news to tell."

"Great. Thanks."

"But if he cheated on you . . . you need to address the issue somehow. It isn't fair to ask them to bankroll a marriage that's already headed for divorce."

"I know. I just...I need a little time. But you promise you won't say anything?"

Her question dangles in the air, one in a long list of secrets I've been asked to keep over the past few months: my dad's job loss, my mom's job search, the Green Grocers pilot project, the horsemeat scandal. I hate secrets, the way they eat me up inside and cloud my judgment, the way they make me lie to people I care about. I hate that I can't unknow them, that I can't talk about them or get help in making sense of them. But Libby is my baby sister, and she trusts me, so I take a deep breath and say, "Yeah, I promise," because at least that's something true.

Two days later, I decide: Tonight is the night. The night I will tell Jeremy the truth. The night I will tell him about the "big story" I've been working on. I've waited as long as I can—probably too long—but now that I've taken my name off the story, there is no reason to wait any longer. I have to tell him, and I have to do it tonight.

In the afternoon, before I head out for my weekly Wednesday shift at the Foggy Bottom farmers' market, I check my in-box to see if I have any updates from Jeremy on our plans for this evening. I don't. I do, however, have an e-mail from the Everly Foods' PR team. As predicted, the one-on-one interview with Louis Frieback will not happen. Instead, they send me the following formal statement:

> "Everly identified the responsible Chinese supplier
> and immediately informed all recipients of
> contaminated products. We have terminated our
> business relationship with the aforementioned
> supplier and can confirm all current products meet
> the highest quality standards."

I call Stu Abbott right away, and when I read him the full statement over the phone, he laughs. "So, in a nutshell: We told Green Grocers there was a problem; it's not our fault they didn't tell you."

"Pretty much."

"Let's get Green Grocers on the record, and after legal has given this a once-over, I think we're ready to roll. How does next Friday sound for a publication date?"

"Sounds perfect," I say.

I hang up with Stu and immediately put in a call to Green Grocers, which—if I had to guess—incites total pandemonium behind the scenes. The call with the head of media relations is short and to the point, but her clipped, sharp tone confirms what I both hoped and feared: They are in deep doo-doo.

While I wait for someone at the company to respond, I set off for Foggy Bottom. The afternoon is busy but otherwise uneventful, and once I've helped Rick break down the tent and pack up the truck, I head to Marvin, a bistro three blocks from my apartment. That's where I've asked Jeremy to meet me, and where I will finally tell him about the horsemeat story. I'm nervous about how he might respond—okay, I'm borderline terrified—but now that his bosses won't be able to trace the story back to him, his reaction won't be *that* bad . . . right?

I am the first to arrive, so I slide into one of the plush leather banquettes and order a glass of Malbec, which I sip as I watch waiters shuttle back and forth from the kitchen to the bar. The décor is part pub, part bistro, with dark wood furniture and floors, butter-colored walls, and candlelit tables. The wall across from me displays a huge stylized portrait of Marvin Gaye, a former DC resident and the restaurant's namesake, and the air around me fills with the percussive sound of clanking silverware and the guttural *ooh* and *ahh* of James Brown, whose soulful voice hums through the restaurant's speakers.

I drink half my glass of wine before Jeremy arrives, and when he does, he pushes toward my table with a distressed look on his face, his tie askew and his hair in disarray.

"Sorry I'm late," he says as he dumps his briefcase on the floor and tosses his phone on the table. "This day—don't get me started."

"What happened?"

"I don't want to talk about it." He waves down the waiter. "Double Maker's Mark."

"Neat?"

"Neat."

The waiter heads for the bar, and I bring my glass to my lips and take a sip. "That's a serious drink order."

"After the day I've had? You're lucky I'm not ordering a triple."

A moment later the waiter returns with Jeremy's drink, which Jeremy throws back in one swig.

"Are you okay?" I ask.

He places the glass on the table and runs his hands through his hair. "Not really."

"Why? What happened?"

He lets out a sigh and rolls his empty glass around in his hand. "Apparently the *Chronicle* is running a story on Green Grocers and the horsemeat scandal."

My breath shortens. I open my mouth to speak, to tell him everything I came here to tell him tonight, but the words get stuck in my throat, and I sit across from him in stunned silence. Why can't I tell him? What is wrong with me?

"The timing couldn't be worse," he says. "My project was just coming together, and now . . ." He trails off.

I clear my throat, making a second attempt to speak, but before I can say anything, Jeremy's phone rings and buzzes on the table. He glances down and sighs. "Sorry, I have to take this."

He picks up the phone and presses it against his ear, but when the noise around us becomes too loud for him to hear, he rushes out of the restaurant. I watch through the front window as he paces back and forth, alternately running his fingers through his hair and rubbing his chin. After he has been outside for a good five minutes, he hangs up, comes back inside, and grabs his briefcase off the floor.

"I hate to do this, but I have to go."

"Now? What's going on?"

"Green Grocers has called us in for crisis management. I'm on the last flight out to Chicago tonight."

"Tonight? You're kidding."

"I wish I were. They want all hands on deck. I'm going to see what I can do to salvage the farmers' market partnership, and the other guys are going to work to minimize reputational damage when the story comes out." He takes a deep breath and lets it out slowly. "This is really bad, Sydney. Really, really bad."

"Not necessarily . . ."

"Yes, necessarily. Bob Young is panicking. The company's stock is about to take a huge hit. My bosses are up my ass, asking if I said anything. It's a total disaster—not just for the company but potentially for me, too." He glances at his watch. "I need to get out of here. I'll call when I can."

He leans in and kisses me, his soft lips pressing gently against mine. I pull away and fix my eyes on his. I want to tell him the truth—*It's my story! I found your e-mails! This is all for the greater good!*—but the words get caught in my throat again, and I can't.

"I'll text when I land, okay? Man, whoever leaked this story from within Green Grocers is about to get into some *serious* trouble."

He gives me another peck on the forehead and then rushes out, leaving me at the table alone. And that's when I realize Green Grocers isn't the only one who's screwed. Apparently I am, too.

CHAPTER 35

Everything is spiraling out of control. I should have told Jeremy the truth, but I panicked, and I didn't, and now he is in Chicago, and he is angry, and everything is terrible.

Heidi, of course, finds all of this endlessly amusing, a point she emphasizes repeatedly as we work together at the farmers' market Saturday morning.

"Didn't I tell you this would go nuclear?"

"You did."

"If you'd stuck with Drew like I suggested, you wouldn't be in this quandary."

I unload a stack of buttery shortbread into a basket. "If I'd stuck with Drew, I'd be telling you about the short-tailed albatross and habitat loss."

"What's wrong with that?"

"Nothing. But I wouldn't have a story on the front page of the *Washington Chronicle*." I dust my hands on my jeans. "And I wouldn't be with someone who makes me as happy as Jeremy does."

"If he finds out you snooped through his stuff and wrote the story, my guess is you will soon be very *un*happy."

"Not necessarily. I still have time to fix this."

"How? By developing a time machine?"

I glare at her as I heave a crate of cinnamon raisin bread onto the table. "Remind me not to come to you for sympathy."

She breaks off a small piece of one of Rick's snickerdoodles and pops it into her mouth. "Do you want sympathy or honesty?"

"Both."

"Listen, it's hard to have a lot of sympathy when you went into this with your eyes open. It's not as if you walked into Jeremy's bedroom, and those e-mails jumped out and attacked you. You didn't have to take photos of them."

"But people have a right to know the truth. It was the responsible thing to do."

She hands me a piece of cookie. "Sure. But that was your choice. And it was your choice not to tell him and then to take your name off the story. I'm not saying those were the wrong choices, but I'm also not going to feel sorry for you for making them."

I take the piece of cookie from Heidi's hand and stuff it in my mouth. "Fair enough."

"Hey, what the hell are you two doing?"

I whirl around and face Rick, my mouth covered in cakey snickerdoodle crumbs.

"Are you eating my freaking cookies?" he says.

"It fell on the ground," I lie.

He grunts. "Well, get back to work. I want this table ready in the next ten minutes. Got it?"

I hurry my way through unloading crate after crate: carrot cupcakes, strawberry ricotta muffins, blueberry lemon pound cake, oatmeal raisin cookies. The early morning clouds break around eight o'clock, and the warm, late-May sun shines bright in the pale blue sky, casting shadows from our tent down the winding dirt path. When the bell rings at nine, the market is already teeming with hungry shoppers, who stroll up and down the market thoroughfare, curly carrot tops and wild garlic scapes peeking out from their canvas bags. A customer passes carrying a box filled with baskets of strawberries, and the sweet smell of fresh berries trails behind him like perfume.

By ten o'clock, we've sold nearly half the chocolate chip cookies and almost all of the oatmeal raisin cookies, so I consolidate the two into one basket. As I bend down to tuck the empty one beneath the table, I see a pair of feet approach and stop in front of where I am squatting.

"Sydney?"

My fingers begin to tremble at the sound of a familiar voice, a smooth baritone I haven't heard in years. I study the pair of feet in front of me, the size ten Nikes pointing at me, the bows of the laces staring at me like eyes. Only when my quads begin to burn from squatting do I realize I've been holding my breath.

I slowly bring myself to a standing position, and as my head rises above the stack of blueberry lemon loaves, Zach's face comes into view.

"Hey," he says. "I hoped I'd find you here."

He flashes a smile, the same goofy, sideways grin he had when we were fourteen-year-olds making out in his parents' basement. He still has the same doe eyes, big and round and dark as chocolate truffles, but his pin-straight hair, which for so many years stuck up in front with an unruly cowlick, is smoothed in a conservative side part. I'd be lying if I said I haven't tried checking up on him on Facebook over the years, but since I de-friended him, I've been limited in what I can see. Having his face so close to mine—those eyes, that smile—takes my breath away.

An uncomfortable silence hangs between us as we stare at each other, my heart racing in my chest.

"It's been a while," he finally says.

"Five years," I manage to say, my voice tight.

He nods. "Yeah. I know."

I stand stiff behind the basket of cookies, unable to move or speak. Every time I think about opening my mouth to say something, a thick lump develops in my throat, and the words dissolve into dust. What do you say to the person who broke your heart? Who never gave you a proper good-bye? Who screwed you up for life?

"So . . . I'm living in DC now," he says after another protracted silence. "Moved down last weekend from New York. I start my new job at DOJ on Monday."

I nod, my lips pressed together. The one saving grace of our breakup was that he was in New York and I was in Philly, then DC, so I never had to worry about running into him. The idea of living in the same city is pretty much the worst thing I can imagine.

"Listen," he says, after I've stood in silence for a good three minutes, letting him fumble in the awkwardness. "This isn't a coincidence, me running into you here. When I knew I'd be moving to DC, I Googled you. I saw you were writing the farmers' market newsletter and worked here. I wanted to see you again—needed to see you again."

"Why?"

"Because I've been thinking about you. A lot, actually. I've had plenty of time to think over the past five years. What I did to you was really shitty. I still feel bad about it."

"You should," I say.

"I do." He glances at his feet, then back up at me. "And I'm sorry."

Those words—the words I've longed to hear him say for years—send a chill up my spine. "A little late for that, isn't it?"

"I guess. But I've changed."

"Good for you."

He takes a deep breath and presses his hands together. "I miss you, Sydney. I miss my best friend."

I blink to keep my eyes from welling up with tears. "Yeah, well..." I trail off.

"I was hoping... Well, do you think we could grab a cup of coffee after the market? Just to talk."

"I have nothing to say to you."

"Then you can just listen. Because I have a lot I want to say to you."

I tear my eyes away from his. "I'm busy. Heidi and I already have plans."

"What about tomorrow?"

"I'm busy then, too."

"Monday?"

I let out an exasperated sigh. "What aren't you getting? I don't want to talk to you."

He takes a deep breath and fixes his dark brown eyes on mine.

"Okay. Then how about this: My new boss gave me two tickets to the orchestra next week as a welcome gift, and I don't have anyone to go with. Why don't you come with me? That way we don't even have to talk—we can just listen to the music, like old times."

"Zach . . ."

"Please. I'm not asking you to forgive me. Just . . . don't shut me out."

I gaze into his eyes, my heart racing wildly in my chest. Why should I give him a second chance? Has he earned it? Does he deserve it? My gut tells me no: I should run as far away from him as I can. Inviting him back into my life is only asking for trouble. But as I run my eyes across his face, the face I loved so deeply for so many years, the face that has tortured me in my thoughts and dreams, my resolve crumbles.

"Okay," I finally say. "Okay," because apparently I hate myself.

CHAPTER 36

"I'm sorry, *WHAT?*"

Libby's high-pitched shriek blasts through my phone, nearly deafening me.

"Zach is taking me to the Kennedy Center next Thursday. They're playing Berlioz's *Symphonie Fantastique.*"

"I don't care if they're playing *Symphonie Orgasmique.* This is the worst idea I've ever heard. EVER."

"Somehow I doubt that."

"Well, I mean, honestly. I can't be the only one who feels this way. Did you tell Heidi? What does she think?"

"She's . . . not a fan."

In fact, Heidi's exact words were, "Why don't you just go stab yourself in the chest with Rick's rusty bread knife? It'll be faster and less painful."

"See?" Libby grumbles. "Heidi agrees with me. Anyone in his or her right mind would agree with me. This is ridiculous. Zach is a lying, cheating asshole. Why would you forgive him so easily?"

"I'm not forgiving him. We're just going to the orchestra."

"Oh. Right. 'Just' the orchestra. And then it will 'just' be his apartment. And then 'just' his bed."

"It isn't like that, Libby. I swear."

"Then what is it like?"

"Everyone deserves a second chance."

"No, they don't."

"Oh, really? And what about Matt?"

She hesitates. "That's different."

"How?"

"I don't even know whether Matt did anything wrong."

"You still haven't confronted him?"

"Not yet."

"Okay, and what if he did do something wrong?"

"It's still different."

"Why? Because it's you and not me?"

"Because it's you and Zach. There's too much history there."

I let out a bitter laugh. "Are you joking? You and Matt are *engaged*."

"So?"

I rest my forehead on my hand and let out a loud groan. "You know what? Never mind. I'm sorry I told you."

"You're only sorry because I'm not telling you it's a great idea. It's a terrible fucking idea, and you know it, and when he breaks your heart a second time, you'll have no one to blame but yourself."

"Hey, Lib? This is me hanging up. Good-bye."

I end the call and throw my phone on my couch, wishing for once I had a regular landline so that I could actually slam the phone down with force. I don't know what makes me angrier: that Libby is probably right, or that the irony of her admonition is completely lost on her. What gives her the right to choose who gets a second chance and who doesn't? What makes her so freaking special?

Heidi, of course, happens to share Libby's view, though Heidi also believes Jeremy never deserved a second chance either after his professional misdeeds. Frankly, the only person she encourages me to give a second chance to is Drew, the only man among the three with a conflict-free past and, whether despite or because of this, the only one in whom I no longer have any interest.

As I navigate my way through my very own soap opera, Green

Grocers finally sends me a statement Wednesday afternoon, adding more fuel to my emotional firestorm.

> Green Grocers has always prided itself on the quality of its products and the integrity of its people. Unfortunately, we and one of our suppliers have let down our customers, and for that we are sorry. The lapse in quality standards lasted for an isolated period of time, and we have since resolved the issue and are working hard to ensure such a lapse never occurs again.

The statement doesn't say whether Bob Young will remain CEO, but when I follow up to ask, the PR representative gives me a typically formal response about how the company stands behind its leaders—which, in my experience, companies do until they don't.

With Green Grocers' statement in hand, I finish writing up my story and shoot it off to Stu Abbott, who calls me in an excited tizzy a few hours later.

"We're good to go," he says. "Legal is looking it over right now, but so far everything looks solid. We should be all set for Friday. Oh, and I'm going to help Charles with a piece for *The Morning Show* as part of our content-sharing agreement. He has some . . . interesting ideas."

"He usually does . . ."

To be honest, I'd forgotten about Charles. Now that my name isn't on the story, he'll probably claim the whole thing was his idea.

"But you'll be happy to know my managing editor is thrilled with the story," Stu says. "Once the dust settles, she wants to discuss bringing you on board in a more serious way."

"Really?"

"Really. She's also impressed with your morals—taking your own name off the story to protect your source. That shows integrity." He lets out a contented sigh. "You're a good apple, Sydney Strauss. We'd be lucky to have you as part of our team."

My gut sours as his words echo in my ears, the words "morals" and "integrity" ringing like sirens, and as I hang up, I have to wonder: If I'm such a good apple, then why do I feel so unquestionably rotten?

Later that evening, Jeremy calls me for the first time in a week.

"Finally coming up for air?" I say, trying to mask the nervous edge in my voice. We've texted and e-mailed since he left, but without hearing his voice, I haven't been able to gauge how work is going or whether he knows about my involvement with the horsemeat story. I still want to tell him myself, in person, but the longer he stays in Chicago, the harder that becomes.

"Kind of," he says. "It's total chaos over here."

"Yeah?"

"To be honest, I don't know half of what's going on. We're all working in silos. All I know is I've been busting my ass for the past week, trying to salvage this pilot program, and from what I'm hearing, it's probably going to fall through anyway."

My heart sinks. "Really?"

"That's the buzz around the office. I mean, publicly, they'll say all projects are going forward as planned, but internally they'll just keep postponing and postponing until everything falls through. Which, considering how hard I've worked, really pisses me off."

"Wouldn't it make more sense for them to go forward with the program? So they could point to something good they're doing to take the spotlight off the horsemeat scandal?"

"One would think. But I don't make the decisions. I just do what I'm told. All I know is the *Chronicle* plans to run the story Friday, so I'm heading back to DC tomorrow night." He lets out a long sigh. "But enough about me. I've missed you. Maybe we can grab a drink after I land tomorrow night."

A knot develops in my chest. Tomorrow night I'm supposed to meet Zach at the Kennedy Center. "What time are you supposed to land?"

"Not sure. I think around nine? I can give you a call when I get in."

"Okay. Sure." Given that the performance begins at seven, I can make that work. And anyway, it will be good to have an excuse to get away from Zach—and to have a chance to talk to Jeremy in person before the story comes out.

"Great. I could use some Sydney time. I meant to tell you before I left, but everything was so crazy. . . . The past few months have been really special. Ever since I met you, my life has been . . . I don't know. Better. Fuller. I know that sounds cheesy, but I mean it. I'm the happiest I've been in a really long time."

His words swell inside me and fill me alternately with joy and terror, seeming to sweep me away and knock me down at the same time. My hand shakes as I press the phone against my ear, my palms slick and my heart racing.

"Me too," I say.

I'm not sure what scares me more: the fact that those words are true, or that in two days, they might not be.

CHAPTER 37

In less than twenty-four hours, my story will be on the front page of the *Washington Chronicle*. In less than twelve hours, it will be up on the Web site. And in less than six hours, I will meet Zach at the Kennedy Center.

There is not a silo of Pepto-Bismol big enough to get me through this day.

I manage to find someone to cover my shift at the Penn Quarter farmers' market, giving me ample time to prepare physically and mentally for tonight's potentially calamitous meeting with Zach. I try not to let Libby's and Heidi's negativity infiltrate my psyche, but I am not very successful. What if they're right? What if this is a huge mistake?

The problem is that even if it is, I cannot stop myself from making it. Zach is my kryptonite. When I look at him, I don't see twenty-six-year-old Zach, with a sleek side part and laugh lines and a law degree under his belt. I see fourteen-year-old Zach, the one I fell in love with, the one who bought me my first bouquet of roses and sent me my first box of chocolates. Maybe if I could see him through some other lens, I wouldn't have agreed to this rendezvous, but it is impossible for me to look at him without getting bitten by the nostalgia bug. If I'm being honest with myself, I didn't agree to this meeting because I wanted to give him a second chance; I wanted to give a second chance to myself, a second chance to *us*.

I spend most of the day working myself into a borderline psychotic lather, trying on no fewer than six outfits and five hairstyles. I wish I didn't care so much about how I look this evening, but part of me wants Zach to see what he has been missing the past five years. Admittedly, if I were being more forthright about the situation, I would show up braless, in sweatpants, with unshaven legs and a seriously questionable bikini line. But he doesn't need to know I let myself go in his absence. What he needs to see is Sexy Sydney, the woman he could have had if he hadn't foolishly thrown it all away.

Somewhere around five thirty, between vetoing a black shift dress and squeezing into a too-tight pair of gray capri pants, I realize I haven't eaten anything but a bowl of cereal all day. I scan my refrigerator, which offers precious little in terms of lunch or dinner options, but I spot leftover chicken salad sitting in the back corner of the top shelf. I lift off the lid of the Tupperware and take a whiff. It doesn't smell . . . bad, per se, but it doesn't smell particularly good either. I bought it from Whole Foods before Jeremy left for Chicago, which means it is more than a week old.

As I stare at the limp lettuce, my phone buzzes on my countertop. A text from Jeremy:

Flight running on time. See you in a few hours?

I pick up the phone and reply:

Sure. Talk to you soon.

Then I grab a fork, stab at the salad, and shovel a huge helping into my mouth. Because tonight I'm going to need all the sustenance I can get.

Due either to the mild weather or a temporary lapse in sanity, or possibly both, I decide to walk to the Kennedy Center from my apartment. It's a straight shot down New Hampshire Avenue, crossing through Dupont and Washington Circles, but I am Sydney, the least fit woman in Washington, and so halfway through the journey it becomes abundantly clear I have made a huge mistake. Sweat stains have already begun to develop beneath the arms of the gray silk top I so carefully chose, and thanks to the light June breeze that blows my hair to and fro, the front strands of my hair are caked in sticky lip gloss.

I eventually pass the Watergate building, whose curved rows of white concrete and dark windows make it look like a lumbering spacecraft, and wind my way toward the Kennedy Center, located around the corner. I hurry up the wide steps and head for the entrance, taking cover beneath the soaring, hundred-foot overhang. The building is rectangular in shape, made of white Carrara marble, and lies along the Potomac River, just beyond the National Mall. At night, a series of lights sets the white marble exterior aglow, and from a distance, the building appears to hover atop the flickering water. Heidi, never missing an opportunity for snark, likes to call it "the Kleenex box on the Potomac."

I push through the glass doors and head down the magnificent main hallway, where the ceiling rises sixty-three feet and a plush red carpet extends from end to end. Flags from around the world dangle on either side of the hall, abutted by smooth gold columns, which lead toward the main lobby. The lobby stretches six hundred feet, set parallel to the Potomac, and features floor-to-ceiling windows, which look out onto the river and a broad terrace, where patrons often gather at intermission. A small crowd of concert attendees congregates in front of the refreshment stand, buying snacks and wine before the concert begins, but, as far as I can tell, Zach is not among them.

I scan the vast lobby from end to end, searching for Zach's face among the swarm of guests, but I do not see him anywhere. I cool my heels beneath the elongated crystal chandeliers, glancing at my watch as my stomach gurgles from a combination of leftover salad and nerves. He wouldn't bail without telling me, would he? I'm not sure what makes me feel sicker: the thought of his not showing, or the realization of how much I care.

As I wait, I pull out my phone and refresh the *Washington Chronicle* Web site. No sign of my story yet. Stu said it wouldn't be up until ten o'clock, but something in my gut tells me that in the age of *get there first* reporting, he will post it earlier if he can. Even though no one else will know the story is mine, I'll know, and part of me won't believe any of this is real until I see my work in print on the *Chronicle*'s site. Some days all of this feels like a strange dream.

Finally, at 6:45, I spot Zach hurrying down the main hallway. He clutches a briefcase in one hand and a huge bouquet of red roses in the other, the same sort of roses he used to send me every year on our anniversary. My knees weaken as he approaches, his golden yellow tie bright and shiny against his pale blue oxford shirt.

"Sorry I'm late," he says. He extends the flowers in my direction. "These are for you."

I take the roses from his hand and lift them to my nose, trying to mask my quivering lip. Why did he have to bring roses? Why does he get to be the good guy?

"Thanks," I say, gripping the crinkly cellophane.

He studies my face. "Your makeup looks nice. I like the navy eyeliner."

My cheeks flush. I know he means that as a compliment, or at least I think he does, but somehow pointing out that I'm wearing makeup—that I cared about how I looked tonight, that maybe I even tried a little too hard—rubs me the wrong way.

"Thanks," I say again.

He scratches his temple, then glances down at his watch. "Should we head inside, or do you want a glass of wine?"

"We should probably find our seats."

He nods. "Let me just grab the tickets."

He reaches into his briefcase, and as he searches for them, I glance at my phone again. Still no sign of the story.

"You got somewhere else you need to be?" he says with a smirk as I flick through my phone.

I look up. "Sorry. No. I just . . . It's a work thing."

"Did Old MacDonald lose his chickens or something?"

I bristle. "No. It's a story I've been working on."

"You're still writing? About what?"

"Food stuff."

He grins. "That's my girl."

His girl. Since when am I his girl?

A loud chime interrupts my train of thought—*do, mi, so*—an ascending arpeggio that rings throughout the lobby to encourage us to take our seats. Zach glances over his shoulder. "We'd better take our seats before they close the doors. Come on."

As we hurry down the hallway, he gently rests his hand on the small of my back, and I feel myself shrink away. I'm not ready for him to touch me yet. Merely being in the same room as him is more than I can handle.

We run up the carpeted steps toward the usher, who points us to the right, and as the chime sounds again, Zach grabs my hand and rushes us toward the stairs to the first-tier seats. I yank my arm free.

"Stop," I say.

Zach slows his step. "Stop what?"

"The flowers, the touching, the hand-holding—just . . . *stop.*"

He flushes and raises his hands defensively. "Sorry. I was trying to be nice."

"Well, don't."

"Don't be nice?"

"No . . . what I mean is . . ." I stop in front of the stairway and let out a sigh. "We can't just pick up where we left off."

"I know."

"Do you?"

"Sure. I screwed up. I know that."

Part of me wishes this admission of fault were enough, that I could leave the past in the past and give us both a fresh start. But I can't. Letting him off with a bouquet of roses makes all of my tears and pain seem silly and pointless, and that isn't fair. He hurt me. That was real. And even if that doesn't matter to him, it matters to me.

I am about to tell him all of this when the chime sounds for a final time.

"Come on," he says. "We can talk about this during intermission."

We run up the stairs side by side, and when we reach the top, the first-tier usher directs us to our seats. We slide past two other couples before sinking into our plush velvet seats, and I slide my roses into my tote and lay the bag at my feet. Zach looks over at me, but I can't bring myself to make eye contact right now. There is so much I want to say to him, but I can't say it here, now, and I refuse to let him disarm me with a touch or a gentle smile. So instead, I root through my tote and, since it's been fifteen minutes since I looked at the *Chronicle*'s site, I check my phone one last time.

And that's when I see it, on the landing page of the *Washington Chronicle*:

GREEN GROCERS' CEO IMPLICATED IN HORSEMEAT SCANDAL

By Sydney Strauss and Stu Abbott

My stomach curdles.

Oh my God.

Oh. My. God.

No. No, no, no, no, no. This can't be happening. *My name.* Stu told me he removed it. He *told* me. But when I click on the link, there it is again: *Sydney Strauss and Stu Abbott,* our names sitting like a crown above our thousand-word bombshell. The story has been up for fifteen minutes, which means for a quarter of an hour, anyone with an Internet connection could see my name attached to this story. Anyone in the world. Anyone at Green Grocers.

My heart races, but before I can contemplate what this means—for me, for my career, for Jeremy—the lights dim. A hush falls over the crowd, and an announcement booms through the speakers, telling people to turn off their cell phones. I flick the silent switch on my phone, but as I do, a text from Jeremy pops up on my screen.

ARE YOU FUCKING KIDDING ME????? Can't talk now, about to take off, but WHAT THE FUCK?

All the blood drains from my face as the room darkens, and the crowd bursts into applause as the violin soloist and the conductor walk on stage.

Zach rests his hand on my knee. "Everything okay?"

I stare ahead in stunned silence, my leg tingling from his touch, and as the violinist raises her bow, I reply in a strained whisper.

"No," I say. "Not at all."

CHAPTER 38

The violinist dances with her violin, bowing and bobbing in her bright green satin dress as she attacks the strings with her bow. The music surrounds me, my emotions churning and swirling with each rapid-fire arpeggio, as the music builds in speed and intensity through the first-movement cadenza. I ride each frantic scale, rising and falling and crashing into a pit of despair. No matter how loudly the horns blare and the cellos groan, they cannot drown the voice in my head shouting, "*You are so fuuuuucked!*"

How? How did my name end up on that story? And how could Jeremy have already seen it? The Green Grocers PR machine must be crapping their pants with even more gut-wrenching intensity than I thought. They probably had some intern refreshing the *Chronicle*'s site every five seconds, some lackey who e-mailed the story to everyone on their team—Jeremy, his bosses, Green Grocers' in-house department. And now, thanks to some idiot on the *Chronicle*'s Web team, they all know my name.

I can't believe this is happening.

The whirling violinist comes to a standstill, and as the tempo slows for the second movement, Zach looks at me and winks, as if to say, "Isn't this great?" But it isn't great. It's terrible. I'm on a date with my philandering ex-boyfriend, who keeps making passes at me in the hope that we can rekindle our old flame, while my current boyfriend flies through the air, most likely plotting my murder. I don't want to be here. I don't want to be anywhere, for that matter. I want to evaporate.

The conductor waves his arms in broad, billowy movements, coaxing along the strings. I have to call Stu. No, first I have to call Jeremy. The damage has already been done. Even if Stu removes my name now, Jeremy and everyone at his company have already seen it, so at this point, it hardly matters. But if I could talk to Jeremy, if I could get him on the phone, I could explain how all of this happened. He would probably still be angry—as, let's be honest, he has every right to be—but at least he would understand why I did what I did. Or if he didn't understand, at least he would know my reasoning. Whether that will make the situation better or worse, I don't know, but I can't imagine many situations worse than having him stew in his own angry juices for two hours as he flies from Chicago to Washington. Which, I remind myself, is exactly what is happening at this very moment.

The orchestra moves into the exuberant final movement, and the soloist's bow flies across her violin as she races through the upbeat melody. I glance down at my phone and notice I have twelve unread e-mails and four texts. Old professors, college friends, my parents, Charles—everyone is chiming in with kudos and praise. I surreptitiously log on to Facebook, where two people I haven't spoken with in at least four years have linked to the story and tagged me, claiming fame for themselves by association. The story has already spread like wildfire. My name is everywhere.

The music slows briefly as the violinist trills on her strings, and then the tempo begins to increase, measure by measure. The conductor waves his arms excitedly, and the violinist hugs her instrument close to her, as if the violin is speaking to her, telling her how to play. She charges toward the coda, and as the music gets faster and faster, beads of sweat form on my upper lip. I have to call Jeremy. Immediately. I know he is on a plane, and I know he won't pick up, but I have to leave a message so that when he lands, my voice is the first voice he hears, rather than that of some jerk from Green Grocers telling him I am the devil. Because I'm not the devil. I'm a good person. Aren't I?

My heart beats faster than all of the violins, which race up and down the scale together as the timpani bang excitedly in the background. The conductor stabs his baton in the direction of the orchestra as the players pound out the final three notes in unison. As soon as the stage goes silent, Zach leaps to his feet and joins the applause as the crowd cheers and shouts, "Bravo!"

Holding my phone tightly in my slick hand, I stand with Zach and the rest of the audience, my legs like jelly. I feel cold and hot at the same time, shivering and shaking as the sweat drips down my back, and the floor seems to rock back and forth. The violinist takes three encore bows, and then the crowd begins to move toward the lobby for intermission. Zach rests his hand on my back and smiles. "Pretty amazing, huh?"

I nod. I wish he would stop touching me.

"Want to have a drink on the terrace?" he says.

"Sure." Alcohol may not save me, but it certainly couldn't hurt.

While Zach waits in line, I make my way to the sprawling terrace, in the middle of which sits a huge, square fountain and two rectangular blocks of planted trees. I walk to the edge and stare out at the river, hoping the serenity of the placid water will abate my queasiness before I call Jeremy. The terrace juts out over the Rock Creek Parkway, and I close my eyes and listen to the northbound traffic whoosh below me, car after car after car, as the water in the fountain behind me spurts up and crashes down. This, unfortunately, does not make me feel better, and if anything, the cacophony of sounds makes me feel worse. I wish I could blame all of this nausea on my nerves, but I'm beginning to wonder if the week-old salad I ate was, in fact, a colossal mistake.

Since an end to my nausea is nowhere in sight, I pull out my phone and dial Jeremy. As expected, the call goes straight to voice mail.

"Jeremy—hey, it's Sydney. Listen, the horsemeat story . . . Oh God, I'm so sorry all of this happened the way it did. I've been meaning to talk to you about it, and my name wasn't even supposed to be on the story, but someone at the *Chronicle* screwed up—"

"I hope you're okay with red."

I spin around and face Zach, who is standing in front of me holding two plastic cups filled with red wine. I wave him quiet with my hand as I carry on with my message.

". . . and now everything is a mess, and . . . Oh, God, I'm so, so sorry. Please call me as soon as you get this. I really need to talk to you."

Zach hands me a cup of wine. "Who was that?"

"No one," I say.

He raises an eyebrow. "Didn't sound like no one."

I bring the cup to my lips, but the strong, musky smell turns my stomach inside out, and I pull it away. "You're right. It wasn't no one. It was the guy I've been seeing, who made me really happy before you swept into town and tried to confuse me."

"I'm not trying to confuse you."

"Then what, exactly, are you trying to do?"

He shrugs. "To make a fresh start. To do CPR on what was probably the most meaningful relationship of my life."

I bring the cup to my lips a second time, but again the smell overwhelms me, and I gag.

"Are you okay?" Zach lays the back of his hand on my forehead. "You don't look so good."

I recoil and brush his hand away. "I'm fine."

"You sure?" He sweeps my hair away from my face. "You look . . . green."

"It's just the lighting out here. I'm okay." He goes to tuck my hair behind my ear, but I whack away his arm before he can. "Stop touching me."

"Jesus, Sydney, what's your problem?"

"What's my problem? What's my *problem?*" Zach's cheeks flush as my voice rises. "Oh, I don't know. Maybe it's the fact that you broke my fucking heart. Or maybe it's the fact that you never apologized, until five years later, when you suddenly realized what a dick you'd been. Or maybe, just maybe, it's the fact that I haven't stopped thinking about you for five years—*five fucking years*—and now that you're here, I can't quite figure out why I bothered."

"What if I told you I'm still in love with you," he says.

The words land between us with a loud thud, and the air around me suddenly feels too thick to breathe.

"I . . . I . . ."

I need wine to answer that question. I force myself to take a sip, but as soon as I do, I know I've made a mistake. The wine only makes it halfway down my throat before it is met by the contents of my stomach, erupting in the opposite direction. The terrace goes blurry, and I slap my hand over my mouth to keep the chicken salad from ending up all over Zach's bright yellow tie. I have mere seconds to spare before the horrible occurs, and so, with few options left and none of them good, I stumble past Zach and charge straight ahead and, in what I am sure is a first for this illustrious institution, I throw up in the Kennedy Center fountain.

CHAPTER 39

Of all of the embarrassing moments in my life, and I have had many, none quite measures up to heaving into a fountain in front of Washington's cultural elite. Chunky bits of salad leaves spew from my mouth into the fountain's basin as the men and women around me gasp and clutch their chests and back away slowly. Zach rushes up beside me, resting his hand on my shoulder as I wipe my lips with the back of my hand. I stare down at the water and watch the half-digested scraps of cucumbers and carrots disperse in the wake created by the fountain jets.

"Do you need me to get a doctor?" Zach says.

I shake my head. I don't need a doctor. I need a magician. Or a time machine.

"I'll take you home," he says.

I shrug off his hand. "I can take care of myself."

"Sydney. You're sick. Let me help you."

"I don't need your help. It's just the salad I ate for dinner. I'll be . . . I'll be . . ."

My stomach gurgles, and I pull my hair away from my face and vomit into the fountain a second time.

"You'll be nothing," Zach says. "Stay here, and I'll talk to one of the ushers about getting us a cab."

"No—Zach, don't—"

But before I can finish my sentence, he has already left in search of an usher. And as I sit in front of the fountain, blotting the drool from my chin as the crowd stares at me with pitying eyes, I wonder if this is karma coming back to bite me in the ass and, if it is, why her teeth are so damn sharp.

The cab ride is torture.

Every bump, every turn jostles my insides, threatening to send whatever remains in my stomach onto the driver's head. At this point, I don't think I have much left to give.

As the cab flies around Washington Circle like a Tilt-a-Whirl, I hold onto the door handle and press my face against the window, hoping the cool glass will soothe my queasiness. It doesn't, but it's better than leaning on Zach's shoulder, which he offered in what I can only assume was an attempt at chivalry.

When the cab stops in front of my house, Zach pays the driver and rushes to help me out. With his arm wrapped around me, he guides me up the walkway toward my front door, carrying my tote bag on his other arm, the flowers he bought me stuffed inside. Even through my nausea, I notice Simon's doorbell is still covered by a hideous wad of silvery tape.

"What's up with the duct tape?" Zach asks as we reach the top of my front stoop.

"My downstairs neighbor. He's crazy."

Zach tries to peer through Simon's windows, which are covered with blackout shades. "What's his deal?"

"I don't know. He's just the sketchy creep who lives downstairs." I wriggle from Zach's grasp. "I can take it from here. Thanks."

"I'm not sending you up there alone. At least let me get you situated."

"I can take care of myself. I've been taking care of myself just fine for the past five years."

He sighs. "I know. But I'm here, and I want to help you."

"Too bad. I don't want your help. I'm . . ." My stomach gurgles. "I'm . . . I'm . . ." I grab the wrought-iron railing next to my front door and heave into the bushes.

"That's it. I'm taking you upstairs. Where are your keys?"

"Small pocket in the back," I groan as I grip the railing.

He rummages through my bag and eventually finds my collection of keys, which looks as if it should belong to a janitor or a jail warden.

"It's the silver one with the square top," I mutter.

He pops the key into the door and unlocks it, and then he unlocks the second door in my entryway and helps me up the flight of stairs to my apartment. When we reach the top, he removes the roses from inside my bag, sets them on the coffee table, and dumps the bag next to my couch.

"Why don't you get into bed, and I'll grab an emergency trashcan to put beside you."

"Zach, you really don't have to do this."

"I know I don't."

We lock eyes, and for a brief moment, I catch a glimpse of what we used to be, so real and raw it slices me down the middle. Then he tears his eyes away, and the moment vanishes into the air like smoke.

"So where would I find an extra trashcan around here?" he asks.

I hesitate, then relent. "Bathroom. First door on the left."

He heads off, and I pick up my tote bag and trail behind him, making my way to the bedroom, where I change into an oversize Northwestern T-shirt and a pair of red flannel shorts and crawl into bed.

Zach knocks on the door. "Okay if I come in?"

"Sure. Whatever."

He opens the door and glances around my room, a grin tattooed on his face as he studies the clothing racks lining the walls.

"It's like coat racks at a bar mitzvah," he says with a laugh. He comes around to my side of the bed, setting the bathroom trashcan beside me. "I'll be on the couch out there, so if you need anything, just give a shout."

"You're not staying."

"Of course I'm staying."

"Zach, how many times do I have to repeat myself?"

He lets out a big sigh. "You have food poisoning, and I'm worried about you. Why can't you let me take care of you?"

"Because it isn't fair."

"To whom?"

"To me. You can't just swoop in and play the hero. You haven't earned it, and you don't deserve it."

He shifts his gaze to the floor, then looks up at me. "I'm not trying to play the hero."

I pull the comforter up around my shoulders. "I don't feel like arguing about this right now."

"Then don't. Get some rest, let me crash on your couch, and we can talk about everything in the morning."

I'm about to launch into one final protest, but instead I flick off the lamp and bury my head in my pillow.

"Fine," I say, because I no longer have the energy to fight him.

The next morning, around seven thirty, I awake to the shrill buzzing of my doorbell. I wait a few seconds, hoping the sound was part of a dream, but a moment later, it buzzes again. Given my mother's penchant for sending flowers at every opportunity—birthdays, anniversaries, graduations, Tuesdays—my guess is that it's someone from 1-800-FLOWERS making a delivery to congratulate me on my story. Why the delivery man feels the need to wake me before eight in the morning, I have no idea.

Moving sluggishly and with caution, I roll out of bed, my hand pressed against my stomach, which still aches from last night's barf-fest. I haven't thrown up since 1:00 a.m., but the trashcan next to my bed reeks of bile and barf, and my hair is matted to my head, full of kinks and knots. I slip into my blue terry cloth robe and tie it loosely around my waist, taking care not to cinch my sore belly, and slide my feet into my fluffy gray slippers. Before leaving my bedroom, I take a long look at myself in the full-length mirror. If Mrs. Doubtfire and Chewbacca mated, their offspring might look something like this.

Before I leave my room, I spot my tote bag sitting next to my bed, and suddenly I panic. *Jeremy.* I rush to my bag and rummage through it in search of my phone, and when I find it, I discover I have fifteen missed calls from him and five voice mails, on top of twelve text messages, the last of which reads,

If you want to talk to me so bad, then where the hell are you?????

Oh, God. Oh, God, oh, God, oh, God.

I start calling him back when my doorbell rings for a third time. Crap. Phone pressed against my ear, I hurry toward my living room, where I find Zach sitting on my couch in his undershirt and boxers.

"Good morning," he says. "Sounds like you have a visitor."

I hustle toward the stairway. "I think it's a flower delivery from my parents. Give me one second."

Jeremy answers his phone as I rush down the front steps. "Hello?" he says.

"Jeremy—hey, it's Sydney. Listen, I'm so sorry I missed your calls last night. I got food poisoning, and my phone was on silent from being at the orchestra, and—"

I yank open my front door, expecting to see a surly delivery boy from 1-800-FLOWERS, but instead, I see Jeremy. He stands in front of me, phone in hand, face white as snow.

"I . . . oh," I stammer, letting the phone slide down my face. "I didn't realize it was you."

He stares at me in silence, his jaw tight.

I clear my throat and glance down at my furry slippers. "So . . . like I was saying . . . I got food poisoning at the orchestra last night, from a salad I bought last week, and . . . well—"

"When were you going to tell me you were working on that story?"

I gulp. "I wanted to tell you last week."

"But you didn't."

"But I wanted to."

"Oh, well, in that case: gold fucking star for you. Do you have any idea the massive amount of shit I'm in? Do you even care?"

"Of course I care. I never meant for any of this to happen."

"Yeah, getting a story on the front page of the *Washington Chron-*

icle is usually an accident. 'Whoops! There goes another thousand-word story flying out my asshole! I hate when that happens!' "

"You don't understand—my name wasn't supposed to appear on the story."

"But it did."

"But it wasn't supposed to."

He lets out a bitter laugh. "You really think that makes a difference to me at this point? How long have you been working on this story behind my back?"

I clear my throat. "About two months."

"Two *months?* How did you even get your hands on those e-mails?"

"You had copies."

"Not that I shared with you."

"You told me about them. And you didn't exactly hide them."

He glares at me. "You went snooping through my stuff?"

"Not . . . snooping, no." I play with the belt on my robe. "It was more like—"

"Sydney? Everything okay down there?" Zach calls down from the top of the stairs.

Jeremy cranes his neck in an attempt to see who it is. "Who the fuck is that?"

"Oh. That." I clear my throat. "It's kind of a long story."

"Sydney?" Zach trundles down the stairs and stops when he gets to the bottom, still dressed in his undershirt and blue-and-white plaid boxers. "Hey," he says, looking at Jeremy. "Are you the flower guy?"

"The *flower* guy?" Jeremy's expression hardens. "No, I'm not the fucking flower guy. Who the fuck are you?"

"I'm Zach."

Jeremy's eyes shift between Zach and me. "Wait, Zach? As in *Zach* Zach?"

I scratch behind my ear. "Well . . . technically . . . yes . . ."

"Perfect. Just perfect." Jeremy sticks out his jaw. "I leave town for a week, and my lying, conniving girlfriend proceeds to sabotage my career and cheat on me with the weenie she dated in college."

"Hey!" Zach says. "Watch it."

"Maybe we should move this conversation inside. . . ." I say, eyeing Simon's door.

"I'm not moving anywhere," Jeremy says.

"Neither am I," says Zach.

"Oh, see, that's where you're wrong," Jeremy says. He points up my stairway. "You're going back upstairs, putting on some damn clothes, and getting the hell out of here."

"Thanks, but I'll stay right where I am."

Jeremy's cheeks flush. "Don't make me come over there and take you upstairs myself."

"I'd like to see you try."

"Guys!"

But it's too late. Jeremy rushes toward Zach, and before I know it, the two of them are a tangled mess of limbs on my stairway. The two of them wrestle their way up my stairs—Jeremy pushing Zach, Zach bashing Jeremy's head into the railing, Jeremy heaving Zach by the waist, Zach kicking Jeremy in the shoulder. At one point I try to break them apart by throwing myself on Jeremy's back, but Jeremy just stands, wearing me like a cape, and proceeds to rip Zach's undershirt. Soon, all three of us are in my living room, my legs flailing in every direction as Jeremy and Zach grab and poke at each other like kindergarteners.

"Guys—stop! Please!"

I slide off Jeremy, and Zach backs away toward my couch, examining the rip in his shirt.

"I didn't cheat on you with Zach," I say. "I promise."

Jeremy wipes his forehead with the back of his hand and tries to catch his breath. "Why should I believe you? Why should I believe anything you say now?"

"Because it's the truth. There's nothing between Zach and me anymore."

Zach tosses his hair out of his eyes. "Bullshit."

My cheeks redden. "Bullshit? *Bullshit?* I'll tell you what's bullshit: you thinking you can waltz back into my life like nothing happened."

"I'm not waltzing in like nothing happened. That's the point. A lot happened. We have a long history. And I still love you."

The doorbell rings, its high-pitched whine filling my apartment, and someone starts banging at the front door. Now the 1-800-FLOWERS guy shows up. Of course.

"You don't even know me anymore," I say.

"Sydney, I know you better than almost anyone. Certainly better than this clown."

"Hey!" Jeremy lunges for Zach again, but I push him back with my arm.

The doorbell rings again.

"Well, I would hope someone who dated me for *eight freaking years* would know me a little better than someone who's dated me for a few months," I say. "But he knows me now—the Sydney who worked in TV news and lost her job and works at the farmers' market and had her heart broken by a guy who cheated on her with some bimbo named Georgina. You don't know that Sydney. You gave up on her a long time ago."

"You forgot to add the Sydney who used her boyfriend as a pawn in her quest for fame and fortune," Jeremy says.

More banging on the front door. "It isn't like that. I swear."

"So you didn't steal my private e-mails without permission?"

I stare at him for a long while. My lip trembles. "I didn't really steal them. . . ."

"Oh, okay. You just borrowed them, right?"

"I . . . well . . ."

"I'm out of here. I don't have time for this."

"Jeremy, please—don't go. Let me explain."

"Explain what? That you've been lying to me for months? That's probably the only reason you kept dating me, isn't it? To get your big scoop."

"That isn't true! I didn't want any of this."

"Then what did you want?"

The doorbell rings a fourth time, this time with more banging. Seriously? This 1-800-FLOWERS guy must be the biggest dumbass on the planet. Just leave me a freaking note and try to deliver the flowers later. I do not have time for this.

"I wanted . . . I wanted . . ." A fifth round of ringing. Sweet lord.

This flower guy is going down. "Let me get that. But please—stay here. I want to talk about this."

"I'm not staying anywhere," Jeremy says.

"Just ten seconds—please."

Before he can argue, I run down the stairs in my robe and slippers, scurry through the entryway, and unlock the front door.

I yank it open. And then I panic.

Twenty men dressed in black are standing right in front of me, their guns pointed directly at my face. A man at the back shines a huge, round light at me.

"FBI!" they shout as they barge in. "Put your hands in the air!"

I stick up my hands as one of the officers busts into Simon's apartment. "Is anyone else upstairs?" one of the officers shouts.

"My . . . my boyfriend." I pause. "And my ex-boyfriend." The officer looks at me quizzically. "It's complicated," I say.

An agent immediately runs up my stairway, and another whirls me around, presses my hands behind my back, and slaps a pair of handcuffs around my wrists.

And that's when I decide, without question, this is the worst day of my entire life.

CHAPTER 40

The FBI agent grabs my arm and marches me down my front steps. He forces me onto my knees, facing the sidewalk, and my furry robe bunches up beneath me as he presses a gun into the small of my back. When I look over my shoulder, I see another agent pushing Simon out of the building, followed by Jeremy and Zach. Like me, they are all handcuffed. Zach is also still wearing nothing but an undershirt and boxers.

As Jeremy and Zach approach, Jeremy's eyes flit between me and the FBI agents. "What the hell is going on?"

"We have a warrant to search the premises," one of the officers says.

Jeremy balks. "On what grounds?"

The officer doesn't flinch. "Down on the ground, sir. We'll explain once we've secured the building."

The officers force Jeremy and Zach to their knees, one on either side of me, and press guns into their backs. Simon kneels next to Jeremy, with yet another officer watching over him.

"Do you have any idea what this is about?" I whisper across Jeremy to Simon. Simon stares straight ahead and doesn't respond. I try again. "Why are they searching our building?"

Simon shrugs without looking at me.

"All clear!" shouts an officer standing on the front stoop.

The officer behind Simon lifts him to his feet. "Could you please come with me, sir?"

He drags Simon into the house and several other agents follow, while Jeremy, Zach, and I continue to kneel on the front lawn.

"Can we go inside, too?" Zach asks, shivering in the early morning air.

"In a minute," the officer behind me says.

"Can you at least tell us what all of this is about?"

A fourth officer approaches, his hands on his hips. "The possession and dissemination of child pornography."

"WHAT?" all three of us say in unison.

"We have records of multiple downloads of pornographic images at this address," the officer says.

"This is some sort of mix-up," I say, my voice tense and pleading. "I've never done anything like that—ever, ever, ever."

"And what about your half-naked friend over here?"

I glance at Zach. "He never even visited my apartment until last night."

"And this fellow?" he says, nodding at Jeremy.

"He'd never do anything like that."

"You're sure?"

"I—of course I'm sure."

"Well, we have documentation of multiple downloads as recently as last night on wireless network SwannStream, beginning at 7:46 p.m."

"I wasn't even home at 7:46," I say. "I was at the Kennedy Center."

"With me," Zach adds.

"Oh, so you two were on a date?" Jeremy huffs. "Fucking perfect."

"It wasn't a date," I say.

"Like hell it wasn't," Zach says.

The officer holds up his hand, his eyes shut. "There are other instances besides last night."

"I'm telling you—the three of us have nothing to do with this."

The officer pulls out a piece of paper. "The warrant is for this address. This house."

"This isn't a house—it's two separate apartments." The pieces start coming together. "Don't you see? It's all a big misunderstanding. I share a wireless network with my downstairs neighbor. This has nothing to do with us."

"The house is deeded as a single-family home, and we have a warrant to search the entire premises."

"But it *isn't* a single-family home. It's two separate apartments. My landlord, Al, never changed the deed."

The officer stares at me coolly. "Well, there's only one functional doorbell, and according to the legal record, it's a single residence."

Zach jumps in. "I still have the ticket stubs from last night's concert upstairs. If you let me back inside, I can show them to you."

"Oh, you'd like that, wouldn't you?" Jeremy says.

The agent narrows his eyes. "We'll let you inside when we want to let you inside. Until then, you're not going anywhere."

The agent walks back toward the house, but the other three officers continue to stand behind us, still pressing guns into our backs. Only now, with my view no longer obstructed, do I notice how many people have gathered around my front gate, staring at us.

"Like this wasn't already the shittiest morning of all time," Jeremy mumbles under his breath, eyeing the crowd.

I sigh. "Tell me about it."

"Tell you about it? Tell *you* about it? I'm the one who found out his girlfriend has been keeping secrets from him for months."

"I told you—I didn't mean for any of this to turn out the way it did."

"How did you think it would turn out?"

I pull at the handcuffs around my wrists. "I don't know. I guess I hoped I'd finally have the career I've always wanted. And you'd be glad this story finally came out."

"Glad? Why would I be glad?"

"Because the whole cover-up made you uncomfortable. You said so yourself. Now the public knows the truth. They had a right to know."

"Of course they did. But so did I."

"Okay, well, what about me? Why weren't you upfront about your past?"

"I was."

"Not until I dragged the truth out of you. Would you even have told me about the whole 'cash for comment' scandal if I hadn't brought it up?"

"Whoa, 'cash for comment'?" Zach's eyes light up. "As in the scandal at the *Chronicle*? That was you?"

Jeremy grimaces. "Butt out, dude."

Zach looks at me, apparently disgusted. "So you'll date some slimeball, but you won't give me a second chance. Nice."

"He isn't a slimeball," I say.

"I beg to differ."

"Like you're one to talk! You slept with someone else and lied about it. What does that make you?"

"A guy who made a mistake." He locks his eyes on mine. "Sounds like you might know what that's like."

My insides twist into knots, and I turn to Jeremy, who is staring at the ground. "I'm sorry, Jeremy. I should have told you about the story."

He sniffs as he looks up and scans the crowd, which is slowly growing in number. "Why didn't you, then?"

I open my mouth to answer, but nothing comes out. Why hadn't I told him? Because I didn't want him to be mad at me? Because I worried he'd talk me out of doing the story? God, how lame am I?

"Because I was afraid of losing you," I say.

Jeremy goes silent for a long while as a gentle June breeze blows across my front lawn. A few more people gather in front of our house, whispering and shrugging shoulders as the FBI agents walk in and out of the building.

"Did it ever occur to you that maybe if you'd told me the truth, I could have helped you with the story?"

I screw up my face. "You made it pretty clear you had no interest in doing that."

"But if you were so passionate about it . . . All I'm saying is, I might have changed my mind."

I fumble over my words, but before I can put together a complete sentence, I let out a small gasp. Along the fringes of the growing crowd, I spot Melanie, my former *Morning Show* producer, her spectacled face peeking out from behind a tall man's shoulder.

Melanie catches my stare and pushes her way through the horde of nosey neighbors.

"Boogerface??"

She hunches her shoulders conspiratorially, as if the fact that I am kneeling on my front lawn in my robe and slippers, looking like Chewbacca Doubtfire, is some sort of secret between the two of us. This, of course, only heightens the mob's interest in me and my boyfriends present and past.

I smile nervously, hoping Melanie will understand I am in no position to talk right now. She doesn't take the hint.

"Hey, Boogerface!" she half yells, half whispers. "What *is* all this?"

The FBI agent behind me clears his throat. "Ma'am, I'm going to have to ask you to step back."

"I'm with the press," Melanie says, one leg over the fence.

"I don't care who you are," he says, pushing his gun harder against me. "Step back."

Melanie sticks her nose in the air. She sniffs loudly. "Is that police militarization I smell?"

"Ma'am, I will say this one more time: Step. Back."

She sighs. "Fine, fine." She looks at me and starts to leave, but then her eyes land on Jeremy, and she freezes. "Hey, why do I recognize you? What's your name?"

Jeremy's entire face turns red, out of embarrassment or anger or, more likely, a combination of both. Melanie's eyes dart between the two of us, and she reaches into her bag, grabs her phone, and points it at Zach, Jeremy, and me.

"No—Melanie!"

She snaps a photo, then another, and stuffs the phone back in her bag. She scampers off as the FBI agent shouts after her, while Zach, Jeremy, and I kneel handcuffed on my front lawn, on display like zoo animals in front of the growing mob.

If there is a way this day could get any worse, I don't want to know what it is.

* * *

But there is an endless number of ways in which this day can get worse, and the universe is determined to ram them up my ass in the most painful way possible. After a mortifying twenty minutes of kneeling in handcuffs on my front lawn, over which period I see no fewer than five other people I know, the FBI agents finally escort the three of us back into my apartment. On the way, we pass Simon, whose lanky arms are still handcuffed behind his back as an FBI agent guides him out the front door. The agent escorts Simon into the back of a marked police vehicle parked out front and slams the door before getting into the front seat. If they know Simon is the suspect, then why are they still treating the three of us like criminals? And why did this need to happen on a day when I look like a rabid squirrel?

When we reach the top of the stairway in my apartment, the floor is littered with old folders, books, and papers, some of which I'd forgotten I owned, all of which I will have to sort through and reorganize once the officers leave. When I look down, I see a stack of notes from the Green Grocers story splayed out like a pile of autumn leaves.

One officer scans the material on my laptop, and another makes a copy of my hard drive to take back for further analysis. Despite our repeated attempts to explain what happened—despite the display of our NSO ticket stubs and the fact that they've already carted away the perpetrator of these alleged downloads—the agents proceed with their interrogation undeterred. At no point is Zach offered the opportunity to put on pants, nor am I given the option of wearing something other than a hideous furry robe, and so the three of us sit on my couch looking like a bunch of crackheads while a team of FBI agents ransacks my apartment.

Finally, once they have inspected every last piece of furniture and electronic equipment, they leave almost as quickly as they came. As the last officer departs, Jeremy gets up from the couch and heads for the stairs.

"Jeremy—wait. Please don't go."

"Why, so I can get firebombed by SEAL Team Six? No thanks."

"Please. Just . . . stay for a few minutes so we can talk."

Zach cups my shoulder. "If he wants to go, let him."

270 • Dana Bate

I shrug off his hand with a violent twitch and stand up, pointing my finger at him. "Shut up. This has nothing to do with you."

"All I'm saying is . . . I think it's over."

"You know what's over? You and me."

"Syd . . ."

"Don't 'Syd' me. We're through. We've been through for years."

Zach opens his mouth to say something, but Jeremy's phone rings and interrupts him. Jeremy glances at it. "It's work. I have to go."

"Can you call them back?"

"Seriously? What part of this don't you understand? Your story has upended my client's entire company."

"You can take the call in my bedroom. I just . . . I need to talk to you."

He sighs. "Fine. Whatever. This is such bullshit."

He traipses through the mess on the floor and slams my bedroom door shut behind him.

"You'd seriously rather date that shill than me?" Zach says.

"Jesus Christ, Zach, get over yourself. He isn't a shill. Frankly, he's probably a better guy than you are."

"I have never, ever compromised my integrity the way that guy did, nor would I."

"You cheated on me and broke my heart. Right now? To me? That's worse."

"But I'm still in love with you."

I clench my fists and stomp my foot on the floor. "No! You're in love with what we had in high school. And you know what? I am, too. But those people are gone. *Gone.* They grew up. And it's time we both accepted that and moved on."

"Why do we have to move on? Don't you think we owe it to each other to see if we can make a fresh start?"

"I don't owe you anything."

"Yeah, but—"

"But nothing. And as for you—you owe me an apology."

"I said I was sorry."

"Yeah, five years later!"

"Why does that matter?"

I bury my face in my hands and let out a loud groan. "Because! You never apologized when it mattered. When I was heartbroken and distraught, when I thought I'd never fall in love again. Well, I am falling in love again, and now it's too late for you. For us."

"I don't believe that."

"You don't believe that? You don't *believe* that?" I rush across the room and gather up his pants, shirt, and tie in a ball and grab his briefcase off the floor. "Well, maybe you'll believe this."

I hurl all of his belongings down my stairway, and they land in the entryway with a loud thud. Then I snatch the roses he gave me off the coffee table and chuck them down the stairway, too, followed by a melamine vase that, frankly, has nothing to do with Zach but makes a glorious crash as it strikes the ground.

"If it weren't for you, maybe I would have covered that Professor Ferguson scandal in college. Maybe I would have taken that food-writing job in Fort Lauderdale. Maybe I wouldn't have needed to write some juicy horsemeat story in the first place."

"Oh, so now it's my fault that jerkwad is mad at you?"

"Yeah, kind of."

"At some point, you need to stop blaming me for your misery," he says. "The fact that your life is screwed up isn't all my fault."

The blood rushes to my face, and I grab him by his ripped undershirt and drag him toward my stairway. "Fuck you, Zach."

Zach opens his mouth as if to say something, but I slap him across the face before he can. He stares at me with glassy eyes.

"You know what? Forget it," he says. "I'm sorry I bothered."

He trudges down my steps, collects his things, and disappears through my front door.

As I turn around, Jeremy charges out of my bedroom. "Well, thanks to you, it looks like I'm about to get fired," he says. "Which, given the events of the past twenty-four hours, is the icing on the fucking cake."

"Fired? But . . . why?"

"*Why?* Why do you think? I'll be lucky if Green Grocers doesn't sue me—which, by the way, they totally could."

"But how would they know you were the one who leaked the documents?"

"Because someone already posted a photo of the three of us on the Web. It doesn't take a genius to put the pieces together."

Melanie. Damn it.

"Maybe they'll understand—you were trying to do the right thing."

"No, *you* were trying to do the right thing, and you handled it in the worst way possible."

"I know, but . . . you could use this as a chance to redeem yourself—to be the good guy."

He lets out a bitter grunt. "Why? So you can feel better about dating me? So that you don't have to explain to all your friends and family that I'm not really as bad as my Wikipedia entry says I am?"

I shrug helplessly and open my mouth to respond, but nothing comes out. Jeremy stares at me for a long time without saying anything, letting me stew in the awkward silence, and then he turns around and walks toward my stairway.

"I'm not proud of what I did, but I'm not ashamed of who I am. Obviously you are."

"That's not what I said. I didn't—"

Jeremy holds up his hand. "Enough."

He holds my stare with unblinking eyes, and when I don't say anything, he grips my banister tightly, until I can see the whites of his knuckles. "I think it would be better for both of us if we didn't see each other anymore," he says.

Then he starts walking down the stairs and, without turning to look at me or say good-bye, marches out the front door.

CHAPTER 41

It's official: Everyone hates me.

Jeremy blames me for losing his job, Zach blames me for choosing a disgraced journalist over him, and my landlord Al blames me for getting him into trouble with the DC government for using a single-family house as an apartment building. Apparently, I am the worst person alive.

Even my compatriots at the farmers' market no longer hold me in their good graces. When I show up at the West End farmers' market Saturday, the day after the story appears in the *Chronicle*, I pass Drew as he sets up beneath the Broad Tree Orchards tent. I have avoided him ever since our date at Tryst two months ago, but now he seems to be the one avoiding me, his eyes glued to the crate of black cherries he is arranging on one of the tables.

"Hey, Drew. Long time no speak."

He looks up and acts surprised, as if he didn't know I'd been standing there. "Oh. Hey."

"How's it going?"

"Okay. Busy."

"I hear that." I fiddle with the strap on my tote bag. "Sorry I've been MIA. Things have been a little nuts on my end."

"Yeah, I saw your story in the *Chronicle*."

Him and half the planet. Once I realized Jeremy and his superiors had seen my name associated with the horsemeat story, I didn't see the point in removing myself or concealing my involvement. The whole point of taking my name off the story was to protect Jeremy, and now that I've failed at that, the whole exercise in anonymity seems pointless.

Drew unloads a crate of gooseberries. "I'm surprised you're willing to associate with us lowly market folk, now that you're all famous."

"I'm not famous." Infamous is more like it.

"Whatever. You obviously have an agenda."

"An agenda? What are you talking about?"

"You're obviously just working here to dig up material for your writing career."

"That isn't true. I needed this job. And I like working here."

"You have a funny way of showing it. You do realize Green Grocers is pulling the plug on the pilot program, right?"

My heart sinks. "The company told me all projects were going forward as planned."

"That's not what we're hearing. Julie is being told there are 'unspecified delays' to the program, and her contact at the company has backtracked on all of his commitments."

Just what Jeremy said would happen. Damn it.

I clear my throat. "But it would have been wrong for me to keep the horsemeat story a secret."

"Totally. I get that. But a bunch of the people around here feel a little used. Like, you cared about them until a bigger story came along. All those new trees Maggie showed you? Thanks to your story, she has to find a new buyer."

"But if I'd kept this story a secret, I'd be as bad as Bob Young."

"Again, I get that. Doesn't change the way a lot of us feel."

My face grows hot. "But . . . but . . ." I trail off.

"But what?"

I fumble over my words, trying to think of anything I can say to keep Drew—handsome, caring, boring Drew—from hating me. Surely there is something?

"The . . . short-tailed albatross," I finally squeak out in a faint voice.

"Yeah? What about it?"

I stare at him stupidly, willing myself to say something compassionate or insightful or, at the very least, sane. But nothing comes out, and instead I simply walk away, because as long as I'm burning bridges, I might as well light another match.

When I show up at Wild Yeast's tent, Rick greets me by throwing a baguette at my head.

"Fuck you very much," he says as I rub my forehead.

"Rick—what the hell?"

"Thanks to your little screed in the *Chronicle,* Green Grocers has put our deal on hold."

I sigh. Another addition to my legion of haters.

"I know. But that doesn't mean the deal is off forever. Once the uproar dies down, there's a good chance they'll revive the program." I have no idea if this is true, but it sounds better than affirming the alternative.

"Fuck of a lot of good that does me now. Do you have any idea the sort of investment I made to give them the volume they wanted? I'm even more screwed now than I was before."

"But . . . they put horse meat in their lasagna. . . ."

"La-di-frickin'-da." He heaves a crate of rye onto one of the tables. "They could've put Rin Tin Tin in their beef stew, and I wouldn't have given a crap, as long as they made good on their promises."

"But you're an artisan—a craftsman. Surely you wouldn't want to associate with an organization like that."

He throws another crate on the table and rests his hands on his hips. "I bake bread. Damn good bread, but let's be honest: It's bread. And at the end of the day, it doesn't matter a lick how good it is if no one buys it."

"Maybe there are other markets willing to carry your stuff. Have you thought about Dean and DeLuca? Or Marvelous Market?"

He rolls his eyes as he wraps one of his meaty paws around an oatmeal loaf. "Oh, yes, just what I need: More companies to make my life hell. Stop wasting my time with your explanations and cocka-mamie ideas and unload the rest of this crap like you're supposed to. I don't have all frickin' day."

He kicks one of the crates beneath the table with a loud thwack, and I wonder if there is a way I could fix things for Rick and Maggie and the others, or if I'm destined to alienate everyone in my life, until I have no friends left.

I do have at least two friends, the first being Heidi, and the second being Stu Abbott, who apologizes profusely when he finally speaks to me Saturday afternoon.

"I don't know how all of this happened," he says. "I could have sworn the version of the story I sent didn't have your name on it. Honest."

"Yeah, well, the damage is done."

"I know. And I'm sorry." He pauses. "Was Jeremy Brauer really your source?"

"He was."

Stu hesitates, then hums into the phone. "I never would have guessed. Given what happened when he worked for me, I'm surprised Bob Young's e-mails even bothered him."

"Why? Because he made some bad decisions six years ago?"

"Yeah, I guess that isn't really fair, huh?" He sighs. "Anyway, the good news is that your story is a massive success. Did you see how many times the link was posted and re-tweeted?"

"I have a vague idea," I say. The answer: a lot.

"This story is perfect for updating our food page's brand. It has everything: food, scandal, intrigue, meat—both literally and figuratively. You did an excellent job."

"Thanks." I scribble on one of my notepads. "It sounds like the farmers' market partnership is off, though. At least for now."

"Yeah, I heard. That's unfortunate. But sort of inevitable with a story like this. On a brighter note . . ." He pauses for dramatic effect. "Now that your name is out there, you're the young food writer everyone is talking about. My managing editor is really excited with the reception this story has gotten and would love more stuff like this from you."

I sit up straight. Finally some good news. "Really?"

"Really. I take it you're game?"

"Yes—definitely." I flip my notepad to a blank page. "I already have a bunch of ideas. One is on the rising popularity of home-brewing, and another is about urban gardening, and—"

"Yeah . . ." Stu interrupts me. "When I said my managing editor wanted more stuff from you, I meant more stuff like the horsemeat story. We're looking for sexier stuff—stuff that'll get tons of page hits."

"Oh." I lean back in my chair. That isn't the kind of stuff I've ever wanted to write. "But . . . what about stories with a human ele-ment? Not everything is doom and gloom. Not every story has to dismantle a company."

"But if it could, that would be great." Stu gives a stilted laugh. "I'm kidding. Sort of. Anyway, we have plenty of reporters on staff who do the regular features and human-interest stories. We need you to be our muckraker. That seems to be your specialty."

My chest tightens. My specialty? What have I gotten myself into?

When I don't speak up, Stu chimes in. "I thought this was what you wanted—a chance to run with the big boys."

"It is. It's just . . ."

"It's just what?"

I gnaw at the end of my pinky nail. "Nothing," I say. "Never mind."

Because I can't bring myself to say out loud that at the moment when everything is at my fingertips, when I could have everything I've always wanted—Zach, a food-writing job at the *Chronicle,* re-spect from my food-writing peers—I've never felt more lost or alone.

CHAPTER 42

A muckraker? Since when am I a muckraker? That's never what I wanted to be. I wanted to write about heirloom apples and crazy bakers and eccentric food artisans. I figured the Green Grocers story would gain me entry into the exclusive cadre of food writers, but then I could write about whatever I wanted. How could I have been so naïve? And now I'm the scandalmonger. The scandalmonger with no boyfriend and a dwindling number of friends. Great.

Just when my morale hits an all-time low, I board a train to Philadelphia, where I will join my parents, my sister, and her shady fiancé for their wedding tasting at The Rittenhouse Hotel. At this point, all I need is a funeral and a house fire, and this will officially be the worst week of my life.

My mom picks me up Friday afternoon at Philadelphia's Thirtieth Street Station, meeting me in the middle of the vast marble concourse. The grandeur of the hall swallows me up, the five-story rectangular windows and travertine walls dwarfing me as they climb toward the ninety-five-foot-high ceiling. As I push my way through the bustling horde of travelers, my eyes land on a large banner hanging above the doorway leading to Market Street, welcoming visitors to the 35th Annual Homebrewers Conference this weekend. I stop in my tracks. The Homebrew Competition. *Je-*

remy. Is he here this weekend? He must be. Didn't he say he goes every year?

Before I can fully process the idea of Jeremy and me running into each other, my mom approaches me from in front of the timetable, which *flick-flick-flicks* through its series of trains and departure times. She is dressed in a pair of black capri pants, a sleeveless blue tunic, and black sandals. As usual, she looks a thousand times more stylish than I do, even though she is more than twice my age.

"Hi, sweetie," she says, beaming as she reaches out her arms and throws them around me.

She pulls me in tight, enveloping me in the powdery, sweet smell of her Shalimar perfume, the same scent she has worn for the past twenty-odd years. She pulls away and grips my upper arms, scanning me from head to toe. I haven't slept well in a week and have been subsisting on large quantities of leftover muffins, cookies, and brioche.

"You look terrible," she says, brushing my hair off my face.

"Thanks . . ."

"No, I mean really. You look like you haven't slept in days. Are you okay?"

"I don't want to talk about it."

"About what?"

"Why I look like a mess."

She studies my face. "You're sure?"

"Positive."

"If you say so. Oh, but I've been meaning to tell you—our phone has been ringing off the hook ever since your story came out. Everyone is so impressed. We never knew you were such a sleuth!"

"Neither did I . . ."

"Well, we think it's wonderful. We're so proud of you."

She kisses my forehead and then, with her arm wrapped around my shoulder, whisks me through the marble concourse and out the glass doors to the pick-up and drop-off area. I scan the rows of cars for her white Ford Explorer, but her signature mode of transportation is nowhere to be found. Instead, we head straight for a Toyota Prius the color of a pumpkin.

I slow my step as we approach the car. "Is this yours?"

"It is," she says.

"Since when?"

"Since last month." She pops the trunk. "With the dealership closing and everything else that's going on . . . Well, we figured something smaller with better fuel economy made more sense right now."

"But a Toyota? I thought Dad only bought Fords."

She purses her lips. "That was before the company decided to close his business. But it looks like he'll be able to start at the Toyota dealership next month after all, so the Toyota folks cut him a deal."

"That's great. Dad must be thrilled."

"Thrilled is a little strong. But he's happy. It isn't the perfect job, but it's something."

She stuffs my suitcase into the trunk, and we hop into the car, which powers on with the push of a button.

"What about you?" I ask. "Any leads on the job front?"

She looks over her shoulder and pulls out of the waiting area. "Kitchen Kapers in Suburban Square has an opening for a sales associate. I should hear by the end of the week."

"That's exciting."

"I guess. A little nerve-wracking, though. It's been so long since I've been out there." She takes a deep breath and shakes out her shoulders as she turns onto Market Street. "I guess change can be good, right?"

I glance at my mom as she grips the steering wheel with both hands, the skin around her eyes tense as she maneuvers the car down the street. Then I look out my window and watch the cars whiz by as I take a deep breath.

"Let's hope so," I say.

We pull into the circular driveway in front of The Rittenhouse Hotel, which rises thirty-three stories, the edifice zigzagging back and forth like jagged teeth, giving each room a view of the eponymous square. A bellman in a black suit with gold trim and matching cap opens my door for me.

"Welcome," he says. "Are you a guest of the hotel?"

"We're here for a wedding tasting," I say.

He smiles. "Ah. Congratulations on your engagement."

"It isn't for me. It's for my sister."

"Oh." He fumbles with the door handle. "Well, best wishes to your sister."

"My guess is she'll need more than wishes. Her fiancé is an ass."

The doorman blushes and closes the car door behind me. He smiles uncomfortably, apparently at a loss for words. Great. Now I'm alienating total strangers.

"Sydney? Come on," my mom calls from the front entrance. "We're going to be late."

I follow her through the lobby, with its beige inlaid marble floors and warm, blond wood columns, and scurry up the marble stairway to the second floor. We pass the grand ballroom and continue down a carpeted hallway to a boardroom whose door is propped open.

"There they are!"

Libby skips toward us, her golden-brown waves bouncing off her toned shoulders. She wears a cream silk shantung shift dress and pearls, looking conservative and bridal and very, very Libby.

"We were beginning to think you'd gotten lost."

"Traffic on Market Street was terrible," my mom says. "Is your father here yet?"

"Yep. He's in there talking to Matt. I was shocked he beat you two. You know Dad—always running fifteen minutes late because he had to close 'one more deal.'"

I lock eyes with my mom, who clutches her purse strap against her shoulder. "Yes, well . . ." She clears her throat. "Let's get started with this tasting, hmm?"

She heads into the room, and I follow her until Libby grabs me by the elbow and pulls me aside. "You didn't say anything to her, did you? About Matt?"

"Of course I didn't. You told me not to."

"Good." She takes a deep breath and lets it out quickly.

"I assume you talked to him?"

She nods. "Yep. Everything's fine."

"So what was the deal? Whose earring was it?"

Her cheeks turn pink. "It's a long story. Not important."

"Not important because it was his mother's? Or not important because you're afraid of telling me the truth?"

"I'm not afraid."

"Then whose was it?"

She presses her lips together, then lets out a sigh. "One of the first-year associates at his firm. But it's not a big deal—it's not as bad as it sounds."

"Did it fall into his briefcase like I suggested?"

"Not exactly..."

"Then what happened?"

She waves me off with a flick of her manicured hand. "I told you—it's not a big deal. It was just one night."

My eyes widen. "Libby."

"What? Listen, he said he was sorry. And I believe him. He *cried,* Sydney. Like, actual tears."

"Well, whoop-dee-doo."

She purses her lips. "You're just jealous because Matt apologized, and Zach never apologized to you."

"He did, actually. Last week."

"Five years too late..."

I clench my jaw. "This isn't a competition, Libby. Zach versus Matt, me versus you. This is about your life. Your happiness."

"Exactly," she says. "So stop making me talk about this and get your butt in that boardroom and help me pick out a wedding menu."

She turns on her heel and marches down the hallway, and all I can think is there isn't enough vodka in this entire hotel to get me through this weekend.

"To begin, we present you with our lobster bisque."

The wedding coordinator beams as three waiters emerge from behind a swinging door carrying a small white bowl in each hand. The waiters place the bowls in front of the five of us, and we each pick up a small spoon and lap up the creamy soup.

"Wow," my dad says, blotting the corners of his mouth with a napkin. "This is dynamite."

The bisque is silky and rich, infused with the intoxicating combination of lobster, sherry, and a hint of saffron. I have to restrain myself from licking the bowl.

"There is, of course, a small supplement for the bisque, given that it's made with lobster," the wedding coordinator says, tucking a lock of white-blond hair behind her ear.

My mom and dad eye each other uncomfortably.

"But it would be worth every penny," Libby says, oblivious to my parents' uneasiness. "It's *soooo* good."

Matt sits next to her in silence, stirring his spoon awkwardly in circles around his bowl. His thick, almost black hair is gelled to the side, and his bushy eyebrows jut over his eyes, which are cast downward. He hasn't taken a single mouthful.

The wedding coordinator announces the next menu option: a chilled lobster salad dressed in a light chive vinaigrette.

"Oh, my," my mom says between bites of supple lobster meat, each succulent chunk nearly the size of a golf ball. "This is lovely."

"Again, there would be a slight supplement for this dish," the coordinator says.

"But *totally* worth it," Libby says.

Matt pokes at the bits of lobster with his fork and says nothing as the rest of us clean our plates.

The next course arrives: lobster ravioli bathed in a creamy rose sauce, the pasta so fresh and tender it nearly melts on my tongue.

"Again," the coordinator begins.

"Let me guess," I interrupt. "A small supplement."

She smiles. "Yes. For the lobster."

We next try a lobster empanada, followed by a dish of lobster and grits, followed by lobster tempura so delicate and crisp it's like handling blown glass. When I say "we" try these dishes, I mean Libby, my parents, and I. Matt merely pushes the food around his plate, a sullen expression painted on his angular face.

Before the next course arrives, I clear my throat. "Are we going to try anything that doesn't involve lobster?"

The wedding coordinator dons a pair of bifocals and skims a piece of paper in front of her. "Hmm...I don't think so.... Though one of the entrées is a surf and turf—filet mignon and lobster tail."

I lock eyes with Libby. "You're joking, right? After everything we talked about?"

Her cheeks flush. "I thought we'd do a lobster menu. What's wrong with that?"

"Seriously? Do you have any idea how much it would cost to do a lobster-themed dinner for a hundred-some people?"

"I thought you said two hundred," the wedding coordinator interjects.

I roll my eyes. "Even better."

"It's my wedding," Libby says. "I can do what I want."

"It's your wedding, as in you and Matt. Your fiancé hasn't touched a single thing that has come out of that kitchen. Matt, do you even *like* lobster?"

"Not really," he mumbles.

Libby clicks her tongue. "Matt doesn't like anything but pizza and chicken fingers. That's why he's letting me choose the menu."

"But does every course really need to revolve around lobster? There wasn't a chicken dish that looked decent? A green salad, perhaps?"

"I'm not letting you ruin my big day just because you're jealous of me."

"Libby, how many times do I need to say this? I'm not jealous of you! This isn't a competition."

"*Girls,*" my dad says. "Enough. Sydney, if your sister wants lobster, she can have lobster. We'll find a way to make it work."

I rub my temples. "This is insane."

"What's insane? That Dad wants to make my day special?"

My hands clench into fists. "No, that he is willing to bankrupt himself so you can marry this jerk."

"Hey!" Matt says.

My mom shifts uncomfortably in her seat. "I'm sorry, Matt. Sydney isn't herself today." She turns to me. "No one is going bankrupt over anything."

"And Matt isn't a jerk," Libby adds.

I look at Libby, then at my parents, then at Libby again. I can't take this anymore. The secrets, the hypocrisy—I wasn't built for this. I kept the secret about the horsemeat story from Jeremy, and look how that turned out. If I have to eat one more bite of lobster, while my adulterer of a future brother-in-law sits sullenly across from my cash-strapped parents, I am going to scream.

"I'm tired of keeping everyone's secrets!" I shout, seemingly out of nowhere.

Libby and my parents freeze in their seats. The wedding coordinator's eyes flit around the room.

"I'm sick of it," I say. "I'm sick of this fucking charade."

"Sydney . . ." Libby starts to say.

"No. I've had enough." I thrust my seat away from the table and stand up, my napkin clutched in my hand. "There are too many secrets floating around this room, and if people don't start telling the truth, I'm going to do it for you. Because I can't take another second of this." I throw the napkin in the middle of the table. "Matt, maybe you can start."

Then I storm out of the boardroom, slam the door behind me, and tear down the hallway, not knowing where I'm headed but realizing anyplace I end up is better than here.

CHAPTER 43

I probably could have handled that situation a little more delicately. Like slamming the door? That might have been overkill. And did I really need to throw the napkin? Probably not. But I'm tired of playing the bad guy while everyone else pretends everything is okay. Everything isn't okay. Everything is a mess, and my family needs to know that.

The problem with making such a dramatic exit is that I am now charging down the streets of Philadelphia, without a clue as to where I am heading. I don't have a car, my parents live in the suburbs, and I don't know anyone who lives downtown. I didn't really think this through.

I press onward along Walnut Street and eventually turn onto Broad Street, heading toward City Hall, the nine-story Beaux Arts building looming a few blocks ahead of me, a bronze statue of William Penn perched atop its clock tower. In high school, Zach and I would go for drives at night, swerving along Kelly Drive to look at the twinkling boathouses or circling City Hall to see if William Penn was wearing an Eagles jersey as the playoffs approached. The clocks turned bright yellow at night, and Zach always said it looked as if good old Billy had taken a leak through the clock tower.

As I get closer to City Hall, I curse myself for thinking about

Zach, for tethering yet another experience in the present to an experience with him in my past. Why can't I let him go? Why do I keep trying to jam everything—my relationships, my career, my visions of the future—into the narrow framework of what I thought I wanted in high school?

The traffic on Broad Street curves around City Hall, and I dart across the street as I continue my aimless journey. For so long, Zach was a crutch, an easy excuse for why I gave up on my food-writing dreams and felt so alone. But I don't blame Zach anymore. I blame myself. And I don't want him anymore. I want Jeremy.

Jeremy.

I look up as I round City Hall and see a lumpy, middle-aged man moving toward me, a laminated pass dangling around his neck by a long, black cord. Upon closer inspection, I notice the large seal and lettering above the man's name: 35TH ANNUAL NATIONAL HOMEBREWERS CONFERENCE.

I rush up to him before he can cross the street. "Excuse me—are you heading to the Homebrewers Conference?"

"You betcha," he says. "You?"

"I . . ." I clear my throat. "Yes. Mind if I follow you?"

"Sure thing."

I hustle along with him as he crosses Broad onto Market Street, realizing I have no idea where we are going or who this guy is.

"So where are you coming from?" he asks as we wait on the corner of Thirteenth and Market.

"Washington, DC."

"Ah. Nice. Couldn't get a room at the Marriott either, huh?"

"Nope . . ."

He casts a sideways glance at me as we cross to the other side of Market Street and approach the Marriott. "What brew club are you with?"

"Um . . . It's a really small one. We're not very well-known."

"Well, you gotta start somewhere, right?" He laughs as he gestures in front of the Marriott's front door. "After you, m'lady."

I swing through the circular door, which empties me into the Marriott's vast lobby, where throngs of guests of varying descriptions shuttle back and forth along the cream marble floor. Various signs pepper the waiting area, directing guests to the events taking place there this weekend, including the Homebrewers Conference.

"Better get out your badge," the man says as he sidles up beside me. "They're real sticklers when it comes to that."

"I . . . actually have to run to the ladies' room first. I'll catch you up there."

"Okeydokey. But I'd hurry if I were you, before it gets too crowded."

He heads for the elevators, and I slip into the bathroom, where I park myself in front of one of the mirrors and try to make myself look presentable. Given that my carb, sugar, and fat consumption over the past week has rivaled that of a small country, there's a limit to what I can do. I'm also not exactly sure what my plan is. And let's be honest: My track record in devising plans while in the bathroom is less than stellar. My only saving grace is that there is no baby powder in here.

Once I've given my cheeks a pinch and my hair a quick tousle, I make my way out of the bathroom and up to the fourth floor to Franklin Hall, where the Beer Expo is taking place. Dozens of tables line the room, showcasing anything and everything related to homebrewing: exotic strains of malt and yeast, high-tech brewing gadgets, free beer from local breweries, specialty beer glasses, and on and on. Radical facial hair pervades the room, everything from handlebar mustaches to Santa-like beards, a fashion statement outclassed only by the Hawaiian shirts in varying shades of neon and one man who, inexplicably, is dressed as Bigfoot.

The crowds move from stand to stand, sampling different kinds of beer made with whatever sort of specialty ingredients or equipment is on exhibit. In the back of the room, a few homebrewing clubs offer samples of their beers in a makeshift suite, clubs with names like Barley Legal and Yeast of Eden and San Andreas Malts.

I manage to slip in without being asked to show my badge and scan the room for Jeremy. I don't see him anywhere. Maybe he isn't here. Even if he were, the crowd is so thick I don't know how I'd find him. There are hundreds of people in this room.

As I snake through the crowd, unsure where I am going or why, I casually drape my arm across my torso, trying to disguise the fact that I don't have an entry badge and therefore have no business being here. Is this really what my life has come to? Crashing a beer conference? What the hell am I doing?

Just as I am about to bail on what is surely a bad idea, I spot Jeremy in the back corner of the room, listening to a poster presentation beside the Yeast of Eden table. He wears a baby blue polo shirt and strokes his chin as he listens to the presenter, his eyes twinkling. He is rapt.

I slink along the fringes of the crowd and make my way toward the poster presentation, where some guy is talking about glutathione and a bunch of other long, chemical-sounding words I do not understand. I am about to reach out and tug Jeremy's shirt, when he raises his hand to ask a question.

"So what are we talking, in terms of shelf life?" he asks.

"Good question," the presenter says, and proceeds to respond to an intrigued Jeremy.

When it seems the presenter has moved on, I crane my head in Jeremy's direction. "Pssst!"

He doesn't hear me. I inch a little closer and tap him on the shoulder.

"Pssst!"

This time, Jeremy and the entire crowd turn to look at me, everyone appearing equally perplexed by my presence. Jeremy's cheeks flush, and his jaw tightens. He does not look happy to see me.

"Sorry." I hold up my hands defensively as I meet the gaze of the man presenting his poster. "Carry on."

He resumes his talk, and Jeremy drags me out of the hall and into the area immediately outside. His grip on my arm isn't rough or painful, but it isn't tender and welcoming either. It is not the grip of a man who is about to say, "Sydney, I missed you. I hoped you'd come and find me here."

He pushes me into a quiet corner and lets go of me. "What are you *doing* here?"

"I . . . I don't know."

"You don't know?" He snorts. "You came all the way to Philadelphia, but you don't know why you're here."

"I was in town for my sister's wedding tasting."

"Ah." He nods solemnly. "Well."

I wait for him to continue, but he doesn't.

"I wanted to see you. Needed to see you." I glance down at my shoes, then look up again. "I miss you."

Jeremy stares back at me, his expression blank.

"Aren't you going to say anything?"

Jeremy keeps his eyes fixed on mine. "What am I supposed to say?"

"I don't know. That you're mad at me. That you hate me. That you miss me, too."

He sighs. "I don't hate you. But am I mad at you? Yeah. I'm really fucking mad at you. And I don't feel like talking to you."

"You mean right now?"

"No, I mean like ever."

"Oh."

I wait for him to say more, but he doesn't. He just stands there, staring at me with cool, impassive eyes.

"I made a huge mistake," I say. "I know that. I broke your trust. And I'm not sure there's anything I can do to get it back." My voice quavers, and I take a deep breath to collect myself. "But I feel terrible about what I did, and I'm asking for forgiveness. You know what that's like."

He presses his lips together. "Why should I forgive you?"

"Because . . ." I take a deep breath and collect myself. "Because I'm falling in love with you."

Jeremy stares at me for a long while, and the silence hangs between us, thick and poisonous like a dense acid cloud. After a few moments, his shoulders slump. "Sydney," he says, his voice soft. "I . . ."

"Jeremy?" A guy in a tie-dyed T-shirt and clip-on bowtie pokes his head out from behind me.

Jeremy studies the man's face, as if he is trying to remember who this guy is. "Yeah?"

"Aw, man, I thought that was you!" He slaps Jeremy on the back. "It's me—Vince. Vince Stone. From last year? In Minneapolis?"

Jeremy nods slowly, then a smile blooms on his face. "*Vince.* Right. Wow, how've you been? You competing again this year?"

Vince pretends to wiggle his clip-on bowtie. "Indubitably. You?"

"Yep. My Munich Helles and oatmeal stout both made the final cut."

"That's amazing," I interject. "You never told me."

Vince shifts his gaze to me, as if he is noticing me for the first time. "Pardon my rudeness," he says, reaching out for my hand. "It's a pleasure meeting you, Ms. . . . ?"

"Strauss. Sydney Strauss."

"She was just leaving," Jeremy says.

Vince scowls. "What? The party's just getting started. Come on. A bunch of us are going to check out the Spiegelau tasting before we get ready for Club Night."

"Maybe in a minute," I say, keeping my gaze on Jeremy.

"Okay, but when the room is too packed, don't say I didn't warn you." I feel his eyes on me. "You'd better put on your badge, though. The enforcers are out en masse."

"She was just leaving," Jeremy repeats.

Vince studies me quizzically and hesitates before heading into Franklin Hall, and Jeremy glances over his shoulder toward the door. "Listen, I have to go. And so do you."

"But . . . don't you want to talk?"

"Talk? About what?"

"About us."

He sighs. "There is no us."

"I know. And that's my fault." I take a deep breath and close my eyes, then open them again. "Is there anything I could do to win back your trust? Because I'll do it. Whatever it takes."

He looks at the floor and sighs, but before he can say anything, I feel a forceful tap on my shoulder.

"Excuse me. Ma'am?" I whirl around and face a stocky man in a rust-colored Hawaiian shirt, who is standing next to a security guard dressed in black. "Could I please see your badge?"

"I . . . oh . . ." I pat my hands up and down my torso and around my pockets, as if—*whoops!*—I somehow managed to misplace it. "I must have forgotten to put it on."

The man in the Hawaiian shirt pulls out an iPad. "Name?"

I mumble my name under my breath.

"Sorry? I didn't catch that."

I glance up at Jeremy, hoping he will jump in and save me, but he doesn't. My shoulders slump. "Sydney Strauss," I say.

The man flicks through his iPad. "Did you register for this event?"

"I . . . well . . ." I clear my throat. "The thing is—"

"No." Jeremy jumps in. "She didn't."

The man looks up. "Then I'm going to need you to come with me."

"Just give me a minute," I say.

"I'm sorry, ma'am, but you need to leave now."

"You don't understand—the two of us were dating, and I made a huge mistake, but I'm really sorry and need to talk to him before it's too—"

"Ma'am? I'll ask you one more time."

"But . . . I still need to—"

But before I can continue, the security guard grabs one of my arms and the guy in the Hawaiian shirt grabs the other, and the two of them drag me down the hallway while I kick and shout and beg them to let me go. I peer over my shoulder at Jeremy, who watches, along with fifty-some other homebrewers, as the two men wrestle me toward the elevators.

"Jeremy!" I shout back at him. "I'm sorry!"

He stands frozen and says nothing as I trip and flail down the corridor.

Finally, when we reach the elevator bay, I call out to him one last time: "I'll wait for you in the lobby!"

He stares at me, his sad eyes fixed on mine. "Please don't," he calls back.

Then he walks back into the conference, disappearing as the two men shove me into the elevator and the doors close in front of my face.

CHAPTER 44

I think it's safe to say that was a disaster.

Given that I had neither a plan nor any right to be there, I shouldn't be surprised. But I thought maybe if Jeremy saw me, if he knew how sorry I was and that I was falling for him, he'd give me a second chance. How could I have been so stupid?

Once the two burly gentlemen have deposited me in the lobby of the Marriott, I stumble through the lobby and out the front door, my arms still aching from their tight grips. This is the second time in eight days that I've been forcibly dragged around by enforcement agents of one kind or another, and quite frankly, I've had enough. Did they really need to create such a scene? I will concede that I was the one kicking and screaming, but still. It's a beer conference. What were they so worried about? That I'd drink all of the Weizenbock?

I massage my throbbing biceps as I wander along Market Street, heading back toward City Hall. Once again, I'm not really sure where I'm going. Back to The Rittenhouse? Where my family is probably waiting to strangle me, if they haven't already strangled each other? Uh, no thank you. Then again, could it really be worse than making an ass of myself in front of a bunch of drunk porkers in Hawaiian shirts? Tough call.

When I finally reach Rittenhouse Square, I decide to take a seat on a bench along the fringes of the park, by the cobblestone path lined by tall elm, oak, and sycamore trees, whose leaves flutter and sparkle in the late afternoon light. I close my eyes and soak up the sounds of the city, the high-pitched squeals of children playing by the giant frog sculpture and the jingle-jangle of dog tags as the pooches and their owners trot through the square. I love the way every city has its own sounds, its own cadence, a timbre that reverberates through its streets and squares like a living, breathing soundtrack. I've missed the sounds of this city, the sound of being home.

"Mind if I join you?"

I open my eyes and see Libby standing in front of me, her hands clasped in front of her.

"Sure." I scoot over, as if to make room, although I have the whole bench to myself.

Libby brushes off the bench, smoothes her stiff cream dress, and sits beside me. We sit in silence for a few minutes before Libby breaks the calm between us.

"So . . . where have you been?" she asks.

"Off ruining more lives. My own, mostly."

She fiddles with the edge of her skirt. "Matt and I are putting the wedding on hold. At least for a little while."

I look up at her. "I'm sorry."

"Don't be. Wait, I take that back. You definitely could have handled things better in there."

I sigh. "I know."

She twirls a long strand of hair around her finger and then starts picking at the split ends. "Why didn't you tell me Dad lost his business?"

"He didn't want you to know. At least until after the wedding."

"But if I'd known . . ." She kicks at a small pebble. "I feel like such an ass—the special chairs, the lobster menu. I would have been happy with a picnic in the backyard."

"Libby, come on. A picnic?"

She wrinkles her nose. "Okay, fine. That's a stretch. But I would have been okay scaling everything way back. I'm not a total diva."

I chuckle. "Since when?"

"Since . . . I don't know." She leans back against the bench. "God, I guess I am a diva, aren't I? No wonder Matt cheated on me."

"Libby, don't say that—it isn't your fault."

"It's never just one person's fault," she says.

I think back to the betrayals in my own relationships. Did I bear some of the responsibility for Zach's duplicity? Does Jeremy bear some of the responsibility for mine?

"I guess that's true," I say. "But cheating on someone, lying to him or her—that's the coward's way out."

She frowns as she twists her ankle back and forth, studying her hot pink toenails. "Yeah. I know."

"So what do you think you'll do?"

"I don't know. I can't really think about it right now. I get too upset."

"Okay. We don't have to talk about it."

"Matt and I were supposed to go for a drink with Mom and Dad after the tasting, but I don't think the three of them should be in the same room right now."

"They're not his biggest fans at the moment?"

She casts a sideways glance. "That's putting it mildly."

"So what's the plan? You heading home?"

"I think I'll stay at Mom and Dad's tonight. I need my old bed. My old room." She rests her hand on my knee. "You're staying too, right?"

"I don't know. I should probably head back to DC before I wreck any more lives."

"Please stay? We can hang like old times."

I snort. "Like what old times?"

"When we were younger. Before Zach came along."

"We didn't really hang out much then either. You were always too cool for your dorky older sister."

"That isn't true. We were just . . . different."

"Yeah, different as in you were pretty and cool, and I wasn't."

"First of all, that isn't true. You're totally pretty, and you're cool in that geek chic way. And how do you think I felt? I had an older sister who was an all-star student and won writing awards and landed a job at a major news network. Teachers would always say, 'Oh, you're Sydney's sister!' and expect me to be like you. But then I'd bomb a math test, and I could tell what they were thinking: 'Ah. She's just the dumb little sister.'"

"You're not dumb. No one ever thought that."

She sighs. "Whatever. The point is, I knew I couldn't be you, so I didn't try. I tried to be me. That worked out pretty well for me in high school. But now . . . I don't know."

"What are you talking about? You have a job and tons of friends, and, until an hour or two ago, you were engaged to a successful lawyer."

"I know. But sometimes I wonder if maybe I peaked in high school. A few high school friends and I had brunch a few weekends ago for a little reunion, and all we talked about were things that happened years ago. All I could think was, 'Wow, is this all we have to talk about? Was that as good as it gets?'"

"Trust me—high school is definitely *not* as good as it gets."

"For you it wasn't. You've done all sorts of amazing things. Like the horsemeat story? The whole country is talking about it, and that's down to you."

"Yeah, well, success has a price. Thanks to that story, I've alienated the one guy I've legitimately cared about since Zach."

"The PR guy?"

I nod. "I'm pretty sure I destroyed any chance of making that relationship work."

"How bad?"

"Like a grenade in a petroleum factory."

"Sorry. That sucks."

"Not gonna argue with you there." I glance at Libby and picture what we must look like to an outsider. "Man, are we a couple of losers or what?"

"Speak for yourself, sister. You're the one I found sitting on a park bench like a bag lady."

I elbow her. "Hey!"

"I'm just trying to put things in perspective." She flashes a wry grin as she knocks her knee against mine.

We fall into a comfortable silence next to each other, our knees touching as we stare out at the square. Two little girls crawl onto the frog statue, the older one kissing it like a princess hoping it will turn into a prince, and the younger one follows suit, slobbering all over the smooth, granite amphibian. Their mother rushes up to them and wipes the younger one's mouth with a moistened tissue.

"I wish we hung out more like this," I say. "Just you and me."

She nods. "Me too."

"We should do it more often."

She nods again. "We will."

I reach out, grab her hand, and hold it in mine. "Good," I say. "I really hope so."

CHAPTER 45

At Libby's urging, I agree to spend the weekend at my parents' house like I'd originally planned. The two of us pile into the back of the bright orange Prius, and my mom zips out of The Rittenhouse driveway and follows my dad in his gray Ford Focus back to the suburbs.

My dad peels off to pick up some light bulbs as we pass the neighborhood hardware store, but my mom keeps driving, zipping past the houses and shops I remember from my childhood. As we turn down my old street, Stu Abbott calls. We have been e-mailing back and forth for the past week about future stories, but so far he hasn't liked any of my ideas.

"I'm meeting with my managing editor Monday, and I'd love to have something I can pitch to her," he says. "Have you been able to come up with anything meatier? No pun intended."

I bite my thumbnail as my mom pulls into the driveway and approaches the house I grew up in, a white brick colonial with pale green shutters and an arched overhang above the pale green door.

"You didn't like the story on homebrewing? Because I think that could make for a great multimedia piece—lots of visuals."

He makes a snoring sound. "Boring. Is there anything we can

do to further the horsemeat story? Other than the obvious follow-up stuff?"

I think back to the conversations I had with Drew and Rick the day after the story came out. "What about a piece on the farmers' market partnership that fell through? We could talk about the impact the scandal is having on some of the company's other initiatives."

"Meh. Sounds fluffy."

"It doesn't have to be." I hold the phone between my shoulder and my ear as I follow my sister into the house, dragging my suitcase by the handle. "The financial ripple effects are huge. Like that woman, Maggie, at Broad Tree Orchards? She planted a field full of new trees, expecting the pilot program to take off. But now that it isn't, she has a bunch of fruit she can't sell, and she's screwed."

"I told you, we have the human interest stuff covered. We need you for the juicy stuff."

"I know. But . . ."

"But what?"

"That isn't the kind of food writer I want to be."

"You don't want to expose the bad guys? You don't want to make a difference?"

"I do want to make a difference." I feel my mom's and sister's eyes on me. "Just not like that."

"Listen, that's the kind of reporter we're looking for, so if you can't deliver, then maybe you should look elsewhere. Call me if and when you come up with a serious story idea. What you've sent me so far isn't going to cut it."

He hangs up, and I groan as I toss my phone in my bag and take a seat on one of the barstools along my parents' kitchen island.

"What was that about?" Libby asks.

"Oh, nothing, just my future livelihood." I hold my head in my hands. "I could finally have the job I've always wanted, but it turns out it isn't what I thought it would be."

"No?" my mom says. "What's the problem?"

"They want me to be someone I'm not."

"Then don't be that person."

I look up at her. "You make it sound so easy."

"I never said it was easy. Sometimes being yourself is the hardest thing."

I fold my arms on the counter and rest my chin on them. "Lately I can't even remember who I am."

"You're the geek who tries to put a human face on the food system," Libby says. "And who has an extremely limited fashion sense."

I lift my head and glare at her.

"Sorry," she says. "I had to. You make it too easy."

"Libby, why don't you take Sydney's things upstairs while I talk to your sister for a second, okay?"

Libby opens her mouth, about to balk at the idea, but something about my mom's expression stops her and she relents, grabbing my suitcase and disappearing upstairs.

"All this talk about your food-writing career . . . There's something I've been meaning to talk to you about," my mom says.

"Yeah?"

"A few months ago, when we talked on the phone, you said something that . . . well, I haven't been able to stop thinking about it."

"Uh oh. What'd I say?"

"We were talking about Libby's wedding, and you referred to the 'Bank of Strauss,' and when I said it was never closed you said, 'Except if your name is Sydney and you want to pursue a career in food journalism.'"

"Oh. Right."

"Do you really feel that way?"

I shrug. "I mean . . . yeah. Why do you think I took such a detour with the job at *The Morning Show*?"

"Because I thought that's what you wanted."

"Really? You thought I wanted to work with a jackass whose idea of a fun story involved crashing into a camera on skis?"

"It was one of the most popular morning shows in the country. Who wouldn't want to work on that show? We figured, when you turned down the one food-writing opportunity that came your way—"

"That was because of Zach."

"Right. But you never really pursued another food-writing job after that, so we thought you'd lost interest."

"I realized I could never afford it, and you guys would never help me."

She frowns. "You never asked."

"You never offered."

"That's because we thought you didn't want our help."

I sit up straight. "What would make you think that?"

"You've always been so . . . independent. Even in high school, you did your own thing, marched to your own beat, never really . . . *needed* us, the way your sister did."

"Of course I needed you. You're my parents."

"But not in the way Libby did."

"Right. Because Libby has always been the favorite."

"No," my mom says, her tone stern. "Because she lived in Libby Land, and your father and I needed to watch over her, or God knows where she'd have ended up. We never had to worry about you. We knew you'd be fine."

I run my hand along the edge of the counter. "Sometimes I wish you'd watched over me a little, too. Just because I was independent doesn't mean I didn't need you."

Her shoulders slump, and she looks at me for a long while. "You don't make it easy for people to help you, Sydney. Whenever we tried, you made us feel like we were intruding. You wanted to do everything on your own."

"Not everything."

"Well, if you needed help, you certainly never asked for it."

I glance down at the counter. "I didn't think I'd have to. You're my mom. Moms are supposed to know these things."

"Even moms make mistakes. We're not perfect."

"I know. I just . . . Sometimes I felt a little like the ugly duckling. Like you wished I could be more like Libby."

"I never felt that way. Ever. You were my superstar—are my superstar." She comes to my side of the counter and wraps her arms around me, pulling me in for a tight hug. "I'm sorry," she says. "I never meant to give you that impression."

"It's okay."

She pulls away and lets out a deep sigh. "No, it's not. With you and your sister . . . I didn't always do the right thing. Libby was so needy, but sometimes a mom wants to feel needed—to feel necessary. After all the bottles and diapers and sleepless nights, to wake up one morning and realize your little babies are young women, who have their own lives and don't really need you anymore . . . It isn't easy, especially for a stay-at-home mom like me. If my daughters didn't need me, then what good was I? Did I even have a purpose? You seemed ready to fly the nest when you were fourteen. But Libby was more helpless, and looking back on it now, I probably took advantage of that."

I gaze into my mom's eyes, which glisten in the light above the island. "I didn't mean to make you feel unnecessary. I did need you. I still do. I just never knew how to tell you that."

She brings me in for another hug. "I hope you know how much I love you. How much your father and I both love you."

I hug her back. "I do. I love you, too."

Libby comes crashing down the stairs and bursts into the kitchen, interrupting with the sort of obliviousness that has become both predictable and endearing.

"Hey—sorry to break up this hugfest, but who feels like brownies? We didn't get to try any cake at the tasting, and I'm in need of chocolate."

My mom pulls away, the scent of her perfume lingering on my shoulder. "Okay. Did you want to bake a batch?"

"Yeah." Her eyes land on me. "The three of us. Together."

My mom looks at Libby, then at me, and smiles. "Let's hurry, then," she says. "It's getting late, and we don't want to waste any more time."

Over the next two days, my family recrystallizes into a unit, each of us falling into variations of our former roles. Libby and I are still the children, and my parents are still the parents, but our attitudes and responsibilities have shifted. Now my mom, Libby, and I cook together, starting a new tradition with all three of us in the kitchen. While they peel and chop and truss, I season and slice and sear.

We're a team—the Strauss women—and with us behind the stove, there's no telling what we can do.

On Sunday morning, my mom bursts into the kitchen as the rest of us eat breakfast, a smile plastered on her face.

"Kitchen Kapers just called," she says. "I got the job!"

It's the happiest I've seen her in months, and although I know she'd rather not have to reenter the workforce at fifty-six years of age, she seems ready for a change.

"Congratulations!" we say in unison.

"We should celebrate tonight," Libby says. "Something special."

"Why don't I cook dinner?" I suggest.

My parents and Libby stare at me. I cannot tell if their expressions reveal astonishment, skepticism, interest, or all three.

"Sure," my mom says. "What would you like to make?"

I pause. "Spaghetti carbonara."

Libby hesitates. "You sure?"

"Yes," I say. "I'm positive."

That night, I whip up a dinner of spaghetti carbonara, using the same recipe Zach and I attempted all those years ago. I fry the bits of pancetta in my mom's stainless steel frying pan, filling the kitchen with the rich smell of fried pork and the pop and hiss of sputtering grease. I whip together the eggs and cheese, and when the pasta is perfectly al dente, I dump it into the pan with the pancetta, pouring the eggs on top and tossing everything together until the spaghetti glistens in a thick, creamy sauce.

My family gobbles up the silky noodles studded with flecks of salty pancetta, washing down mouthfuls with glasses of cheap champagne. At one point, as my mom slurps down a long noodle, she looks at me and winks.

"Thank you," she says. "This is perfect."

I twirl the velvety pasta around my fork, take a bite, and swallow it with relish. "You're right," I say. "It is."

CHAPTER 46

When I return to Washington the next day, I have made a decision: I am not going to be a muckraker. That isn't me. I want to write about people—about farmers like Rick and Maggie and home-brewers like Jeremy. If the *Chronicle* doesn't want to run those stories, fine, but someone else might. And if not, well, maybe I'm not cut out for this line of work. But I'll never know unless I try.

I start working on the story I pitched to Stu, about the ripple effects of the horsemeat scandal on local farmers and artisans. Given that Rick pays me to work for him, I focus on Maggie, since I don't have a conflict of interest with her or her business.

As I help Rick unload the truck at the Foggy Bottom market on Wednesday, Maggie pokes her head out from behind it, her spiky hair even wilder than usual.

"So are we on for Monday?" she asks.

"Yep. My friend is letting me borrow her car. I should be there by ten."

"What's happening Monday?" Rick grumbles as he grabs a crate off the truck.

"Sydney is visiting my orchard for a story she's writing."

"What, she hasn't kicked us in the balls hard enough already? Why the hell would you help her?"

Maggie shrugs. "Hey, at this point it couldn't get much worse, right?"

Rick throws a crate of blueberry muffins on the table, their craggy tops bursting with hunks of buttery streusel. "Like hell it couldn't. One more juicy story from this *chiquita,* and I could be out of business."

"This isn't that kind of story," I tell him.

"That's what they all say. And the next thing I know, my creditors are calling me up, and some debt collector named Obadiah is banging on my door, and my hip starts making that popping sound again, and my wife is pissing blood."

Maggie and I make brief eye contact, both of us flummoxed by Rick's explanation. "This isn't that kind of story," I say again.

"Then what kind of story is it?"

"It's . . . a people story. A look at the impact one person's bad decision can have on others."

"Whose bad decision are we talking about, here?"

"Bob Young's."

Rick grumbles. "That bastard?"

"Call him what you will, but he's the one who wanted to take your bread to the next level."

"Yeah, but then he went and screwed it all up with his lies."

I heave a long sigh. "Yes. That is the point of my story."

He grips the handles on a crate of brioche with his meaty paws. "Fine," he says. "Whatever. Go spin your little yarn. But so help me God, if I lose more business because of you, I will come after you for all you're worth."

"Understood," I say, because I hate to break it to him: At the moment, I'm not worth all that much.

Everything about this story feels right.

When I visit Maggie's farm on Monday, she takes me from field to field in her pickup truck, showing me the fruit they just started harvesting for the summer markets: yellow Sentry peaches, white nectarines, red plums, baby apricots. We spin past patches of Chantenay carrots and orchards of Honeycrisp apples, both of which they'll pick later in the season, after the raspberries, the canes already bursting with ruby and gold fruit. Back in April, the peach trees bore masses of fluffy, sweet-smelling pink blossoms, but now dozens of fuzzy, round fruits hang from their branches like Christmas ornaments, the ripe ones so juicy you can't eat them without wearing a bib.

I interview Maggie and her husband and talk to them about the financial hardships they've endured running their farm and the impact a sales agreement with Green Grocers would have on their business. We talk about the realities of operating a farm, from pests to labor, and the dreams they have for their family. I meet with their production manager and foreman, their marketing manager and market coordinator, everyone who assists with getting an apple from the tree to a customer's hand. With every person I meet, all I can think is, *This. This is what I want to be doing.* Meeting people and hearing their stories, learning about the difference between a plumcot and a pluot, tasting the difference between a yellow and a white peach—this is what I've always wanted to do, and what I should have been doing all along. I lost my way, but for the first time in a very long time, I feel as if I'm where I belong.

Once I'm back home, I get Drew's number from Heidi and interview him about working for Maggie, and he manages to go a full thirty minutes without working an obscure Alaskan bird or mammal into the conversation. When he eventually brings up the caribou, I close the lid to my laptop, take a deep breath, and thank him for his time. I wish there could be a future for Drew and me, but if I have to spend the next fifty years talking about the horned puffin, I might try to take my own life.

I spend the week pulling together all the pieces of my story and creating a companion video, and on Friday I send them to Stu Abbott. He shoots back a kind but tepid reply: "Nice angle, but not really what we're looking for. We could post on the Web, but you'll only get the blogger rate. Sorry."

Though I could probably hold out for more, I decide to take the hundred bucks from Stu. It's the *Chronicle,* after all. I could certainly do worse. And in my gut, I know there's a better fit waiting for me, and I need to work as hard as I can until I find it.

In the meantime, I continue working for Rick and writing the market newsletter. At Julie's suggestion, I make another trip to Rick's bakehouse to show people how he makes his pain au chocolat, that magical, flaky pastry filled with heavenly bites of chocolate. I shoot video of Rick laminating croissant dough, rolling and flattening and folding the butter-filled slab of pastry until the dough is as long as a beach towel and stratified with butter like canyon rock. He cuts it into rectangles and stuffs each one with two fat chunks of bittersweet chocolate, rolling up the edges and tucking the chocolate inside. He bakes off five sheets in his convection oven, filling the bakehouse with the sweet perfume of browning pastry, and when the croissants emerge, their golden tops glistening, I have to restrain myself from reaching out from behind the camera to stuff three or five in my face.

As soon as the newsletter goes out the next week, Rick's customer base goes crazy. People line up and down the market thoroughfare, undeterred by the stifling July heat, clamoring for flaky pain au chocolat and crusty sourdough loaves. Day after day, he sells out of everything at least thirty minutes before closing, and the chocolate croissants sell out in the first hour.

"You know what, sweet cheeks?" he says Saturday morning, dabbing his forehead with a balled-up white towel as he eyes the growing crowd at the West End market. "You're not actually the worst person alive."

"Thanks. You really know how to make a girl feel special."

He flashes his pervy grin. "Don't I know it."

We work at breakneck speed, bagging up loaf after muffin after loaf, sweat dripping down our backs. Seven months after a record-breaking snowstorm, Mother Nature has careened in the other direction, and the temperature has skyrocketed to an unbearable ninety-five degrees. Sweat trickles down Rick's face and neck, and his light gray T-shirt looks as if it's tie-dyed with sweat stains. My white tank top clings to my moist, slippery skin, and my hair is slicked with sweat. I'm also pretty sure I smell like a pet store.

I wait on a young couple who orders the last of the chocolate croissants, which in this weather ooze melted chocolate, their once-flaky exteriors soggy in the hot, muggy air. As I shove the melting pastries into a paper bag, I glance up and see a familiar face at the end of the market—a face with a narrow chin and soft blue eyes and milk-chocolate hair.

Jeremy.

My stomach somersaults. I haven't seen or heard from him in a month, though I've thought about him almost constantly. As I follow his path, the paper bag slips through my slick fingers, sending the pastries tumbling to the ground.

"Christ Almighty," Rick mutters, dabbing his forehead with the back of his arm.

I squat down and fumble with the bag, my eyes trained on Jeremy, who is moving closer and closer to the Wild Yeast tent. He hasn't seen me.

The woman hands me six bucks, and I pass her the bag, and as she and her companion walk away, Jeremy's eyes land on mine, and he stops. His cheeks flush, though whether that's from the heat or me I cannot tell. I think back to the first time I ran into him at the market like this—how little I knew about him, how little I knew about myself, how much I still have to learn about both of us.

Jeremy glances at the ground, then up again at me, his expression charged but unreadable. Sweat pours down my forehead and my back, and just when I think my heart can't beat any faster, he starts moving slowly in my direction, smoothly and steadily, as if he is gliding on ice. He drifts toward the Wild Yeast tent and stops directly across from me, on the other side of the table. His eyes are still fixed on mine, his expression still inscrutable. There is so much I want to say, so much I want to tell him, but I'm on my side of the table, and he is on his, and there doesn't appear to be any way for us to meet in the middle.

He stares at me for a long time in silence, while the blistering air pricks my skin. I've missed his face. I've missed his smile.

"Hi," I say, my voice scratchy. "How have you been?"

He looks down, then up again, his expression softening. "Lonely."

My heart races. "Me too."

He surveys the baked goods displayed along the table. "I saw the profile you did of Maggie and her farm. It was a nice piece."

"Thanks."

"Sounds like things aren't so great for her right now, but . . . Who knows? Maybe your profile will make a difference."

I shift my weight back and forth as I wait for him to say something more, but he doesn't.

"Listen, Jeremy—"

He holds up his hand and cuts me off. "I know," he says.

"You know . . . what?"

"All of it."

"I don't think you do."

He smirks. "You're challenging me now?"

"No—it's just . . . You don't understand how sorry I am, how much I've missed you, how often I think about you, how much I—"

He reaches out and presses a finger to my lips. "Yes," he says. "I do." A beat passes, and then he says, "Because I've missed you, too."

My lip starts to tremble, my eyes welling with tears. He holds my gaze, his blue eyes fixed on mine, and then, as his finger slides from my lips, he leans over the table and kisses me. His lips are soft and warm, and I realize how much I've missed the comfort of his kiss, its warmth and familiarity, like a favorite pair of shoes that have molded to the shape of my feet. I don't want him to leave—not now, not for a long time—so I lean toward him, my lips pressed against his, my heart dancing with joy.

"WHAT THE HELL IS THIS?" Rick shouts from across the tent. "Oh, no, no, no. Not on my damn watch."

I pull away from Jeremy and look at Rick, who is swearing and sweating like a wild beast. Then I look back at Jeremy, grab him by the shirt and pull him in for another kiss, because for the first time in a very long time, I'm exactly where I want to be.

CHAPTER 47

"Psst. You're going to be late."

Jeremy pokes me, and I grudgingly open one eyelid, then the other, and glance at the clock on his nightstand.

"So are you."

"My meeting isn't until eleven," he says. "And I don't take thirty minutes to blow dry my hair."

"Maybe that's because yours is thinning. . . ."

"Oh, so that's how it's gonna be?" He throws off the covers, grabs me by the waist, and tosses me over his shoulder. "To the showers with you."

"Hey—let me go," I shout, kicking as he marches me into his bathroom.

"Listen, maybe you don't remember what it's like to go on a job interview, but I do, and let me tell you: BO and morning breath are discouraged."

He puts me down once we reach the bathroom, and I readjust his Han Solo T-shirt, which I wore to bed last night.

"These guys sound like hipsters," I say. "I'm pretty sure they wouldn't care."

"Yeah, what kind of magazine is called *Washagrarian* anyway?"

"Don't knock it 'til you read it."

"Do they print it on recycled corn stalks? Is their Web domain powered by chickens?"

I roll my eyes and push him out of the bathroom. "All right, enough out of you. Good-bye."

I shut the door behind him and flick on his shower. "Be careful with the baby powder," he shouts from behind the closed door.

"Not funny!"

"I disagree." He chuckles to himself. "I'll put on some coffee. See you in a few."

I hop in the shower and let the warm spray trickle down my back as I run through my plan for the day. At ten, I'm meeting with the editors of *Washagrarian,* a new DC-based digital and print magazine that will focus on local food, urban and rural farming, and the connection between what we eat and how we live. They plan to launch their first issue in September and contacted me after reading my profile of Maggie last month. They saw my horsemeat story too, but they are looking for someone to write what they call "people stories"—which, I emphasized to them, are precisely the kinds of stories I like to write. They haven't offered me a job yet, but given what they've told me so far, I have a good feeling.

After my meeting, I'll grab a quick bite before hopping on the Metro and heading to the Penn Quarter farmers' market, where I'll meet Rick for my usual Thursday afternoon shift. If I end up getting a job with *Washagrarian,* I'll need to scale back my hours with Wild Yeast, but ever since Green Grocers resumed their plans for a farmers' market partnership, I've had Rick's blessing to do pretty much whatever I want. Nothing is set in stone, and the new management has tweaked the terms of the deal, but Rick, Maggie, and the others are breathing a lot easier knowing they might not have to flush their investments down the drain. I'd like to say my Broad Tree Orchards profile turned the tide in their favor, but I know better than to overstate my role. I'm just glad one misdeed didn't cause irreparable harm—and that applies as much to Green Grocers as it does to myself.

I flick off the water and wrap myself in one of Jeremy's plush towels, and then I step out of the shower and wipe the steam off the fogged up mirror with my fist. *Geek chic,* I think as I stare at my reflection, recalling Libby's backhanded compliment. I smile. *Geek chic.* I'll take it.

Once I've dried my hair and put on my makeup, I throw on my outfit, which Libby helped me choose: skinny black capris with white polka dots, a sleeveless white wrap shirt, and red heels. When I'd mentioned I had an interview with a food magazine, her first question, in typical Libby style, was, "What are you going to wear?" And then, before I could answer, she said, "Forget it—let me help you." She sent me an e-mail with four different options ("You want to look hip but professional—NO POWER SUITS and NO STRETCHED OUT PANTS"), and we decided on this one together.

I smooth a little serum into my hair, and then I go into Jeremy's living room, where I find him sitting at his breakfast bar with his laptop and a mug of coffee.

"Well, *hellooo,*" he says, grinning.

"Don't get any ideas."

He glances at the clock. "You have a little time. . . ."

"Not for that. Do you have any idea how long it took me to straighten this hair?"

He looks at the clock again. "A really long time."

"Exactly. We'll revisit this later. Don't worry. I'll make it worth your while."

"I like the sound of that." He smiles. "You know, this whole being on probation thing is working out pretty well for me."

Ever since Jeremy decided to give me a second chance, he has told me I'm on "probation." He always says this with an air of seriousness, and though I know I have a long way to go in fully earning back his trust, I feel myself getting closer every day. If I can learn to trust and let go after Zach, I guess anything is possible.

I pour myself a cup of coffee, and as I hold the warm mug between my palms and take a sip, I eye Jeremy's T-shirt: another *Star Wars* getup, this one featuring an image of Darth Vader holding a picket sign that reads, GIVE EMPIRES A CHANCE.

"You're going to change before your meeting, right . . . ?"

He peeks down at his shirt, and his lips curl to the side. "What? Not okay?"

"You want these guys to give you money, right?"

He shrugs. "They're nerds like me. That's why they love me."

I take another sip of coffee. Apparently, Jeremy won "Home-brewer of the Year" at the Homebrewers Conference for his Munich Helles, and a few investors and fellow DC-based brewers at the conference approached him about starting a microbrewery. At first he hesitated, not wanting to embark on yet another road to professional failure, but ultimately he relented because deep down, this is what he has always wanted to do. It doesn't hurt that he is also really good at it.

I throw back the rest of my coffee, dump the mug in the sink, and walk around to Jeremy's side of the counter and lean in for a long kiss.

"Wish me luck," I say as I pull away.

"No breakfast?"

"No time."

"We're still on for dinner?"

"You bet. I should be back from the market by seven thirty. I was thinking we could try the new Mexican place on Fourteenth Street. They're supposed to have a good beer list."

He wiggles an imaginary tie. "None as good as mine, I'm sure...."

"Well, obviously. But it's a big day for both of us. We can either celebrate, or drown our sorrows."

"Sounds like a brilliant plan to me."

I lean in for one more kiss and then head for the doorway.

"Hey, Syd?" he calls after me.

I stop and look over my shoulder. "Yeah?"

He stares at me for a beat. "I'm glad I gave us a second chance."

I smile. "Me too."

Then I blow him another kiss and, with a smile so big it could take up the entire city, I head out the door.

As I walk along M Street toward Dupont Circle, my phone buzzes in my pocket. A text from Libby.

GOOD LUCK TODAY! Are u wearing the outfit we discussed???

I text back.

Yep. Even the red shoes. Look at me—fashion forward!

A few minutes pass, and Libby sends one last message.

Sweetie, red shoes r older than the Lord. But yay! U will rock this!

I laugh to myself. Libby will be Libby, and for that I love her.

The street forks as I hit Connecticut Avenue, a sunburst of roads heading north, south, east, and west. I rush across the street as the light turns yellow, holding my bag close to my body as I breathe in the thick summer air. Last month's spell of sky-high temperatures has passed, but it's still August in Washington, which means I'm already sweating buckets.

I turn onto Seventeenth Street and make my way toward *Washagrarian*'s office. They are renting temporary space just off M Street, in an eight-story tower of muted gray concrete, with receding rectangular windows that make the edifice look like a big Belgian waffle.

I stand in front of the doorway, letting the hurried masses hustle around me on the sidewalk, and glance up to the sixth floor. In a few minutes, I will sit in that office. In a few weeks, I might even call it my own. And maybe in a few years, I'll be the one running it. There are no guarantees—not with this job, not with Jeremy, not with anything in life, really—but guarantees are overrated. I'd rather trade in adventure. In chance. In opportunity. It's a scarier way to live, demanding trust in myself and others that I'm still trying to master, but I'd rather ask for a second chance than not take any chances at all. It's been a long time since I took such a leap of faith, but hot damn, it feels good to jump.

I rest my hand on the cool metal door handle and take one last look up the building's face. Then I pull open the door and walk inside, ready for anything.

ACKNOWLEDGMENTS

Many thanks to my amazing editors: Esi Sogah at Kensington and Victoria Hughes-Williams at Constable & Robinson. Your keen insights and suggestions helped take this story to the next level. Thanks also to Dominic Wakeford for taking over so seamlessly and with such enthusiasm.

A big thank-you to the rest of my publishing team: Vida Engstrand, Alexandra Nicolajsen, Kristine Noble, Paula Reedy, and Steven Zacharius at Kensington, and Grace Vincent, James Gurbutt, Louise Cullen, Hazel Orme, and the rest of the gang at Constable & Robinson. I am so lucky to have such a great team on both sides of the Atlantic.

To Scott Miller, Sylvie Rosokoff, Stephanie Hoover, and everyone at Trident: You are the best in the business, and I am beyond thankful for all that you do.

Thanks to Sophie McKenzie and Mandi Schweitzer for reading early, messy drafts of this book. Your thoughts and critiques helped immeasurably.

A hat tip to Sallie James Dimitri for giving me insight into a real-life FBI raid. Sometimes truth really is stranger than fiction.

I couldn't have done any of this if it weren't for my parents, who instilled in me a strong work ethic and the self-confidence to achieve my dreams. Thank you for your support, your honesty, and your love. And a huge thank-you to my brother, Brian, for making me laugh and teaching me not to take myself too seriously.

To Alex: Thank you for making my days brighter, my life fuller, and my heart bigger. You burst into my life halfway through the writing of this book, and I see your tiny little fingerprints all over the pages of this story. Thank you for the naps that allowed me to write.

And finally, to Roger: You are my best critic, my biggest champion, and my best friend. Thank you for making every day a gift.

Keep reading for
recipes from and inspired by
A Second Bite at the Apple.

(For the Salted Fudge Brownie
recipe, see foodandwine.com.)

Spaghetti Carbonara

Serves 4

Authentic carbonara contains only four ingredients, aside from salt and pepper: guanciale (or pancetta), cheese, eggs, and pasta. No cream. No peas. No onions. You can, of course, add these things, but part of what makes this dish so delicious is its simplicity.

Oh, and as a fun, nerdy aside: There are many theories as to where the dish got its name, but my favorite is that *alla carbonara* means "in the manner of the coal miner," and the flecks of ground black pepper in the dish are supposed to mimic the soot that would fall off the miners' clothing as they ate their meals.

Ingredients

Extra-virgin olive oil
8 ounces thickly sliced guanciale or pancetta (or even bacon), cut into ¼-inch pieces
3 large eggs plus 1 large egg yolk, well beaten
1 cup grated Parmigiano-Reggiano cheese (or a combination of Parmigiano-Reggiano and Pecorino Romano)
Kosher salt
1 pound spaghetti
Freshly ground black pepper

Heat a little bit of olive oil in a large skillet over medium heat until it ripples. Add the guanciale or pancetta and cook, stirring often, until crisp. Remove the pan from the heat and set it aside.

Bring 6 quarts of water to a boil in a large pot. While the water is heating, whisk the eggs, egg yolk, and three quarters of the cheese together in a bowl.

Once the water comes to a boil, add a liberal amount of salt—about 2 tablespoons should do it. Add the spaghetti and cook, stirring often to prevent the pasta from clumping, until al dente (refer to the side of the package for exact timing). Drain, reserving ¾ cup of the pasta cooking water.

Working quickly, dump the hot spaghetti into the skillet with the pancetta and place over *very* low heat. Add the egg mixture and just enough of the reserved pasta water to make the mixture lusciously creamy. Stir quickly—you don't want to end up with scrambled eggs!

Remove the skillet from the heat, add a bit of ground pepper to taste, and serve, passing the remaining grated cheese at the table.

Philadelphia Italian Hoagie

Makes 4 hoagies

Technically, for an authentic Philadelphia hoagie, you need to use Amoroso's rolls or buy rolls from Sarcone's Deli in Philadelphia. But any oblong roll should do the job.

Ingredients

½ large red onion, thinly sliced
2 tablespoons red wine vinegar
1 tablespoon dried oregano, divided
¼ cup extra-virgin olive oil
4 submarine-style sandwich rolls
Kosher salt and freshly ground pepper
¼ pound thinly sliced Genoa salami
¼ pound thinly sliced prosciutto
¼ pound thinly sliced capocollo
¼ pound thinly sliced provolone cheese
½ head iceberg lettuce, finely shredded
3 plum tomatoes, thinly sliced
¼ to ½ cup sliced pickled hot or sweet peppers (optional)

Soak the onion slices in a bowl of cold water for 15 minutes.

Stir together the vinegar and half the oregano; then whisk in the olive oil until emulsified.

Split the rolls lengthwise, pulling out some of the bread from the inside if desired. Brush the interior of the rolls with some of the oil and vinegar mixture. Season with salt and pepper.

Layer the meat and cheese on the bottom half of the bread. Drain the onion and pat dry and layer on top of the meat and cheese, followed by the lettuce, tomato, and pickled peppers (if using). Brush with more vinaigrette and, if desired, sprinkle with additional oregano. Season generously with salt and pepper. Place the top half of the roll on the sandwich and serve.

Almond Poppy Seed Muffins

Makes 24 muffins

Rick's almond poppy seed muffins are actually my mother's poppy seed muffins, and she has made them ever since I was a little girl. As Rick says, they are more cake than muffin, but in my book, that's hardly a strike against.

Ingredients

3 cups all-purpose flour
2¼ cups granulated sugar
1½ teaspoons baking powder
1½ teaspoons salt
1½ cups vegetable oil
1½ cups milk
3 eggs
½ teaspoon almond extract
1½ tablespoons poppy seeds

Center a rack in the middle of the oven and preheat the oven to 350 degrees Fahrenheit. Grease two 12-cup muffin tins or line with cupcake liners.

Combine the flour, sugar, baking powder, and salt in a large bowl. In another large bowl, whisk together the oil, milk, eggs, and almond extract until smooth. Add the dry ingredients to the wet ingredients and mix only until evenly moistened. Stir in the poppy seeds.

Divide the batter among the muffin cups. Bake the muffins until they are golden brown, about 30 minutes. Serve warm or at room temperature.

Rick's Oatmeal Raisin Cookies

Makes about 15 cookies (recipe can easily be doubled)

For big cookies à la Rick, use an ice-cream scoop with a 2-inch diameter to scoop the dough onto the cookie sheets. For smaller cookies, reduce the baking time. You can use dark raisins if you like, but Rick and I prefer golden ones.

Ingredients

¾ cup all-purpose flour
½ teaspoon baking powder
½ teaspoon ground cinnamon
½ teaspoon kosher salt
8 tablespoons (¼ pound) unsalted butter, at room temperature
½ cup light brown sugar, lightly packed
½ cup granulated sugar
1 large egg, at room temperature
1 teaspoon pure vanilla extract
1½ cups rolled oats (old-fashioned, not quick-cooking)
¾ cup golden raisins

Preheat the oven to 350 degrees Fahrenheit. Line two baking sheets with parchment paper or a silicone baking mat.

In a small bowl, mix together the flour, baking powder, cinnamon, and salt.

In a large bowl, beat the butter, brown sugar, and granulated sugar together with an electric mixer on medium-high speed until light and fluffy. Turn the mixer to low and add the egg, followed by the vanilla.

With the mixer still on low, slowly add the dry ingredients to the butter mixture. Add the oats and raisins and mix just until combined.

Using a 2-inch ice-cream scoop, drop the dough on the baking sheets, spacing the scoops 2–3 inches apart. Flatten the tops slightly with a damp hand. Bake for 15–20 minutes, until lightly browned but still slightly soft in the center. Let the cookies cool on the baking sheet for a minute or so, then transfer the cookies to a baking rack and cool completely.

Rick's Millet Muffins

Makes 12 muffins

These muffins were inspired by the millet muffins at Philadelphia's Metropolitan Bakery, one of my favorite spots to grab a muffin and a coffee. Millet is a whole grain that is often used as birdseed, and it gives baked goods a delicious crunch. (Try adding it to banana bread or waffles!) If you don't have whole wheat pastry flour, you can easily substitute another cup of all-purpose flour. Also, if you want to toast the millet beforehand, you can, but I find that it's an unnecessary step.

Ingredients

1 cup all-purpose flour
1 cup whole wheat pastry flour
1 cup millet
1¼ teaspoons baking powder
½ teaspoon baking soda
¾ teaspoon kosher salt
6 tablespoons (3 ounces) unsalted butter, melted and cooled slightly
1 cup dark brown sugar
3 large eggs, at room temperature
⅓ cup milk, warmed in the microwave until tepid (about 10 seconds)
1 teaspoon vanilla extract

Preheat the oven to 375 degrees Fahrenheit. Grease two 12-cup muffin tins or line with cupcake liners.

In a large bowl, mix together the flours, millet, baking powder, baking soda, and salt.

In a medium bowl, combine the melted and cooled butter, brown sugar, eggs, milk, and vanilla.

Make a well in the dry ingredients and pour in the wet ingredients. Stir together, mixing only until the dry ingredients completely disappear into the batter.

Divide batter into the prepared muffin cups and bake for 15–20 minutes, until golden brown and a toothpick inserted into the center comes out clean. Cool in the pan for 5 minutes, then turn onto a wire rack. Serve warm or at room temperature, with butter and jam.

Whole Grain Bread

Makes two 9" x 5" loaves

Technically this isn't one of Rick's loaves mentioned in the book, but it's one of my favorite breads to make at home. It was inspired by the OSM (oats, sunflower, millet) Bread I tried at The Bunnery in Jackson Hole, Wyoming.

Ingredients

2¼ cups lukewarm water
½ cup honey
1 package (2½ teaspoons) active dry yeast
½ cup canola or safflower oil
2 cups bread flour (or all-purpose flour)
3–4 cups whole wheat flour
1½ tablespoons salt
½ cup rolled oats
¼ cup sunflower seeds
¼ cup millet

Mix together the lukewarm water and honey in a large bowl or the bowl of a stand mixer. Sprinkle the yeast over the top and stir until dissolved. Allow the yeast to proof for 5–10 minutes, until the yeast rises to the surface and starts to foam.

Stir the oil into the yeast mixture. Then add 1 cup of bread (or all-purpose) flour and 2 cups whole wheat flour and beat with a wooden spoon or the paddle attachment until the batter is smooth and glossy. Cover the bowl and let the dough rest for 20 minutes.

Add the salt, oats, sunflower seeds, and millet to the bowl; stir down the dough and blend in. Add the remaining cup of bread flour and stir well. Gradually add in enough whole wheat flour until you have a stiff dough that comes away from the sides of the bowl. When the dough becomes too stiff to stir, switch to the dough hook on your mixer until the dough is soft, but not sticky, 5–10 minutes (or transfer to the counter and knead by hand for 10 minutes). Place the dough in a large, oiled bowl, cover lightly, and allow to rise in a warm place until doubled in bulk, about 1½ hours.

Grease two 9″ x 5″ loaf pans and line with parchment paper, allowing the parchment to hang over the longer sides of the pan. (This will make it easier for you to lift the loaves out of the pans.) Punch down the dough and knead lightly and briefly to deflate. Divide the dough in half and form each half into a loaf, and place a loaf in each pan. Allow the loaves to rise in a warm place until doubled, about 45 minutes.

About 20 minutes before you bake, preheat the oven to 350 degrees Fahrenheit. Bake the loaves for about 40 minutes, until they are nicely browned and sound hollow when tapped. (The internal temperature should be around 200 degrees Fahrenheit.) Allow the loaves to cool in the pans for a few minutes, then lift out of the pans using the parchment paper and let them cool completely.